P9-DEK-464

TRESPASSING

3 8467 10022 6882

TRESPASSING

A NOVEL

BRANDI REEDS

LAKE UNION
PUBLISHING

This is a work of fiction. Names, characters, organizations, places, events, and incidents are either products of the author's imagination or are used fictitiously. Any resemblance to actual persons, living or dead, or actual events is purely coincidental.

Text copyright © 2018 by Brandi Reeds
All rights reserved.

No part of this book may be reproduced, or stored in a retrieval system, or transmitted in any form or by any means, electronic, mechanical, photocopying, recording, or otherwise, without express written permission of the publisher.

Published by Lake Union Publishing, Seattle

www.apub.com

Amazon, the Amazon logo, and Lake Union Publishing are trademarks of Amazon.com, Inc., or its affiliates.

ISBN-13: 9781503950108 (hardcover)
ISBN-10: 1503950107 (hardcover)
ISBN-13: 9781503949072 (paperback)
ISBN-10: 1503949079 (paperback)

Cover design by PEPE *nymi*

Printed in the United States of America

First edition

For my husband, who shines in Key West,
and our daughters, who thrive in artistic circles.
You are my moon and stars.
La Vita in Rosa

He who knows nothing is closer to the truth

than he whose mind is filled with falsehood and errors.

—*Thomas Jefferson*

Chapter 1

November 10

I know kids have active imaginations—and I have actually heard of invisible playmates—but this goes beyond what I'd consider normal.

"Who's to say what's normal?" Dr. Russo chuckles. "Kids *do* have wild imaginations, and your child is exceptionally creative. Artistic."

Not once have the educators at the Westlake School referred to her this way.

I glance at the table, where three-year-old Elizabella is engaged in her favorite activity—coloring. I lower my voice. "Doctor, if I fail to set a plate at the table for Nini, Nini gets mad. If Elizabella gets into trouble at preschool, it was Nini who made her do it. Sometimes," I continue, "in the middle of the night, she laughs loud enough to wake me, and when I check on her, she's sitting down to a tea party in her room, saying, 'Nini just said something so funny, Mommy.'"

"Have you considered removing toys from her bedroom?"

My brow wrinkles, intensifying my headache. He doesn't get it. That's not the point. "I just thought, you know, considering the family history . . ."

He fills in the blanks. "Schizophrenia is extremely rare. It affects only one percent of the population, and in children, especially children of Elizabella's age, it's practically unheard of. And based on what you've told me, your mother struggled more with depression than with voices in her head."

Sure. Based on what I've said, it's a logical conclusion to reach. But I haven't told him everything yet. I haven't even told Micah everything, and not because I don't want him to know. I can't explain what I don't understand. I don't like to think of my mother that way, anyway. It's better to remember her at her best.

"And even if your mother had been properly diagnosed as a schizophrenic, which I doubt—the due diligence just wasn't given to the case—the fact that you don't exhibit signs of the disorder means a less than ten percent chance Elizabella will be affected."

Would anyone, though, think herself crazy . . . if she's crazy?

"Creative minds usually run in families," the shrink continues. "Are you creative?"

"Not exceptionally." I majored in women's studies in college—not that I'm using my diploma for a damned thing since my little bundle of restless energy arrived. Ironic, now that I think about it.

"Your husband?"

I hold the doctor's gaze. He already knows the answer to this one. Micah, who wears only shades of gray because he doesn't know which colors go with which, is anything but artistic. I know where this line of questioning is headed, and I know he won't quit until we get there.

"My mother designed jewelry," I admit.

"I suspect you're a little artistic, too, but you're afraid to follow in your mother's footsteps, no matter the capacity in which you do so."

It's a ridiculous thing to say, an overgeneralization. *Anyone* would be afraid to become what my mother became. She had her way at the end: a short service beneath a lovely pane of stained glass.

"You're under a lot of pressure, with the fertility treatment, with Micah's traveling," Dr. Russo says. "Would this be easier to deal with if I prescribed you an antianxiety?"

I shake my head. I still have the pills he prescribed after the miscarriage in April. I don't like to take them—it's hard to be a mother when I'm on them—but it's out of the question in the midst of in vitro.

"Perfectly normal." Dr. Russo massages a hand over his beard. "This is the optimum age for the development of a 'friend'"—he uses air quotes—"like this. Sometimes, the child creates the imaginary friend to deal with some sort of shift in the household. Moving, for example. The onset of preschool."

I look again to the corner table where Elizabella is coloring. Dr. Russo is our family therapist; we've been seeing him together for about six months now, since April—since Nini made her debut . . . which coincided with the miscarriage. Not long after, we moved to the Shadowlands, a full-service, gated golf course community on the outskirts of Chicago. And Bella started preschool last month.

I twist my wedding ring around my finger; it's tighter than usual.

"You're trying to have another baby," he says.

Always. I wish someone had told me in college it would be this difficult to knock me up.

"Have you begun . . ."

His inquiry fades with the images in my mind, always just a trigger away from revisiting me. Sticky sheets. Blood everywhere.

"Veronica?"

"I'm sorry." I chase away the pain of the loss. "Yes. Yes, we just aspirated for eggs yesterday morning."

"Elizabella has been part of the process," he says. "She's seen you take the shots. You've been preparing her for a baby brother or sister most of her life. She doesn't know life *without* that preparation."

"We're getting her ready, yes. Just like all the books say." And I've read them all. "We've even prepared her for the possibility a baby won't

3

come, you know, just in case . . ." I look away, out the window, at a brilliant display of gold-and-russet foliage.

"Considering this past April . . . that's even more of a reason for her to create a sort of sister in the meantime, isn't it?"

He has a point, I suppose, but still . . .

"Imaginary friends don't last forever. Most disappear by age five or six. I suggest you document this time in her life. It'll make for an interesting story for your new baby."

"Nini!" My daughter reaches across the table and grasps a crayon that's rolled away. "I'm using the red. You have to share!"

"And it's normal for her to fight with this friend, too?" I ask.

Dr. Russo lets out another chuckle. "A good sign she's learning right from wrong. She's a very articulate, very intelligent three-year-old. She'll be fine."

Resigned, I stand. "Come on, Ellie-Belle. Time to get you to school." She'll be only a few minutes late, if traffic cooperates. This time of day, it could take half an hour to get out of Evanston.

"You're preparing for the worst," Russo says, "so subconsciously you feel you'll be able to handle it, should the worst come to pass. It's understandable, given all you've been through. Your mother, the falling out with your college roommate. Especially considering the miscarriage—"

"Thank you." I extend a hand, which he shakes, before he can opt to lengthen the list of my trials. Then I wrap an arm around Bella's waist and pull her, kicking and screaming, from the table.

She fights me all the way to the car, to the point I'm nearly dragging her down the hall, down the stairs, through the parking lot.

"No school! No school!"

"Yes, you're going." When I lift her to her car seat, she arches her back and slips from my grasp to a crumpled mass of girl on the floor of the SUV. "Elizabella, stop! You're going to hurt yourself."

No sooner said than done, she whacks her shoulder against the console between the passenger and driver seats and lets out an excruciating wail.

But at least it incapacitates her for a moment, and I'm able to wrestle her into her seat and fasten the buckle.

"No school," she says again.

"Yes, school," I retort.

Amid her sniffling and whispering blame on Nini, I drive.

At the second set of railroad tracks, when I'm stopped for another commuter train, a wave of nausea washes over me. This is the worst part of fertility treatment . . . feeling pregnant when I'm not. It makes sense. I'm pumping my body full of hormones, and just two and a half days ago, I took a shot of hCG to the ass. It's a lot to go through for a very real chance that it will get us absolutely nowhere.

I take a sip of lukewarm water and cradle my head. A glance in the rearview mirror shows Bella twirling her chestnut hair around a finger.

"Don't be scared," she says. "School isn't bad."

"Nini's going to school with you today?"

"She doesn't want to." And then speaking to her coil of hair where Nini lives: "I won't let them put us in a time-out again. It was the boy in the red shoes. His fault."

Perfectly normal. Okay, Dr. Russo. I'll take your word for it.

We arrive at the Westlake School twelve minutes past start time, a big no-no, according to the director, and yes, those are the words she used. Late arrivals disrupt the morning routine, but I might guess that Bella's late arrival, in particular, will cause an uproar. She's been having trouble with separation lately.

With Bella's hand in mine, and her backpack in my other hand, I step quickly toward the door.

The autumn breeze is uncomfortably cool at my back, bordering on biting. Soon, we'll be trudging through snow. Still, it's a festive time of year. I hope we'll have some good baby news to share by Christmas.

"Mommy, wait! Nini's not out of the car yet."

"She's right there, baby." I play along like Dr. Russo suggested. "Right in your hair. Like usual."

"We have to go back and get her!" She resists and yanks on my hand. "Mommy, please! She's all alone! She's scared!"

I glance down to see Bella in the midst of tantrum number three of the day, stomping and crying and shrieking. My head pounds.

Fatigue. Nausea. And an invisible friend locked in the car.

I don't need this right now. I have half a mind to load my daughter up and lug her back home. Just for today.

But Dr. Russo also said consistency in regards to preschool was best. If I give in once, she'll only become more resistant to going in the future.

I take a deep breath. "Okay, if we go back for Nini, you'll be good once we go into school, right?" I crouch and tuck a tear-soaked tendril of hair behind her ear. "If Nini goes with you, there's no crying at the door."

Bella sniffles. Her lower lip trembles. "Mommy? Are you scared?"

I laugh a little. "No, baby. There's nothing to be scared of."

"Yes, there is." Her little hands grip mine. "Nini says when Daddy went to God Land, he left us all alone."

Slivers of ice dart through my veins. "Nini said what?"

Fat tears well up in her big, brown eyes. "We're all alone."

"Why do you think we're alone?"

"Daddy. He went to God Land."

"Baby, Nini doesn't know what she's—"

"Nini knows."

Baffled, I do nothing for a second or two. "Come on, baby girl. Everything's okay." I gather her into my arms, and while the fertility doctors tell me not to lift more than a gallon of milk, sometimes their advice isn't quite practical. I prop her on my hip and make a show of going back to the car for Nini, and even pretend to hold the kid's hand—as if I'm not holding enough—as we make our way to the door.

We've already missed attendance, calendar time, weather report, and meet-a-new-friend. Well, they'll just have to understand. I should've thought to bring a note from Dr. Russo. Maybe they'd spare me the lecture if they knew I'd been attempting to help my child adjust to this preschool routine.

I lower Bella to her feet and punch in the access code at the door. A red light blinks at me. I try again to no avail. Great. I buzz for help.

Through the intercom: "May I help you?"

I push the button again. "This is Veronica Cavanaugh. The code doesn't seem to be working."

"One moment."

A minute or two later, Miss Wendy, the director of the school, appears at the door to admit us. "I'm surprised to see you today." Her eyebrows slant downward, and her pink lips bend into a pout.

"Oh. I know we're a touch late, but Bella had an appointment." We walk into the foyer, decorated with a painted mural of a picket fence and flowers and blue skies that belie today's overcast cloud cover.

"How are you holding up?"

"I'm . . ." Did I tell them about the egg retrieval yesterday? I don't think so. But Claudette Winters knows, and since she picked up Bella for us yesterday, I wonder if she spilled the beans. It would be unlike her if she didn't. "I'm hanging in there." The generic response is easier than explaining that I feel like shit, thanks to the aching caused by my ovaries blasted to the size of tennis balls and the constant headache. I've learned that while people ask, they don't really care about the specifics anyway. I help my daughter remove her coat.

"Such a tough time." Wendy crouches in front of Bella and wipes tears from her cheeks. "And how are you, sweetie?" She looks up from my daughter. "You know, I think bringing her today is best. Sometimes a distraction, especially when that distraction is learning, is just what the doctor ordered."

Just as I'm about to tell Wendy that beyond knowing that *Mommy takes baby shots*, Bella isn't all that involved in the IVF process, a classroom coordinator appears to take my kid by the hand and lead her to class.

"Wait!" Bella says. "Wait! *Mommy!*"

I open my arms and allow her in for one last hug. "See you in a few hours, Ellie-Belle."

Her little arms are tight around my neck, and I feel her trembling. "Nini's scared."

"You and Nini will have a good time today," I remind her. "You always do."

"I love you, Mommy."

"I love you, too."

She separates of her own volition—sometimes I have to pry her hands off me—and voluntarily takes the coordinator's hand. She looks over her shoulder at me and rubs a tear into her left cheek.

"We'll call you if it doesn't go well." Wendy takes the backpack from my hand. "And if you're a bit late picking her up today, we understand, given the circumstances."

All right, this is just getting weird.

"Or . . . if it'll help . . . Miss Jennifer doesn't live too far from the Shadowlands. She's offered to drop her off after class, and with a signed release—"

"I'm okay," I say. "We've been through this twice before, and it isn't glamorous, but IVF is more common today than—"

"IVF?" Her face corkscrews into a confused-looking frown. "I thought . . . Elizabella said yesterday . . . *IVF?*"

"It's the reason Claudette Winters picked her up for me yesterday. We went through the retrieval process in the morning."

"Oh." Her smile melts away the tension. "Well, that's a little different. Bella gave us the impression that"—she waves a hand—"oh, never mind."

"What did Elizabella tell you?"

"She said . . ." Wendy covers her laugh. "It's not funny. I don't know why I'm amused. She told Miss Jennifer yesterday that your husband died."

I freeze. "Did you say . . . my daughter told you—"

"That your husband passed away." She's nodding. "I'm relieved to know she was mistaken." Again, she giggles. "Children and their imaginations."

I cross my arms over my chest to ward off a shiver. "She told you my husband died?"

"Her exact words? *My daddy went to God Land.* She must have misunderstood something she overheard, but anyhow . . . the new code. You obviously didn't get the memo." She hands me a quarter sheet of paper with the new code and instructions for using it.

"Wait a minute." I shove the scrap into my tote. "My daughter told you . . ."

"Believe it or not, telling tall tales at this age is more common than you might think. If you'd like, I can arrange an appointment with our staff social worker, but aside from a little anxiety, and the *tardiness*, Bella's doing really well. And when Claudette came for her yesterday . . . well, let's just say the transition process went more smoothly."

Of course it did. Claudette does everything better than me in Mom World.

"I think your daughter knows how to get your goat. The social worker might be able to help with that, too."

"We've just come from our family therapist."

"Oh." Her brows dent a little again. "So you don't need a referral, then. But perhaps our social worker can offer a new perspective or . . ." She trails off, unable to effectively suggest anything that might explain away Bella's whacked stories.

"I'm sorry. I don't know why she'd say such a thing."

An uncomfortable silence fills the space between us, tripped up only with the sound of music down the hall. *The wheels on the bus go 'round and 'round.*

"If you think a meeting with the social worker will help . . . ," I begin.

"A different point of view can't hurt."

My phone chimes the special alert set for the embryologist—a rendition of "Rock-a-bye Baby." My stomach hollows out. It's either good news or bad news. I have to take the call.

"Listen," Miss Wendy says. "Who knows why she said it? Often, we never know. Let's see how today goes."

I clench my phone. "Call if there's trouble?"

"Of course."

With that, I'm out the door, the phone at my ear.

And I know I have to listen carefully to everything the embryologist says, but Elizabella's words are on repeat in my head:

Daddy went to God Land.

Daddy went to God Land.

Daddy went to God Land.

Chapter 2

My husband, alive and nowhere near God Land, despite our daughter's insistence, wraps an arm around my waist and spins me across the kitchen floor in his own version of a ballroom dance, which is hopelessly without rhythm. "Stay with me . . . Stay some more . . ." He sings—incorrectly and a bit off key—the classic ballroom ballad.

"*Sway* with me," I join in.

Funny that he can maneuver a jet through cloudy skies and touch down anywhere on this vast planet, but he can't make his way across a dance floor.

"*Stay* with me," he sings. "Stay, stay, stay . . ."

"*Sway!*"

"Let me lead."

We're both laughing now.

"Micah, stop. About what Bella said. She's insisting Nini told her—"

"Obviously, it's her imagination." Micah gives me one last twirl.

"That you *died*."

"Do I look dead? There are days she insists she's a mermaid. Why are you letting this bother you?" He kisses my lips and dips me in a dramatic end to our dance.

He guides me to a seat at the kitchen table, where I laid out the picture Bella drew at preschool this morning.

She's watching a movie on demand in the great room. Even as we're discussing Nini, Bella carries on a conversation with her.

Micah is standing behind me now, his strong hands working their magic on my shoulders. "And about this picture"—when he leans in closer, I catch the scent of Dolce & Gabbana The One Sport—"you're seeing things."

He sees scribbles.

I see death.

"So she drew something that looks like the flames of hell." My husband takes the chair next to mine but maintains contact, his thumb lightly caressing the back of my neck.

"Correction." I can't stop looking at the stick figure in the midst of jagged red-and-orange lines. "*Nini* drew it."

"Last time she drew something that looked like the devil incarnate, it turned out to be a picture of her teacher."

"Same difference, if you ask me."

"Nicki-girl." He's the only one who shortens my name this way, and his *Nicki-girl* gives me a rush every time he says it. He brushes a kiss over my lips. "You're overreacting."

"What if Nini's more than an imaginary friend?"

"Okay." His thumb still feathers over my skin. "Indulge me. What do you think Nini is?"

At first, I thought maybe Nini was an alternate personality or a voice in Bella's head, but Dr. Russo is right. I looked it up. Even the most severe cases of schizophrenia don't usually rear up until adulthood. A rare case was reported in a nine-year-old girl who couldn't control the expanding number of her imaginary friends, but never has a three-year-old been thusly diagnosed.

Now, considering my daughter's insistence this morning that *Daddy went to God Land*, I wonder if Nini isn't something else.

Something not even doctors can explain. "What if she's a ghost? Or a demon?"

Micah grins. "Really?"

"Yes, really." I stiffen and pull a few inches away. "Look, I know it's farfetched, but—"

"Are you telling me you think our three-year-old is clairvoyant? That she opened a door to the great beyond and plays with Satan's minions?" He pretends to reach for my cell phone. "Let's call Oprah. She'll know what to do."

"You don't think I know how crazy it sounds?" I attempt to rub away my headache. "Maybe it's me. Maybe I'm the crazy one, if everyone else thinks this is normal."

He grips the back of my neck. "It's crazy, all right. As crazy as I am about you."

I try not to laugh, but while he's working my neck with one hand, he tickles my ribs with the other and gives my earlobe a nibble. "Stop!" I say on a breathy giggle. "This is serious."

"Listen." He scoots his chair closer. "I don't want you worrying about anything." His hand settles on my abdomen. "Think about two little embryos. Still kicking in their test tubes."

"Not great odds." The lab's call this morning informed us that of six, only two eggs fertilized. I'm thirty-one years old. Too young to be going through this.

"If these two fresh ones don't make it, we still have one more shot to batch," he reminds me. "And if we don't have anything to show for that attempt, *we still have two frozen at the lab*. All it takes is one, babycakes. All it takes is one, and we already have two. One is silver, the other's gold, all right?"

I rest my head on his shoulder. I don't tell him so, but I can't handle the prospect of having to endure this again—the shots, the medications, the side effects—perpetually hungover and queasy, without the benefit of the drink, for months on end. Especially because I'm becoming less and less confident in the process. Sure, IVF worked when we conceived Bella, but I'm four years older now, and things are different. On our second try, I miscarried twins at thirteen weeks. Brutal. Painful. Not fair. To go through it all for nothing but heartache.

"Do you think it's going to happen for us?" I ask. "Do you think we'll have another baby?"

"No two people on this planet deserve it more."

I don't disagree with him, but that's not what I asked. "I know you want a big family—"

"If this is it, if all we have is Bella, I'd die a happy man. Having the two of you is more important than anything in this world." He tickles my ribs. "Or even in *God Land*."

I roll my eyes at his bad joke. "It's just that I don't feel good. And even a simple trip to the park turns into a stressful situation."

"Maybe go *with* someone, give yourself an opportunity to socialize, have adult conversations. Set something up with Claudette."

Claudette is the closest thing I have to a friend, but she's one of those supermoms, always toting organic snacks, always with firm control of her children . . . I can't measure up. Sometimes being with her feels a little less like socialization and a lot more like judgment day. But I know Micah's trying to help, and it's good advice. "Maybe I'll do that."

But my husband must sense my hesitation because he tickles the back of my neck. "Whatcha thinking?"

"Sometimes I wonder if I'm up to the task, all right? I'm not as *good* at this as Claudette is. I just want to push my daughter on a swing. I want to enjoy her, let her have fun. But being with Claudette sometimes reminds me of all the reasons I'm not quite the mother she is."

"Then I'll put a swing in Bella's room. You won't have to leave the house."

I shake my head and smile ruefully. Micah's mind is methodical. Even when our pregnancy tests kept turning up negative, he researched infertility tirelessly and found a solution, and in time, it worked. But I wish he'd see that not everything is fixable. Sometimes life just sucks, and there's nothing to do but cope—and coping is hard work.

"I wonder sometimes . . ." I hesitate. "Natasha and I were good friends."

His brow peaks with the mention of my college roommate. He drapes a curl over my ear. "You don't have to beat yourself up for the rest of your life, you know. Natasha moved on. There's nothing you could've done."

"I know, but being friends with her was *easy*. Not like it is with Claudette or even anyone in Old Town. Is friendship supposed to be so . . . forced?"

"You've got a lot on your plate. Things will fall into place for us. I promise. We'll have more babies. We'll have friends . . ."

I hold my tongue, but I want to tell him he can't will these things to be.

"My mom'll be back from Europe in a couple of weeks," he says. "Maybe she can come help for a while after our embryos are implanted, until we're out of the woods, until we see little blips of heartbeats on sonograms."

"I'm sure she'll be in the throes of another benefit for the hospital group before long, and besides, she won't leave your father for more than a week anyway. If only you'd consider reconciling with him—"

"Man's a tyrant."

"They could both come, is what I'm saying. I could meet him. He could get to know his granddaughter while Shell plans her next seminar or charity event."

"Nicki. No."

I stare into his clouded eyes. I never knew my father; to think Micah has one and doesn't care to know him . . .

"I know he made some mistakes," I say, "but if Shell's forgiven him, maybe, with time . . . I just think a man should have a relationship with his father, shouldn't he? If it's at all possible?"

"We're better off," Micah says crisply. "I don't want to talk about it."

I figured as much, and I have no choice but to understand and accept his decision. Whatever happened, happened long ago. I have my own demons of memories locked behind doors.

"My mother will come," he says. "You'll make it in the meantime."

"I'm so tired."

"I know. You're not sleeping."

It's another side effect of the medication.

"Take a pill tonight."

"No." The last time I took a pill, I woke up in a panic, feeling as if someone had been inside the house and I'd been too zonked out to notice. "What would happen if Bella needed me and I couldn't wake up?"

"You have to sleep."

"Well, you're leaving, and I'm on my own, so I guess I'll have to sleep when you come back."

"Nicki."

A cheap shot. I knew constant travel was part of the package when I married a pilot. I also know Micah would take the shots and gain baby weight if he could. *He'd* have the baby for *me* if he could. "It's just that I have a headache all the time, and those people at Bella's school . . . if they knew, some days, how difficult it is to get that child ready and out the door—with Nini, to boot—"

"What do you have to do to get Nini ready?" He's laughing, still rubbing my belly. "Tie her shoes? Braid her hair?"

"You laugh. But yes. She makes everything more difficult."

"And Doctor Russo thinks it's best to play along," Micah confirms. "Pretend this demon child living in our daughter's hair is really there."

"That's what he said."

"Okay." He drums his fingers against my tummy. "Then let's set some ground rules. Just like we did when Bella got her tricycle."

Before I have a chance to respond, he's calling into the great room: "Bella? Bella, can you come here for a minute?"

"No," she pips.

"Come on, sugar cube."

She glances over her shoulder at us—"We're busy"—and turns back to her coloring table. "Nini, that's mean."

I raise an eyebrow in a silent I-told-you-so.

He tries again: "Bella? Do you want ice cream?"

"Yes, yes, yes!" She's jumping up and down now. "For Nini, too!"

"Of course Nini can have ice cream. Come on into the kitchen." I'm on my way to the freezer.

"Can you bring it in here? We're *busy*."

"No," Micah says. "You know the rules."

"Nini says *you* don't follow the rules."

My head snaps up the moment I hear her tone. "Elizabella!"

"Well, I'm a grown-up," Micah says. "Sometimes I don't have to follow the rules. And if you don't come into the kitchen, you won't get ice cream at all."

"Thanks a lot." Bella slams a crayon down on the table. "Mommy's mad all the time, but now you made Daddy mad, too." With her arms across her chest, she puffs out her darling, chubby cheeks so they look like pink apples and makes her way toward us.

I bite back a laugh—she's so dramatic—but Micah doesn't contain his, which only serves to frustrate Bella more.

"No laughing!"

"Ice cream, Mike?" Just as I turn to pull three dishes from the cabinet, I hear a crash and a wail. By the time I turn around, he's already scooped up our daughter, who is a cuddly, weepy ball in his arms. "What happened?"

Bella screeches, "Nini pushed me!" just as Micah explains that she tripped.

"It's okay." Micah sits at the table, still holding Bella on his lap. "Ice cream makes it all better."

I scoop out one heap of strawberry into a silver dessert dish, then another, and two into the third for my husband, who makes ice cream part of his daily routine—not that his waistline tells the tale. He'll eat Nini's ice cream, as well as whatever Bella doesn't finish, but he'll be no worse for wear on the scale tomorrow.

I slide one dish in front of Bella, one toward an empty chair, and the dish with two scoops I hand to Micah.

"None for you?" he asks.

"I'm up seventeen pounds with the treatment." I show him my left hand. "I can't even take off my ring."

"It's for a good cause," he reminds me. "And you're still stunning."

"And you're blind with love."

"So. Why don't you tell Daddy about this picture Nini drew?" He nods toward the drawing we've been perusing, and spoons a bit of ice cream for Bella and offers to feed her.

She allows it, despite the fact that she's a *big girl now* and wouldn't tolerate such an offer from me on her best day. I take the seat next to them.

"You like it?" Elizabella turns her head to look up at her daddy. Her angel-soft hair brushes against his chin, snagging on the whiskers of a five-o'clock shadow.

"I love it. Nini must be an artist."

"She is."

An artist. Like my mother.

"What's the story behind it? Who's this?" He points to a figure I assume is human, floating in the middle of the page amid black chevrons and red swirls.

"That's you, Daddy."

"What am I doing?"

"Flying."

This makes sense. Micah has been a pilot with Diamond Corporation for only a few months, but before that, he flew with a commercial airline. He's flown since before she was born. She doesn't know a life without planes.

"Flying without his plane?" I ask, although Bella and I have been through this conversation before.

"Silly Mommy. The plane went to God Land in the water."

I freeze, and a chill runs through my system. She did *not* say that the first time I asked. Micah looks up and meets my gaze. He's wearing a look of concern.

"And here's the water, where the plane is," Bella says, as matter-of-fact as if she were telling me the water is wet. Her chubby finger travels over the page. "And the place over here is where the big house is."

I swallow over the lump in my throat. "There's a big house?"

"A very big house," she tells me.

"Is it an imaginary house?" Micah asks. "Or a real house?"

"Real."

"Real like Nini?"

"Nini goed there once."

This time, when my husband looks at me, it's with relief, as if to say, *There you have it. God Land is a haven for her imaginary friend.*

But because I'm not especially comfortable with Nini, knowing my daughter has now created an imaginary place to put her does little to calm my anxieties.

"Want me to draw it for you?"

"Would you do that?" My fingers tremble as I push the morbid scribblings a few inches forward on the table. "It's a beautiful drawing."

From Micah's lap, she reaches for me and presses a hand to each of my cheeks. "We can 'member him when he's gone."

All is silent, except for the sound of the neighbor's landscaping crew blowing leaves.

I'm staring into my daughter's eyes.

My breath catches in my throat, and tears prick my eyes.

I don't know what to say, so I go with the old standby: "Mommy loves you, Ellie-Belle."

"All right, sugar cube." Micah pulls her back into his lap. "Let's eat this ice cream and get you in the tub."

I suppose we'll set those ground rules about Nini another time.

Chapter 3

"If I were you, I'd nip it in the bud," Claudette says.

Claudette and I shared the same whim, which I'm beginning to regret, and spontaneously met at Centennial Park after preschool today.

"I don't tolerate imaginary friends."

Of course she doesn't. She doesn't allow her kids to eat when they're hungry, either. They eat at seven, noon, and five, with snacks at ten and two, whether they're hungry or not.

I check my watch now. It's almost two.

Like clockwork, she's unzipping an insulated cooler and calling over her shoulder to Crew and Fendi—her children, who know better than to delay responding—before she turns back to me. "Listen. If you put on like this Nini is real, it's going to encourage her."

I'm sorry I mentioned Nini at all. "The professionals say it will encourage her imagination."

"Professionals don't always know what they're talking about. A *professional* plumber fixed my garbage disposal last month, but it's on the fritz again. I told him what was wrong, and he insisted otherwise, so . . ." She shudders, as if a colony of ants just wandered out of her hair. "Sometimes you have to take charge of what's going on in your own household, if you know what I mean."

The kids, Bella included, are running toward us.

Claudette spreads a red-and-white gingham tablecloth over a picnic table and is pulling snacks from her cooler—homemade and prepackaged in tiny, resealable containers with matching forest-green lids—and placing them into three neat piles. "I always bring extra," she says. "Just in case. Don't want to leave anyone out. I assume you didn't plan to have snacks at the park today?"

I feel my brow knit. I want to tell her that my kid is perfectly all right to gnaw on whatever stale crackers or fuzzy, high-fructose fruit snack I happen to find at the bottom of my purse, but the fact of the matter is that I don't even have a crumbling saltine to offer Elizabella.

It's not like this outing was a planned picnic. If it were, I'd surely have sliced grapes into quarters and mixed an organic peanut butter spread for celery sticks and . . . whatever else Claudette does when she isn't listing and selling houses. We were simply driving by, and Bella said Nini wanted to stop for a swing. So here we are. I can't deny my daughter an offered snack when her playmates are bellying up to a table set more for a ladies' luncheon than a quick snack at a park.

Claudette's son reaches for a container labeled with his name, but Claudette pulls it just out of reach. "Set the table first, Crew."

He begins to set out biodegradable paper plates and even proceeds to fold the napkins in half.

"Say thank you," I remind Bella.

She glances up at me, then down at the foods in the containers, which must look foreign to her. "Where's Nini's?"

"You'll have to share your plate with Nini," I say.

Claudette lets out an exasperated sigh, and if I took the time to look at her, I'm sure she'd be treating me to her best mom stare.

"Not fair," Bella says. "Fendi has her own, Crew has his—"

"Bella—"

"Nini wants her own."

My phone rings—"Rock-a-bye Baby"—and my heart flutters. It's the lab, calling with today's news. "Share for a second, okay?" I dig in my purse while Bella protests. "We'll talk about it—"

"Not fair." Bella crosses her arms over her chest.

I find my phone, press the "Answer" button, and hook an arm around my daughter's waist to pull her off the picnic bench. I'm not supposed to lift her, but I can't very well leave her having a tantrum at Claudette's table. Neither can I deal with her and the lab at the same time. I lead her away from the playground and picnic area toward a line of pines, where it's quieter.

Bella's squealing and kicking. "Not fair, not fair, not fair."

"Is now a good time?" the woman from the fertility clinic asks.

No. But I can't not take the call. Waiting for news is nearly as stressful as the shots and procedures. "It's fine. Just a moment." I lower Bella to the ground and pull the phone from my ear for a second. "Bella, this is the baby doctor, and Mommy has to talk to her for a minute. Please."

She's in tears now, wailing at the top of her lungs.

But what can I do? I turn a few degrees to the left, walk a few steps so I can hear, and put my phone to my ear. "Sorry about that. What's the news?"

"Mrs. Cavanaugh, of the oocytes we managed to fertilize, only one is developing. By the second day, we like to see a cell count of four to six, and the one that is developing, I'm sorry to say, is at only two."

Numbness spreads from my heart to my fingertips. Deep breath. "So that means . . . wait. How . . . I'm not sure I under—" I press a hand to my other ear to deaden Bella's screams. "We had six eggs. Twenty-five percent develop. That's what you said. So how is it that we don't have a single healthy embryo this cycle?"

"Twenty-five percent is the likely outcome, but as you know, assisted reproduction is an inexact science, and—"

I'm pacing now, wearing a trench in the grass around a tree. "It has only two cells?" Anger rises like bile in my throat. We've been cheated. It isn't fair. I did everything right. Not once did I miss a dose of medication, not once did I neglect the needles, not once did I miss a pill.

And if I did everything right, how is it possible things have gone wrong?

"We'll watch it," the tech is saying. "There's a chance it will still develop, but—"

A *chance?* I—*we*—deserve more than a fleeting chance! I hear about people all the time, "cursed" with unwanted pregnancies, women begrudging that it happened *now* instead of six months from now, couples pondering abortions because their kids are older, and they were almost *out of the woods* when they were surprised with an *oops*, despite their methods of birth control. But me . . . I'm a good mother, and yet it's always a struggle for me to conceive.

"And no measured correlation between cell number and gestation." The technician's voice is flat, dry. I know she isn't supposed to give me a sense of false hope or even prepare me for the worst. Just the facts.

"But even if it does develop"—I take another deep breath—"doesn't that mean there's something wrong with the embryo?"

"Not necessarily."

It worked once, I remind myself. We have Bella. We have two embryos frozen at the lab. I spin to look at the proof that everything is going to be okay.

But Bella isn't where I left her. A quick scan of the area turns up no sign of my daughter. "Bella!"

Another spin. She's nowhere to be seen. "Bella!"

I realize I've hung up on the lab, but at the moment, I don't care about anything as much as I care about glimpsing my kid.

My heart is beating like mad. My pulse throbs in my ears, and I feel my legs trembling as they carry me toward the playground.

Please, let her be there!

But the swings sway in the light autumn breeze, and only a pair of boys occupies the merry-go-round. Claudette is pouring juice for her kids, right where we left them, but my daughter is not seated at their table.

I scream at the top of my lungs: "Elizabella!"

Chapter 4

Centennial Park is a blur of colors spinning all around me, as if I'm at the hub of the merry-go-round. The auburn spread of leaves awaiting raking at the far end of the playground, the still-green grass, the knobby gray-brown trunks of decades-old maple trees, the offensively yellow ladder on the slide . . . Everything is a kaleidoscope of paint streaks on canvas, but I don't register the one color I desperately need to see: the lilac of my daughter's coat.

I can scarcely hear anything beyond the rapid beat of my heart, and even drawing a breath is difficult, but I scream at the top of my lungs: "Elizabella!"

And suddenly, I see her elbow, poking out beyond the massive trunk of a tree.

I dart to her, sweep her up into my arms, and feel her warm little body against me, her cool cheek pressed against mine.

Tears of relief blur my vision, and the faint ache of swollen ovaries rears its head again, as if reminding me, *Don't lift more than a gallon of milk.*

"Don't do that," I say. "You can't just run away like that."

Bella places her hands on my cheeks, cupping my face. "Nini said she saw Daddy."

And despite the panic of the moment, I touch my forehead to hers, and I laugh. "Let's try to do what's right. Okay, Ellie-Belle? And not what Nini tells us to do."

She puckers her pretty pink lips and kisses me. Wipes away more of my tears. "I miss Daddy."

"I miss Daddy, too. He'll be home tomorrow." Meanwhile I have to call to tell him about the unfortunate news from the lab. "Come on, baby. Let's go home."

She shakes her head—"Want to play with Fendi and Crew"—and wiggles until I put her down.

Before I have half a second to compose myself, she's running over to the picnic bench and climbing between the model children, demanding another snack and place setting so Nini can have her own.

I follow. "No. Nini—"

"Nini isn't real," Claudette says. "I don't feed children who aren't real."

My headache pierces. I glance at Claudette. "I can handle—"

"Is so real!" Bella frowns and puffs out her cheeks again.

Claudette finishes popping little paper straws into small cups of organic apple juice, oblivious to my protest against her parenting my child. "Let me give you some advice." Supermom of the Year plants her hands on her lean hips, raises an eyebrow, and continues before I can tell her I'm not in the mood to hear it. "Now, you know I wouldn't say this unless I truly *cared* about your family, Veronica. It takes two to raise a toddler, and because your husband is gone a lot, I want you to rely on me. I know you're exhausted, but you need to establish and enforce some boundaries. You're letting her control you. Who's in charge?"

I wrap an arm around Bella's waist and pull her, kicking, off the picnic bench. "Stop. Before you hurt someone."

Bella doesn't stop.

"Maybe you should find an outlet," Claudette says. "Something for *you*. I was the same way before I got my realty license. The feelings of inadequacy, the overblown concentration on spoiling the children—"

"Excuse me?"

"I know you're under a lot of pressure with IVF and with Micah's being out of town. And it's giving your daughter an opportunity to act out. Have you ever considered the fact that you're trying too hard to get pregnant?"

I plant Bella on the ground next to me and meet Claudette's gaze.

"Relax and it'll happen," she says. "My children are living proof of that."

It probably took her a whole month or two of trying before a little plus sign appeared on the sticks in her bathroom. Some of us aren't that lucky.

"Why don't you let me take Elizabella for the afternoon? Go home, have a glass of wine—"

"I can't drink during treatment."

"And relax, and it'll happen."

"Do you honestly think we *weren't* relaxed for the first year?" I tug on Bella's hand. "Who *isn't* relaxed for the first several months?"

"I'm just saying—"

"Well, don't." My daughter is at the onset of another tantrum, but I tighten my grip on her hand and give her my best *Mommy's serious* look. "If Nini's coming, she has to come now." And we begin toward the parking lot.

"Veronica. Sometimes positive thoughts—"

"Yeah, yeah. I've read *The Secret*."

"Veronica!"

I picture Claudette staring after me, hands on hips, but I don't turn back to confirm it. Instead, I look down at Bella. "Let's give Daddy a call." I try a tone with more sweetness, and it seems to work.

"Yay!" Bella skips alongside me.

Aside from emitting a dramatic sigh, Claudette seems to have already forgotten her quest to educate me in the ways of easy, carefree conception. A quick glance over my shoulder proves she's busy with her robotic children, who obediently grasp her hands to thank Jesus for the snacks before they gobble them up.

The nerve of that woman, thinking I'd be shooting up Follistim night after freaking night because it's more convenient than having sex at just the right time, as if I prefer the drama of infertility to simply giving my husband a roll midcycle.

No one goes through what I'm going through unless there are no other options.

Rationally, I know I shouldn't fault Claudette for what she doesn't understand. No one understands, unless she's gone through the shots, the egg retrievals, the intracytoplasmic sperm injection, the inch-and-a-half-long needles filled with enough progesterone to ensure the embryos transferred into their faulty uteri stick . . . and she does it all only to see another negative result or even to miscarry.

No baby at the end of it all.

I might be one of those women now. Only one fertilized egg survived the night. And it isn't doing well.

Once Bella and Nini are settled in the back seat, and we're far enough away from Centennial Park that I can no longer see Claudette's prayer circle, a feeling of utter exhaustion overcomes me. Suddenly, I'm bawling.

Guilt over my behavior and the way I treated Claudette begins to prick at me. I'll have to call her to smooth things over.

"Nini, Mommy's sad."

Yes, I am.

I push the Bluetooth button on my dashboard. "Call Micah."

"Calling Micah." The computerized voice confirms my command.

His phone doesn't ring; rather, it goes straight to voice mail: "You have reached the mobile phone of Micah Cavanaugh—"

In a knee-jerk reaction, I terminate the call. My tears intensify, not with despair as much as irritation. How convenient that he has the luxury of turning off his cell phone. I'll bet he's enjoying a late lunch and a cocktail, despite our agreement that if I can't drink, he shouldn't drink. And I'm stuck here with a sassy three-year-old, her mischievous imaginary friend, and Claudette Winters as my only acquaintance.

I take a deep breath and try again. "Call Micah."

"Calling Micah."

Again, voice mail picks up before the phone rings. This time, I leave a message, trying to hold my tears at bay: "It's me. I have news from the lab and . . . it's been a rather rough day. I hope you had a nice flight. We can't wait to see you, so hurry home. Love you. Bye."

I hang up.

"I know," Elizabella is saying. "I told her, but she won't believe me."

I glance in the rearview mirror and witness Bella in deep conversation with no one. "What doesn't Mommy believe, baby?"

"You don't believe what Nini says. About Daddy."

"What about Daddy?"

"You tell her, Nini." Bella fiddles with the belt on her car seat. "I don't want to make her mad."

"Mommy won't get mad," I promise.

"I *told* you," Bella says. "We're all alone."

"Daddy's coming home tomorrow."

"No." She follows it up with a dramatic sigh. "No, Mommy. He went to God Land in his plane."

I stomp on the brake at a red light. "Bella, you have to stop saying that! You know it isn't true!"

"Is so."

She sounds sleepy. I glance at her again and confirm it when I see her heavy eyelids. By the time I turn into the Shadowlands and punch in the access code at the gate, the kid is out cold.

I drive along the winding paths leading to Hidden Creek Lane, where our home sits just south of the eleventh fairway—across from Claudette Winters's.

I park in the garage and have no choice but to carry Bella inside. I can't leave her sleeping in the car. Nor can I wake her, unless I want to deal with an even crankier version of Miss Mind of Her Own. But when I lift her, I feel a subtle strain in my lower back, as well as in my abdomen. This is one of those times life would be easier if Micah had a normal job. If he were due home at six o'clock, I might not care about a challenging, overly tired three-year-old. I'd wake her up, let her have a fit or two, and let Micah take a turn dealing with it when he came home.

But as things stand, I carry her in, gently lower her to the sofa, unzip her coat, and remove her shoes. I watch her for a moment, time suspended, in absolute awe of her beauty.

Every parent thinks her child is exceptional, and from a certain point of view, it's true. Every child is a miracle—of science, of faith, of whatever keeps us going in the still of the night. Claudette spends thousands of dollars on head shots for her daughter and son, insistent they'll be the next Disney stars . . . and they're not especially cute kids. Some moms go overboard believing their children are special, but Elizabella *is*. Especially considering the news from the lab today. No one can convince me she's anything short of a miracle.

I snap a photo and text it to my husband, in order to document what he's missing. Sometimes, he comes home earlier if he can arrange it, and especially given the news from the lab, I desperately need him to try.

I lower myself to a chair and prop my feet on the oversize ottoman. When I glance around this house, I realize, and not for the first time, that it has yet to feel like home.

But the Shadowlands is a good place for kids to grow up. *And you can't raise children in the city,* Claudette has told me. As if she'd ever tried.

Still, I miss our condo in Old Town. The white-bearded man who sets up his folding chair and draws the charming buildings from the corner . . . the wrought iron scrolled gateway arching over the side-walk to announce your arrival into the quaintest neighborhood in Chicago . . . the fresh produce market just around the corner.

I want to move back. When Micah calls, I'll tell him. Let's just pack up and go. Leave this snooty neighborhood and the eleventh fairway behind us. Chalk it up as a mistake. And I miss having friends like Natasha. Has enough time passed? If I were to reach out to her now, would she be open to meeting for lunch?

With the very thought of going back home and reconnecting with my college roommate, my one true friend besides my husband, my heart quickens, but I know it won't happen. I remember why Natasha and I parted ways, and I know why we moved out to the 'burbs. More space for our growing family. Little did we know the only addition might come not in a bundle of joy in receiving blankets, but in the form of Nini.

Chapter 5

Somewhere between dreamland and wakefulness, a memory surfaces, as clear as if it happened only yesterday.

My mother sits on a stool at our kitchen table, which she's recently painted blue.

She's wearing the sweatpants smudged with every color of paint she's opened the past few years, and a men's tank-style undershirt, which she says used to belong to my father.

Every time she wears it, I find myself staring at the worn material, hoping to find a clue somewhere within the threads. Something that might tell me where my father is, what kind of man he used to be.

The pants practically hang off her hips. She's so thin. Her nubs of breasts are like tiny topographical bumps on a map now, but I remember when she looked like an hourglass. I remember when she looked like a woman.

Her hair hasn't been washed in over a week, and lately she's been pulling at it, strand by strand. There's a scabby bald patch at her right temple now.

But she's still my mother.

I long to feel the warmth of her embrace, to hear the pretty sound of her voice—almost musical—when she speaks to me.

The radio is broken, so I wind the crank on my music box to play a tinkling version of some Broadway hit—something from *Cats*, maybe?—and Mama hums along with the melody.

She places a tiny red crystal into a pronged opening. Two more stones to go before the pair of earrings is complete. Quietly, I watch from a distance. Can't disturb her; I learned my lesson last time.

A whisper in my ear. *She's watching you, waiting for the right time to strike.*

I flinch when I realize it's my mother at my side, her lips brushing against my ear as she speaks.

Be careful, little Veri. They don't want you here.

And they're looking at me now.

I feel it, that tingling sensation that settles into the back of my neck whenever I sense someone looking at me.

Someone's in the house.

I can't open my eyes.

Can't move.

Wake up! Wake up!

"Mommy?"

I startle out of the deepest sleep I've had in more than a month.

Bella. She's standing over me in her purple jacket in the dim, still room. Her hair is mussed, and she's backlit by the setting sun filtering in through the patio doors. In this light, she looks like an angelic messenger.

"I told you, Nini," she whispers to no one at her side. "She's asleep."

"Hi, baby," I say through a yawn. I straighten in the chair and feel an instant ache in my back from the awkward position I slept in. An overwhelming sense of loss sucker-punches me square in the chest—the feeling that something horrible happened before I fell asleep.

It's an oppressive feeling. Instantly, my mind travels back to April, when I awoke in a puddle of blood. Bleeding out my babies. Elizabella's brothers. Our family. A sticky, scarlet mess on our white cotton sheets.

It's the embryos, I remember. Sad news. Only one survived, and it doesn't look good.

My daughter is staring at me, head cocked to one side, the same way she did when Micah and I told her the sad news about the miscarriage—as if she doesn't understand why we couldn't make it better, why we couldn't fix it.

"Are you hungry, Bella?"

"Yes!" Her concerned, if not somber, expression dissipates, and she jumps into my lap and cuddles against me, all warm and sweet.

There's a smudge of something on her cheek, and when I wipe it off, I catch the scent of chocolate.

"Nini and I ate chocolate pudding!"

I glance to the child-size table in the corner to see the evidence of two now-empty pudding cups and spoons littering the scattering of papers. How long has Bella been awake and entertaining herself? I forego reprimanding her for eating in the great room, which is against the rules. Claudette wouldn't approve, but I'm picking my battles today.

"How about dinner?" I touch a button on my phone, which brightens the screen. It's after five. And no call from Micah. "Come on, munchkin. Let's get some real food in that tummy."

Bella scrambles off my lap and into the kitchen. "Ronis!"

"Okay, macaroni and cheese it is." Claudette wouldn't approve of this meal, either—high in sodium, chock-full of preservatives—but children have been subsisting on this crap for years. I take out a pot and fill it with water. Once it's on to boil, I try Micah again, hitting the "Speaker" button so Bella can talk, too.

"You have reached the mobile phone of Micah Cavanaugh . . ."

I hang up.

Screw him, if he won't turn his phone on.

"Mommy, he won't answer."

"I can see that. We'll try him again before bed."

"He won't at bedtime, either."

I crouch to look my daughter in the eye. "Of course he will."

She shakes her head, tears rimming her eyes. "Nini says you don't listen. Daddy is gone. He went to God Land."

My grip tightens on her arms. "Stop saying that!"

Fat tears now glisten on her thick lashes. "Nini says you don't believe it, but it's true. He won't answer. He won't come home."

I give her a sharp shake. "Don't say things like that!"

"It's not my fault, Mommy." A sob escapes her. "But it's true."

I pull her tightly to me and smooth her hair, press a kiss to the crown of her head. "Maybe he's had a busy day, or maybe his phone broke. But he'll call."

Her hair catches on my sweater when she shakes her head. "No, Mommy."

"I love you, Bella."

"Love you, too."

"Do you and Nini want to color while I finish the ronis?"

"Okay."

"Make Mommy a nice picture. We'll hang it on the refrig—" I stop. This refrigerator has panels to match the cabinetry. It looks more like an armoire than an appliance. Nothing will stick to it without tape. "We'll hang it on the bulletin board in the mudroom."

"Okay." She backhands her nose, just as I reach for a tissue to dry her tears.

I give her another kiss. "Daddy is fine." I peel the lilac Windbreaker from her shoulders and drape it over a chair at the island. "You'll see."

She looks at me skeptically, as if she thinks I'm lying. "Okay." And finally, she turns toward the great room. "Come on, Nini. Let's color. And I use the red first this time."

I turn on the news, listening for any report of a small corporate jet not reaching its destination.

The anchors report nothing but city shootings and legislative arguments; during a commercial break, an ad for a cell phone company fills the screen. Hmmm . . .

I open my laptop on the kitchen island and log on to our mobile phone carrier's site. I've never tracked Micah's activity before—and doing it now, I feel a bit like a psycho who doesn't trust her husband—but I'm not worried about whom he's called or why. I just want to know that his phone has been in use. Period. Because if he's used it, it means he's okay.

But there's no record of any calls after six thirty this morning. I jot down the last number, which begins with area code 305, in case I have to follow his trail. I won't have to—he'll call—but just in case.

Then I look up the number to Diamond Corporation. If I haven't heard from Micah by tomorrow morning, I'll call the company. A butterfly of relief flutters in my stomach. Of course Micah is fine. If anything had happened, if his plane hadn't reached . . . where did he say he was going? . . . New York, the company would have called me. He's fine.

Perhaps he's being a bit irresponsible or negligent, but he's fine. If he'd crashed, as Nini suggests, the company would have sent a representative, or the police would be here. Surely, if someone had to be in New York City in the morning and the plane hadn't arrived, I'd know it by now.

I close the laptop, feeling ridiculous. No news is good news. Isn't that what they say?

I pour the box of noodles into the boiling water and reduce the heat.

"Well, if he's not at God Land," Elizabella's saying, "where is he?"

I glance at the numbers I wrote down on the pad of paper.

Bella giggles. "That's funny, Nini. I don't think my daddy knows any dolphins."

A chill dances in my veins. I snatch up my phone and dial Micah again.

"You have reached the mobile phone of Micah Cavanaugh . . ."

Hang up. Dial.

"Hello. And thank you for calling Diamond Corporation. Our normal business hours are nine to five, Monday through Friday. If you're calling during these hours, we are away from the switchboard or tending to other callers. If you know your party's extension, you may dial it now."

I press zero.

"Hello. And thank you for calling Diamond Corporation. Our normal business hours are—"

Hang up. Dial the last number on record for Micah's phone.

A series of three high-pitched tones pierce my ear. A computerized voice: "The number you have reached . . . three . . . oh . . . five—"

You've got to be kidding me.

"Has been disconnected."

Bella is giggling up a storm.

My heart is pounding so rampantly that I can scarcely hear anything beyond its beat. Who can I call? Who can help me find my husband?

My mother-in-law seems the obvious choice, but she's in Europe with Micah's father. I don't want to worry her if I'm overreacting. Besides, it's the middle of the night across the pond. If I'm going to call, it'll have to wait until morning.

I consider calling Claudette—what are friends for?—but I feel sheepish after the way I stormed out of the park. I have to apologize to her, face-to-face, before I go to her for help.

A familiar dread rises up from the dark places of my past, and suddenly, I'm back there again, in the waiting room at Loyola University Medical. Eighteen and alone, staring at an approaching doctor, the one who'd been caring for my mother, knowing well before he reaches me what he's about to say.

"Silly Nini."

My daughter's voice zaps me from the memory.

"My daddy doesn't know that man in the kitchen."

I flinch. My God, my God, my God.

"Bella."

"*No.* He didn't."

"Bella, listen." I crouch in front of her and hold her elbows. She looks at me.

"Tell me about the man in the kitchen."

"Nini says Daddy knowed him."

"Is it pretend, Bella?"

"Nini's real."

"I know that, baby. But the man in the kitchen—"

"I was too little, Mommy." She practically rolls her eyes. "Don't 'member him."

"Does Nini remember?"

"Nini knows."

"There was a man in the kitchen? When you were little?"

"Yes, Mommy."

My mouth is instantly dry. It's not just the dream I had this evening. I remember waking up months ago, at our place in Old Town, feeling as if someone was looking at me, as if someone had been in the house while I was asleep.

What if—I swallow over the lump in my throat—what if it's true? What if everything Nini says to my daughter is true? What if there really was a man in my house? A man no one but my husband knows?

Chapter 6

November 12

It's past three in the morning. My head pounds, and every muscle aches with insomnia.

After doing some quick math, I ascertain that it's about nine where Shell and Mick are vacationing. I don't want to worry them, but I'm going crazy waiting for information to come to me. I have to try *something*. Perhaps Micah called his mother. Or sent her an e-mail, letting her know what's going on. Especially if he needed to get away from me, away from the drama of fertility treatments, for a while.

What the hell. I dial.

After a few rings, Shell's voice mail picks up. I leave a message:

"Hi, Shell." I take a deep breath. I can't just disclose all my fears in a voice mail. *Keep it easy.* "Hope you're having a good time. I'm just wondering if you've heard from Micah . . . or if you know if he had any plans he maybe forgot to tell me about. Give me a call when you can. Love you."

When I hang up, I feel lonelier than ever.

Bella is asleep in my bed next to me, and my laptop is open on my lap.

I've gone through nearly an entire box of tissues, and while I don't know where I'm finding more tears to cry, they keep coming.

The Diamond Corporation website is displayed on the screen. It's a professional creation of plum and navy, with an eye-catching bolt of lightning lasing down from nowhere to scrawl the word *Diamond* across the top of the page.

For the eightieth time, I click on the tab ABOUT DIAMOND, and I'm redirected to a page displaying a picture of a woman in a couture business suit seated in a high-backed chair. DIAMOND: CONNECTING THE WORLD THROUGH CUTTING-EDGE COMMUNICATION.

It's vague. All of it is.

The page apologizes, but it's under construction, as are the other pages on the site. The CONTACT DIAMOND page offers up an e-mail address and an eight-hundred number, which I've already called, but no names of corporate gods or generals who might be able to help me track down Micah and his plane.

Bella lets out a chuckle in her sleep. "So funny, Nini."

Nini.

I click to open another tab and search for *Nini.*

It comes up in a baby name dictionary. It means "little girl" or "little sister." My heart warms when I consider what Dr. Russo said about Bella's creating a sister while waiting for IVF to work its magic.

I should leave it at that. But a nagging sensation tugs at me. Nini appeared one day, out of the blue and unexplained. It was a week or so after the miscarriage. Micah's parents were out of town, and Micah had taken Elizabella to his parents' lake house up north, and they came back with Nini. She isn't a good child, a good influence, a good playmate.

I type in, if only to see the comfort of no results returned, *Nini Demon.* Images from anime pop up and pages of comic books beckon. I click on a small cartoon of the Nini demon, who looks almost sweet. She's seven years old—*not little*, Bella said earlier of her imaginary friend. In the world of comics, Nini is a child spirit who makes trouble.

It's true enough in my house, and I nearly smile through my tears at the coincidence of it.

How Elizabella managed to come up with Nini as a name—either meaning "little sister" or in reference to the mischievous influence with whom she spends her days—is a mystery.

I return to the search results and am just about to close the browser when a link at the bottom of the page catches my eye. I click, and it takes me to a reference page—a dictionary cataloging the legacy of Native American dialects—and my heart nearly stops.

The root *nini* can be a verb or a noun, but however it is used, it's a reference to fear, synonymous with the verbs "to thunder" and "to scare." Nini is also an evil being, used in folklore to scare unruly children—like the bogeyman of my childhood.

But the bogeyman never spoke to me. The bogeyman never stole my red crayon or talked me into eating chocolate pudding in the great room—or insisted there was a man in my kitchen or told me Daddy went to God Land.

Schizophrenia. I don't have to google it to know it's a condition marked by not knowing what's real and what's not. By hearing voices in one's head. One of my last conversations with my mother involved her confessing the terrible things she'd been instructed to do.

"No," I whisper to myself. "Don't remember her that way. Remember the good years." But I'm raw and vulnerable. I can't help feeling as if she's still here sometimes, still looking at me like that . . . like she'd bury an ax in my skull, if she'd had strength enough to lift it.

She's been gone so long, but sometimes her absence is bitingly fresh. Sometimes I miss her as if she died only yesterday. On those days, Micah helps. He makes everything better. He doesn't know about everything I went through with my mother, but he reminds me that the past is in the past. We're the future, and I'm no longer alone.

I pick up the phone and dial him again. No answer. I have to admit that even if his phone had died, he would've called from his hotel room. Either he's not calling because he's doing something he shouldn't be doing, or Nini is right.

For a split second, I find myself hoping it's the latter. If he isn't calling because he's busy with another woman, I'd either die myself or kill him.

Both scenarios are preposterous. He's fine, and he isn't with another woman. He just forgot to turn his phone on. I kept him up late last night with what Micah calls saying goodbye with mind, body, and soul, and he left early this morning. He's exhausted. That's all. He didn't get to take a long nap after the park like I did. Maybe he laid down, thinking he'd call later, and he fell asleep. Micah and I wouldn't be trudging through fertility treatment if he were having an affair. He wouldn't pretend to want a family with me if he were sleeping with someone else—

"Stop!" I say it aloud, as if it's the only way to stop the thoughts racing through my head.

Bella stirs but rolls over and sighs a pretty little sound that further convinces me she's nothing but angelic, despite the demon child in her imagination.

I put the phone and my laptop aside and tiptoe out of the room and down the hall to the blank slate of bedroom three of four, which someday will house our next baby. I'm hoping for a boy to carry on Micah's family name. An only child, he's the last of the Cavanaughs if we don't produce one. Then again, considering Elizabella's strong will, I'll bet whomever she lowers herself to marry will be taking her name.

Twin boys again.

That's what I want.

This time, we'll name them.

I close my eyes and envision a pale-blue stripe racing around the beige walls. Two chestnuts cribs, with a changing table between them.

Their names hanging letter by letter on the walls above the cribs: **DYLAN** and **DOMINIC**. We'll have them both at the same time. We deserve it. We've worked hard. Done everything we're supposed to do. We love each other, and we're good parents.

Maybe the results of this IVF round are trying to tell us something. Don't get greedy. Take what you have: a beautiful daughter and two frozen embryos at the lab.

But if the unthinkable happens again . . .

I lower myself to the plush carpeting, an arm cradling my still-flat tummy, ghost pains of miscarriage racking my abdomen. And the blood . . . so much blood.

It's one reason leaving our condo in Old Town was acceptable. I never again wanted to sleep in that room where it happened, where my body ceased caring for the twins I was carrying, where they cracked free from their warm and safe station.

It won't happen here.

A fresh start, a new beginning, a new life.

Micah promised.

No one can keep a promise like that. But if anyone can, it's Micah. It's why I believed him when he said it.

Standing, I walk to the window and gaze out at the eleventh fairway, lit only with the haze of the moon and stars. I remember Micah's commentary the day we moved in: *Guess I'll have to start golfing again.*

He's next to me now, wrapping his arms around me in our would-be nursery, dreaming of tomorrow with me. I close my eyes and sink into the comfort of my imaginary husband.

Can't live on the eleventh fairway and never land a ball there. You should golf with me.

"I've never swung a club," I remind him, although I know he isn't here to hear me.

I never danced before we took cha-cha lessons and look at me now.

"You still don't dance," I say, swaying in time with him.

It'll be something fun for us to do together. I'll sign us up for golf lessons in the spring.

"Unless I'm pregnant."

Of course. Everything changes when you're pregnant.

I lean against the window, trying to believe. It'll happen. The lab will call tomorrow with miraculous news: the embryo will have survived another night, and maybe we'll have another couple after the next round of batching. I'll be pregnant by the new year. Micah will golf without me. I'll drive the cart, with Bella and her naughty imaginary friend coloring in the back.

An orange glow appears in the middle of the fairway. Just a dot in the expanse of blackness. I straighten and try to zero in on where I saw it, but it's gone again. Out of the corner of my eye, I see it to the right, farther north on the fairway, but just like the first time, it's gone again.

I open the window. Listen.

Nothing but the sounds of night insects and the mild breeze and—*crack.*

The snap of a twig.

There it is again: the orange glow.

The faint scent of cigarette smoke filters up from the fairway.

Someone's walking the golf course at night, that's all.

Smoking.

Probably some Shadowlands resident who's lying to his wife about his habits, escaping in the middle of the night to indulge.

But it's a strange, if not random, place to stop. Why stop at all? Why not walk the streets instead of the course? Who would do such a thing?

The Shadowlands is a safe place. No one can be admitted unless a resident permits it. However, the property backs a forest preserve, which is blockaded with a privacy fence. If someone wanted to gain entry and couldn't get past the gates out front, it wouldn't be impossible for him to come in through the county preserve.

The orange glow now comes and goes at measured intervals, brightening when the smoker inhales. Whoever he is, he's copped a squat and stopped walking. I wonder if he's looking at me the way I'm looking at him.

I wonder if he stopped walking because he can see me silhouetted in the window.

Or—I shudder with the thought—if he came looking for me in the first place.

Chapter 7

"I'm sorry. Who are you looking for, ma'am?"

I take another deep breath and prepare to explain the situation again to the third person to whom I've been transferred. "My name is Veronica Cavanaugh. My husband is a pilot for your corporation. He left yesterday morning for New York, and I haven't been able to get ahold of him since. Can someone tell me, maybe, what hotel he's in? Or . . . or at least confirm that he landed all right?"

"You said your husband is a *pilot*?"

"Yes."

"With *our* corporation?"

"Yes. His name is Micah Cavanaugh, and he left yesterday—"

"I don't see an extension for anyone with that name in this office. Or for either of our satellites."

"He isn't *in* the office. I don't think he's ever *been* to the office, but he's—"

"Just a minute, Miss . . . Cavanaugh, did you say?"

"Yes. C-a-v-a—"

"Just a minute." Elevator music interrupts my spelling. I bite on my thumbnail to keep from screaming.

"No, Nini," Bella is saying. "That would be bad. If we do that, Mommy will never let us stay home from school again."

I'm sure Miss Wendy will fill my ears about Bella's absence today, but until I find Micah, my daughter is staying put. No learning, no routine, no Westlake School rules, and if that stick with a pocketful of sunshine doesn't like it, she can kiss my ass. This is a bona fide emergency.

While I'm on hold, my other line blips. It's the lab. It's awfully early for them to be calling. This can't be good news.

I have half a mind to let it go to voice mail. They're allowed to leave me detailed messages; I signed a waiver permitting it. However, it's been my experience that they prefer to deliver bad news to a live person. I could call them back if they don't leave a message, but the phones go off the switchboard at four. There's no guarantee I'll reach anyone, and I can't bear the thought of not knowing until tomorrow whether or not our meek two-celled near-embryo made it out of the gate.

I click over and hold my breath.

"Well," the lab technician says, "we had some progress overnight. It's at five cells now, and we'll continue to watch it."

"Five?" A bubble of elation rises in my heart. "That's good, right?"

"It's progress, but it's still behind schedule. I'll call you tomorrow with an update either way, but your embryo had a productive day."

"Which means . . . what? It might be viable?"

She continues: "I'm surprised to see this progress, truth be told. But some of these little guys have minds of their own. We've had five cells that become babies, and some eight that don't."

"So . . . I guess we wait and see?"

"That's about all we can do."

Knowing nothing more than I used to know—we *might* have an embryo—I click back to the elevator music and remain on hold.

It feels as if I'm living in limbo, as if my entire life is wait and see. No good news or even definitive bad news regarding the embryo. No word from Micah. No information from whomever put me on hold at Diamond Corporation.

After a glance at Bella, who is deep in conversation with Nini while a Disney flick plays in the background, I head out to the screened porch. It's cold, and I'm wearing only a light sweater over a T-shirt, but I don't want my daughter to watch me unravel.

Micah has been gone now for almost thirty hours. Since we met, we haven't gone a solid twenty-four without speaking.

Something terrible has happened. Even if he needed a time-out, a vacation from the rat race of hormone shots and imaginary children— not that I'd immediately forgive his seeking such a thing, but I'd certainly understand—wouldn't he at least have texted? To let me know he's okay?

Maybe it's worse than I assume. Maybe the constant battle for conception finally got the best of him. Before Elizabella was born, I feared he'd leave me for someone he could more easily impregnate. He talked me down off the ledge countless times, assured me I was more important, told me we would adopt if all else failed. Even if he'd changed his mind about me, about us, he couldn't possibly turn his back on our daughter—especially after all we went through to have her.

"Ma'am?"

I catch my breath. "Yes. Yes, I'm here."

"Ma'am, are you sure you have the right Diamond Corporation?"

"Headquarters in Chicago," I say. "With satellites in New York and Miami."

"That's right," the receptionist says. "The trouble is . . ."

I wait a moment for her to gather her thoughts.

"The trouble is . . . what?" I finally ask.

"Well, it's just . . . Do you know, by any chance, who hired your husband? Who's the head of his department?"

"I don't know." It's not like other jobs, where he reports to an office, punches a time clock with familiar faces, and complains about

49

the wages over lunch pails. "Can't you look it up for me? Who's the head of aviation?"

"Ma'am, bear with me, all right? We're a small communications corporation, and—"

"Who's in charge of your pilots? Micah is new, so maybe you don't know him. He was hired this past spring, but someone, any pilot . . . If you talk to any pilot, he should be able to point you in the right direction, shouldn't he? Somewhere along the chain of command, someone is going to know my husband, and—"

"It's just that we don't have any planes, ma'am."

Her words knock the wind clear out of me. "Wh-what?"

"Planes. I'm unaware of any aviation department here at Diamond Corporation. I've asked around, and no one knows anything about pilots on our payroll. Are you sure that's what your husband does for us?"

"Of course I'm sure! He flies planes! That's what he does! First for United Airlines, and now for you. Maybe your supervisor knows him or her supervisor or hers. Put me in touch with the goddamned president of the corporation, for all I care. This is important!"

"I'm trying to help you, Mrs. Cavanaugh, but I'm not sure you have the right company."

I storm into the house.

Bella startles.

I skid to a stop at the cabinets between the kitchen and the great room, which Claudette called the family planning center the first time she brought us here. I tear through the mail and find proof that I'm not insane.

"I'm looking at his pay stub right now. Is this Diamond Corporation at ten fifty-eight LaSalle, suite F twenty-two, in Chicago?"

"We are on LaSalle, ma'am—"

"What if I give you his employee ID number? Will that help?"

"But we aren't on the twenty-second floor. This building has only fifteen."

"ID number one-oh-three-two-nine-seven. Can you look him up that way?"

She sighs. "Look, honey. Your husband doesn't work for us."

"I have his pay stub. His name is on it. It says Diamond Corporation."

"Mommy?"

I spin around to see Bella holding a picture of a plane in what looks likes silvery water in her outstretched hand. "Nini says she told you. God Land."

I hang up the phone.

Gather my daughter into my arms.

Feel her tears against my neck when she buries her face there.

"Bella, why are you saying things like that?"

Her little arms tighten around me. "Not me. Nini."

Chapter 8

"And when did he leave?"

Our formal living room is packed with agents of the law—some in uniform and some in plain clothes. While a couple of officers occupy Bella, I'm speaking with a detective wearing faded blue jeans, a backward baseball cap, and a University of Miami T-shirt. He looks more like a high school sports coach than someone who belongs on *CSI*, but the badge hanging around his neck says his name is Jason Guidry, with the Lake County Police Department.

"Two days ago. Just before six in the morning."

He squints as he writes down everything I say in a handheld notebook. "And when is he supposed to come back?"

"Two hours ago." Before the detective can draw the obvious conclusion—that he's not technically missing; he's only late—I blurt out: "I haven't heard from him, and his company . . . the Diamond Corporation . . . they're pretending they don't know who he is. They're pretending he doesn't exist."

"Has this ever happened before?" Guidry nibbles on his lower lip, still writing. "He forgets to call? Goes off radar?"

"Of course not! He always calls. *Always.*"

"I believe you." He glances up at me. "Have you been in touch with members of his family? Parents? Brothers and sisters? To see if they've heard from him?"

"He's an only child." I open my laptop to show the detective what I've done. "His parents are . . . well, they're in Europe. They aren't due back for another week, and I don't know if their phones are working over there, but I left a voice mail for his mother and sent an e-mail. I also messaged her on Facebook, but she's not in the habit of checking it."

"What's her name?"

"Shell. Shell Cavanaugh."

"I'd like her phone number, if you don't mind. And your father-in-law?"

"Micah Senior. He goes by Mick."

"Have you attempted to reach Mick?"

"I don't have his number."

The detective awards me with only a momentary glance, but I see something in his eyes in that split second—suspicion, maybe?—that propels me to explain. "He and Shell are together. In Europe."

Guidry is unfazed.

"He and Micah don't get along. We don't have a relationship."

"I see."

"He and Shell were separated when Micah and I met. They're back together now, but Micah never forgave his father for whatever it was he put his mother through."

"A shame."

He's looking at me like he wants more elaboration, but I don't know much more than that. I know Mick had found someone else. I know he came to his senses just in time to save his marriage. Typical midlife crisis stuff: motorcycle, sports car, younger woman. Shell forgave him, or maybe she simply chose to overlook it, but Micah wrote him off.

That's the way it is with Micah. He's your biggest fan until you do something unforgiveable.

"Mick practically lives up north now, at their lake house. Shell's a butterfly. When she isn't planning charity events, she travels quite a bit and sometimes drags Mick with her. This time, he went."

"Mick doesn't see your daughter?"

I shake my head. "Micah wouldn't allow it . . . he doesn't want him in our lives."

Guidry nods. "And it's because of whatever happened between his parents."

"That's what he said."

"The rift had nothing to do with Micah's stealing money from his father ten years ago?"

"What money?" My eyes widen. "Ten years ago was right around the time we were graduating from college. We were together then, but I . . . I don't know anything about that."

"There was a report filed. Your father-in-law pressed charges. Dropped them shortly after."

I chew on a nail. I can't picture Micah stealing, but why would he have kept the accusation from me? "I don't know. I mean, he never mentioned anything like that. What kind of money are we talking?"

"Quite a bit."

"There's a record of it? Of the filed charges?"

"When your call came through, the first thing I did was enter your husband's name into the system. This old charge popped up."

"Anything else?"

Guidry shakes his head. "No, ma'am."

I've bitten my nail off. Is it possible there's more to Micah—and his relationship with his father—than I understand? But I don't have time to ponder it because Guidry's continuing.

"And you've contacted Micah's employer?"

I hand over all the correspondence I've found from Diamond Corporation during the past hour. Bundled with a rubber band are salary transfer confirmations and his offer letter, as well as the corporate employee handbook, which I'd never seen Micah open. But it's proof that he was, indeed, hired and employed by Diamond.

"You said *the* Diamond Corporation," Guidry says.

"Yes."

"There's no *the*."

"What?"

"The automatic deposit stubs. The stationery. There's no *the*. It's just Diamond Corporation."

"Okay."

"So maybe you were in touch with the wrong company."

"The wrong company based in Chicago *on LaSalle Street*, with satellites in New York and Miami?"

"It seems silly, but sometimes, things are as simple as a word out of line. We'll follow up on it."

"Detective?"

I look over my shoulder to see an officer standing over me. Suddenly, Bella is climbing onto my lap—I wince as one of her knees presses too hard against my swollen left ovary—and one of the officers laden with the task of entertaining her is leaning down to whisper into Guidry's ear.

His split-second glance again flickers over me but then settles on my daughter. "Elizabella?"

She's pressing her hands against my cheeks. "It's okay, Mommy."

"Elizabella?" Guidry tries again. "Can you show me what you drew?"

She nudges my stomach again when she spins and plops her bottom down on my lap. "I didn't draw it. Nini did."

"Your mommy did?" Guidry asks.

"No! *Nini.*"

"It's her imaginary friend," I say.

"She's *real*."

"And she drew this picture?" Guidry asks, gesturing to the page an officer plants in front of him.

"We took photos of it, Lieutenant," the officer says.

"What did she draw?" I ask. Guidry peruses the sketch, which appears to be a lighthouse of sorts—a bullet-shaped object of red, yellow, and black horizontal stripes, with water in the background.

"I told Nini it was bad," Elizabella says. "Markers are off-limits."

"Are you sure your mommy didn't draw this?"

I shake my head, confused. It looks like a *child's* drawing. "Why would I . . . unless you're trying to insinuate I'm putting thoughts into my daughter's head—"

"Not Mommy! *Nini!*"

"She draws pictures all the time," I say.

"It isn't this one picture, per se." The detective shares a glance with his officer, then says to Elizabella, "Did you tell the officer this is where your daddy is?"

"Uh-huh."

"Where is he?"

"He went to God Land."

"When did he go to God Land?"

"When I was sleeping. He gave me a kiss bye-bye."

"He stops in her room to kiss her before he goes out of town," I explain. If I'd ever stopped crying, the tears are full force again now. I tighten my grip on Elizabella and allow my head to fall on her shoulder.

She gives my hand a pat.

"Elizabella, can you do me a favor?" Guidry asks. "Can you draw me a picture?"

"Yes." Bella is swinging her legs playfully, but she doesn't attempt to climb off my lap.

"Can you do it now? I'm not going to be here for very much longer, and I'd like to take it home with me tonight to show my kids."

He's a father. A tiny speck of heat warms my heart. He's a father! He'll understand how important it is for a man to come home to his family. He'll help me. And while I can't bear the thought of releasing my daughter, even to let her draw in a room forty feet away, I loosen my grip. "It's okay, Bella. Go ahead."

"Some concerns," Guidry says when she's on her way to her table. This time, his gaze settles directly on me. It's an uncomfortable, thousand-mile deadpan that tells me he could win a staring contest with a corpse.

My heart tightens, and tears storm down my cheeks. I drop my head into my hands, if only to escape the intensity of the stare, which feels accusatory, demanding.

"Your daughter knows something, and she's trying to communicate it. What I want to know is whether she learned the secret from you."

I snap my gaze up to his. "Are you saying—"

"Has she ever been on vacation with you? Along the shore of Lake Michigan, perhaps? Ever been to the ocean?"

"She's seen Lake Michigan—of course, she's seen it—and Micah took her to his family's cottage once."

"You didn't go."

"No." I don't tell him it was because I'd checked myself into a recovery retreat after the miscarriage. I don't tell him it was because I thought I was losing my grip on reality. "But it's on a tiny lake in northern Wisconsin."

"Any chance she means God's country?" Guidry licks his lips and squints at me, as if he can bore into my brain with his eyes and learn the truth. "It's a common euphemism for northern Wisconsin."

"If he were in Wisconsin, he would've told me he was going to Wisconsin. And besides, this isn't the best time of year to be heading up there."

"Any chance he called and you missed the call?"

"We've been home all day, waiting for the phone to ring. I can't imagine . . ." My head is spinning and pounding and aching, but I try to think. "We stopped at the park after school the day before yesterday. My friend Claudette and her kids were there . . ." I run through the past two days' events, offering as much detail as possible, and even admitting that I let Bella sleep last night in the soft, velveteen dress she'd worn to school—that she'd been wearing it since the morning Micah left.

"So your daughter was out of your sight the day before yesterday while you were on the phone with the embryology lab at the park, again while you were napping, and once more yesterday, while you spoke with Diamond Corporation on your screened porch. No one else has seen her, to your knowledge. No one else who may be putting these thoughts and images into her head."

I nod. The detective is a blurry mass through my tears. The tissues in my hands are drenched with snot, but I wipe them against my eyes anyway. "I'm sorry. It's been a tough couple of days with Micah's going MIA, the news from the lab . . ."

Guidry gives me a nearly imperceptible nod.

"Are you going to find my husband?"

He squints at me. "Yes."

I let out a violent, relieving sob. "Thank you."

"As long as you tell me everything I need to know."

"Of course, I'll—"

He reaches into his back pocket and pulls out a small leather billfold, from which he extracts a crisp business card. "This number here"—he points to the one on the very bottom—"is my personal cell phone. You think of anything—anything at all—you call me."

I sniffle and nod. "Bella told me . . . she has an active imagination, but she said something about there being a man in the kitchen. When she was little."

"Not recently?"

"Well, she *said* it recently, but she said it *happened* when she was little."

"She ever say anything about that before?"

"No."

"You have reason to believe anyone could've been in your kitchen?"

I think of the rare nights after the miscarriage I'd popped a sleeping pill and could've slept through someone coming in. I consider telling him about the feeling I had earlier, a glimpse of a memory about it happening in Old Town, but I don't want him to think I'm losing it. I shake my head. "No."

"You sure about that?"

"I just don't know why she'd say it."

"You're in a gated community. We should have record of anyone coming in."

"Unless they came in with the gate code. Or came through the county forest preserve. But we haven't lived here very long. I wonder if she might even mean our kitchen in Old Town."

"When did you leave Old Town?"

"This past spring."

"Is there anyone who can help you out tonight? Anyone who can come stay with you while you wait for him to come home?"

"You think he'll come home."

For the first time, Detective Guidry cracks a smile. "I do."

I hope he's right, that I've overreacted, that I did contact the wrong company.

"Can you call your mother maybe?"

My heart plummets to the hollow of my gut. "I wish I could."

He continues. "Even if she isn't local—"

"She died when I was eighteen."

"I'm sorry. Father? Siblings? Aunt? Cousins?"

I shake my head. There's no one. I never knew my father, and when my mother died, I officially became a wolf without a pack.

"Your friend . . ." He checks his notes. "Claudette Winters. Give her a call maybe."

I take a deep breath and mentally debate whether or not I should explain the difference between friends like my estranged college roommate and friends like my neighbor. Some friends you can entrust with anything and everything that crosses your heart and mind. Others, you tread carefully with, in order to decide what information to disclose. I just don't know Claudette well enough yet to determine which of the two categories she falls into. However, given my lack of options here . . . "Yes. That's a possibility."

"Keep calling him, check credit card statements, cell phone records, what have you, for recent activity. Keep me informed. But in the meantime, you shouldn't be alone. This IVF business sounds like quite an ordeal. Maybe that's why your husband checked out. Maybe the news about this embryo—"

"He was gone by the time I got the call. He still doesn't know."

"Lieutenant?" The call comes from across the house.

Guidry raises a finger to delay whatever the beckoning officer needs, then pockets his notebook. "You'll call Claudette Winters?"

"Sure." I won't do it tonight. I'm not *together* enough for a visit from Claudette. But I don't see an end to the conversation without my acquiescing.

"Got a minute, Lieutenant?"

I'm already on my way to the great room when Guidry falls in step behind me.

Elizabella is sitting at her table with a uniformed officer, pointing out details in her drawings. "This is the water where his plane is. And over here is where the big house is, by the big boat. And here's my daddy at God Land and my baby brothers, who went to God before they were born."

"Where's Nini?" the officer asks.

"Silly. Nini is on your lap."

"On my lap?"

"She's being good."

"Is she usually naughty?"

"She gets us in trouble all the time."

"And she's the one who told you Daddy went to God?"

"Not to *God*. He's at God *Land*."

"Does Mommy know he's at God Land?"

"Yes."

"How does Mommy know?"

I stiffen. This officer is insinuating that I know what happened to my husband. Furthermore, that I'm responsible.

"She watched. He kissed me bye-bye, and she watched."

Chapter 9

November 14

"I need to leave a message for Lieutenant Jason Guidry." I say the name as articulately as I can, given I'm choking on tears. I pull the phone away for a split second, to blow my nose again.

"I can connect you to his voice mail," the switchboard operator says, "but the schedule has him out until Tuesday."

"Out? As in . . . *on vacation*?" I've tried his cell phone. I left three messages for him already. "How can he be on vacation when my husband is missing?"

No one can tell me Micah isn't missing now. He was supposed to be home over twenty-four hours ago. There's been no activity on his credit cards. No activity on his cell phone. And Diamond Corporation—I'm certain I've reached the correct company after calling at least seven others with similar names—still denies knowing him.

"Would you like his voice mail?"

After a stuttering inhalation, I say, "Yes. Thank you." I wait for the machined voice to prompt me to leave a message.

"Detective, this is Veronica Cavanaugh calling again. Please call me back." A sob escapes me. "No word from Micah."

I stand there stupidly, with the phone to my ear, as if I expect the voice mail to comfort or console me. "I just—" But there's nothing else to say. I hang up the phone and drop my head into my hands.

Nearly instantly, the phone begins to ring. I answer without looking at the caller ID. "Hello?"

It's the IVF clinic. I vaguely remember listening to the details of yesterday's report: "Not generating at an acceptable rate." I repeat the news matter-of-factly. Without Micah, there's no reason to generate embryos at all. But I repeat what I remember from the clinic's last call: "Cautiously optimistic about the embryo."

"Someone with the lab will be calling you soon, but—"

"Mommy." Elizabella climbs onto my lap.

I wrap an arm around her and prepare to hear the words no one wants to say: our last embryo is gone. I wipe my raw nose with a paper towel—I'm out of tissues—and swallow a few more tears. "It's okay."

"But I'm calling about your outstanding balance, Mrs. Cavanaugh."

"I'm sorry . . . what?"

"There's an outstanding balance on your account."

"Our insurance will cover four cycles. This is the third. There shouldn't be—"

"Mr. Cavanaugh's been paying out of pocket."

"But we have a new insurance plan," I explain. "My husband took a new job—" Wait. I stop myself. "What insurance card do you have?"

"The last on record is Blue Cross of Illinois, but the policy lapsed. Mr. Cavanaugh has been paying—"

"That's our old card. Didn't he get you a new one?"

"No, ma'am. As I said, the invoices have been paid out of pocket."

I'm back at the family planning station, opening a file drawer and pulling out a file with *IVF* written on the tab.

"Maybe that was when he was between jobs," she continues. "If you scan and e-mail the new card, I'll resubmit the claims to your insurance company."

There was no time between jobs. Diamond headhunted him straight from United.

Tucked inside the file are the yellow copies of the bills we receive after every appointment at the IVF lab. Scrawled in red at the top of each is a credit card confirmation number and Micah's chicken scratch—*paid*—and the date. He's been paying for the services out of pocket?

"But . . . why," I say aloud, "when it's covered by insurance?"

"You've explained it, Mrs. Cavanaugh. You have new insurance. Scan and e-mail the new card, or next time you come in, if you wouldn't mind bringing it—"

"Sure."

"And I'm sure everything will go through. Recent charges, I mean. Insurance doesn't cover the storage fee for Mr. Cavanaugh's specimen."

"Thank you." I wait, even after her *you're welcome*. Because something isn't making sense. "Specimen? You mean the two embryos? I thought we paid storage fees up front for—"

"For the embryos, yes, you're paying monthly, but there's an annual renewal fee for the storage of the spermatozoa."

"The . . . we're storing Micah's *sperm*? But why would we—"

"It renews every year, ma'am, unless you send written notice."

"I was unaware we were storing . . ." Why would we be storing something he produces, without fail, every time we batch eggs? "I apologize about the account, but I'll find the new insurance and get you a copy of the card."

As I hang up, the doorbell rings.

Detective Guidry. It has to be. Of course! That's why he hasn't returned my calls; he's in the field. Stopping by is better than a call back.

Halfway down the hall, however, when it's too late to pretend I haven't heard the bell, I spy Claudette Winters and her no-nonsense bob, perfectly coiffed, on my doorstep. She's cradling a casserole and waving frantically through the seeded glass window in the door.

I swear under my breath. She knows there's a problem or she wouldn't be bearing a casserole. What are the odds she assumes my recent avoidance has something to do with my infertility issues? Or maybe she's here to make amends for lecturing me—for calling my child *spoiled*—at the park.

"No hiding that there's trouble," I mutter, once I catch a glimpse of my reflection in the mirror hanging in the hallway. I'm a mess.

"Are *you* talking to Nini, too?" Bella asks.

"I guess I am." I scoop up my daughter and balance her in the perfectly accustomed place on my hip. "Nini says Mommy looks terrible."

"No. Mommy's pretty." Bella presses a wet kiss to my cheek, and I tighten my grip on her little body.

The second I open the door, Claudette steps into my foyer, with Crew and Fendi in perfect cadence a pace behind her. "Veronica, you should have called." She whisks past me, down the hall and into my kitchen. By the time I catch up with her, she's making room in my refrigerator for her casserole. "This is gluten-free pasta with farm-raised chicken and organic peas and carrots. Nothing fancy, but it's the best I could do on such short notice."

Crew locks me in a blank-expression staring contest, while his sister smirks. I imagine they've never had a mother who skipped a shower or cried off all her mascara.

I say nothing to the children but mutter a thanks to Claudette when she turns to face me, head cocked, brows slightly knit. "Imagine my surprise when the *police department* calls me and asks me to check in on you."

Wait. They've called *her* but haven't had a moment to return my calls?

"Honey, listen." She drums manicured fingernails against the black granite countertop on my island, which is at the moment strewn with files I've perused and torn apart in pursuit of Micah. "Whatever it is you're going through, you can count on me. I won't judge you—"

65

Right. A hard blink prohibits my rolling my eyes.

"I might offer an opinion or two, but I'll never judge you." Her gaze travels to my hip, where my daughter is securely stationed, and I know it's killing her not to lecture me about allowing my perfectly capable three-year-old to walk.

I challenge her stare with silence.

"The police said . . ." She momentarily glances away. "Micah didn't come home?"

"He's at God Land," Elizabella pipes in.

I lower my daughter to the floor. Some magnetic pull takes her attention directly to the robotic children standing half in my hallway, half in my kitchen. Suddenly, I want to pull her back, keep her separated from them, as if she might catch their overly obedient tendencies like a disease.

"Why didn't you call?" Claudette persists.

The best response I can come up with is a sigh. I sniffle over tears I'm choking back.

"Why don't you draw a hot bath? I'll straighten up and get dinner going."

Before I can take a breath to respond, her finger points in Bella's direction. "Take Crew and Fendi to your table. Keep busy until I call you."

Crew and Fendi are already glancing at the child-size table in the great room, their eyes wide with disbelief that Elizabella didn't immediately jump to their mother's orders. Quite the contrary, she sidles up against me and wraps her little arms around my right leg.

That's right, I assure her with a glance and a smoothing of her hair, *it's you and me now. You and me against the world.*

She tightens her grip.

"I don't want to take a bath," I tell my neighbor, "and I don't want you to straighten up. There's a method to my mess here, and—"

"Then let me help you sort it. But you'll feel better after a shower."

"Would *you* feel better if I showered?"

"Kids." Claudette gives her two a stern look. "Give Mrs. Cavanaugh and me some privacy."

Crew and Fendi hesitantly walk toward the great room. Bella watches them for a few paces, then rips herself from my side to join them. *Traitor.*

"Listen," Claudette says in a low-volume voice. "Brad pulled this once. It happens more often than you might think."

She thinks Micah chose to leave, that he didn't come home because he's been keeping secrets from me. But I know better.

I catch a tear on the tip of a finger. "He isn't screwing around."

"Maybe not screwing." Claudette turns her back on me but only to preheat my oven. "But playing. Let me tell you something no one knows." Now she's straightening the papers on my island, organizing them into little piles. "A few years ago, right after Fendi was born, Brad had an affair. One of those skinny bitches—you know the type, willowy, like an underwear model, and with a name that sounds like one of those candles from Bathworks. Misty Morningside. Can you imagine?"

"I'm sorry to hear, Claudette, but Micah isn't—"

"The moment I figured it out, I was hysterical. Just like you. But once I calmed down, I realized something. This wasn't a statement about *my* shortcomings. It's a message about *his.* Truthfully, it's the best thing that could've happened to us. The guilt is nearly overwhelming for him, and he's been a model husband ever since. The key is to make this work to your advantage. Don't let him off too easy. Put him in purgatory for a while."

I look at her for a few seconds, to make sure she's done with her dissertation.

She's not.

"So much depends on this consequence. I know you're hurting, and the first thing you're going to want to do is throw your arms around him—because you miss him, you love him, you're worried about him—but what message does that send? It tells him you understand what he's done! That all is forgiven. But you don't, do you? And it isn't, is it? If you welcome him home, by the time you've managed to send the right message, it will be too late. You *must* make it *clear* that this behavior is unacceptable."

When she's attentively staring back at me, one eyebrow peaked in an arc, lips pursed as if she's just tasted something tart and can't decide if she likes it, I speak: "Micah isn't having an affair. He's missing."

She answers with a slow blink.

"He left to take some executive on a trip to New York, and I haven't heard from him since." My voice breaks a little, but I swallow my grief and continue. "The company he works for . . . they're pretending they don't know who he is, but I have proof. Pay stubs. The company policy handbook. If they don't know who he is, why would they have been paying him every other week for six months?"

"That's really what you think?" She crosses her arms over her chest and leans a thin hip against my island. "There's something bigger going on here?"

"Yes." I dab at my eyes with an already moist paper towel I find in my hand.

"Then why didn't you call me? There's no shame in Micah's being in an accident."

"I'm not ashamed. Something's happened to my husband! Why would I be ashamed of that?"

"If that's really what you think, you would've called me." She pushes away from the island. "Where do you keep the glasses?"

I frown, which intensifies my constant headache.

Claudette is already opening doors in search of what she's looking for. "Here we go!" She helps herself to ice and filtered water, filling two glasses. One she slides across the countertop to me; the other she sips herself.

"Look, honey." She leans in closer. "I know we're different people. But I'm the only friend you've got right now. Micah was your everything, right? Your lover, your partner, your best friend. You didn't need anyone else. He was it."

I nod and finally take a sip of water. It's true. Since we found each other, Micah and I have been inseparable. We didn't really have friends, so much as casual acquaintances we'd see occasionally, whenever we felt the need to prove to the world that we were capable of interacting.

"I'm going to go downstairs to the wine cellar and pull a dusty old bottle off the shelf, and you and I are going to toast to our strength, and—"

"I can't drink."

"And then you're going to eat, take a hot shower, and start thinking rationally. Toss Elizabella in the tub and change her clothes, for Chrissake. She needs a sense of structure right now. Pull yourself together."

A million words stir in my brain, and my tongue fights to form even a fraction of them. Nothing's right. Micah's gone. My world is spinning out of control, and it's not because I'm being irrational.

Or is it?

As if she hears the question in my mind, Claudette sighs. "I never wanted to tell you this—how do you make accusations like this?—but you've been blind, Veronica. I've seen the signs. Half the neighborhood has seen him walking the streets in the middle of the night."

An icy sensation rushes through me. I think of the figure I saw on the green the night Micah left. The one with the lit cigarette. Someone walking the course, I'd thought. Someone who's being dishonest with his wife. Watching me in the window.

"He's always on the phone." Claudette is at the stairs that lead to the basement. With a toss of her head, she beckons me to join her in the wine cellar.

I stay planted.

"Now tell me. Why would he be on the phone at that hour? And who do you think he's talking to? I overheard the name Gabrielle."

I flinch. The name is a specific detail. It lends credence to Claudette's theory.

She probes further: "Do you *know* a Gabrielle?"

I want nothing more than to scream at her to leave me alone. "You're mistaken. It wasn't Micah." But I don't sound convincing. I gravitate toward the basement stairs and, against my better judgment, follow her.

"I'd tell you to check the phone records, but you might not find anything. Brad had a second phone when he was screwing around. Men are very good at this—smart men, anyway—and they know how to cover their tracks. And a man like Micah? Traveling for his job? I'm sure it's only made things easier for him. He wants to go see the tramp? Wants to spend the night with her? All he has to do is conjure some sort of business trip."

I might throw up. Could he? *Would* he?

"I tell you"—Claudette raises a finger to illustrate she's about to make a point—"the cell phone has made serial cheating possible. Our mothers didn't find themselves in this position. And why? Because the little sluts had to call on the landline, and it was over with the first ring."

By now, we're in the wine cellar, which is more of a showcase, complete with a tasting table and carved moldings, than the hole in the wall its name suggests. A floor-to-ceiling wine rack graces the far wall for reds, and a full-size wine cooler for whites is built into a walk-behind bar. Leaded glass panes adorn the cabinetry doors, and when the light hits the glass, a spray of color splashes the wall.

I pause, feeling as if I'm back in Fourth Presbyterian, staring at the stained glass raining colors down on my mother's casket. Never had I felt as alone as I did in that minute, and the feeling revisits me now, pulsing in my veins with every heartbeat.

And it's happening again. The clouds of despair gather over my head.

My feet pad over the uneven, bricked floor to the wine rack, where I select a bottle of pinot noir.

"Oh. Red?" Claudette pauses on her way behind the bar, but after a second, she reaches for the door of the wine cooler.

I step between her and the appliance.

She blinks at me—"White really works better with poultry"—and reaches for it a second time.

Again, I interfere. "Are you joining me or not?"

I may have let her take charge of my kitchen the moment she set foot in it, but I'm not about to let her dictate the wine I drink, too. And I just might serve prepackaged snacks to her children to prove a point. Oreos maybe. Without another word, I turn out of the cellar and make my way upstairs.

She's right that white pairs better with chicken, but I haven't had a drink in years. If I'm going to drink, I'm going to sip on whatever I damn well please, whether it brings out the flavor of the food or not.

She's right about something else, too: Micah has opportunities to have an affair, and he's smart enough to pull it off.

Chapter 10

November 15

When my eyes finally close, my thoughts drift to my mother, and I'm hurtling back through the annals of time.

Wake up, little Veri.

I've been awake for hours, despite the fact that it's barely four in the morning, but I pretend to be asleep when she's like this.

I lay as still as possible, even when she sticks the sharp end of the brooch through my nightshirt and drags the straight pin—an accident? Or done purposefully?—over the skin near my clavicle.

She's humming some strange melody, something I've never heard before, and she's rocking back and forth.

The humming crescendos, and my head starts to ache.

While my little one sleeps, she says.

I feel the pillow come down over my face.

The pressure I feel in my ears, in my chest, when I can't breathe.

The panic.

I try to relax, try to conjure the sounds of my music box, but I can't hear anything beyond my own heartbeat.

The blurry line between life and death seems to constrict around my windpipe.

It feels as if my eyes might burst from my head, and the ache is unbearable.

Worse than usual.

In the distance, I hear the pealing of a ringtone.

It jars me from deep sleep. I gasp and struggle to catch my breath. Back to the here and now.

Ring, ring.

But this ringtone isn't the one I preset for Micah's cell, so I don't make a move right away to answer it. I'm too tired. Too comfortable, despite the fact that I'm sleeping on the sofa in the great room. But it might be news about my husband. I should get it.

I sit up and press a few fingers to my right temple. It's a wine head-ache. I had only a glass and a half last night—Claudette drained the rest of the bottle—but through the trials and tribulations of IVF treatment, I guess I've forgotten how to imbibe.

"Hello?" Elizabella's voice echoes in the dim house.

I spin my head toward the kitchen, where Bella has my phone pressed to her ear.

"Ellie-Belle, bring Mommy the phone."

"Hiiiii," Bella says into the phone. Gradually, she's moving toward me. "Nini says Mommy's sick. Mmm-hmm. She threw up last night."

I did. Not because of the wine, but rather because it's impossible to eat while sobbing hysterically, and between the situation with Micah and the hormones, it's hard to breathe without hiccupping over tears.

I'm on my feet now, padding over the cold floor to where Elizabella is dawdling in the kitchen.

"Nini," she says. "The little girl who lives in my hair."

I take the phone and scoop her up and head back to the sofa. "Hello?"

"Veronica, is everything all right?" It's my mother-in-law.

"Shell!" My voice breaks a little. Finally, someone who will believe me, someone who loves Micah just as much as I do, someone who will help!

"Are you okay?"

"No. No, I'm not. Micah." I swallow tears and will myself to keep it together. But I can't. Fresh tears come faster than I attempt to stop them.

I press a kiss to the top of my daughter's head—her hair is a mess of tangles, and we both need a bath—and try to compose myself. "Micah."

"What about Micah?"

"He went to God Land," Bella chimes.

"Veronica?"

"I'm here. Just . . ." It takes a few long seconds for me to find constitution enough to say what I need to say. "He left for work Tuesday, and I haven't heard from him since. He was supposed to be back on the thirteenth."

"That isn't like him," Shell agrees. But she isn't panicking. "Are you sure you had the timeline right? You know, sometimes, when Mick was traveling, he'd run into some flyspeck town, and he'd be hard-pressed to find a *pay phone*—back when people expected to see pay phones—let alone a cell tower. Maybe it's just that he's in an area—"

"He said he was going to New York City."

"Oh."

"And he *never* stays through the weekend. *Never.*" A few beats of silence follow, while we both let it sink in: if he really is where he says he is, there's no way he wouldn't have called.

"The police don't believe me. They say give him time, that he must have needed a break—from me, from our life—but I know him, Shell. I know he wouldn't forget to call, and if his cell phone is on the fritz, he'd call from a phone at the hotel—I know he would, and—"

"He went to God Land," my daughter says again.

"What's Bella saying?"

74

"She seems to think he . . ." A violent sob escapes me, despite my attempt to hold it back with a hand over my mouth. "Elizabella seems to think he isn't coming home. She keeps saying he went to God Land."

"God's land?" A wave of static on the line nearly deafens me for a moment. "The north woods of Wisconsin."

"What?"

"The north woods of Wisconsin. God's country. His cell phone doesn't work up at the lake. No one's cell phone works up at the—"

"That's what the detective said." My heart pounds in my ears, a contrast to my mother-in-law's calm demeanor. "But why? Why would he go there and lie about it?"

"Maybe the police are right. Maybe he just needed a break. Give the house a call." Shell rattles off a number. "Or . . . if he doesn't answer, maybe he's out fishing. Maybe one of the neighbors could let us know if someone's been at the house, though we don't regularly see most of them past Labor Day."

"I'll call the lake house, but—"

"He has a key," Shell says. "Don't you keep a spare set in the desk drawer? There should be four or five keys on the ring—one to our condo downtown, one for our mailbox."

I know the keys. Our safe-deposit box key is on the same ring.

"The lake house key is labeled with a green cap."

I'm at the desk drawer now. "He wouldn't go to the lake house. Not without Bella. Not without telling me." I finger through the keys. One, two, three, four.

"There's no green-capped key," I say.

"Maybe he's up north then. Maybe he drove up for the weekend. You're *sure* he didn't say anything about taking a weekend to himself?"

"*Positive.* Shell, he's *never* done that sort of thing."

"Hmm."

"You don't think he'd . . ." Images of underwear models flash in my mind. *No.* He wouldn't . . .

My call waiting blips. I give it a glance. "I know you're overseas, but the police are calling. Just a minute."

"The police? Honey—"

I click over, a sense of dread balling up in my stomach. What if I don't want to know what they're about to tell me? Still, a dry *hello* sputters out.

"Mrs. Cavanaugh, this is Jason Guidry. Do you have a minute?"

"They told me you're out until Tuesday."

"Officially, yes. But I'm in the neighborhood, and I'd like to stop by."

"Of course. *Please.*"

"I'll be there in a few minutes."

"Thank you." I click back over. "Shell? If he's at the lake, do you think there's any way he might not be there alone?"

"You don't mean—"

"Cheating on me. Yes."

"Honey, after the way he turned his father out after Mick's affair . . . God, no. He *loves* you."

My tears sprout anew. "Thank you. No one else seems to remember that. And my neighbor Claudette . . . she says she overheard him talking to some other woman late at night. Gabrielle."

"Gabrielle."

"I think that's what she said. We don't even *know* a Gabrielle."

"Well . . . *I* do. She's a nurse at Children's Memorial. But Micah wouldn't be . . ." She sighs. "Then again . . ."

My gut clenches. Then again *what*?

"Sometimes it's not a question of how much he loves you."

"Oh God. You think he and this Gabrielle—"

"Not the Gabby *I* know, but . . ."

I get the feeling she's debating whether or not to tell me something. Maybe it's possible after all. Maybe Micah is truly not who I thought he was.

"I'm coming home," she says. "As soon as I can get a flight."

The instant relief washing over me is short-lived. What if I'm over-reacting? What if there's a logical explanation for all of this? What if Claudette is right, and he's running around with an underwear model, and because of my unfounded panic, Shell cuts her European vacation short? I imagine her racing home to find Micah safe in the confines of our gated community . . . fresh from the north woods of Wisconsin, with another woman's lipstick on his boxer shorts. As much as I need Shell here . . .

"If something's wrong," Shell says, "and Micah—"

"What if it *is* just an affair? I'd hate for you to rush home, if he's just . . ." I take a deep breath. "Let's just . . ." He wouldn't be doing what Claudette assumes. He *wouldn't*. And Shell can't possibly believe it, either. But I can't explain his being gone this long without calling if he's not. The detective is on his way. Maybe he'll have news. "Let's give him a couple of hours. Call me back around noon?"

"I'm sure he'll call. He's probably up at the lake."

"I hope so. I'll call the lake house and let you know. I'd hate for you to cut your trip short . . ."

"Will you call me? Let me know what's going on? We'll have a seven-hour drive from the airport to the lake. We'll be there for the week of Thanksgiving," Shell says. "Right when we get home. But if you need me sooner . . . if you need me to come back . . . you'll let me know?"

The doorbell is ringing.

"I'm sure everything is going to be okay," Shell says. But she doesn't sound convincing. "If he's up north without telling you, and heaven forbid, he's doing something he shouldn't be doing, he'll hear about it from me, I promise you. Kiss my grandbaby."

"I will."

"Love you, hon."

"We love you, too."

I gather my hair, which isn't in much better condition than my daughter's, and try to smooth it. I could use a breath mint. The house is a mess. Bella's artwork is scattered over the great room floor. Micah's receipts from the past year are haphazardly piled like paper buildings in a village erected on the kitchen island.

Claudette's crusty casserole dish collects dust on the cooktop. She was too tipsy to clean up, and I was too sick to care.

The detective doesn't appear fazed by the picture of death warmed over. He doesn't lecture me about the fact that Bella is still in the same long-sleeved velour dress she was wearing when he met her. He simply steps inside and says, "Any word?"

I shake my head and move aside. While I'm closing the door, he's walking down the hallway.

"Looks like you had a party last night."

I trace his gaze to the empty bottle and two wineglasses on the island. "Claudette." I want to explain that she was persistent, that the wine was her idea. "She seems to think Micah is having an affair."

"So she told me."

"Have a seat." I gather papers scattered over the breakfast table and make room for him. "I appreciate your coming out on a . . . God, is it Sunday?"

"It's Saturday. Comes with the job, ma'am. I take the information as it comes, whether it's Sunday, Tuesday, or Christmas Day."

"Information? So you know something?"

He sits. "You're right about the job. They have no record of employing a Micah Cavanaugh at Diamond Corporation."

"The checks . . . the pay stubs—"

"I'm working on that."

"But how do you explain his getting a paycheck from a company that insists they never hired him?"

"The payment receipts were formatted on a basic publishing program. Anyone could've printed them."

"You think Micah made his own deposit receipts? And brought them home to fool me into thinking he had a job?"

"Stranger things have happened." Guidry shrugs, yet before he can offer another ridiculous comment, I cut him off.

"I've checked the account at the bank. The deposit amounts match the pay stubs. *Someone* was paying him."

He nods. "Could be that he was just transferring money from one account to another."

"But that kind of money? Where would he get money like that to transfer? Regularly?"

"You don't know of any other accounts? Stocks, bonds, mutual funds?"

"Micah handled all of that."

"I'm looking into this business with his father and the money. The old charges he pressed against your husband. Could be these deposits were generated from the monies he allegedly stole from his father."

"What about flight records? He usually flew out of the business airport in Des Plaines."

There's a long pause before he says, "Have you ever seen his plane, Mrs. Cavanaugh?"

"Of course I have. When he worked for United, before the miscarriage, Bella and I used to fly with him from time to time. Domestic flights. Here to Philly, here to Boston."

"The plane he supposedly flew for Diamond, I mean. Would you be able to identify it if you saw it?"

"I think so. I mean, maybe. He texted me a picture of it a few times."

"I'm going to need copies of those pictures."

"Of course." I tap an icon on my phone and begin to scroll through thumbnails—mostly of Bella.

"If you could text them, I'd appreciate it."

I nod, and a sense of dread rises from my stomach to my heart. "But . . . if you're telling me he never flew for Diamond—"

"It's a long shot." The detective presses his lips together and bobs his head. "But the remains of a small plane were discovered yesterday just off the Atlantic coast—"

"Oh my God." My heart seizes. "Oh God, oh God."

"Off the southern coast of Florida. Did he have his own plane? One he flew for leisure?"

I shake my head. "He'd wished for one . . ."

"He *had* wished?"

"From time to time." Tears prick my eyes, and everything feels numb. Remains of a plane. *Remains.* I'm texting pictures that may help identify my husband's mangled plane off the Florida coastline. My fingers shake as I tap the screen.

"All planes of that size with recorded flight patterns in the area are safe and accounted for. And since we can't trace your husband's flight pattern without knowing more about the plane he was flying—"

"But he wasn't going to Florida. He said New York. Wait. The last time he used his cell phone . . . the morning he left. He called a number with a three-oh-five area code. Florida."

"Do you know how many times he called it?"

I shake my head. "I'll try to get access through the carrier, but the online records don't give me much information. I did try to call the number, but it was disconnected."

"Do you still have the number?"

"Yeah." I dig through a pile of papers on my island until I find it.

"I'll see if I can trace the number. It could mean something, being it's a Florida number. And you think he was leaving from Chicago Business Airport in Des Plaines?"

"I didn't ask, but I assumed."

"A car with his plates was found early this morning just over the border in Wisconsin."

"His car? So he flew out of Wisconsin?" I think about what Shell said. God's country.

"It wasn't his car, Mrs. Cavanaugh. Just the plates. According to the secretary of state and I-Pass records, your husband drives a Chevy Impala."

"Yes."

"Dark blue."

"Yes."

"And these are his plates?" He slides an eight-by-ten color photograph across the table at me. It accumulates Oreo crumbs on its journey.

"Yes." Even though the picture is a close-up of the license plate, I can tell it's not on Micah's car but on a bronze-colored vehicle. I frown.

"The plates were on a gold Honda Civic, reported stolen yesterday." He slaps another photograph onto the table, one of the entire car bearing Micah's vanity plates: I FLY 3. "We're searching for the Civic's plates, hoping when we find them, they'll be on your husband's car. So far, it hasn't been found in any parking lot in any airport in northern Illinois, southern Wisconsin, or northwest Indiana. Ground crews recognize his picture, or at least his name, but they haven't seen him in some time."

"So are you telling me—"

"I'm not telling you anything," Guidry says. "I wish I had something to give you."

Bella's voice carries from the great room: "That's mean, Nini! Take it back!"

Guidry looks over his shoulder.

"Fighting with her imaginary friend," I explain.

He returns his corpselike stare to me. "I'd like to go to the press to get the word out." The detective gathers his photos. "Maybe someone out there knows something that can help us. Someone might've seen something. Sometimes it's a seemingly innocuous detail that blows a case wide open."

"Yes. It makes sense, I guess."

"The press can be especially cruel with spouses in this sort of situation. They may start hounding you with questions."

"I'll answer them. I have nothing to hide."

"Mommy!" Bella screeches. "Nini's glad Daddy's gone! She says *she'd* rather be at God Land, too."

I'm on my feet now, and my daughter propels herself toward me and catapults into my arms.

Her tears dampen my shoulder. "She needs a time-out!"

"I think she does." I cradle Bella against me, feel her soft warmth. I resume my seat, rocking her like I did when she was a newborn. "It's okay. It's okay. He'll come back."

The detective shifts his gaze from Bella to me. "No charges have gone through on his I-Pass. Which means he stayed off the toll roads or removed the transponder from his car and paid the tolls in cash. We can't trace his route that morning, but we're looking into his past records. Studying his patterns, so we can approximate where he might've gone, what roads he might've taken to get there."

"Do you have a picture of the plane that was found? What was, you know, left?" I can't say the word. I can't say *remains*.

"Yes." But he doesn't pull it from his file.

"Can I see it?"

He reaches into his coat pocket and produces his cell phone. Soon, the picture fills the screen: a mangled mass of metal bobbing in the silvery waters of the Atlantic.

My breath catches in my throat. I have no idea if it's Micah's plane. I'd have no idea if it were a commercial jetliner or scrap metal, for that matter. "Were there . . . you know . . . any bodies inside?"

He's shaking his head. "I haven't seen the report."

"Is that the water where the plane is?" Bella points to the screen.

"Yes," I say over a sob.

"And over here . . ." She waves a hand to the right. "Here is where the big house is. At God Land."

The detective squints.

A chill darts through me, like ice water in my veins.

"Elizabella," Guidry says. "Do you know where your father is?"

"Nini says he's at God Land."

"That's what your mother told you?"

"I didn't say—"

Bella interrupts me. "Not *Mommy. Nini.*" She's using her frustrated tone. "The girl who lives in my hair."

"Okay. The girl who lives in your hair," Guidry says. "Does your mommy know where your daddy is?"

"Uh-huh."

"No, baby." I tighten my grip on my girl. "I don't." But somehow Nini drew a picture of the plane crash days before it happened.

"She knows?" The detective glances at me but quickly turns back to my daughter. "Your mommy knows where Daddy is?"

"No," I say again.

"I *told* you," Elizabella says over her shoulder to me. Then to Guidry: "I *told* her. God Land."

"His mother seems to think she means God's country. They have a house on Plum Lake in Wisconsin—"

"What town?"

"I don't know. Just north of Minocqua. Maybe you could ask the police up there—"

"What's the address of the lake house?"

"I don't know. I've never been there. But it's on Plum Lake." There can't be more than one Plum Lake in the northern woods, and there can't be too many properties deeded to Micah Cavanaugh Senior. If Guidry is any kind of detective, he'll find it easily.

"I'll check it out."

"Thank you."

"Anything else?"

Again, I shake my head.

He fixes me with a stare that's almost accusatory. "Are you sure? There's nothing else you'd like to tell me?"

"I wish I *knew* what else to tell you, but he's just . . . gone. I wish I knew where to find him, but . . . look, no one in her right mind would choose to go through this."

"Okay, then." He drums his fingertips on the table. "Does he have a computer?"

"A laptop, but I assume he took it with him. And there's a desktop upstairs, but he hardly uses it. It's more for Bella. Her games."

"It would be helpful . . . and this is voluntary, you understand . . . could we take his computer? Analyze the files? The Internet searches, that sort of thing?"

I wipe at my eyes. "If you think it'll help bring him home, you can take the whole house." I choke over a sob. "Just bring him home, okay?"

"I'll send a team of techs." He moves to get up. "I'll be in touch."

But I see it in the detective's eyes. He thinks I know something I'm not telling.

Chapter 11

November 16

Shower.

Dishes.

Another box of tissues.

News from the lab: a week after fertilization, the embryo is officially gone. I can stop the hormone injections, as there won't be an embryo transfer this month. Sit back. Wait for a menstrual period. Call the office when it comes and try for another retrieval to see if we get better numbers.

I hear Micah's voice in my head: *We still have two frozen at the lab. All it takes is one.*

But does it matter anymore? If Micah isn't coming home, there's no reason to have another child. When I lost the twins last spring, everyone at the hospital tried to comfort me with generic sentiments like *God has a better plan for you.* Or *Maybe God is looking out for your family in ways you don't understand.*

For the first time, I consider they might've been right. Maybe I lost the boys then to save my sanity now. I'd been beside myself with grief. There's a limit to what a human being can endure, after all, and I'd felt as if I were well over that limit with the miscarriage. But what position would I be in now with a missing husband and three children to care for instead of one?

As soon as the thought enters my mind, I cast it out. Shame on me for feeling a modicum of relief at losing my sons!

My tears, which never stop but for a minute here and there, intensify.

Elizabella's been bathed, and half a bottle of detangle spray later, she looks presentable again. She and Nini are watching a morning cartoon.

I'm on hold with our cell phone carrier, who is reluctant to give me any information, as my name isn't on the account. Everything is in Micah's name. "I just need to know," I say. "How many times did he call the number with the three-oh-five area code?" If there's a connection to the plane found off the Florida coast, I need to know.

"You can access the account online."

"Only the current billing period. I need to know historically how many times he called the number."

"And I can't disclose that information without you being an authorized user on the account, ma'am. I'm sorry."

"But it's my phone plan. I should have access to the account information."

"If that's true, you'd have the required password."

"My husband is missing," I say. "Missing! This information could help me find him!"

"We can release the information with a court order, but—"

"Can you tell me if anyone's ordered the records yet?"

"I can tell the *authorized user* of the account whether the records have been ordered, but—"

I hang up in frustration. I'm looking at the past few months of cell phone bills, which Micah apparently hadn't paid, as we had an outstanding balance of nearly $400 until a few minutes ago, when I paid it by credit card over the phone. Apparently, I'm authorized to pay a bill, even if I'm not authorized to peruse the records. There are no itemized calls or texts on the bill. Just total minutes used, total texts sent, and total texts received for each number.

Light bulb.

There are 334 more texts sent from Micah's number than those received on mine, which means he wasn't texting me exclusively. Who might he have texted? Roughly ten times a day?

I know what Claudette would say. That he's been texting the proverbial Misty Morningside.

I shake away the possibility. Maybe he was texting colleagues. What colleagues? According to Detective Guidry, Diamond had not hired him once he left United.

Friends from Old Town? We hardly had any. None that we'd text with, anyway.

His mother maybe. I'll send a quick note asking her about it.

I open my laptop.

Maybe Micah's e-mailed.

I click on the icon that will take me to my mail server, and a second later, the sign-in page is brilliant with today's headlines:

LOCAL PILOT MISSING, REMAINS OF PLANE FOUND.

Everything is moving in fast-forward. My finger running over the mouse pad to click the link, the words flashing before my eyes, the verdict of the press: he's dead.

But no one's come to tell me he's gone. Surely, the police would *tell* me if they found him dead. I scan through another paragraph.

No confirmation that the two cases are linked, but there is a strong possibility . . .

It's just the press. I try to catch my breath. It's just the press making an inference, connecting the two cases that might coincidentally overlap, even if they're not related. The press is trying to stir up excitement, trying to get people's attention.

A small blip of relief. What they're reporting is just a possibility. Not certain. Not yet.

The phone is ringing.

The number is blocked.

But I should get it.

Might be Micah.

Or it could be someone *calling* about Micah.

I take a deep breath. Center myself. It's okay. It's okay until I hear otherwise.

Pictures flash in my head: ice cream at the table, scribbled drawings of water and lighthouses, organic chicken casserole.

"Hello?"

A whispered voice answers me: "Veronica Cavanaugh."

Bills unpaid.

Fertility fees paid out of pocket.

The mysterious Diamond Corporation.

The dead embryo in the lab dish.

"Who's calling?"

A pause. Static. A whisper: "Veronica."

I can't identify the voice.

"Who's calling?" I say again.

"Listen to your daughter."

My fingers tense around the phone; I feel my hands trembling, feel my brain rattling. "Who is this?"

Click.

Chapter 12

Listen to my daughter.

Listen to my daughter.

Listen to her rag on her imaginary friend?

I look to Bella, who is singing along with the cartoon: "A-B-C-D . . . E-F-G . . ."

The phone is still in my hand, blaring its dial tone. And suddenly, I feel as if I'm spiraling down a psychedelic corkscrew slide—everything is black-and-white checkerboard, everything's vibrating—with the tone of a ready telephone ringing in my ears to the point I can't hear anything else.

Elizabella is suddenly standing in front of me. Her lips are moving. *H-I-J-K-ella-menno-P . . .*

I'm a puddle on the kitchen floor.

What's going on?

She tugs on my sweater. *"Mommy!"*

Her voice is distant, as if she's speaking to me through a tunnel, but she's right here, right with me.

Focus. I focus on her little lips moving.

God Land.

The water where the plane is.

I blink hard.

"Mommy, look!"

Bella is pointing to the television. Breaking news.

"Daddy's on the TV."

I feel my jaw go lax, and I'm staring agape at Micah's driver's license photo, which fills the left half of the screen.

A clip of Guidry's voice, a statement given over the phone, crackles on-screen. A transcript of his words appears in the blank space to the right of Micah's photo. "Naturally, the first step in a missing persons case is to thoroughly question the spouse of the missing. Very often, we don't have to look further."

"Detective, can you confirm Veronica Cavanaugh is a suspect in his disappearance?"

"I can*not.*"

My fingertips tingle. My legs feel like rubber. I can't get my feet under me, or maybe my muscles won't hold me. But I stumble to the family room, where I trip on my way to the sofa, and land a hand on what I'm looking for—the remote control.

The reporter continues: "Police are investigating a small plane crash off the southeastern coast of Florida. The remains are consistent with the type of plane Micah Cavanaugh allegedly flew, but no confirmation yet that there's a connection."

I aim the remote control at the television, finger poised on the "Power" button.

"More news as it comes to us. Reporting live—"

Zap.

I collapse onto the sofa.

A phone is ringing again. This time, it's my cell. Detective Guidry. I slide my finger over the screen to answer, but I don't bother saying hello. "What the hell is happening? Have you seen the news? You said going to the press would help bring him home. Instead they're acting like *he's already dead.* People aren't going to be looking for him if they think he's dead."

"Veronica—"

"Find. My. Husband. Can you do that?"

The doorbell rings, too.

"I warned you about the press," the detective says. "I need you to keep calm."

"Calm? Calm? You warned me the press would be invading my privacy and bombarding me with questions, not throwing me under the bus."

"At this point, any press is good. Believe it or not, that clip—not saying I condone it—will have people rushing to their computer screens to research the missing man from Shadowlands."

"I just got a call," I blurt out.

"Let's take a deep breath and calm down."

"Mommy!" Elizabella calls from the hallway. "Crew and Fendi are here!"

"Don't you answer that door, Bella." And to the cop: "I can't stay calm! I just got a call. Whoever it was told me to listen to my daughter and—"

"Who?"

"I don't know, but they knew my name, and they told me to listen to my daughter."

"Listen to her about what?"

"I don't—"

"You didn't recognize the voice?"

"It was a whisper."

"Man or woman?"

"I don't know. A whisper."

"I'll check your phone records for incoming calls. It might be a good idea to put a wiretap on."

"A wiretap?" An ache in my chest practically consumes me, as if I'm caving in. Despite the fact that the call rattled me to no end, Guidry is calm and cool. Aloof. As if he's immune to my unraveling. As if he thinks I'm putting on an act. "You want to listen to my conversations?"

"In order to filter—"

"You think I know something." My fingertips pulsate with my heartbeat during the space of silence that follows.

Guidry coughs. Finally: "Do you?"

"You think I know what happened to him. Where he is. You think I know."

"Veronica."

I swallow a sob.

Guidry asks, "Is there a chance Claudette Winters could be right?"

"Claudette?"

"Hello-o!" I hear her voice through the door.

"Is there a chance there's another woman?"

Gabrielle.

The door squeaks a little as Bella disobeys me and opens it.

"No!" I say to both the detective and my daughter. I charge to the foyer, still on trembling stems.

"I—" Claudette shuts up the moment our eyes meet.

"What?" I ask her.

"I came for my casserole dish." She thrusts a handful of envelopes at me. "And I brought your mail."

I scoop up my errant kid and allow my neighbor access.

"Have you followed up on Plum Lake?" I ask Guidry.

"I put the word out. Haven't heard back yet if anyone's been to the house or seen your husband. Things move a little more slowly up north than they do here. But I've personally called the lake house phone dozens of times."

So have I.

"If he's there," Guidry continues, "he's ignoring the calls."

Bella squirms in my arms. "Want to play with Crew and Fendi."

I tighten my grip on her. "I'm going to look into it myself. If it's too much for you to do your job, too much for you to protect my daughter and me while you do it, I guess I'll have to do it for you."

"We're on top of it. The best thing for you to do is stay home and wait—"

"Down," Bella whispers and plants a sweet kiss on my cheek.

I acquiesce and lower her to the floor. "And if I don't?"

"Mrs. Cavanaugh." The detective sighs.

"Let's have a snack, shall we?" Claudette's bustling in my semiclean kitchen.

I glance over my shoulder to see she's managed to seat all three children at the table. Crew is doling out napkins.

"I'm going up north to the lake house. And if he isn't there, I'll come right back. It'll help, right? Please. I can't just sit here anymore."

Silence fills the other end of the line for a second or two. Finally: "Veronica."

"Hmm?"

"Who is Natasha Markham?"

I let out a little gasp the moment I hear her name. Instantly, her image appears in my mind. Auburn hair, dark-green eyes. Even in my memory, she's looking right through me. "She's . . . an old friend of Micah's."

"A girlfriend?"

"She was Micah's girlfriend," I admit. "She was my college roommate." For a brief moment, I relive a montage of memories: the day Micah leaned in and kissed me for the first time in our tiny dorm room while Natasha was at class, Natasha's interrupting a study session at the library we hadn't told her about, the look of realization on her face when she figured out her boyfriend had fallen for her best friend. "But we haven't seen her in years. What does Natasha have to do with anything?"

"Maybe nothing. We're just following up on any possible lead. And Micah? You have no reason to believe he's been in contact with Natasha?"

"No." My mother had been dead less than a year when I started college, but being with Natasha made it feel like I still had family. "We just talked about her. The night before he left. I mentioned her. Micah gave no indication he even knew where she was."

But just speaking her name aloud brings back memories.

Thursdays were movie night. We rented old eighties flicks and ate microwave popcorn and shared blankets. We ate ice cream out of the same tub, passing it back and forth. We shared toothpaste and laundry detergent.

But all that ended when Micah and I got closer.

"It was a dramatic few weeks all those years ago, but we made a clean break." I catch Claudette's glance. As if she can hear the detective's line of questioning on the other end of the line, she raises a brow and almost imperceptibly shakes her head in a silent *it's a shame, but I told you so*. "Why? Do *you* have reason to believe he's been in contact with Natasha?"

"I'm not ruling anything out at this point."

"Any word on the plane off the Atlantic coast?"

"Not yet, but we should know soon. As soon as I know, you'll know." He clears his throat. "You're a person of interest in the case, Veronica, and while that isn't the same as being a suspect . . . Look, I can't force you not to go to the lake house, but at this point, if you do, think how it'll look, your taking off right as the news breaks. I'd appreciate it if you stayed local."

But the police up there don't even care enough to drive by the lake house in a timely manner. And I have to find Micah. This wretchedness could be over in a few hours if he's on the lake. I envision it—Micah bundled by a fireside, a week past a shave, getting his head together. *Hey, Nicki-girl. You found me.* Relief fills my system. Of course he's up at the lake. He's taking a breather. He's spent the days on the water, with a fishing pole in his hand. That's why he isn't answering the phone. Everything's been building lately; he's been living in a pressure cooker.

And I've been a hormonal mess.

"*Call* the lake house again, all right?" Guidry says. "If he answers, great. Give us a call and go see him. But if he doesn't . . ."

I take a deep breath. "Thank you for calling."

"We'll be in touch."

He hangs up. There's plenty he didn't say, but I heard every word.

Natasha was my college roommate. Micah chose me over her all those years ago. The detective assumes Micah has gone back to her, and the local press thinks he's dead.

It's ridiculous.

Maybe Natasha can confirm they're wasting their time if they're trying to pin something on me. She knows how I feel about Micah, how I've *always* felt about him. I haven't had a phone number for her in years, and I doubt she's still using her college e-mail account, so I open my laptop and navigate to Facebook. I locate her page, but it appears as if she hasn't been on the site since May—at least that's the date of her last posting. There are no pictures available for viewing beyond her profile picture, which is perhaps her as a baby. I leave her a direct message with my phone number, then google her to see if anything pops up. A LinkedIn account and other avenues of social media appear, which I'll investigate once Claudette leaves.

"Are you all right?" Claudette asks.

I shake my head but can't manage a verbal response.

Guidry doesn't know my husband, and the press doesn't know anything about us.

Of course Micah went to the lake to decompress. Just like he did when I nearly lost my mind after the miscarriage. And I'll prove it to the world.

Chapter 13

November 17

The "new" insurance card Micah gave me, the one I thought we'd given to the fertility clinic, is invalid. The group number doesn't exist. Micah fabricated the insurance, I suppose, so I'd think we were still covered, so as not to interrupt our mission for another baby. And because he'd been paying the bills out of pocket—$5,000 here, $2,000 there—the balance in our savings account is dangerously low.

It's more proof that he never took a job with Diamond Corporation . . . at least not a job that offered health insurance. But given our plans to attempt IVF again after the miscarriage, why would he have left United without a decent health care plan?

So maybe there's another secret Diamond Corporation, but he's apparently gotten pretty good at using a print shop, seeing as I'm holding a believable insurance card with a faulty group number. Not to mention the deposit receipts complete with a Diamond logo.

And then there's the fact that we're two months behind on our mortgage, which I just now learned when I opened the mail.

So what's going on?

The job he wasn't offered . . . I can only assume he invented it to keep me at ease during the IVF process.

We're going into debt to grow our family . . . and to live in this family-appropriate house, in this safe, enclosed neighborhood. Leaving Old Town was my idea. I couldn't stay there anymore. The bad energy . . . the miscarriage . . . I'd needed to put it all behind me.

I glance at Claudette, who is practically purring over her cup of green tea, sweetened only with natural stevia. "I've put too much on his shoulders," I say. "He's under a lot of pressure."

"It's perfectly all right to demand what you deserve."

"I would've been all right in a two-bedroom condo."

"Honey. No one's all right in a two-bedroom condo."

I wonder if she's ever lived in one.

"Have you looked through his things yet?"

I scoop another heaping teaspoon of sugar from the bowl and stir it into my mug. It's my first caffeinated beverage since before we conceived the twins. "He doesn't have anything to hide." It sounds like a lie, even to my own ears, considering he's been hiding plenty.

She lifts a shoulder in a subtle shrug. "Then there's no harm in looking, is there?"

"My dad comes home on the train," Crew is saying across the room. "Maybe he's on a train."

"My daddy doesn't go on trains. He's on a *plane*." Elizabella takes a bite of her peanut-butter-topped celery, which Claudette provided. "It's in the water."

I shiver a little every time she references it. Remembering how eerily her drawing predicted the accident churns my stomach.

"Why do you think she's saying that?" Claudette asks.

I haven't the slightest idea. "She knows about the remains of a small jet off the coast of Florida, and her dad flies. Maybe she's assuming—"

"Or maybe she knows something." Her eyes zero in on me. "When Brad was involved with the tramp, he was extremely careless around the children. He took phone calls in front of them, even talked about her to them."

"That must have been awful, but—"

"*But nothing*, Veronica. The way Bella's behaving . . . she's dealing with something she doesn't understand, and one thing little girls don't understand is that their fathers can be complete and utter assholes."

"Or maybe it's exactly what the doctors say. An imaginary friend."

"An imaginary friend who draws plane crashes?" After another long, thoughtful slurp of tea, my neighbor calmly places her mug on the table and dabs her glossed lips with her napkin. "Maybe she overheard Micah talking to that other woman."

"No." Memories of our last twenty-four hours together zing through my system. The cha-cha in the kitchen. The sex we had before he left. "He wouldn't have."

Then I think about what Shell said. I glance at Claudette, quickly assess her, and decide to trust her with a tidbit: "Except his mother admits to knowing a Gabrielle."

Claudette raises a brow. "It's time to delve into his secrets, if you want to get to the truth."

I blink, and I'm back in a bungalow in Maywood at eighteen, digging through boxes of my mother's things while she was stashed in a drawer down the road at Loyola University Medical. The musty scent of that old attic revisits me now, along with the bite of tears that welled the moment I found the paperwork—old medical records. My mother's grandmother had been institutionalized. The doctors suspected schizophrenia.

We had a history of schizophrenia in the family, and I'd never known it.

And my mother had just taken her own life at the behest of mysterious voices who told her to do it. Learning of the family history after her death helped explain it.

Maybe learning Micah's secrets—and I'm starting to think he had a lot of them—will help me deal with his disappearance.

The chime of the doorbell—church bells, which remind me of the day I buried my mother—jolts me from the memory.

"I'll get that." Claudette is halfway there by the time I think to insist on answering my own door.

"Nini," Bella's saying from the next room over. "That's not nice. Tell Fendi you're sorry."

And a deep voice from the foyer: "Good day, ma'am. I'm Special Agent Lincoln with the Federal Bureau of Investigation, and this is . . ."

Clumsily, I pull myself out of my chair and stumble on the first step down the hallway.

". . . here to discuss your husband's accident."

Claudette, shaking the taller one's hand: "Come in."

The shorter fed, as he takes my neighbor's hand: "Veronica Cavanaugh?"

"I'm . . . it's *me. I'm* Veronica Cavanaugh." My toes are numb. My fingertips tingle. *Federal agents?* I stop several feet away from the two gentlemen, smartly dressed in black suits and striped ties, as if they happened by on their way to a funeral.

"Mrs. Cavanaugh." The taller one—Lennon? Lincoln—folds his hands in front of him, perhaps when he realizes I'm not going to shake his hand. I'm too afraid of what he's here to tell me to remember social graces. "May we come in?"

"Of course." My voice sounds weak, more like a few pips than words.

Everything feels cloudy for the next few seconds as I lead the gentlemen, Claudette following close behind, to my kitchen.

Lincoln's partner pulls out a chair and presents it with an abrupt palm up. "Would you like to sit down?"

Maybe I should. But I can't seem to propel myself forward. I'm glued to my spot. Everything echoes and blurs.

"Sit." Claudette guides me onto a barstool. "I'll take the children outside."

I meet her gaze, see her lips moving, but I don't know what else she's saying. Then suddenly, she's gone, and the kids are gone, and Lincoln is talking with me.

I catch only a few words:

Accident.

Plane.

Debris.

Identified.

Declared.

Dead.

Chapter 14

November 18

I awaken from a fitful nap.

An hour has passed.

Or maybe a day or two.

I check the time on my phone. Just after seven at night, over twenty-four hours since my husband has been declared dead.

My call log tells me I missed a call from Shell, who must have been returning the call I made just after I heard the devastating news about Micah.

Her message: "I'm sorry I missed your call. Honey, you've got me worried. Call me back."

I will. But she deserves to sleep through the rest of the night. Her world can end in the morning.

I glance at Claudette, who is busy with the dishes in my sink, and try to remember what she was wearing the last time I looked at her to determine if it's the same day as the last time I saw her in my kitchen.

Can't remember.

Or maybe I never paid attention.

Without a body, I can't bury my husband, and his remains are still en route. He'll be delivered to the same funeral home that took my mother. Lincoln and his partner have made the arrangements for me.

It's surreal. I won't believe Micah's really gone until I'm holding his death certificate, until he's officially stamped *not alive*. And maybe even then I won't believe it.

If I'd known that cha-cha would be our last . . .

If I'd known, if I'd known, if I'd known . . .

A blink later, I look toward the sink, and Claudette is no longer there.

It's dark outside.

Despite the late hour, Bella is coloring at her table, and a syndicated sitcom blares from the television set. A witty line—*Actually, it's Miss Chanandler Bong*—precedes laughter.

My abdomen is still tender with yellowing bruises from weeks of IVF needles, and I'm nauseous with the drastic hormonal shifts taking place in my body now that I've abruptly stopped the injections.

The shift in this house is just as drastic. One minute, I was prepping for a baby with my husband, and now I'm . . .

I don't know what I'm doing now.

I'm not decorating the nursery. I'm not shopping for onesies and tiny Chicago White Sox wind suits. I'm not doing much of anything . . . including being a mother.

"She is *not*, Nini." Elizabella's voice isn't much more than a whisper. "She's just sad."

I suddenly realize I can't remember the last time I interacted with my daughter. Judging by the plethora of wrappers littering her table and the floor around it, she's been grabbing snacks when she's hungry. I have vague recollections of opening a juice box or two, but beyond that . . . I swallow a sob . . . I've been nearly catatonic. "Bella."

She startles a little when I call her name. Her eyes widen.

"Bella, come here." I'm out of my chair, gravitating toward her.

Pick up the pieces.

Just like after Mama died.

Like after the miscarriage.

Bella needs me.

"Mommy."

Her body feels smaller than ever in my embrace.

"It's okay," I say.

"He's at God Land."

That's what they tell me.

She pecks a tiny, wet kiss onto my cheek.

I stare out over the fairway and imagine the energy of summer on the course. Early tee times. Fair play. The faint scent of cigarette smoke drifts on the air.

A split second later, I see it: the intermittent orange glow against a black felt sky. Someone puffing on a smoke.

I lock my gaze on it, and somehow I know he's staring at us. Watching us.

Or . . . I tighten my arms around Elizabella.

Maybe it's not me he's looking at.

I could call the police. But I can't prove he's casing our house, and I don't know what they would charge him with if they apprehended him.

Still, I hike Bella onto my hip and slink toward the sliding glass door. I turn the bolt and yank down the Roman shade to shut out the rest of the world. But then, I catch sight of the windows in the breakfast room. We live in a fishbowl. All these windows!

She wiggles. "Down."

I let her down, when all I really want to do is keep her next to me in one of those slings I used when she was a baby.

"Just a minute, baby. Stay right with me."

Frantically, I pull on cords, lower blinds. Rip at tiebacks. Catch sight of more glass in the kitchen, then in the dining room. Curtains fall over the windowpanes.

My legs are shaking as I dart to the front door and engage and reengage the two locks on it.

Bella's shriek sends an adrenaline shot to my heart.

"Mommmmmmy!"

I trip on the rug in the foyer but catch myself against the wall to prevent a fall.

"Mommmmmmy!"

"Bella!" I'm nearly out of breath by the time I see her, screaming, pointing at the shades I just lowered over the patio doors. "Bella! What's wrong?"

She's sniffling over her words: "Nini. Nini saw."

I fold my arms around her and pull her to the sofa. "What, baby? What did Nini see?"

Bella's brown eyes, reddened at the rims with either fatigue or tears, widen. "Mommy." A pair of fat tears curb over her pink cheeks.

I tighten my grip.

"I'm gonna go be with Daddy."

Chapter 15

"Bella, listen to Mama." I take a deep breath. "Daddy is at God Land. It's true, but you're safe at home with me."

Her cheeks puff out in frustration.

I reach for my phone when it rings and recognize the number as Detective Guidry's.

Elizabella settles in on my lap.

I take the call. "Hello."

"Mrs. Cavanaugh, we have a lead on your husband's car."

My mouth is dry, as if I'm about to cough. I don't know why his car matters, if his plane has crashed, if he's dead.

"Mrs. Cavanaugh?"

"I'm here," I manage to say.

"I know it's getting late, but would you mind if I stopped by?"

"It's not too late." Time is relative at this point, anyway. "There's a man . . . he's on the fairway . . . I think he's spying on us."

"I'll send someone to check it out. Probably a member of the press, looking for a photo op. Keep your shades drawn."

"A member of the press?"

"Probably. They're desperate for human-interest stories."

That's what we've become? A human-interest story?

"No one can get in past the guard," he continues. "Or without the gate code. And we've doubled the patrols at the county preserve just in case. If someone's out there who shouldn't be, we'll know."

A few minutes later, the detective is seated at my kitchen table, opening a file folder. "Is this your husband's car?" He glances up at me.

With Bella on my hip, I award the photograph in his file a once-over.

Dark-blue Chevy Impala.

"Yes. But that's not his plate."

"The VIN matches. It's at C-Way."

"C-Way?"

"C-Way. An airport. It's between here and the north woods of Wisconsin. About ninety minutes southwest of your father-in-law's lake house."

The familiar, dull ache in my lower back registers just then. I shift my weight to accommodate the bulk of kid in my arms, but she's my security blanket, and I don't want to let go of her.

"Mrs. Cavanaugh."

"Yeah."

The detective places a warm hand on my elbow. "Veronica."

We lock gazes.

"Why don't you sit down?"

Fresh tears swell in my eyes. I lower my tired body to a chair. Bella touches the glossy photograph in the detective's file. "Daddy."

Guidry tears off a few sheets from his legal pad and slides them across the table to my daughter, along with a pen. Bella isn't usually allowed to write with ink, but I help her click it open and give a nod toward the paper.

"Could be he drove up north for some alone time before he took his flight." Guidry's voice is soft, assuring. "Security at C-Way says the car's been there at least twenty-four hours, maybe longer. It doesn't fill all the gaps—the license plate switch, for example—but . . ." He sighs. "It's something."

"I don't know why he would've left from up there." I feel my brow creasing. As much as I don't want to lose it—again—in front of Guidry, I'm powerless to stop the continuous flood of tears.

"I'm sorry for what you're going through," he says.

I wipe tears from my cheeks and again meet his gaze. "I never know what to say when people say that."

"You don't have to say anything."

"I mean, I appreciate the sentiment. You can't *not* say you're sorry, but—"

"You're holding up okay? You need anything?"

It isn't like I have a choice. I have to *hold up okay*, don't I? And I don't need anything, except my husband. But no one can bring him back to me.

"Detective, I'm . . ."

He narrows his gaze, but this time it comes off more concerned than usual.

"I'm . . ." I catch my breath over a sob. "My world is falling apart."

"I'm sorry. I'm doing everything I can."

Nothing makes sense.

"Perhaps if you dig deep," he continues. "*Think.* What are you not telling me?"

I wish I knew what he wanted me to say. But all I'm *thinking* is that if the police can't answer these questions, I have to find the answers myself.

They think I'm not telling everything I know, but I think it's just the opposite, actually. *They're* keeping something from *me*.

If Guidry is saying Micah never took a job with Diamond, then whose plane was he flying? And if he wasn't a pilot anymore, then how did he die in a plane crash?

Chapter 16

"I don't believe it," Shell says through tears. "There has to be a mistake."

I keep hoping the phone will ring, and that's all this mess will have been—one big mistake.

"My son, my son, my son," she murmurs. "God, why? And Bella . . ."

My tears intensify.

"What happened?"

"I don't know. Except they found remains of a plane . . ."

"No, no, no."

"It was off the coast of Florida. Atlantic side."

"No, no, you said he was going to New York. There's some mistake. There's got to be—"

"That's what he told me, Shell, but there were obviously things he didn't—"

"We'll figure it out. Someone's made a mistake."

"They sent federal officers to tell me." I don't say so, but it sure doesn't *look* like anyone made a mistake.

"And Bella . . . she had a feeling. What was it she said?"

"God Land." I hiccup over the words. "She said he went to God Land, and we know now she didn't mean Wisconsin."

"Jesus, Mary, and Joseph. How do you suppose—"

"I don't know." But I'd rather not think about it.

"So much life ahead of him," Shell says. "So many years ahead for *you,* for *Bella*. You were trying to have another *baby!*"

"He was a good father," I say.

"Good, *period*. He had plans. For you. For your family."

"I know. I can't believe it," I say. "I don't *want* to believe it."

Until I'm holding the death certificate or until I see his dead body, I won't believe he's gone. Nothing adds up. Short of his flying a plane for some secret government agency, no two pieces of this puzzle fit together.

"But what happened?"

"I don't know."

"Surely, they've told you what they think—"

"If I knew, I'd tell you. They said they'd share the report, but—"

"What will you do?" Her tears rattle through the phone, which only leaves me falling apart into even smaller fragments. "With Bella . . . how will you . . . how will you manage?"

Just as Micah would've wanted me to. But I know what Shell means. Being a single parent—especially to a handful like Bella—is going to be hard. But even if I'd known eventually I'd be doing it all on my own, I still would have fought to have her.

"I'll be there for you, for both of you."

"I'll never be the same," I whisper. I'll never be able to hold him again, to kiss his lips, to tell him I love him. I'll never see Bella climb into his lap again. And that terrible truth keeps playing on repeat in my head. I keep seeing her climb into his arms. I keep seeing her eat ice cream off the spoon he held out for her.

For the last time.

And it hurts to know I wasted those last few hours with him. Bitching about preschool, about Nini, about how his life was so easy compared to mine. I feel cold inside, as if someone is taking an ice pick to my heart, carving out the places reserved for my husband, the father of my only child. And to think that Shell lost her only son . . .

"Not the natural order of things," Shell says. "A son shouldn't go before his parents."

They say sharing grief helps, but I can't believe anything helps now. As a mother, I see Micah's death as doubly unfair. Take a father from his daughter. Take a husband from his wife. But how must it feel to have a child taken from his mother? How would I feel to have Elizabella taken from me?

"I'm . . . God, Shell, I'm lost. I can't believe it."

"The service will help."

"I suppose." My only experience with memorials—my mother's—didn't provide closure, and the prospect of holding one for Micah feels as if I'm spiraling down into nothingness.

"We'll do it right," she says. "Something special to honor him."

No anniversary parties are on the horizon. No graduations. No giving Bella away with her father on her wedding day.

Will anything be special enough?

"When will it be?" Shell asks. "The memorial."

"The crematorium is supposed to call when he arrives. But I thought I'd wait for you," I say, although I haven't wanted to think about *anything* of the sort. "To plan the memorial. To find the right time."

"Our flight is tomorrow. I can't get on an earlier flight, with the holiday next week, but, honey, come to the lake. We'll plan the memorial together."

At first, the prospect of being with Shell is like a warm blanket on a cold night. But a heartbeat later, the chill seeps back into my skin. "Is Mick all right with that?"

"He'll *have* to be. I'll talk with him. We should be getting there sometime Saturday."

We cry together and talk for a while. But eventually, she has to go. She has to tell Mick that their only son, with whom he hadn't spoken in years, is dead.

"Love you," she says.

"Love you, too."

Maybe I will find closure if I plan a memorial. Micah and I had planned for this sort of thing, only we'd figured we would be in our seventies or eighties or even nineties when it happened.

I'm an island, drifting in a horrific sea.

Thanksgivings of my youth flit in and out of my mind. Mama and me. Just the two of us, alone. I never wanted to repeat that pattern. Would Mick object to two more for Thanksgiving at the lake? Might he learn to consider us family even if he couldn't mend fences with his son? If this year goes well, I hope we can count on holidays with Shell and Mick from here on. I can't bear the thought of celebrating at a table for two.

I look to Elizabella, who's struggling with the zipper on her coat. I wanted so much more for her. I wanted a big family, so we'd have each other when tragedy struck. I never wanted to leave my daughter alone, never wanted her to endure the hell that I went through.

"Where are we going?" Bella attempts again to zip her coat.

I take over and zip it up for her. "Warm and cozy?"

"Nini doesn't want to go to school."

I haven't sent her to the Westlake School since it all happened. I don't know why she'd assume I'd send her now. Come to think of it, pre-school was Micah's idea, and it made sense because we assumed I'd need some Bella-free time once IVF worked its magic and I was pregnant again. Now that another baby isn't in the plan, and now that Micah isn't here to persuade me otherwise, there's no reason to rush Bella out the door to a school she obviously hates.

"We're not going to the school, Ellie-Belle."

"Yay! To the park?"

111

"We're going to the bank."

She frowns a little. "Oh."

"They have lollipops."

She softens a little. "Pink ones?"

"We'll have to see." Micah and I have an emergency stash of cash in our safe-deposit box. It isn't much—a few thousand, maybe five, assuming he hasn't spent all of it—but it'll carry us until the death certificate arrives and the insurance comes through. And in order to file for the insurance, I have to find the policy numbers. I'm hoping the paperwork is still in the safe-deposit box, where we stashed it when we moved here from the city.

I hold my daughter a little too closely.

"Mommy? Do you miss Daddy?" She's staring me right in the eyes. Sometimes, I think she's too little to comprehend what's happening, but other times, like now, it's apparent she knows the permanence of our predicament.

"Yes." I kiss her baby cheeks. "I will *always* miss Daddy."

The ride to the bank is a blur—almost everything is cloudy since Micah left—and the walk to the vault and safe-deposit box isn't crystal clear, either. But I must've turned the key in the lock when the bank manager turned hers because Elizabella and I are now staring into the box.

"Ooooh, pretty," she coos when I hold up a ring I've never seen before. It's white gold, or platinum maybe, with a pretty bluish-green stone—a fairly large princess-cut set amid a diamond halo.

I don't know where the ring came from or why Micah would've been hiding it in this vault. Unless . . .

A space in my chest warms with a thought: Maybe it's a final gift from my husband. One he never had the chance to give me.

I pull the ring from its velvet bed and slip it onto my finger, but it's too small, even for my pinkie. Micah knows my size. If it were a gift, he'd surely have purchased a larger band. Then again, my fingers have been swollen, and I've gained a fair amount of weight—upward of twenty pounds at the height of IVF treatment. Maybe he was going to have the ring sized, once my hormones leveled out.

Or maybe he never intended for me to wear it.

Gabrielle.

I stuff the ring back into the cushion, snap the box closed, and drop it into my purse. When I'm up at the lake with Shell, I'll ask about her friend, Gabrielle. I'll find out why, if what Claudette says is true, my husband would be talking to Gabrielle in the middle of the night.

But I can't ponder possibilities now.

Just get what you came for and get out of here.

A few manila envelopes sit at the bottom of the box. I peek into the first, and relief rushes through me. Insurance policies.

The cash is there, too, just as it's always been, just as it was in our box in the city before we moved here, bound with yellow paper straps. I count them as I place them, too, into my shoulder bag. One, two, three, four, five bundles of tens.

But then I notice something.

The bundles . . . their straps are more mustard than yellow. They aren't bundles of tens but *hundreds*. Which means . . .

I'm dizzy for a good half minute.

I have $50,000 in my bag, when I came expecting five.

Fifty thousand dollars.

"Micah," I whisper. "What were you thinking?"

He may as well have shoved the money under the floorboards! Who, in this day and age, keeps *this much cash* at the ready? Why wouldn't he have kept it in a savings account, where it would accrue interest? Or, better yet, in stocks and bonds?

"Mommy."

"Just a minute, baby."

And why wouldn't he have told me how much was here? When we rented the box in the city, we put a few thousand in it, and even then

I hadn't understood the purpose. Micah said it was a good idea to have cash on hand. For emergencies. But *$50,000*?

Have we always stashed this much away? Or . . . is this the money Micah stole from his father? The money that caused the rift between them?

"Mommy, Nini's hungry."

"I'll get her a lollipop in a second."

The urge to flee the bank smacks me dead between the eyes, as if I'm doing something I shouldn't be doing. As if this money isn't really mine, and if I don't rush out of here—now—someone will either take it from me or take me from it.

The thought is ridiculous, of course, but so is not telling your wife about fifty grand. I was going to simply deposit the cash into our checking account, to use it for bills and necessities until the estate was settled, but now . . . I can't deposit this much money! How could I explain where it came from? I slip a few hundreds from one of the bundles. I'll deposit a thousand, maybe two. But the rest, I'll keep here.

Safe.

Only suddenly, I don't feel so safe anymore. Our credit cards are all but maxed. There's not enough in our checking account to carry Bella and me for more than a week. Like it or not, I might need this money.

The image of the man on the eleventh fairway flashes in my mind as if he's a recurrent memory. The cigarette glowing in the black of night . . .

The voice on the phone that night: *Listen to your daughter.*

And I can't help thinking that maybe Micah is gone because of this money. Maybe the man with the cigarette knows what happened. Or maybe he wants what I've just dropped into my purse.

I have to get out of the Shadowlands. Tonight.

Maybe I'm being ridiculous.

But I can't take any chances.

We'll just go up north a few days early. We can stay at a hotel until Shell and Mick arrive. I'm sure Shell will understand. She's the only one who could possibly fathom the gargantuan crater Micah's death leaves in my soul. She's the only one grieving the way I am. Maybe Bella and I can stay at the lake house until I get my head together, until I figure out what to do, and maybe Shell can help me figure things out.

But the money. I can't talk to anyone about that.

I can't even tell Shell I found it, if his having it proves he stole from Mick.

If Detective Guidry knew, he might assume Micah was involved in something illegal, whether this money is tied to Mick or not, especially given all the evidence of a fabricated life my husband left in his wake. And I have to admit now that maybe it's true. If Micah wasn't working, how did he come across this much cash? And why, if he had this money stashed away, have we fallen behind on our bills?

My hands tremble as I scoop up the other things at the bottom of the box: the insurance policy for my engagement ring, the deed to our Impala and the Explorer I drive, our wills and declaration of trust.

And an eight-by-ten manila envelope, addressed to Micah at our place in Old Town.

"Nini's *hungry.*" Elizabella tugs on my coat. "Lollipops."

"Okay."

"Pink ones."

"Of course. Any color you want."

I drop the rest of the things into my bag and tear open the last envelope.

A deed of title with my name on it slips into my hands, along with a palm tree keychain, on which three keys are hooked.

I own a piece of property.

In Key West, Florida.

What?

"Mommmmmy."

"Okay, Bella. We're going."

I shove the safe-deposit box back into its slot, like a drawer in a morgue.

I'll deposit a couple thousand, maybe fifteen hundred, get Bella a lollipop, and get out of here, so I can start putting two and two together.

The moment I step out of the vault, however, I catch sight of a man in a suit. He's perched on one of the leather chairs in the atrium of the lobby—and he's staring right at me.

Agent Lincoln.

I'm certain of it. I'll never forget the face of the man who told me my husband is dead.

Something in the way he looks at me and the way he avoids looking at everyone else sends up warning signals. If he wanted to speak with me again—maybe to share the report on Micah's death—he wouldn't be *here*. He'd meet me at my home.

I make a move toward the teller, but Lincoln stands up and takes a step in that direction, too.

His expression . . . accusatory.

"He was in the kitchen," Bella says.

"Yes."

What is he doing here? Is he looking to see if I'd take the money? What if Micah stole it and was under investigation? God, suppose they think I'm in on whatever scheme Micah pulled off?

"Loll-ee-pop."

I imagine agents descending on me, right here in the bank lobby. I can't let that happen. Not here, not now. And not on the street outside, either.

Or . . .

He was in the kitchen.

What if he's the man Bella was talking about? *My daddy doesn't know that man in the kitchen.*

I scan the area. The bank is crowded. Unless he bowled people over, he wouldn't be able to get to me if I beelined out the closest door. If I try to stop at the teller, though, he could stop me—or see that I'm carrying a ton of cash. "On second thought," I say, more to myself than to my daughter, "we're going home."

"Lollipop."

I scoop her into my arms before she has a chance to throw a tantrum, and the look in my eyes must be convincing enough, because she's instantly silent.

We slip out the side door and into the car.

I don't see Lincoln exit the bank because we're already driving away.

Chapter 17

The moment I pull past the gate at the Shadowlands, Bella says, "Nini says you lied. You promised lollipops."

"Yep." It's not my finest mothering moment, but I don't want to get into this with a figment of my child's imagination. "I lied."

It's a minuscule lie, compared to those her father told by omission.

Then, softening, as I make the turn onto Hidden Creek: "But I might have some gummy bears at home."

"Okay."

"But you have to tell me, Bella. The man at the bank. You said he was in the kitchen."

"He *was*."

"When?"

"With Crew and Fendi."

Okay, so she's talking about seeing him recently.

"Silly Mommy. He *talked* to you."

Notwithstanding running into Lincoln at the bank—and who's to say he was there to see me at all? Couldn't his expression have been indicative of regret for the news he'd delivered?—I need to pull myself together before I completely unravel. If he were there on official business, wouldn't his partner have been with him? Wouldn't one of them have been waiting at my car for me?

I suppose time will tell. If this money was obtained illegally, they know where to find me.

I pull into the garage and close the door before we get out of the car, so as to avoid any glances from the neighbors, and once Elizabella is settled with some gummy bears, I start to look through the things I found in the safe-deposit box.

I don't remember discussing the purchase of a house in Key West, but my signature is on the form that gives Micah power of attorney to conduct the transaction without my presence. According to the deed, I own it, free and clear. Just me. Not Micah. I purchased the house four and a half years ago. We've been paying property taxes twice a year ever since.

I would have been newly pregnant with Bella at the time and completely preoccupied. It's possible, I suppose, that Micah slid the form in front of me and asked me to sign it at some point, but I'd think I'd remember buying a house. Especially when we apparently paid nearly $1.3 million—cash—for the place.

Cash!

Elizabella now colors at the table next to me, while I search online for a property deeded to me, on Elizabeth Lane, in Key West.

When the house in question pops up on my laptop screen, my heart nearly stops. I've never been to Key West. Elizabella has never been to Key West. But there it is, online—the house she's been drawing since the last night she spent with her dad.

It's pale yellow, with arched windows.

I leaf through my daughter's drawings. Page after page. Yellow house with light-purple flowers in the window boxes.

Bella's voice in my head. *This is the water where the plane is, and over here is the big house.*

I stop paging through the stack of drawings when I hit on the red, black, and yellow sketch that looks something like a lighthouse.

I open another window on my laptop screen and search for *Key West lighthouse image.* While a lighthouse pops up onto the screen, it doesn't resemble Elizabella's drawing. It's pure white, for one thing.

I conduct another search: *Key West lighthouse red black yellow.*

Suggested websites pop up instantly. I click on one, which directs me to tourist sites in Key West. The first image to materialize is the southernmost point in the continental United States, marked with an oversize, concrete buoy, cemented at the corner of South and Whitehead Streets. The page claims this is one of the most photographed sites on the island.

Its horizontal stripes are red, black, and yellow.

I compare it to the crayon rendition.

Her rudimentary shapes, among what appears to be a rocky shore and waves behind it, led me to believe Bella had drawn a lighthouse, but in fact, it's this concrete buoy, a Key West landmark.

"Bella, have you ever seen this? In person?"

"We're coloring."

"Bella." I pull her onto my lap.

A splat of pink, sugary gummy bear drool lands on my sleeve.

"Mommy!"

"Behave," I tell her. "Look." I point to the screen. "Have you ever been there?"

"No." *Chomp, chomp, chomp* on her gummy bear. She wiggles to climb off my lap.

I tighten my grip. "Ellie-Belle, this is important. Why did you draw this?"

"I *didn't.*"

Deep breath. "Was it Nini's drawing?"

"Yes."

"Has Nini been here?" I again point to the buoy on the screen.

"Nini goed there once."

I glance at my shoulder bag, sitting atop the island and stuffed with insurance policies and five bundles of large bills.

My gaze travels to the suitcase I brought up from the basement storage room. I was going to pack for Plum Lake tomorrow morning. But perhaps we should go sooner. Plans are changing quickly these days.

One minute, I'm shooting up progesterone, rooting down in this house, ready to live here until babies number two and three and maybe four graduate from college.

Now I'm shoving things into suitcases, as if I'm not sure I'll be returning.

And maybe I won't have to. We paid too much for this house, and I don't like living at the Shadowlands, anyway, and Micah's driven us up to our elbows in debt.

But I have fifty grand and a house in Key West. No family beyond Bella and the demonic Nini. I have no friends here, save the lone, slightly overbearing but good-hearted acquaintance across the street, and there's a detective who was half a comment away from accusing me of offing my husband before the feds declared him dead. I ought to walk away. Be rid of this place forever.

But this bed beneath my suitcase . . . it's our first. Our queen-size mattress, which barely fit in the bedroom at our college apartment and damn near reached wall-to-wall at our condo in Old Town. It's where Micah made love to me both the first time and the last. It's where we began and ended.

Maybe I can't leave for good, but I can stay up at the lake for a while, either in a hotel or with my in-laws. And after I've had time to think, I'll decide what to do with the mini-mansion on the island. I'll decide what to do with this place . . . and the fifty grand. I wonder if I'll even have to make a decision or if the police will swoop in and take everything I have.

"Shell, it's me again." I lose my composure every time I leave her a message. "Please call as soon as you can. Bella and I"—I swallow over a lump in my throat—"we're heading up north, to Plum Lake, early. I hope that's okay. So if you don't get me on my cell, please just . . . we'll meet you at the lake house when you get there."

I toss my phone to the mattress and resume packing. I usually keep a small photo album containing pictures of our wedding in the drawer in the bedside table. But since Micah went missing, I've kept it on my pillow. I open it now, if only for a glimpse of the happiness we used to share, if only for proof that I didn't imagine it all, despite the secrets he was keeping from me.

Our wedding was an intimate affair. Micah and me traversing the sand on a Lake Michigan beach with a few guests: Shell, of course, and some friends we'd met at UIC, with whom we quickly lost touch once we graduated. Natasha and I were long estranged. Mick hadn't come; Micah hadn't forgiven him for the midlife crisis, during which he'd briefly left Shell.

And now, Micah will never have the chance to mend his relationship with his father. I'd always wanted that for him.

I press the photo book into my suitcase and give it a pat, which seems rather melodramatic. But I want him with me.

I feel him leading me across the kitchen floor in time with his unique cha-cha beat. I want to grasp the memory of those last moments, fold it into a tight square like the notes I used to pass in middle school, and keep it safe and private in my pocket. A piece of us that no one can disturb. Our last dance.

"Mommy?" Bella's lying at the foot of the bed, freshly bathed and in pajamas, and already fed. It's only a few minutes past sundown, but I'm planning to put her in the car in an hour or so and make the drive up north just as she's about to get sleepy. She'll sleep during the drive, and the trip will be easier. "Nini's coming, too?"

"Why wouldn't she?"

"'Cause you don't like Nini."

"I like her just fine, baby."

A big, sweet yawn escapes her. "Me too."

Plum Lake is about seven hours away. I'll be practically brain-dead by the time we arrive, but I'll check into a hotel in Minocqua, try to sleep, and meet Micah's parents at the lake late Saturday. Just the thought of setting foot in the cottage where Micah spent many a childhood summer warms me, as if he's sidling up against me, close to me, breathing with me. Or maybe I want to go to see for myself that he isn't there. That he isn't anywhere anymore.

I cover a sob—the grief comes in waves, it seems—and sink into the memory of his holding me. It's the closest I've come to feeling him—his presence, his essence—since he walked out the door nine and a half days ago.

"I sleep with you, Mommy, okay?"

I wipe away tears, then press a kiss to the crown of her beautiful head. "You'll sleep in the car tonight," I tell her.

Another yawn. "Okay."

Leaving feels urgent now that I know Micah's not coming back. I felt this way after my mother died, too—the need to keep moving, to escape, to never sit still. I'd used her meek life insurance to put myself through college at warp speed. Then, before I knew it, Micah and I were getting married, then trying month after month after month for a baby. Then after medication after medication, Elizabella came, then more trying, more medication, then the twins . . .

Within minutes, Bella is asleep, winding a coil of hair around her finger, rubbing the hair with her thumb. I drape her favorite blanket over her tiny body and hope she stays asleep through the transfer down the stairs and to the car.

I carry suitcases down the stairs one at a time and stow them in the SUV. My body is recovering from the IVF retrieval. I'm not nearly as sore; I'm stronger, physically speaking, than I was a week ago. But emotionally? Mentally? I wonder if I'll ever feel whole again.

The house feels empty now, with three suitcases and a laundry basket full of Bella's toys and art supplies in the car. With my child asleep upstairs, everything is quiet and still. Funeral-like.

I have a long night ahead of me. I sit for a moment at the breakfast table and stare out at the dusky sky, a private mourning session between me and the great beyond, the sky that stole my forever when it swallowed up my husband.

I crack open a window. Take it all in.

A faint hint of smoke drifts in on a chilly breeze.

I stiffen and glance across the eleventh fairway. Where is the smoke coming from? It's distinctly cigarette smoke. Not from a grill or a bonfire.

But I don't see anyone on the course.

I crank the window closed and lower the blinds.

It's time to leave.

I throw my arms into my parka—it'll be cold up north—and bundle Elizabella in more blankets before carrying her down the stairs. She's getting too big to be carried like this. Too heavy.

Once she's strapped into her car seat, I again check my shoulder bag to ensure the stacks of $100 bills remain hidden at the bottom of it. I don't know where I assume they'd go, but I feel better once I count five bundles. I catch sight, also, of the ring box and paperwork I found in the deposit box. I wonder what else Micah was hiding from me.

And soon, we're whisking out of the Shadowlands.

The road stretches before me, still muddled with the last remnants of rush-hour traffic, which spans from three in the afternoon to seven at night, even on the outskirts of Chicago. I'm neck and neck with many of the same motorists, as if we're fish in a school, all narrowing toward the same current—in this case, the Tri-State Tollway—to carry us to faster passage. Black crossover to my left. Blue two-door to my right. Brown sedan behind me. Inch. Inch. Inch. Stoplight after stoplight.

Finally, I exit north on the toll road, which is more populated than I'd anticipated at this hour, but it thins out as we near the state line. I glance in my rearview mirror to catch a glimpse of my sleeping daughter. In the periphery, I see it: the same sedan—I see it's brown when it passes under a streetlight—that's been with me since Half Day Road.

I adjust the mirror so it's aimed more at the car than Bella.

It's a nondescript car. Probably not the same sedan. It isn't following me. Chalk that theory up to my wild imagination and paranoia.

I switch lanes.

So does the sedan.

I slow down to five under the speed limit, which is practically unheard of on a road where everyone goes at least ten over.

Cars whip around me but not the sedan.

I'm in the center lane now. I drift back to the right.

The sedan does the same.

I brave a glance at my shoulder bag and remember that federal agent—Lincoln—at the bank. And even though it sounded as if my daughter was referencing his recent visit, her words haunt me. *Daddy doesn't know the man in the kitchen.*

And then there's the fact that Micah stole money from his father.

Who did I marry? What had he gotten himself into?

If I'd left this money stacked on the back porch, would I still feel as if this sedan were pursuing me?

My hands are damp with perspiration. I lower the heat.

My heart gallops in my chest.

I gun it and whip around a minivan into the left lane.

The sedan stays nearly on my bumper.

Even when I slow down, it's still there.

My breaths come more quickly.

What am I going to do?

There's an off-ramp up ahead. Should I exit and flag down a cop? Call one now?

Yes. I'll call one now.

I press the OnStar button on my mirror. *Beep, beep.*

Another glance in the mirror tells me I can't switch lanes in time to get to the exit. There are too many cars. Maybe I can make it to the ramp if I stomp on the pedal and pray. Or maybe someone will crash into me when I do it. Either way, the police will come. Either way, I suspect I'll be better off than I'd be if this sedan follows me all the way to Plum Lake, which will be practically deserted this time of year.

Noise surrounds me. I can't think.

"Just do it," I say aloud. I guess I'm talking to my own version of Nini now. "One. Two. Three."

I step hard on the gas and yank the wheel toward the exit, nearly clipping the car that had been gaining in the lane to my right.

Horns blow.

High beams flash.

Tires squeal.

I nick the edge of a guardrail—it scrapes against us—and for a second, two tires lift from the pavement.

I take my foot off the gas and ease the vehicle around the cloverleaf. I'm all right. We're all right. I exhale when I realize I'm merging onto the road. Burleigh Avenue, it's called. I did it.

"Mommy?" Bella sounds scared half to death.

I glance back at her. "Everything's all right, baby."

"Promise?"

"I promise."

"Good evening, Mrs. Cavanaugh."

I startle when I hear the voice.

"This is OnStar. How may I assist you?"

A peek at the rearview mirror proves no brown sedan managed to follow me.

For the first time since Micah left, I start to laugh. I'm fine.

Chapter 18

November 21

It's official. I've lost touch with reality.

We've stopped only for snacks and bathroom breaks.

Now, with more than half the country between us and the place we've been calling home, I finally pick up the phone to make a call I should've made before we left. It's a good time to do so. Elizabella is asleep.

"Mrs. Cavanaugh," Detective Guidry says. He clears his throat. "You're on my list of calls today. I spoke with your daughter's preschool teachers." His tone is cold, accusatory. "Your daughter shared something rather suspect. She told them your husband died days before you called to report him missing."

"I told you that."

"No, you didn't."

"I could've sworn I did." My heart bottoms out. This can't look good. Guidry already thinks I'm hiding something. "I'm sorry. But yes. I can't explain what Bella said."

"And now, it's been two days since anyone's heard from you. I left you two messages yesterday—"

"I didn't get any messages. I've been without service a few times."

"And I damn near reported you and your daughter missing, too."

"I'm sorry. I should have called. I had to get out of there. I just couldn't—"

"Where are you, Mrs. Cavanaugh?"

"I'm . . . I'm sorry. I'm on my way to . . . I was on my way up north."

"I asked you not to go."

"Micah's mother invited us for Thanksgiving, and—"

"Yet you haven't arrived. You left a message for your mother-in-law that led her to believe you'd be on Plum Lake by now."

"I've called her to explain. She hasn't returned the call."

A moment of silence precedes his repeated and more staccato: "I asked you not to go."

"Well, as it turned out, I didn't. I was on my way—I was—but someone was following us. A brown sedan."

"Following you?"

"I thought they were, but . . ."

"Did you catch the license plate?"

"It was an Illinois plate, and it started with *S-T-X*."

"Where are you, Mrs. Cavanaugh? Are you going to Plum Lake?"

"No. I'm a little farther south than that." I'd stopped looking in the rearview mirror by the time we crossed the border into Georgia, stopped jumping every time someone else happened to pull up to the gas pump next to mine.

"You're heading to the place in Key West."

A chill races up my spine when he says it, as if it hasn't been real until now. "I guess I am." I hadn't wanted anyone to know about the house in Key West. I didn't want anyone to know where we were going. It was as if I thought we might disappear forever, if we made it safely to the Florida Keys.

But I should've known Guidry would find the property deeded to me. It's his job to dig and find information.

"Why didn't you tell me you owned a house in South Florida? You didn't think it worth mentioning, considering the remains of the plane—"

"I didn't know about the house," I say. "And I need you to believe me. I guess there's a lot I didn't know about, so . . . yeah. I would've told you, but Micah never told me."

I hear the drumming of his fingers against some surface, but he doesn't reply.

"Listen," I say. "If I had anything to do with my husband's disappearance or death, would I have called you?"

"Maybe. Maybe not."

"I'm calling because I'm scared. You can't expect me to believe that everything is okay, when Micah was obviously keeping secrets. Bella said something about a man in the kitchen."

"I remember."

"Well, she said this agent had been *in the kitchen*, when we saw him at the bank."

"What agent is that?"

"Lincoln. With the FBI." A glance at the speedometer tells me I'm driving like a bat out of hell. I ease off the gas. "He was at the bank the day I left, and something in the way he was looking at me *scared* me. And there was a man on the fairway again, smoking. Micah's gone, right? And I don't know what he was dealing with, but I feel like all of you expect me to know the answers. I don't understand any of this. You're supposed to be helping me, but it feels like you're *hunting* me. I left because I'm *terrified*."

"Confirm this for me: you're heading to Key West."

This time, I'm the one who doesn't reply for a moment. "Yes."

"Please stay there until I get to the bottom of things. I'll have local eyes on you, so don't think about skipping town on me again."

"I don't"—I swallow over tears—"I don't have anywhere else to go. We're months behind on the mortgage at Shadowlands. Did you know that? Micah invented a job. Why would he quit a job with a commercial airline if he didn't have another job?"

"I've spoken with other pilots in his class. He didn't quit United for better opportunities. He quit to avoid a criminal investigation."

"He . . . what? What kind of investigation?"

"Criminal. Meaning he did something he wasn't supposed to do."

I rub my temple, which is suddenly aching with the onset of a tension headache.

"And searches on his social security number . . . I've hit a brick wall with that, too. The search showed no legitimate employment since United."

"No employment." Yet he was paying medical bills out of pocket. Depositing cash into our account. Faking pay stubs. A gurgle of a sob escapes me. "I don't understand what's going on."

"As a matter of fact, it's your father-in-law's social security number associated with your mortgage at the bank. Your husband couldn't secure the loan for the house in the Shadowlands. Without traceable income . . . well, that'd be hard to do."

"There has to be a mistake. Check again. Please."

"I *have.*"

"But if that's the social security number on the mortgage papers . . ." Is he saying Micah and I don't actually own the house? That his *father* does? "It's my fault," I whisper. "I kept pushing for more children, more fertility treatment. I pushed and pushed, and I pushed him over the edge." I pushed because I thought he wanted it, but still . . . I can't imagine the pressure he must have felt to provide. Desperate men take desperate measures, but to have fabricated a job and insurance?

"It's Micah's social on your marriage license," Guidry says. "So it's safe to say you married who you thought you were marrying."

I stifle a sob. God, what if I hadn't? What if *my marriage* was as much of a ruse as the rest of this?

"How long did you know your husband before you were married?"

"Two years. It wasn't like we rushed anything. I mean, the engagement was quick, but we waited until after graduation."

After a few moments of silence, he says, "It does mean something that you proactively reached out. I'm grateful you called to tell me where you were going. It saves me some work. But I have to remind you, Mrs. Cavanaugh. You're a person of interest in this case."

"You think I know something I'm not telling."

"Why didn't you tell me about the life insurance policy Micah took out last March?"

"The life insurance? I mean, I guess . . . of course he took out another policy. We were expecting *twins*, detective."

"Twins to the tune of two-point-five million?"

"Two and a half million dollars?" I can barely speak the words. I blink hard. "Why would he need . . . *two and a half million*? I didn't know—"

"Listen," he continues. "You're well within your rights to leave the state. Legally, I can't demand that you stay here, but I asked you not to go. You have to agree this doesn't look good."

"That's not why I left. I was scared."

"Does the name Diamante mean anything to you?"

"Should it?"

"It meant something to your husband. When I traced the routing number on the electronic transfers at the bank, it led me to a corporation by that name. Based in the Dominican Republic."

"*Diamante*. It's Spanish?"

"It means 'diamond,'" he says. "Found it interesting, given you thought your husband worked for Diamond Corporation."

"The pay stubs *said* Diamond. Micah *told* me it was Diamond. I didn't just make it up."

A beat of silence answers me.

"If I agree to share with you everything I find in Key West," I say, "will you believe that I'm not party to a conspiracy? My husband was my *world*—"

"So you've said."

"And losing him is *killing* me. *Killing me.*"

"I'll have eyes on you in Key West," he reminds me.

"Okay. Thank you. I'll feel safer knowing someone's looking out for me."

"Looking out for you, watching you. Whatever you prefer to call it."

Chapter 19

November 22

Every time I close my eyes for the slightest amount of sleep, I remember her, my mother, calling to me. *They're coming for you. Even your earrings have faces.*

And I picture them, the ruby crystals for marquis eyes, the cubic zirconia mouth in a solitaire O. Alien faces from Area 51. A perpetual expression of shock in the gems dangling from my earlobes.

They see. They know. They know what you're doing. They know what you've done.

I hear a tapping at the glass.

Mama stands on the outside, looking in at her blue table, at the stones scattered over the pine surface.

I gather the stones and categorize them by size, shape, and color.

She's pounding on the window with a tight fist, so small and brittle-looking that I fear her bones might shatter before she manages to crack the glass panes. *Don't you touch those stones, little Veri. Your human hands will poison their beauty.*

The pounding grows ferocious. I feel its beat in my bones, hear its ring in my ears, cacophonic in combination with the chirp of the tines raking over the barrel in my music box.

I startle as I awaken.

No one is tapping on the glass.

The car is locked, and we're parked in bright daylight at a rest stop. Safe.

Only seven minutes have passed since I surrendered to my heavy eyelids, but it's enough.

I start the car and put it in gear, ready to blaze down the last stretch of road before me.

The route is self-explanatory. In order to arrive at the southernmost point in the United States, you have to drive south. If you take a wrong turn, you simply take the next fork south. In a way, all roads lead to where I'm going.

Now, we're breezing down A1A amid an apricot sunset.

Water to the left, water to the right.

Everything is green and thriving, despite the apparent "cold snap" rushing through the Florida Keys. It's sixty-eight degrees this evening, the lowest low they've had all week.

I look to my parka and Bella's, stowed on the front passenger seat. The coats seem out of place with the mild breeze whipping through our open windows. I consider the possibility of tossing them into the first trash bin I see, which is silly. It's not as if we're never going back.

Micah's body should be arriving at the funeral home soon. If for no other reason, I have to be back to put him to rest.

"Mommy?" Elizabella says from the back seat. "Nini's hungry."

"Tell Nini we'll get her some nuggets and fries in just a bit." I cross over the last bridge from Boca Chica to Key West. In all, we've been en route for the better part of three days, with a little more than twenty-six hours of driving time, considering I'd traveled into Wisconsin first. Talk about a roundabout route.

After a roll or two around the island—it's only about two-by-four miles—I see the newel post for Elizabeth Street.

A length of road later, I spot a lamppost with a small rectangular sign hanging by chains from a crossbar and boasting the address of the house I own. There is a car coming up behind me, so I turn onto the pink-brick driveway lined with flowering trees. About ten feet in from the street, the drive bends to the right, and I find myself driving through a masonry archway with the words **GODDESS ISLAND GARDENS** lettered along the arc. Some letters are missing, as if they've fallen victim to age: the *DESS* in *goddess*, and *IS* in *island*.

The sight steals my breath. With the letters missing, the archway reads **GOD LAND GARDENS**.

Listen to your daughter.

Elizabella had told me her father was at *God Land*.

My breath catches in my throat.

God Land!

I own this place. I have every right to be here, but it feels as if someone's looking over my shoulder, as if once I'm far enough down this driveway, a SWAT team will descend and demand to know why I've disturbed the peace here. I speed up, as if getting there faster will dissipate the nagging sensation in my gut.

It's a feeling akin to snooping through someone's underwear drawer. Intriguing, yet an invasion of privacy. I'm trespassing through Micah's secrets.

"You own the house," I whisper to myself. The deed is at the bottom of my purse, along with a palm tree keychain and three keys, one of which I hope opens the door. But if I can't get in, which I hadn't considered until this moment, surely someone can come unlock the door—a locksmith, maybe—seeing as I have proof of ownership.

At the next bend of the drive, past a thicket of palms and tropical plants, the house emerges before us.

"It's the big house, Mommy!" Elizabella shrieks.

"It *is* big." I slow our already turtlelike pace to nearly a stop. Pale yellow. Arched windows. Exactly as Bella drew it.

"Nini was here once."

"That's what I hear." I wonder, and not for the first time, if Elizabella has been everywhere Nini's been. "Have *you* been here, Ellie-Belle?"

"Silly Mommy."

"Have you?"

"Hungry!"

The house appears a bit unpolished, perhaps, and the vegetation surrounding it is definitely overgrown, but the patch of wiry lawn appears to have been mowed with regularity. The place is nothing if not large, about the size of the entire building we lived in at Old Town. A two-story stucco with a clay-tile roof, it's not a brick short of charming, despite the obvious neglect and disrepair.

The pink drive terminates to a roundabout, its farthermost tip nudging a wide set of stairs, which lead to a quaint, covered porch.

I stop the car there, at the edge of the arc, and stare up at the place.

My God. What am I doing here? Suppose there are tenants. Or—Claudette Winters's voice echoes in my head—suppose there's a Misty Morningside, or even a Gabrielle, abiding here. The second thought only fuels me to charge up the steps. Not because I want to go head-to-head with whoever happens to answer the door, but because I'm anxious to prove to Claudette-in-my-head that there's no one here.

Or maybe . . . suppose Bella is right? Suppose I find my husband, alive and well, beyond the door?

"Come on, Ellie-Belle." I loop the handles of my shoulder bag over my arm and turn off the ignition.

Bella unclips her seat belt—"Come on, Nini. Undo your belt, too. We're here!"—and climbs into my arms when I open her door.

"Mommy." She presses a sloppy kiss to my cheek. "It's God Land."

I glance around the perimeter of the house—*my house*—and now that I think about it, it's a mini Eden. Whoever named the property did so aptly.

I hike her up a bit higher on my hip—there's only a dull ache around my ovaries now—when we start to climb the porch steps. "Is *this* where Daddy went?"

"Mmm-hmmm."

"When did he come here?"

"In his plane."

"The plane that crashed?"

An exasperated sigh slips between her lips, and she all but rolls her eyes. "It's in the water, Mommy."

I wish now I'd thought to visit Dr. Russo one last time after we received the news. Maybe he could offer insight that makes more sense than what I'm thinking: Elizabella saw the future; she—and Nini—predicted Micah's accident.

I put her down on the porch, and I'm reaching into my purse for the ring of keys when the door whips open before me.

Elizabella startles and grips my hand.

I grip hers but don't take my eyes from the figure in the doorway.

Chapter 20

The moment he steps out onto the porch, Bella shrinks against me. "No, no." Her little fingers are in a death grip on my hand.

He rubs a thumb against an eyebrow, as if he's just roused from a nap. My appearing here must be a big inconvenience for him, seeing as he's hardly dressed for a polite conversation.

Some sort of canvas shorts, the color of an army tent, hang low on his hips, exposing a white line of flesh in contrast to the tanned rest of him. Swim trunks, maybe, with a drawstring pulled not tight enough. His T-shirt, if you can call it that, hangs off him like a flag whipping in the wind, the sleeves and sides scooped away with the jagged snips of scissors, putting his muscled frame on display. If this place is Goddess Island, he must be the resident demigod.

He washes a scarred hand—there's a raised bump of flesh just south of his knuckles—over his chin, which appears about five days past a shave. "Can I help you?"

"I'm Veronica Cavanaugh." Suddenly, I'm warm in jeans and a sweater, not to mention my ankle-high boots.

He shakes his too-long, brown-gold locks from his forehead and squints as if attempting to recognize me, then looks beyond me, toward the driveway. "Land of Lincoln?"

He's reading my license plate.

I guess I don't have to explain why I'm dressed for autumn in a place that appears to be bottoming out at near-paradise-degrees Fahrenheit.

Elizabella's arms now wrap around my thigh.

"I own this property," I say.

"Okay."

"Are you a tenant?"

"Naw. Just looking after the place until Tasha comes back."

"Tasha?" I pry my daughter's hands loose and lift her to my hip. "Do you mean *Na*tasha? Markham?"

"Tasha . . . I-don't-know-Tasha. My neighbor. I live . . ." He thumbs in the general direction of things behind him. "*Who* are you again?"

This time, I offer a hand, which he shakes with a single pump. "Veronica Cavanaugh. And this . . ." I tilt my head to meet Elizabella's. "This is my daughter. I own this place. I have the deed." I shift to open my purse, but I can't risk his seeing the cash—not that he'd ask where I got it, but it isn't something I want to flaunt—and Bella's weight makes it difficult to maneuver anyway.

"I'm sorry . . . come in." He steps aside and opens the door farther.

I shouldn't walk in while he's in the house. The shadow of fear looms over me, and I feel as if a target has been painted on my back, just when I was starting to feel safe again. I glance over my shoulder, although I know no one has been tailing me since the Illinois-Wisconsin border. We're twelve hundred miles from home, and I took a winding path.

No one knows we're here.

Aside from Detective Guidry, that is.

"And you are?" I raise an eyebrow.

"Christian. Renwick."

"Mister Renwick, I—"

"*Christian.* I'm just here to feed the cat."

"Cat?" I enter the cool two-story foyer, my boots clicking against the pale-blue squares of porcelain. The place looks like something out of old world Capri, complete with a plaster-molded fountain niched into the wall with a copper faucet to supply it. The water isn't running now.

"Is she not supposed to have a cat?"

"I don't mind cats," I say.

"When Tasha left, she didn't say you'd be coming."

I didn't know I was coming, either. "When will Tasha be back?"

"She and the kids are usually back by September, for school."

"Kids?"

"They leave late June, come back late August. I feed Papa Hemingway, take care of things, you know, until she calls to tell me they're back. Been a little worried, to tell you the truth. They're not usually gone this long. They're almost three months late."

I'm nodding, as if I understand, but nothing makes sense right now. And my back is killing me, but Elizabella clings to me like a monkey to a tree. I can't put her down.

"So if you're here," Christian says, "I guess you've decided to put the house on the market after all."

"Hmm." It's a nice nondescript reply, I hope.

"I would've thought she would've at least come to pack her stuff. Or . . . or is that why you're here?"

"I . . ."

"Sorry." He puts up a hand, as if he's halting traffic. "None of my business. You'd think she'd at least take her cat, but . . . you want him? Or you want me to take him?"

"I'll . . ." My eye catches a series of framed photos on a long, narrow table tucked against the wall beneath the staircase. I glance at the photos, which appear to be black-and-white images of island-type sites— palm trees, a shoreline. "I don't mind cats."

"Well, if you change your mind . . . Hemingway and I are old buds by now. Never thought of getting a cat. A dog *maybe*, but—"

"Okay. Thanks."

"If you need help slapping some paint on the walls, whatever, to help get the house ready, give me a call. You've got a crack in that pool that needs fixing."

Of course there's a pool with a house like this.

"I've got time. I'm retired."

"Retired?" He doesn't look a day past thirty-five.

"Semi. I'm a writer now. Well"—he shrugs—"to be honest, I do a lot more paddleboarding and surfing than writing."

For a second or two, we stand there in awkward silence. I wonder if he's trying to figure out a way to ask me to leave or maybe if I ought to be asking him. It's my house. I don't have anywhere else to go.

Elizabella squirms in my arms and murmurs, "Nini's hungry."

"I'd better get her something to eat," I say. "Closest restaurant?"

"Follow Southard." He karate-chops the air, demonstrating the straight path I ought to take. "It'll take you directly to Old Town."

I freeze in my tracks at the irony of it. For all my recent pining to return to Old Town in Chicago, I've ended up here, in Old Town, Key West.

"Plenty to choose from," he's saying, "once you hit Duval."

I nod, hoping I don't look like a deer caught in headlights.

"I'm heading out in a bit," he continues, "if you want to tag along."

"I think we'll find it."

"All right. Well, if you need anything . . ."

"Thank you."

"I'm in the pink house. Follow the path through the backyard."

"Thank you."

He's halfway down the hallway. I deduce he's leaving through the back door.

I follow a few steps behind, to the kitchen, which is open to a living room. More picture frames line the built-in shelves there.

He barely lays a hand on the doorknob before he's turning around. "Sorry to do this, but you said you had the deed? To the house?"

"Yes."

"You mind if I see it? Not that I don't believe you, but if someone showed up at my house claiming to own it, I'd want—"

"Of course." I place a reluctant Elizabella atop the white marble countertop in the kitchen and drop my purse next to her. Carefully, I dig through the contents of the bag and extract only the deed.

He takes it from the envelope, gives it a glance—"That's the real deal, all right"—and hands it back. The door is open now, and he's breezing down the path between his door and mine. "If you need anything . . ." He neither turns around nor finishes his sentence, but he starts to whistle a low, soothing melody.

When he's gone beyond the vines, I still hear his whistle. I lock the door.

"Well, Ellie-Belle." I lower my forehead to hers. "Welcome to Key West."

"Hungry."

"We'll find a market." I kiss the tip of her nose. "Maybe some yummy fruit or—"

"Ronis."

"I'm sure there's macaroni in the Florida Keys. I'll just bring in our things, and then we'll get you some dinner." I pull her off the countertop, to the floor. "Stay here, okay? We'll look around together."

My car keys still dangle from my index finger. I flip through the extra few keys I'd looped around the ring when I decided this was where I was heading, the keys Micah had hidden with a deed in our safe-deposit box.

I hope one of the keys unlocks this door. I'll probably change the locks, anyway, but I need to lock the house in the meantime if we're going to leave it to find someplace to eat dinner. Christian Renwick probably has a key I could borrow. He did say he'd help if I needed anything.

But how could I explain my not having a key to a house I own?

I test the first key.

No dice.

The second won't even go in.

The third slides in without effort and turns the tumbler. My initial feeling of elation dampens nearly instantly.

Micah had a key to this house. He kept it in our safe-deposit box, in a bank that holds all the accounts we shared.

I bite my lip.

Why did he keep so many secrets from me?

And why did I never think to question *anything*?

My heart is tearing into pieces. One part longs to feel his arms around me, his whisper in my ear that everything is going to be all right, that we'll have more children. *We still have two frozen at the lab. All it takes is one.*

Another part, however, is gushing with the stab of betrayal. What else was he hiding? And why?

"Daddy."

I spin around when I hear Elizabella's giggle, but she isn't in the kitchen where I told her to stay. "Bella?"

"Nini! It's Daddy!"

Chapter 21

"Daddy, Daddy, and Daddy."

I follow the sound of Bella's joyful voice and trek back down the hallway. Through the kitchen. To a small family room strewn with boxy rattan furniture with turquoise cushions.

Elizabella is on her tiptoes at the built-in cabinetry and shelves, all painted a light gray. Her little fingers grip the edge of the wooden countertop as she struggles to see the pictures on the shelves higher than her line of sight.

Assuming they're more of the same types of pictures as in the hallway—starfish and seashells, maybe—I hardly give them a glance as I lean in closer and wrap an arm around her waist. "No, baby. That's not . . ." I shut up. There's a man in the photograph. He's shown only in profile, looking down at an infant. The baby has a hand on the man's closely cropped beard. It's an image that warms my heart. I have a similar picture of Micah holding Elizabella this way in the weeks after she was born, only Micah shaves every day and never grew facial hair.

Just once, actually. When I was pregnant with Bella.

But then I zero in on the eyes of the man in the picture, on the shape of the nose. It's . . .

"Daddy." Bella points to the picture on the next shelf up.

My heart kicks into high gear.

I feel dizzy.

"Yeah. That's Daddy."

In the second photo, he's posing on the beach with two beautiful boys—they might be twins, about four years old, maybe five—and in other pictures, he's with a gorgeous girl, about seven, with strawberry-blonde hair.

"Nini." Elizabella points to the girl.

Slivers of ice needle my spine. My gaze dances over the frames. The little girl, the twins.

I miscarried twin boys . . . but Micah has them anyway.

Unless . . . did I imagine it all?

I'm losing it. I *did* miscarry, didn't I?

My head spins in an alternate universe where Elizabella is seven and her unborn brothers are four, and *they're* the ones posing in the pictures with the man I married. Not these children. These *strangers.*

I think I'm going to die.

I grip Elizabella's hand and pull her away from the display on the shelves, tuck her behind my body so she can't see what her father has done.

Flames rise all around me—my cheeks are hot, everything's hot—and it feels as if my spine is melting.

My gaze flies from one frame to the next. Micah—or his twin, and *he doesn't have a twin*—engaged in loving embraces with three children.

Three children I couldn't have.

Elizabella chatters about Nini, but I can't focus on her words.

She's tugging on my pant leg.

"Ellie-Belle, wait. Wait a second." I'm nearly breathless. I pick her up, and despite her wriggling in my arms, I walk down the hallway with her and place her, a bit too firmly, on the stairs. "Stay here."

She protests with puffed out cheeks. Arms crossed. Head shaking.

"Stay."

Micah's song rises in my head: *Stay with me. Stay some more.*

"Stay here, Ellie-Belle." My voice sounds as if it's far away, underwater maybe.

She's kicking her feet against the steps.

"Stay!" I say again over my shoulder.

The song continues in my head, a haunting memory of how foolish I was to believe in him, to believe everything he ever told me. "Stop!" I scream to the song. But it won't stop. It keeps playing, and I feel him next to me, stepping on my feet, out of sync with the song he's singing incorrectly. "Stop, stop, stop!"

And I stomp back to the family room to confirm I really saw what I think I saw. It isn't possible. He couldn't have . . .

He's dancing with me, but playing house with another family.

Hands in my hair, I'm pulling on my curls at the roots.

Don't scream. Don't scream. Don't scream.

Can't scare Elizabella.

I look from frame to frame. Micah and a pretty little girl. Micah and a boy and a colorful fish on a hook. At a beach. On a boat. By a red, yellow, and black-striped buoy.

Where is *she*? The woman who bore these babies? Why aren't there any pictures of *her*?

My jaw aches. My teeth hurt from grinding them.

I reach for a frame and slam it to the tile at my feet.

Crash!

I reach for another and another and another.

Crash, crash, crash!

Glass shatters.

Wood frames splinter.

Picture after picture after picture shatters.

And despite my attempts to stifle my rage, I'm screaming.

Screaming at the top of my lungs, like a savage.

Screaming in pain, as if the glass has lodged in my heart, instead of scattered on the floor.

"Mommy?"

I glimpse Elizabella, huddled in the hallway.

Peering around the corner.

Shaking.

I can't catch my breath.

My limbs tremble and remnants of the pictures scatter as I make my way toward her.

She flinches when I reach for her, but her little arms tighten around me the moment I lift her to me.

"Mommy's sorry."

She presses her cheek to mine.

Our tears flow together like a confluence of two rivers.

"Mommy's sorry."

"You broke the pictures of Daddy."

"Mommy's sorry. I lost it, baby. But I'm okay now."

She buries her head in the hollow between my neck and clavicle, like she used to do when she was a newborn.

For a moment, she's that same small baby in my arms, her baby scents so real I swear I smell them: talcum and lavender lotion.

For always, she's my miracle.

"I'm okay," I tell her.

The chime of the doorbell reverberates in the hallway.

Simultaneously, our heads turn toward the door.

"Nini," she whispers.

Chapter 22

I open the door to a uniformed police officer wearing a navy-blue, short-sleeved button-down shirt tucked into shorts in the same fabric. He's leaning against a column on the front portico. A ten-speed bicycle marked with official police department regalia is parked next to my SUV on the motor court.

"Evening," he says, cool as can be.

"Evening," I say over a sniffle.

"Everything all right in there?"

My cheeks flush. He must have heard the breaking glass and screams. I start to nod, but before I can get a word in, he's handing me a business card.

"I'm Officer Laughlin, Key West PD. Got a call from your local department, up in Lake County, Illinois, asking us to check in, keep an eye on you."

Of course. Guidry said they'd be sending someone.

"Your husband is missing, they say."

"We've lost him," I correct the officer, who must not have been thoroughly informed. *Lost.* It appears I lost him before Elizabella was born. I wipe a tear from my cheek.

"He went to God Land," Bella says.

I tighten my grip around her.

"Sorry for your predicament," Laughlin says. "You need anything—anything at all—feel free to call, all right?"

"Yes, thank you."

"And if you're planning to go anywhere . . ." He wipes the back of his neck, then proceeds to give it a good massage. "Well, let's just say you ought to check in with us before you leave on any excursions."

"Where would we go?" I ask. "I mean . . . where do you think—"

He shrugs. "Dry Tortugas. Fort Jefferson. Back to the mainland. Who knows? Just check in before you go. Shows good faith."

"Good faith?" I maneuver the business card beneath my fingernail. A splinter from a wooden picture frame dislodges. "Look, I don't know what Detective Guidry told you, but I don't plan on going anywhere but back home."

He offers a half smile and another nod. "All right."

"And actually . . . maybe you can help me. Do you know the people who used to live here?"

"I don't."

"It's a small island, right? Not too many locals? Mostly tourists? See, I own this house. Only I didn't know anything about it until recently. My husband arranged the purchase, and . . . well, now that I'm here, I'm seeing that maybe the house isn't the only thing I didn't know about."

"Wish I could help. But I haven't had an occasion until tonight to even come up the drive of this place."

"Any of your colleagues then. If they know anything—" I shut up when I catch something in the way he's looking at me. Accusation maybe. Annoyance. Or mistrust.

I swallow over an initial sense of shock building up in my throat. *They, too, think I know something I'm not telling.* "Well, if you think of anything—or if you hear anything, maybe—I wouldn't mind if *you* check in with *me* every once in a while." Maybe now they'll get it through their thick skulls that I'm not trying to hide anything, that I didn't come here to run away—let alone from the law—but to piece together everything that doesn't make sense.

And that includes, apparently, my entire life with Micah.

But Laughlin stiffens, pressing his lips together in a way that makes the muscles in his jaw twitch. "We'll be checking in. I promise you."

"Well"—I clear my throat and cough to hide my intimidation— "I'd appreciate it."

He doesn't budge.

"Is there anything else?" I ask. "I have a hungry three-year-old here."

"This is your first time on the island?"

"Yes."

"Nini goed here once," Bella murmurs into the hollow of my neck.

While the officer glances toward my daughter, he doesn't pry. "Have a nice night, ma'am."

"You too."

"Check in before you go anywhere."

"*If* I go anywhere, I will."

He's walking down the steps now, toward his bicycle.

"I wish I knew what you think I'm hiding," I call after him.

He stops and turns to shoot a disciplined stare right through me.

"If I knew, I'd clear it up for you," I say. "My world is falling to pieces . . . everywhere I turn, just fragments . . . and I don't understand why you're looking at me as if . . ." Unspoken words trail into nothingness.

"Why do you assume I'm looking at you in *any* way?"

"You see?" I wipe a budding tear from my eye. "You're implying I have a guilty conscience. But what if I just want help understanding what happened to Micah?"

"Your husband disappeared under rather mysterious circumstances," Laughlin says. "From what I understand, he left debts behind—debts in only his name. And here you are, in a house you say you never knew you owned. I'm sure you understand. We have to rule out the spouse."

"If there's anything I can do to help you rule me out, then let me do it."

"Will do." He raises his chin. "Evening, ma'am."

Chapter 23

There's a bottle of rum on the front porch. A metallic blue bow is affixed to the label, along with a note: WELCOME TO THE NEIGHBORHOOD!

I look around the property to see who might have left it, but the house is situated away from the road, and the trees shroud this place in privacy, despite the fact that neighbors border nearly all edges of the lot.

It must have been the cat sitter. Who else knows we're here?

The cops, of course, know we've arrived, but they're hardly the welcoming sort.

"So tell me about Nini." I take Bella by the hand, and we saunter down the pink driveway toward town. "The Nini in the picture."

"You broke the picture."

"I know. But Nini's still in it."

Shattered glass won't erase the past, won't erase the proof of Micah's secrets.

"Hungry, Mommy."

And the way Elizabella refuses to talk about being on this island with Nini has me thinking she doesn't want to tell me something—maybe because she's confused. "You can tell Mommy. Were you here with Nini before?"

"Hunnnngry."

My stomach feels hollow, but I can't imagine I'll be able to keep anything down, even if I tried to eat, after seeing those pictures. "We're heading to town," I remind Elizabella. "We'll find a restaurant and stop at a market on the way home."

"Up." She steps in front of me, her little arms stretched to the sky.

I wish I'd thought to shove the umbrella stroller into the car, but I didn't think I'd need it at Plum Lake. Besides, big girls walk. Getting my daughter into a stroller is usually like forcing a cat into a bathtub.

"Up, up!" She jumps, as if she might magically land in arms.

"Mommy can't carry you all the way." My back is aching from three days in the car, and my abdomen is starting to cramp again, as the effects of IVF medication reverse. "Maybe on the way home, okay?"

She crosses her arms over her chest and pouts, but at least she continues to walk.

"We're city chicks, you and me," I tell her.

She takes my hand. "City chicks?"

"We're Old Town girls. We can walk." I would've driven, but zipping around the island, I saw not a single open parking place, and the lots seemed to be as far away from restaurants and shops as my Goddess Island abode. Besides, I don't know the lay of the land yet.

It's cooler now, with the sun beginning to set, and as I opted—in the interest of blending in—to leave my sweater behind, my flesh pricks with chill bumps. If we're going to stay, we're going to need to find some more appropriate clothing. Sundresses. Flip-flops. At the very least, canvas slip-on shoes. These boots are killing my feet.

The walks along Elizabeth Street are sparsely populated, but once we turn onto Southard, the crowd thickens, and by the time we hit Duval Street, the energy of the island practically hums in my veins.

I'm not surprised Micah purchased a home here; he would have loved it. *Must have loved it,* I mentally correct myself, as he obviously spent some time here . . . with the children in the photographs and

Natasha, apparently, if what my neighbor said was true. You don't buy a home on an island you don't love, after all.

And—I draw in a stutter of a breath—he hadn't loved the place alone, if the pictures on the family room floor tell any tales.

Family room.

The house I'll be squatting in once I feed Elizabella—my house—is home to a family, and it appears Micah was part of that family.

The kids . . .

The boys, both only a smidgen older than my daughter, are dark blond and blue-eyed. The girl, whom Bella refers to as Nini, is a gorgeous strawberry blonde.

Perhaps she inherited the red from her mother.

A lump forms in my throat, and tears well in my eyes. I swallow over it and wipe them away. I shouldn't jump to conclusions. There has to be another explanation.

But Micah obviously knew the people living in my house on Elizabeth Street, and he was obviously close to them. And Christian Renwick referred to a Tasha.

The betrayal is doubly painful if he actually means my college roommate. I remember shopping at a thrift store for a murder mystery party we attended our first New Year's Eve. Natasha, emerging from a dressing room in a high-necked calico dress and her hair in a bun: *Aren't I ravishing as a schoolmarm? It's always the quiet ones you have to look out for.*

I shake free from the memory, which raises chill bumps on my arms.

Listen to your daughter.

Someone wanted me to arrive at "God Land" to see for myself. Someone wanted me to see Micah's secrets.

Maybe Claudette was right. Maybe Micah's Misty Morningside came in the form of his ex-girlfriend and three times the children I was able to bear for him.

A pang of jealousy tightens in my gut—envy for those who can conceive, bitter wariness that someone else may have done what I couldn't do for him—but it quickly morphs into something else, something nondescript. Something that borders on *well, can you blame him?*

He wanted a big family. I couldn't provide one.

Bella tugs on my hand.

But he always said that I was more than enough, and Bella was the cherry atop our sundae.

"Mommy! Hungry!"

"I know, baby." We're just off the corner of Duval and Caroline, and as luck would have it, there's a restaurant right here. Palm trees edge the property line, along with a charming, white, may-as-well-be-a-picket fence. I hesitate for a moment, when my gaze locks on the bar at the far end of the place. The Flying Monkey. Maybe this isn't the best place for a child. But a glance to my right reassures me. An enormous, three-story house, complete with a two-tier balcony, sits separate from the rowdy outdoor bar. It's sided in blue-gray and trimmed in bright white, with high-top tables outside. It looks like an old, southern plantation house.

Elizabella clings to me, even begins to yank on my T-shirt in an effort to climb up my torso and into my arms. She doesn't remember living in Old Town, doesn't remember parting our way through crowds denser than this one. The murmur of diners rises all around us. I give in and lift her to my hip.

We weave our way through the tables. Despite her best imitation of a baby monkey clinging to its mother, I manage to lower Elizabella at the wide steps of the house. Her grip is tight on my fingers as we ascend.

I flash back to a time Bella would have had a grip on both my hand and Micah's, and we'd swing her between us as we'd walk—one, two, three, *fly*. More tears surface. Why, why, why?

Why is he suddenly gone? Why did he lie—about everything? Why weren't his daughter and I enough for him?

But we weren't enough for me, either. I took the fertility shots. I took drastic measures to increase our numbers. Even after the miscarriage, even after I swore I couldn't go through it all again, I opted to keep trying.

If I'd known Micah had three island-hopping children before Bella, would I have continued?

"Welcome to Fogarty's. Party of two?"

I catch a tear on a knuckle and smile at the hostess. "Sorry. Yes. Two."

The moment we sit, Bella says, "Ronis and cheese."

"Do you have macaroni and cheese?"

The hostess half shrugs, but fully smiles when she doles out menus. "We have a three-cheese penne pasta."

It'll have to do. I glance about the room, seeking auburn hair, scanning for bright-green eyes that put my brown eyes to shame. Natasha Markham was always striking. I've always marveled at what Micah's choosing me must have meant. He convinced me I was worthy—even went so far as to say that Natasha was more upset over losing me than she was over losing him. He made me believe I was a prize, and that Natasha's distance once we got together was due to her losing her best friend and roommate when I moved out of our apartment and in with Micah, instead of losing her man.

His theory never made any sense. Natasha found another girl to split her rent, and she never looked back—at least not at me. Roommates were easy to replace. Men like Micah, on the other hand . . .

Now I'm not so sure Micah ever found me worthy, either.

The images in those photographs are forever planted in my mind. I suspect I'll see the smiling faces of those children even when I'm sleeping. Even when I'm dead.

"Small world." I look up to see my neighbor, still looking like a surfer, holding a rose-colored, frozen concoction with a pineapple garnish. "Small island, anyway. Saw you walk in, past the Monkey. Thought I'd buy you a drink. Welcome you properly to the island."

"Thank you, but—" I shut up before my standard refusal slips out—*I'm a fertility patient. I don't drink*—because he places the glass in front of Elizabella.

Tentatively, she reaches for it. She may not like our neighbor—she likes few people right off the bat—but she can be bribed, and she's hungry. A split second before she wraps her fingers around the cup, I scoot it just out of her reach. "What's in it?"

"It's nonalcoholic. Naturally."

As if I thought he'd serve her anything else. I'm being ridiculous. I loosen my grip.

"A lot of sugar. She might be wired once it's down the hatch."

I let her take a sip anyway.

"Mmmmm!"

"Say thank you to Mr. Renwick," I remind her.

She shyly glances up at him, a small smile playing on her lips.

"Ellie-Belle."

"Thank you," she says.

Christian gives her a wink. "And you? What's your poison? You like rum?"

So he was responsible for the bottle of coconut rum on the front porch. "Thank you for that. I'm a fertil—" I clear my throat and meet his gaze. I'm not a fertility patient anymore. I can have a drink if I want to, but it's been so long since I've ordered a drink that I don't even know what I like or how it might affect me. And it would be rude to say I don't drink rum after he thoughtfully left a bottle for me. "I don't know."

"Everyone likes rum, right? You'd better, on this island."

I look at him. Really look at him. He looks trustworthy, and we're in a public place. What harm can come of a drink?

And if he's been feeding Tasha's cat, he might know something. Not that I can pounce on him and demand information. I have to build trust if I expect him to tell me what he knows. Besides, theoretically, I ought to know more than I do, considering I own the house she was-slash-is renting.

"Would you like to join us?"

"That's not why I . . . I couldn't impose."

"Don't be silly." I'm already half out of the booth, ready to slide in on the other side next to Bella. "Have a seat."

He looks to my daughter, who stops sipping her treat only long enough to whisper, "Stranger danger."

"He's not a stranger." I glance up at him, but he isn't observing us. He's politely pretending not to hear. "He's our neighbor."

"Like Crew and Fendi?"

"Like Crew and Fendi."

She eyes him. "Do you have little kids?"

"I don't even have big kids," he answers.

My phone buzzes.

Shell! It must be! I left her a message detailing my change of plans; it's taken forever for her to return the call, and *finally* . . .

But *Claudette Winters* spans the screen. I'll have to call her back. I can't take a call just after I invited my neighbor to dinner.

Why hasn't Shell called me back? I know she and Guidry spoke. Maybe she's angry that I changed our plans for Thanksgiving.

"Bella." I silence my phone. "Mr. Renwick is going to join us for dinner."

"Just a drink maybe," he says.

"Nini says okay."

"Oh, you know Nini?" Christian suddenly breaks from his firmly rooted statue routine and slides onto the bench across from us.

I trade glances between my daughter and our new neighbor, anxious to hear the exchange. If Nini is a real little girl . . .

Bella doesn't take her wide-eyed glance from him as he talks about her best friend, and she continues to sip the frothy treat.

"So I don't really *know* Nini," he says, "but she drew me a picture once. On my sidewalk with chalk. Do you like to draw with chalk?"

"Nini did that once."

"Yes. She did."

They're staring at each other across the table, each wearing an amused expression.

"So . . ." I should fill this silence, if only to drown the questions in my mind. "How long have you known Tasha?"

"Few years," he says, while Bella interjects: "Nini's seven."

One corner of his mouth twitches up with a smile. "I guess she *is* seven, but I met her only a few years ago."

"Tasha's daughter . . ." I hedge to see if he fills in the blanks.

He nods. "Good-looking kid."

"Her name is *Nini?*"

"Mimi, maybe?" He shrugs. "I don't . . . the kid . . . I don't have much occasion to talk with her." His tongue wets his lips, and he says again, "Good-looking kid."

It's apparent to me now that's all he knows about her. That she's cute. Why couldn't someone more observant have been feeding Papa Hemingway, the fattest cat on the planet? Someone who might've paid more attention to the children who live—used to live?—at the home I own.

The conversation is a bust if he doesn't know anything, but I'm in it now. Maybe if I get him talking, he'll let small details slip, ones he might not realize he knows. I try again: "What do you write?"

"Write?" His hands still. "Oh. Like I said. Not much of anything lately."

"When you do write, what do you write?"

A waitress approaches with crayons and a paper place mat for Elizabella. "Anything to drink?"

"Rum runner?" Christian asks me.

"Never had one."

"Or . . ." My neighbor offers me only a split-second glance, as if he can assess my preference simply by looking at me. "Mojito?"

"Never had one of those, either."

"Really?" His head tilts, as if in sympathy. "Then it's settled. Two mojitos."

"Two mojitos," she repeats. "Ready to order?"

"My daughter will have the three-cheese pasta, but I need a minute."

"You should try a plate of the conch," Christian pipes in. "Nothing like the conch fritters in Key West."

"Okay." I glance at the menu, but I'm not particularly hungry. Eating has been as much a chore as sleeping lately. A wave of exhaustion hits me full force. My eyes are tired. My feet are tired. Even my little finger is tired. "You know what? The conch sounds good."

The waitress whisks away, our menus in hand, and a silence lingers in her wake, chewing at the air between us.

I must look tired and haggard, despite the light dusting of powder with which I attempted to hide the bags beneath my eyes before we headed out, despite the quick gloss over my lips. No matter what I do, I can't hide the fact that I've been crying for days, even from someone who doesn't know what I look like under usual circumstances.

I straighten my wedding band, white gold with channel-set diamonds, and line it up with my engagement ring, which boasts a round diamond just under a carat. I wonder if I should be wearing the set anymore. If I'd stumbled over Micah's secrets before his plane went down, would I be wearing it still?

I give it a tug again, just to see if it budges, just to see what it feels like to take it off, but it stops at my knuckle. Until I lose the IVF weight, removing my ring is not an option. A thread of relief twines through me. I can't take it off, and I don't want to.

Maybe it's better that he's gone. I don't know if I could have divorced someone I love more than life itself.

"How long will you be in town?"

"Oh." When I invited Christian to join us, I didn't consider he might want to drag as much information out of me as I hope to pull out of him. "Just until I decide what to do with the house, I guess."

It isn't a lie. I do have to decide what to do with it.

"If you're not careful, this island will swallow you whole."

"I'm sorry?" In my mind, I see a black hole enveloping Micah and his plane. Wiping him from existence.

"People come for a week. Some live out their stay on the planet here. It's addictive, this place."

"I can see that." I move Elizabella's drink a bit farther from her reach. She's diligently coloring her place mat and not paying much attention to things that spill.

"So you might not sell, then."

I meet his gaze. Green-gray eyes. "Is that what Tasha said? That we might be selling?"

He glances in the direction of my left hand. Perhaps he's looking at the ring I keep touching. "She mentioned it, yes."

"Maybe we'll have to see if the island swallows us."

"Can I . . ." He massages the scruff on his chin. "This might be out of line. But are you married? Will your husband be joining you? I don't want to . . . well, it looks bad, maybe. My being here. If he's meeting you."

"Oh."

"I didn't see the ring back at the house. I wasn't *looking* for it or anything, but—"

"No."

He shuts up.

"My husband is . . ." *Dead.* I can't say the word aloud, despite its replaying in my mind. *He's dead. He's dead. He's dead.* "He won't be joining us. He's . . ." I can't say it! "We're not together anymore."

"My wife—*ex*-wife, that is—was . . . well, let's just say I respect the institution of marriage. She didn't."

"I'm sorry."

"So if I'd noticed the ring, I probably wouldn't have taken it upon myself—"

"He's dead." I hiccup over the wave of grief that hits me full force, like the water beating against the red, yellow, and black buoy not far from here. "He was a pilot, and there was an accident—"

"God, I'm sorry."

"*I'm* sorry." I dab my napkin at my eyes. "So I don't know how long we'll be here, and I don't know what I'm going to do with the house, and I don't know how I'm going to exist without him, and—"

The waitress appears with drinks, prompting another uncomfortable silence.

I glance at Bella's drawing. A sea creature, judging by the waves of blue crayon. Lots of red squiggles around a circular object. A mermaid maybe. Could be an octopus.

Once the server retreats, Christian raises his glass a few inches off the table. "I know something about how that feels." He clinks the bottom of his glass to mine, which I have yet to touch. "For different reasons, of course. But no matter how it happens, it isn't easy." He takes a sip.

"No, I guess it isn't." I raise my glass to his and offer a *clink* in return.

"You know what worked for me? After throwing things and breaking things—"

I stiffen and feel the flush of embarrassment crawling up my neck to my cheeks. I wonder if he heard my destructive tantrum through the vines in the backyard.

"And after a night in the clink?"

"In . . . in jail?"

"One of the things I broke"—he smiles a little—"the guy's nose."

I feel more than hear my own laugh, brief as it may be. It isn't funny. But it is.

"He came at me first, I swear." His hands rise in an *I surrender* pose. "The judge saw it the same way. But anyway, the point is . . . it's hard to be angry forever in a place like this. I mean, look around you. Nothing's fair in this world, but this place, this island, is a pretty decent consolation prize. You might want to stay."

Echoing in the caverns of my mind is Micah's song, the offbeat cha-cha: *Stay with me. Stay some more.*

"Sway," I whisper to the memory. Tears bead up in my eyes.

"Excuse me?"

I shake off the memory of my last dance with Micah, shake off the fact that it'll never feel warm and fuzzy again, and ward off the tears. "So. Tasha."

My neighbor raises a brow.

"Is she . . ."

This is crazy.

Micah wouldn't have . . . he loved me, loved our daughter, wanted more children.

But I've seen the proof in the pictures I smashed.

I clear my throat. "Is she married? I never met a husband." It isn't a lie. If Tasha is Natasha Markham, I never met her husband.

My phone chimes with a voice mail alert. Claudette left a message.

"I . . ." He bites his lower lip and sort of squints at me for a split second. "I don't know if they were married, but . . ." Again with the squint. "She wasn't always alone."

"Alone," I repeat. I'm alone now.

"I'm sorry for your loss." There's something in the way he's looking at me. Something that tells me I'm a pathetic shadow of what I used to be . . . and lately, I haven't been much of anything beyond a pincushion for IVF needles. "It's recent, huh?"

"Yes."

The warm sensation in my cheeks intensifies, like mercury about to burst a thermometer. I meet the challenge of his stare.

He takes a long draw on his mojito.

His straw becomes a stir-stick, chasing mint leaves around his glass. "I wore my ring for about a year after it was over. Just couldn't bring myself to take it off. It had been part of me for so long that I just . . . I couldn't part with it for a while. Couldn't bear the thought of being with other women, either, but—"

"I heard wearing a ring doesn't quite deter women."

"It wards off the ones who are serious about relationships."

"Oh." I don't know if I actually say the word or if my lips just form it. But either way, his message comes in loud and clear: it wasn't necessarily the *company* of other women he thwarted, so much as a *relationship*.

Could I do something like that? Fill the void Micah left with a casual fling? I take a healthy sip of my drink. Sweet rum mixed with a bitter—yet refreshing—elixir of mint leaves. It burns all the way down, but it chases away the thoughts rushing through my head. Of course I couldn't fill the vacancy with something impermanent, something cheap. I wouldn't know how.

My phone chimes with a different tone. This one alerts me to an incoming text. I glance at my phone. The text is from Claudette. She sent a picture of my house at the Shadowlands. A redheaded figure is on my doorstep.

I tap the screen to enlarge the photo. Blink to ensure I'm seeing things correctly.

But there's no mistaking that red hair.

She's at my house.

Natasha Markham is standing on my doorstep.

Chapter 24

Suddenly the entire world is a tornado rush of colors—the rosy-pink froth spilling across the table from Elizabella's souvenir cup, the purple monkeys adorning it, the green of palm trees, which I see only when I spin to find a member of the waitstaff, in search of a towel. And the memory of the bright-auburn tresses of a woman I last saw in the rearview mirror of Micah's old, beat-up Bronco, rumbling off campus after graduation.

Sticky mess in my lap.

"Mommy's fault, Nini! Mommy's fault!"

Maybe it was. Did I knock over her cup?

With one hand gripping my phone, and the other yanking my daughter out of the booth, as she's now swimming up to her elbows in the mess, a cramping sensation wrings in my pelvis and my lower back strains every time I lift her. She'll have to walk. Out of nowhere, it amplifies into the same stabbing, slashing pain I felt moments before miscarrying the twins.

My knees buckle.

I manage to catch myself with a hand on the back of the booth bench.

Lord.

It's happening now, the dreaded first period—usually god-awful, messy, and painful—after egg retrieval.

A server wedges himself between me and the table.

My eyes lock on his white towel, now bleeding through with reddish-pink slushy.

"Ladies' room?"

"Right behind you, ma'am." He hardly glances over his shoulder at me. "Down the hall."

I give Elizabella a tug in that direction.

"Mommy! Nini isn't—"

"She'll catch up, Ellie-Belle," I whisper.

"No! Nini's still at the table. Stranger danger!"

"Mommy has an emergency."

A blinding pain surges in my abdomen. For a split second, the sensation renders me immobile. Just a breath or so, but it's a productive one.

Bella ricochets off a wall of man—off Christian Renwick's long legs—and lands back against me, gripping my hand.

"I'm sorry," I mutter to Christian, who's now standing at the edge of the booth. I hope he isn't drenched with slushy now, too.

Maybe it's the slushy that's wet in my lap, or maybe it's a bloody mess in my panties, but either way, I need to go. Now.

Elizabella shrieks about Nini not following us when I lead her toward the ladies' room.

"Stop, Bella. Please." Tears prick in my eyes. "Just stop."

My phone is ringing again.

I offer only a glance in Christian's direction before disappearing down the hallway to the ladies' room.

Bella's wail of "Niniiiiiii!" echoes throughout the corridor.

I tighten my grip on her, lest she attempt to escape again, and soon we're in the sanctuary of a blue-and-yellow tiled bathroom. Her snivels and sobs bounce off the walls here, too.

I tend to her first, propping her on the countertop and guiding her hands under a stream of water. Her breaths are staccato, as if she's having trouble inhaling over her tears.

Or maybe that's me.

I gauge my reflection to confirm that I, too, am a sobbing mess of girl covered in sticky red and pink.

And suddenly, I realize how ridiculous we must look, crying over a spill—or so it might seem to the diners beyond the door—and I'm laughing.

And Bella's laughing, too, a moment after I start.

Her brown eyes, wet and rimming with tears, sparkle when she smiles. She tosses her little arms over my shoulders, and I hold her tight to me.

"Love you, Mommy."

"I love you, too, Bella. To the moon and back a hundred billion times plus infinity."

"Is that a lot?" she asks.

"It *is* a lot, baby." I kiss away the tears lingering on her cheeks. "But I think I love you even more than that."

"Ronis," she says.

I laugh even harder and lower my forehead to hers. "Oh, Bella."

Her still-soiled sleeves are wet against the back of my neck.

"You have to stop misbehaving."

"It was Nini's fault."

"Nini has to be a good girl, or she can't stay with us."

After a beat, her little voice sounds: "Nini will try."

"How I miss your daddy." When I close my eyes, I see sun filtering through stained glass, slanting over my mother's casket at Fourth Presbyterian. To think someday Elizabella will be standing alone over a box containing my body . . .

I shove the thought out of my head.

My mother chose to leave me the moment she swallowed the hand-ful of pills in the bathtub with the water running—and then again, later, with her more successful incident with the knife. I don't want to think about that, either.

I'm going to live a long, fruitful life, and by the time I kick it, Bella will be married with droves of children of her own. "You'll never be alone," I promise. "Not for a single second. We'll always have each other."

"And Nini."

"Yes." I smooth my daughter's hair from her forehead and allow myself to laugh at what I'm about to agree to. "Us and Nini. Against the world."

"Against the world," she echoes.

Chapter 25

When we had returned to the table, Christian was gone, and the guests at the table closest to ours had been relocated.

"We sure know how to chase people away, don't we?" I had asked Bella.

But he'd prepaid our entire tab before he took off.

Now that we're back at the house, I wonder if I should knock on his door to thank him. It isn't too late. But tomorrow might be better, or maybe I should wait until our paths cross again. I know what Claudette would do: she'd bring him a casserole.

And maybe that's a good idea. He's a single guy. He provided a dinner for us; I could reciprocate. Wouldn't Claudette be proud?

Her missed call notification still mars my phone screen. I'm about to call her when the picture she sent revisits me . . .

Bella is asleep upstairs in the master bedroom—atop the duvet, as I haven't had time to wash the linens.

I've swept shards of glass and dumped the mess into a small trash can I found beneath the kitchen sink. I washed the travertine tile against which the pictures shattered. There's still plenty to do. I haven't done more than peek at all the rooms in this place, let alone clean them and get to know them.

But I dial Claudette's number.

"Where are you?" No hello.

"Key West."

"Florida?"

"It's a long story."

"Well, I have only a few minutes. Brad's got the bedside candle lit, if you know what I mean."

"I got your text," I say.

"Oh yes. That little hussy tried to convince me she was there to offer support, but I saw it in her eyes."

"You spoke to her?"

"She said she'd called the house and left a message, and when you didn't call back, she thought she'd come. But I could see. She was there to take home a piece of your husband."

"What?"

"A memento. A shirt or . . . or who knows? The hair from his razor for all that's holy. And her name isn't Gabrielle. It's Natasha."

"Wait. You actually talked to her?"

"Briefly, and she said she'd seen the news report, and—"

"She's my college roommate."

"Oh."

"Did she leave a number?"

Another stretch of silence ensues before Claudette clears her throat. "I apologize. I assumed . . . and I'm afraid I wasn't very nice to her. But I stand behind my friends."

"It's okay." For a split second, a longing for home—or maybe for the way things used to be—washes over me. Why didn't Micah and I do couple-related things at the Shadowlands? We could've played golf with Claudette and Brad or at least gone to the clubhouse for lunch.

I realize, maybe for the first time, that I want that sort of life. I want to be sociable, part of a community. I want to have *friends*.

"I'm *sorry*," Claudette says.

"Don't be. She's not exactly innocent, if *you* know what *I* mean."

"Veronica? The police were here, asking all sorts of questions. Did I know about Micah's job? Do I think you two were happy? That sort of thing, and I said . . . I told them you were blissfully happy."

We were. But to hear Claudette say it, it feels more as if she lied for us, as if she expects gratitude for covering for me—which is precisely why I don't thank her.

Or maybe it's that I'm starting to see what a lie my marriage was, even if I didn't realize it until recently.

My cheeks burn with embarrassment, as if the curtain has been pulled back on my life for the whole world to see. As if everyone knows I'm a fraud. Micah's job was no one's business but mine and Micah's. If the police let on that he quit to avoid a criminal investigation, that his job at Diamond didn't exist, that we were paying our bills—the bills we actually paid, that is—with cash from an unknown source . . .

"I . . . I'll let you go, Claudette. Thanks for standing up for me."

"Honey, *wait*. Are you all right? Do you need anything?"

I wish people would stop asking that.

"I'm here for you," she says.

It's an odd sensation, having someone, someone other than Micah, in my corner. My eyes tear up. "Thanks, Claudette. We'll talk soon."

"Call anytime."

I dial my voice mail at the Shadowlands, but there are no messages.

And that's strange. Surely, there'd be a call or two from creditors looking to be paid or reporters maybe. To say nothing of the absence of a message from Natasha. Why would she say she'd left one if she hadn't? And surely, she wouldn't trek all the way out to the 'burbs without at least *trying* to get me on the phone.

A thought worms its way into my head. Could someone be listening to my messages? Could someone have already checked my voice mail and deleted the message from Natasha?

171

I log in to Facebook and navigate to my in-box, but there's nothing new there. The message I left for Natasha sits, not yet read. Next, I click on my wall, in case she posted something there.

My page is laden with nasty messages from people I don't know, accusing me of fleeing the investigation, of not cooperating with the police . . . of *killing my husband*.

Many of the comments are liked, even loved, by dozens of people, even though some kind strangers have posted sensible arguments against the haters. Anything from *don't judge what you don't know* to *try her in court—not on social media*.

A lump of fear and frustration and God-knows-what-else forms in my throat. I nearly whip my phone against the wall, but I don't want to wake Bella, lest she witness my second screaming fit in a matter of hours.

I'm about to exit the app, but I have the presence of mind to open my privacy settings and turn everything to private. I can't help what's already been posted, but no one will be able to do it again or read the nastiness from here on out. I delete all the comments without responding.

Shell.

God, I hope my mother-in-law hasn't visited my page and read such ugly things about her son and me.

I try Shell's cell phone again. Surely, they're back on Plum Lake by now, but the past few times I've called, her voice mail has picked up instantly. Cell service is questionable up at the lake, she'd said. Hit or miss.

Tonight it's a miss.

I leave a message: "Shell, it's Veronica. Again. Please call." I breathe through the tears I feel coming on. But a moment before they fall, I catch sight of the stack of photographs I piled atop the family room built-ins, and my resolve returns. Micah had secrets.

And while I'm hesitant to disturb Mick by ringing the landline—it's getting rather late—I try the number at the lake house. No answer.

Everywhere I look in this place, I imagine Micah dancing with another woman. Maybe even with Natasha Markham.

Micah was so deceitful. This house was a nest he filled with memories . . . memories that may have included Elizabella—depending on whether Nini is a real little girl . . . my daughter's half sister? . . . or just, as Dr. Russo insisted, an imaginary friend. But there is no question that my husband's life here did *not* involve me, despite my name on the deed of this house.

Why didn't he simply put Natasha's name on the deed? If *she* were going to live here, wouldn't it have made more sense to leave me out of this mess? Perhaps I never would've learned Micah's secrets if I'd never found this deed.

Either she stole my husband, or he went to her willingly, but gone is gone. Or maybe, considering her children are older than Bella . . . Was I the thief? I *did* steal him. In college. Micah chose me. But he obviously never completely cut ties with Natasha.

How could that have happened?

I hear Claudette in my head: his traveling made a dual life possible.

I pull a stack of portraits from the shelves and study the children's features. There's no denying their resemblance to the man I married.

But if Micah is the father of these children, they were born during our marriage. After all the frustration of negative pregnancy tests—we had thirty-six before Bella—and poking and prodding and ejaculating into cups, is it possible Micah went the easy route? Impregnated someone else?

Maybe he planned to leave me after these boys were born, but I turned up pregnant—finally—just as he was about to break the news.

Or . . . ironically enough, fertility treatment involves very little actual sex. Our microscopic cells come together; our bodies don't. Nothing about the process is erotic.

Did the lack of sex drive him away?

Did he find himself torn between two families?

If Micah didn't have a job, he probably came here every time I thought he was flying. Sometimes he was gone for three days a week, sometimes four. If he spent as much time here with Tasha as he did with me at the Shadowlands, maybe her life is just as turned upside down as mine is right now.

I look around at the home of Micah's other woman. Flowers and green grass year-round. Beautiful breezes. A variety of places to eat. I'm not sure how anyone isn't happy living in a place like this.

That's one thing I hated about the Shadowlands, I now realize. The rigidity. The lack of options. Sure, it's a safe, hemmed-in neighborhood, beautiful, with plenty of space to spread out. But sushi is a fifteen-minute drive. Ice cream after November? Only at national chains. It was a difficult adjustment after living in the city, where everything was just a block away.

But this place? There's plenty of space here. Plenty of variety. Could I find a happy medium here?

At the moment, I have two options: stay here, in a house I own free and clear, or trek back to Chicago, to mounds of debt and questions no one can answer.

I could let Mick sell the Shadowlands house; that would settle the mortgage debt back home. It's not home anymore without Micah. But I don't know that I can stay here, either. Will I ever be able to look at the shelves across the room without seeing the photographs of his other family?

Not likely.

Maybe if I fill the space with pictures of Bella and me . . .

Or maybe I'll tear the shelves out altogether.

Doubt flickers in my mind. This is the other woman's home. She's bound to be back at some point and find me here.

So what if she does come home? I dare her to try to reason her way back into this place. It's *mine*. And maybe I had to unknowingly share Micah, but there's no way in hell I have to share my house. Let her come.

Papa Hemingway leaps up onto the cushion next to me and nuzzles in for some attention. I massage the top of his head. He paws at me and cuddles on my lap.

Huh. He has six toes on his left front paw. The irony makes me chuckle; this cat proves nothing is right with the world anymore.

But maybe it can be made right. I stare across the room at the blank canvas I created the moment I cleared the shelves. Gray and unassuming, the built-ins blend into the rest of the room. Linear and simple. I don't like the color. And, come to think of it, I don't like the drab taupe walls surrounding me, either.

I abandon the cat and cross the room. The paint is chipping from the edges of the shelves, and the back panel in the cabinet all the way to the left is a little askew, as if installed just a touch out of square, but otherwise, the cabinetry seems to be in decent shape. Sturdy. Might I like this room better if I painted the cabinetry a bright white? If I painted the walls a cheery blue or green?

I open the cabinets and begin to pull out everything inside: issues of home decor magazines, crayons, scissors, art supplies.

Another cabinet holds a wicker basket of what appears to be yellow slipcovers that fit the rattan sectional in this room.

Another houses DVDs of old Disney movies, although a quick glance around the room proves there's nothing to watch it on. I'll head back to the mainland tomorrow to buy a television. I'm going to need something to occupy Bella; I'm going to be busy.

Job one: pack all the personal effects in the house. I won't throw anything away, but I don't want her clothing in the closets. I don't want her blankets tossed over the beds. Come to think of it, I don't want her beds, either.

Once the family room cabinets are empty, I tuck the yellow sofa slipcovers under an arm and take them down the hall to the laundry room. Eventually, I'll purchase a new sofa, but for now, I'll settle for sitting on clean cushion covers. There's only a bit of detergent left—enough for a load or two—so I mentally add it to the list of things to buy.

That and cat food. I spy a nearly empty automatic feeder in the corner of the laundry room.

The cat jumps through an access panel at the bottom of a louvered door. I open it, assuming it leads to a closet, only to be taken aback by the odor of soiled cat litter.

Once I adjust to the smell, however, I flip the light switch at the door, and the space illuminates. I see the litter box is situated in a sort of studio . . . and a generously sized one at that. It's about seven feet wide and at least twice as deep, with three square-shaped windows spaced at equal intervals along the left wall. A good-size pine table occupies the center of the space. An enormous appliance of some sort stares at me from the far end. At first I think it's an extra oven. But then I realize it's an industrial kiln.

A kiln.

Natasha Markham is *not* an artist. She was a finance major. Any half-artsy classes she took as an undergrad, she dreaded.

And she just isn't the type to use, let alone purchase, a potter's wheel, but there's one of those in this room, too.

Maybe I don't know my college roommate as well as I thought. I certainly couldn't know less about my husband; why should I know anything about the woman who took him away from me?

I wonder if she's heard the news, that Micah's been declared dead. Tomorrow I'm going to ask Christian if he knows how to get ahold of her. I think the former resident of this house and I need to have a talk. If not about Micah's dying, about the life he'd been living with Natasha.

Where did she and her children go?

A fleeting thought: maybe she goes north to Chicago every summer. It's the best time to be in the Windy City . . . all the festivals and fairs . . .

Or maybe the whole clan spends summers on Plum Lake.

Micah could pull that off. I've never been to the house on Plum Lake.

And Mick and Shell have been in Europe for six weeks, so maybe Natasha and the kids stayed longer than usual.

Micah's car was at C-Way. Maybe he was paying a visit to the mysterious Tasha and the kids before his trip to New York.

And my daughter recognizes the little girl in the pictures we found in this house, and that little girl just happens to share the name of Bella's imaginary friend. If Bella hasn't been to Key West before, she may have met Nini up north at Plum Lake.

I should call Detective Guidry. I will. First thing in the morning.

A glowing orange light blinks on in the shadows of the garden on the side of the house.

At first, I assume it's a firefly—strange, seeing one in November, as they appear in early summer in Chicago and stay for only a few weeks—but a breath later, I realize it's a cigarette.

Instantly, I turn off the studio light and back away from the windows, ducking into the laundry room.

Someone is smoking in my garden.

Someone is looking into the house.

And the coincidence is too great to ignore. It has to be the same person who was smoking on the fairway back at the Shadowlands.

I was certain no one had followed us.

But apparently, I was wrong.

Chapter 26

I spring toward the back door—it's locked—and flip switches until a light on the porch turns on. I do the same with the front door and at the side entrance, where double doors lead to a patio.

The entire yard is illuminated now, but I don't see a single thing out of place. Just a gate at the back, leading to the alleyway, an empty swimming pool, and Florida foliage. No mysterious smoking man.

Did I imagine it?

The place is deadly silent. Pink and blue and purple blossoms ripple in the breeze, like waves on the sea. Bobbing somewhere out there, however, is a stalker, artfully staying out of sight. Either in the midst of the blooms or hiding away in my subconscious, waiting to drive me completely insane.

I listen hard but hear nothing.

We're too far from Duval Street to be bothered by the hubbub of the tourists; we're too far from the coast to hear the waves breaking on the sand. We're isolated here, in the gardens of a place someone—Micah, maybe?—aptly named Goddess Island.

I draw in a slow breath but can't detect the cigarette smoke. Maybe it was my imagination, or maybe I am slowly slipping into the same sort of world in which my mother lived out the last of her days.

Seeing things that aren't there.

Remembering things vastly different than they happened.

Even the image of Micah is dissipating with every passing hour. I thought he was a golden god of a man. Dedicated to his daughter and me. Beautiful. Caring. Ambitious.

But he was deceitful and manipulative.

How could a sane person have been so wrong about so many things? How could I have been so blind?

All the times I considered worst-case scenarios, I never assumed I'd someday find myself in this predicament.

Then, from out of nowhere, I hear the tinkling tune of a music box.

I make a break for the stairs—my daughter is asleep up there—and take them two at a time, the music box growing in crescendo.

My mother's last hours flash in my mind: my mother and her jewels; the bald spot at her right temple and the blood blooming like tiny buds at her scalp where she habitually ripped hair from the follicles; the blue table; the filthy tank top hanging off her bony frame; the knife in her hand . . .

I skid into the master bedroom, heart beating like mad, only to find no sign of my kid. My ears cloud with the eerie sound of the music. "Ellie-Belle!" I tear her blanket from the bed to confirm she's not hidden beneath it. "Elizabella!"

No, no, no . . .

Flashes of the cigarette glowing on my lawn, on the fairway back home, haunt me as I whip through the room. I peek into the en suite bathroom, in the shower, in the compartmentalized toilet room. I even check in the cabinets under the sinks.

It seems as if the music surrounds me, as if it could be coming through the air vents or echoing off the walls. I can't pinpoint where it's originating, but if I can find the music box, I suspect I'll find my daughter.

I open the closet door to see empty racks and rods . . . but no head-strong three-year-old. "Bella!"

The sound of her laughter is an instant relief.

I follow the resounding joy of her giggling down the travertine-tiled hallway to a dark room at the far end, facing out over the back lawn. She's sitting in the center of the floor, on a round, pink area rug, the texture of which resembles cotton candy. The music box plinks out its song; the pink ballerina in some dancer's pose spins around merrily.

"That's funny, Nini! What else happened?"

"Bella!"

She jumps when I turn on the light. "Mommy!"

"Bella, what are you doing in here?"

Her eyebrows come together in a frown. "I'm playing with Nini."

"It's bedtime," I remind her. "And when I put you to bed in one room, you need to stay in one room, so Mommy doesn't worry."

"Nini said this is *my* room."

"She did, huh?" I crouch down to her level, then sit and pull her into my lap. "Do you like this room?"

"Uh-huh!" She nods enthusiastically.

"This is Nini's room?"

"*My* room. Nini says." A canopy bed, full size, is draped with pink and pale-purple tulle, and an enormous dollhouse is atop a double dresser situated on the opposite wall. In an alcove by the window, its wooden seat tethered to the ceiling with thick, knobby ropes, is an honest-to-goodness swing.

A swing.

In a little girl's bedroom.

Just like Micah suggested we do at the Shadowlands.

"My room, my room, my room."

Of course Elizabella likes this room. It's everything a little girl could dream of. It's her favorite colors: pink and purple. And . . .

I zero in on a framed drawing hanging on the wall near a doorway to a shared bathroom. The picture is of a girl with long brown hair, big brown eyes, strawberry ice-cream cone—Bella's favorite—in hand. It's the work of a child older than Bella, a child who has better control of pencil grip and fine motor skills. Is this caricature of my daughter?

Nini must be an artist.

She is.

A chill darts up my spine. "Let's . . . Bella, let's look at the other rooms. You can pick whichever room you'd like."

"This room." She points to the floor.

"Okay, but let's look at the others, okay?" I scoop her up.

A moment before I carry her toward the attached bath, shared with the room opposite, I opt to open the closet door. A few sundresses—four, now that I count them—hang from the rod. I maneuver a hanger to look at the tag. Size 3T. Bella's just growing out of 3T into the next size up, but I wonder . . . could these dresses have been stocked here for my daughter to wear?

I walk through the shared bath, which is crisp with white fixtures, yellow walls, and a seahorse sculpture—bright purple—hanging on the wall.

"Brush teeth!" she squeals.

I glance down at the double vanity. There are two steps leading up to the sink closest to the pink room.

"This is where you . . ." I hesitate to ask because I'm starting to think I'm not going to like the answer. "Bella, is this where you brush your teeth?"

"Nini did once."

"Nini's been here before?"

"Yes, Mommy."

"Do you go everywhere Nini goes?"

"Sometimes."

"Have you ever been here, Bella?"

"Down!" Emphatically, she shakes her head. "Down, down, down."

I put her down. "Have you been here with Nini?"

"No."

"Never?"

She crosses her arms over her chest and shakes her head, lower lip protruding in an impressive pout.

"Tell Mommy."

"It's a secret," she says.

"A secret you're supposed to keep from Mommy?"

She leans in close: "From *everyone*."

An eerie tickle dances on the back of my neck. "Okay."

She tugs on my hand and leads me to the next room.

This one has a queen-size bed piled with purple and yellow pillows, and carved roses are on the walnut headboard. "Whose room is this?" I ask.

"Nini's."

"This is where Nini sleeps?"

"Sometimes."

I open the closet door, but nothing beyond empty rods and shelves stares back at me.

I know from my first walk through the house that there are five bedrooms. A master, outfitted in shades of gray. A frilly pink bedroom and a purple one, too. One bedroom is painted a slate blue with two double beds and a large model airplane—red—suspended from the ceiling. The last is decked out in white eyelet and neutrals. Despite the made-up beds, it appears the place was permanently evacuated when the mysterious Tasha departed. The closets all open to racks of empty hangers, swaying ghostly in the dark.

Except the closet in the room my daughter's imaginary friend has assigned to her.

Nothing makes sense if Bella hasn't been here before. The only occasion on which Micah took our daughter someplace without me was after I lost the boys in April, and they went—at least, he *said* they went—to the cottage on Plum Lake.

He'd taken over for a few weeks: He'd ordered dinners and researched preschools. He'd even ordered some clothing for Bella's summer wardrobe.

In April, these dresses would have fit my daughter, but it would have been too cold in Chicago for sundresses. Could it be my husband ordered a few extra dresses to keep at his second home?

Could I have been so wrapped up in my own pathetic pity party—poor me; I can't conceive—that I didn't notice my husband was living a life that didn't involve me?

Have I been seeing only what I want to see?

Chapter 27

"You smelled it? You're sure?" Officer Laughlin came to answer the call I made this morning regarding a possible unwanted guest in my garden last night. "Cigarette smoke?"

"I thought I did." This morning, I figured that even if the police don't find anything, I should at least report what I thought I saw.

Not *thought*. I saw it, plain as day: the glow of a recently lit cigarette. The scent was undeniable.

"Why didn't you report it last night?" He's taking notes, writing down everything I say.

I have the sneaking suspicion he, and everyone else in uniform, will eventually try to trip me up, to catch inconsistencies in my story. I have to be careful, have to tell them the absolute truth, even though I don't want to admit that I've been an absolute fool.

"I heard my daughter upstairs," I say. "A music box was playing. She was playing with the music box, I mean, and I panicked. She was asleep last I'd checked on her. If someone was on the property, I had to be sure she was safe."

"And she was?"

"Yes."

"But you didn't call after that? Even though you were worried enough that harm might come to your daughter, you didn't call the department to report a possible intruder."

"I should have," I say. "But . . ." How can I tell this policeman that I was too busy pondering the line between sanity and lunacy to call? That I was busy searching this house for information about the children who live here? This is supposed to be *my house.* A landlord wouldn't have to search for information, and if my daughter has spent time here, what kind of mother am I if I never knew about it?

Besides, if I admit to Laughlin that my husband had another family, won't that supply the investigators with the one piece they need to build a theory around my involvement in Micah's death?

If Micah was playing house with another woman—and it's safe to say he was—I had motive to retaliate.

But I didn't cause his plane to crash.

"Last night, after I didn't see anything with the floodlights on, I assumed it was my imagination," I say. "And maybe it was. But I figured I'd report it just in case."

"Any word on your husband?"

I feel my brows come together. That would be a trick and a half.

The officer probes: "He hasn't contacted you?"

"How would he . . . he's . . . Officer Laughlin . . ." My eyes rim with tears. I shake my head. "They didn't tell you? My husband . . . he's *dead.* He was declared dead."

Laughlin flips closed the cover of his notebook and stares at me for what seems to be an eon. Is he daring me to speak?

I point to the east. "There was a plane crash off the coast." I don't know what else to say. "They came to tell me in Chicago. They're sending his body back. I told you yesterday that we lost him."

I wish he weren't wearing sunglasses. I can't gauge his expression.

Finally, he pockets the notebook. "I'll have a look around the grounds. If I see anything—footprints, cigarette butts—I'll be sure to let you know."

"Thank you." I close the door as he descends the porch stairs.

Elizabella's voice carries down from upstairs, where she is busy playing with the dollhouse in the room she insists is hers. I might have to make an exception to tossing everything in the house. Not only does the dollhouse keep her occupied, it's a healthier option than television. Besides, listening to Nini-isms through the proxy of a dollhouse resident isn't nearly as creepy as hearing my child's one-sided version of their conversations.

But Laughlin's silent stance chews at me. Maybe I should have told him about Micah's infidelity. Or maybe I should tell Guidry first. He's been working the case longer, after all, and Laughlin is here, essentially, to make sure I don't go rogue.

There's so much to do. It's not even ten in the morning, and I'm so tired that it feels like ten at night. I suppose I didn't sleep much. But I did manage to empty the closets and cabinets in every room on the first floor. The place looks like a rummage sale drop-off site. But I'm guessing this house, like my life, is going to go through a period of upheaval before I can put it all back together.

I can't concentrate. The way Laughlin was looking at me . . . the way Guidry expects the worst of me . . . I wish they understood that no one in her right mind would choose to go through what I'm going through.

I pull my cell phone from my pocket and dial Guidry.

Chapter 28

Guidry picks up on the first ring. "Veronica. I just got a call from Key West PD."

That was fast.

"Seems you've insinuated some interesting things," he says.

"Interesting? Well, I wasn't sure anyone was really in the garden last night, so—"

"You informed the responding officer your husband is dead."

"Yes." I'm pacing through the hallway now. "Is that classified information?"

A long pause precedes his clearing his throat. "We received the FAA's investigation report about the small plane crash off the coast of Florida."

"Right." None of this is news.

"If I may ask," Guidry says. "You keep insisting your husband is dead, when we don't know where he is. You've told Claudette Winters your husband is dead. You told your mother-in-law his body would be sent to Paxon Funeral Home and Crematorium, that you'd plan his memorial service. You've inferred, when speaking with me, you don't expect him back. You confirmed it with Officer Laughlin."

"Detective, I'm . . . I'm sorry. I'm confused. Am I not supposed to . . . ?"

"You're telling people he's dead before we have confirmation of that fact."

"But I thought . . . the federal agents . . . they visited me at home. They told me Micah was dead. Is that not confirmation?"

"Veronica."

"I told you about the agent. He was at the bank. He was *in the kitchen*, remember?"

"No federal agents have been assigned to your husband's case."

My knees weaken. I slump against the walls in the hallway. "But they were there. At my house. Claudette was there. She can verify what they said."

I stop myself. Actually, no. She wasn't there for the conversation. She took the kids to the screened porch while I sat down with two men I'd assumed were federal agents. "I didn't invent this, detective."

Or did I? Haven't I had trouble the past few days determining what's real and what's imagined?

Just like Mama at the end, when she told me the voices in her head wanted her to smash my head in with a baseball bat while I slept.

A sob catches in my throat.

What's happening to me?

What if my entire marriage—my entire life—has been nothing more than illusion? Drama created in my head?

"Why would I . . . ," I whisper. "Can you give me one good reason why I would prefer to think my husband is dead?"

"I can give you two and a half million reasons."

"I didn't even know about the insurance policy." I'm pleading with him. "And I *don't want it*. I don't want any of it. His life is worth *more* than that money." I wipe tears from my eyes. "I wish I had him back. Because then he could explain to you all of the things I don't know enough about to explain."

"*That's* why you want him back?"

"I need you to be on my side, detective. I've been cooperative. I've answered your questions, and I've called you several times proactively. I've opened my home to you and your team and done everything I can to help you get to the bottom of this, and you still insist I'm capable of doing the unthinkable."

"Say your husband has a secret."

My heart bottoms out in my gut. He knows. He knows about the children who used to live in this house, and because I didn't have the chance to tell him, he's going to think the worst of me. He's going to think I had motive to make my husband disappear.

Couple that with my telling everyone my husband is dead when maybe he isn't—he might still be alive—and I'm surprised I'm not in cuffs yet.

"Say your husband tells someone—his mother, maybe, his ex-girl-friend—that if you ever found out about this secret, you'd be angry enough to kill him."

Oh God, God, God.

"*Now* say I look into your past. I see the only person close to you before you met your husband—"

Mama.

"She died under mysterious circumstances."

I can't answer his accusations. But he's wrong. I didn't have anything to do with my mother's death, and I didn't have anything to do with whatever happened to Micah.

Guidry continues: "The old case file from Maywood PD suggests something more may have been going on in your mother's house than you let on. You didn't tell me about any of that, either."

My stomach turns, and sweat breaks on my brow. It was so long ago, so far away, but suddenly, I'm back there: My mother is sitting at the table, plying wires and beadwork into art. And out of nowhere, she whips the pliers at my head. She's hissing like a rabid cat, and I'm terrified. Screaming.

"Veronica."

I blink.

"You tell me," Guidry says. "What am I supposed to think?"

I breathe through the confusion, focusing on a crack in the plaster that runs up the wall opposite the stairs.

I startle when I hear Bella's giggle floating down from her room. "Nini, wake up. Connor's being silly."

Connor?

I pull myself to my feet.

Bella is still talking: "Wake up, Nini. Connor's *so* silly!"

Does my daughter have another imaginary friend? How many "friends" are normal? Should one friend make an exit before another arrives?

"Veronica?" Guidry raises his voice.

"Yeah, I'm here." Quietly, I walk up the stairs.

"I may just head down to discuss a few things with you," the detective says. "About your mother. About Micah. You aren't planning on going anywhere, are you?"

"You mistake me for someone who has somewhere else to go."

"There were three bodies identified in the plane crash. They're not releasing the names of the victims, but your husband is not among them."

My sob escapes in a hiccup. I should be relieved he's alive. Grateful. But I'm not. As horrible as it felt hearing his body had been discovered, will it be worse to go on living, possibly for years, without knowing what happened to him? And even if I had him back, I wouldn't have the man I thought he was. He's an illusion.

"You're telling me," I say on broken breath, "that no federal agents came to my house and declared him dead."

"Who visited you that day? Why did you believe them?"

"They had badges." But did they? I don't remember. Claudette answered the door. "They looked official. They were wearing suits. Listen. I can sit down with you and describe them. The tall one, in particular. I've seen him twice now. Lincoln was his name."

I peek in on Elizabella. In her left hand, she's holding a little boy figure. In her right, the little girl. She's talking to Connor and Nini. Just role-playing with her toys.

"Veronica? Have you been in touch with your husband?"

Fresh tears sprout in my eyes. "No."

Guidry's commentary echoes in my head: *Say your husband tells someone—his mother, maybe his ex-girlfriend—that if you ever found out about this secret, you'd be angry enough to kill him . . .*

"But you've talked to Shell," I say.

"She says she didn't know about the house in the Keys."

"I already told you. *I* didn't even know."

He lets another unspoken accusation hang in the air.

"I was going to tell her about the house once we settled in. I was going to ask her to come."

"Really."

"And I've been calling and calling, and she hasn't called back."

"Can you save me some time, Veronica? Help me out?"

"I'll do whatever I can to help. You *know* that."

"You know what my men found on the hard drive of that desktop?"

"Not much, I imagine. Elizabella uses it to play her alphabet games, her counting games."

"Your log in was the primary, the one used most often."

This silences me for a second. Even if I had logged Bella onto the computer, she has her own separate icon to click on to gain Internet access. I would've logged on using *her* sign in. "That's news to me."

He continues. "You searched for—"

"No. If Micah logged in with my account, I can't verify it. But I'm telling you that I have not had occasion to sit and browse the Internet since my daughter was born. I have a laptop. I need to be mobile because my daughter is mobile. You're welcome to search it, too. I can send it or drop it off at the station here. But whatever you've found, however you assume it was me who navigated there, *I didn't do it.*"

"You shared your log-in information with your husband?"

"I shared *everything* with my husband."

"Noted." He pauses, maybe to ensure I'm done ranting. "Under your log in, whoever used it, we found searches for homes to purchase in Italy, Switzerland, and Spain. Were you planning on making a move?"

"I've never even *been* to Italy, Switzerland, or wherever it was. I wouldn't have the first clue *how* to buy a house overseas."

"Did Micah ever talk about it?"

"Not with me. It was a stretch for me to move from Old Town to the 'burbs."

"Yet you took off. You're in Key West."

"Because I don't have a choice. I haven't worked in over five years. I'm entirely dependent on my husband. And almost every credit card is maxed, everything is past due, and the mortgage on a home—which, news to me, we don't even own—is about to go into foreclosure. This house in the Keys is my only asset. It's the only thing in our entire estate that's in my name. Do you know that I can't even access my own phone records? Everything is in Micah's name. Everything except this house."

"Uh-huh."

"Speaking of phone records, have you found anything? How many times Micah called the three-oh-five number?"

"Just once," Guidry says. "It's a cell phone. Untraceable in the day of go-phones."

"Do you think he might be overseas then?" I ask. "In Italy, Switzerland—"

"Is Micah on any medication? Would he have access to any benzo-diazepines? Xanax, that sort of thing?"

My fingertips tingle as if they're going numb. "I had an old pre-scription for Xanax that was filled in April after my miscarriage. I didn't like to take it. Why?"

"The autopsies of those in the plane crash indicated ingestion of benzos and death by drowning."

My blood runs cold. Is he insinuating Micah might have had some-thing to do with the deaths of three people?

"The Xanax was in the medicine cabinet. He had access, but I don't know if he took it with him. You're welcome to check. Check the whole house. I have nothing to hide."

"I put in for a warrant. I'll be in touch when it's signed."

"Detective, wait. I called to acknowledge a few things: I know you've talked with Claudette about Micah, and I know you think—or at least *she* thinks—he was seeing another woman."

He doesn't offer the courtesy of a response, although I'm starting to understand that about him. The less he says, the more information those he's speaking with are inclined to offer.

"She was probably right, and maybe it was even worse than she imagined."

"Worse."

I take a deep breath. "Once I got to the house in the Keys, it was all apparent, right here in front of me, on the shelves in the family room."

"What was apparent, Mrs. Cavanaugh?"

Suddenly, I don't so much *feel* like Micah's wife, and the title throws me. "You can . . . would you mind calling me Veronica?"

"Veronica. What was apparent?"

Man of few words. "There were pictures here. Still *are* here, I guess, but I've packed them away. Pictures of Micah . . . and kids that aren't mine."

"Whose kids are they?"

"I think Natasha Markham's. And probably my husband's, too—the pictures seem to suggest as much."

"Huh."

"I mean, I don't know for *sure*, but these pictures . . . I'll send them to you, if you want . . . It's hard to deny Micah was involved with these children. He was *in their lives*."

"And you didn't suspect any of this beforehand?"

"I feel like a fool. But no. He had me snowed."

A beat of silence follows before Guidry says, "You realize some might see this as giving you motive. Your husband is missing. We always rule out the spouse first. And you might have reason to shake things up. Motive."

"Only if I'd known, and I didn't. Ask anyone. I was blissfully blind to all of this. And I'm angry now—trust me, I'm angry—but even if I'd known back then, before, I wouldn't have been angry enough to kill him."

"Some theorists might disagree. Some say you might not even *remember* being angry enough to kill him."

I grit my teeth. "Anyone who thinks I'd actually *kill* because I lived in a make-believe world, because I was blind, assumes I value Micah's life over mine, over Bella's. And I don't."

Chapter 29

After a quick peek at Elizabella, who has dozed off in front of the dollhouse, I enter the odd little studio through the door in the laundry room.

Papa Hemingway is at my heels, curling around my legs as I step inside.

"What happened here, Papa? Whose space is this?"

The cat stares up at me, blinks, and continues his figure-eight path around my ankles. If he knows anything, he's not telling.

"What do you suppose people do with these?" I pull from a hook on the wall something that looks like a thick thread—fishing line, maybe, or a thin wire—with knobby buttons fastened to either end. I crouch to the cat's level and pet his head while he bats at the strange tool, as if it's merely a toy there for his amusement. "Yeah, I don't know, either."

After hanging it back where I found it—*Why? Shouldn't I simply throw it away?*—I make my way past the shelves along the right end of the room. I feather my fingertips over plastic-wrapped cubes of clay, over mason jars of glazes—among them, cobalt—and some plastic jars of silica, alumina, kaolin, all labeled by hand.

The handwriting is an artsy block, with serifs and ending strokes. Definitely not the no-nonsense style of my ex-roommate, Natasha Markham.

I pull a package off the shelf and blow dust off it. It's a plastic-wrapped cube of clay. The label tells me it's earthenware. Other cubes along the shelf are labeled terra-cotta and porcelain. However long this stash has been sitting upon this shelf, the seals on the plastic wrapping must be airtight because the clay is still malleable. I press my fingers into the mass; even through the plastic, I can make an imprint.

I look to the dusty potter's wheel.

While I've seen people working these things at art fairs back in the city, I wouldn't know how to begin to use it, even if it worked, which I'm not sure it does.

Still, there's an electric outlet just behind the mechanism, and its plug practically dares me to try it out. Balancing the clay in one arm, I bend over to plug in the wheel. Flip the switch to "On." It hums but doesn't move.

Broken, perhaps?

Then I see the pedal. I press it with the tip of my toes, and the wheel starts to turn at a lazy pace.

Old clay residue seems to spiral out at me, like beads in a kaleido-scope, mesmerizing me, playing tricks on my vision.

So the thing works. Good to know, in case I decide to sell it.

Then again . . .

What if I could learn to use it?

I have clay and a kiln . . .

I call up a video on YouTube and watch a few minutes of a tutorial. Seems easy enough. I plunk the cube of earthenware atop the sturdy pine table and twist the plastic wrapping until it starts to unravel.

First, I dig into the stuff with my hands and pack it like a snowball, but the stuff accumulates under my fingernails, and I can only imagine recreating the airtight seal might be difficult without a smooth edge. I retrieve a butter knife from the kitchen and lop off a hunk as evenly as I can manage it.

Now that I have a decent chunk of clay, I fashion it into a ball and plop it down at the center of the wheel. Now what? As soft as the clay is, my hands aren't going to slip around it very easily.

How did the artist in Old Town do this? The guy on YouTube had sponges, a bucket of water.

I retrieve more supplies and sit on a tiny stool behind the potter's wheel. I step on the pedal to start the wheel spinning and cup wet fingers around the clay.

The clay is lopsided, not centered, and I can't manage to control it, let alone shape it into anything with some semblance of style. It hobbles and topples and rips, and I can't seem to get a good pace going. I put either too much pressure on the pedal or not enough. I kick off my shoes. Maybe direct contact between my foot and the pedal will help.

I mash down the clay and try again.

And again.

And again.

I'm filthy, and the diamonds in my wedding ring are caked with earthenware, but eventually I manage to manipulate the clay into a cylinder. With enough water and patience, I pinch the sides of the cylinder so that they thin out and grow taller as they do. I press it back down and try something else, this time molding it into a bulbous shape.

Still lopsided, still ugly. But it's a creation nonetheless.

"You will not defeat me," I say to the machine.

I'll let this whatever-it-is dry, and maybe I'll fire it in the kiln.

I attempt to remove it from the wheel, but it won't budge. If I squeeze it any harder, it'll squish into nothing. If I let it harden on the wheel, I'll never get it off.

The ugly thing stares at me, silently proclaiming victory.

I scan the shelves for some sort of spatula. Then my gaze lands on the weird wire-and-button tool, hanging on the hook.

Worth a try.

I retrieve it, hook it around the clay creation, and with a button in each hand, I scrape the wire along the wheel. Miraculously, the vase-slash-cup-slash-flowerpot liberates itself from the crust of wet clay still stuck to the wheel.

Carefully, I carry it to the shelves and set it there to dry.

Chapter 30

"Baby?" I'm halving grapes and slicing strawberries and placing them on a paper plate for Elizabella. "Come eat some fruit."

Today, we took a walk to a market, where I bought some essentials for lunch and dinner. Living here is similar to living in the city. Nothing is very far away, and for oftentimes unprepared moms like me, life is actually easier when grabbing things on the go. Along the way home, I stopped for a few cheap sundresses and a pair of flip-flop sandals for each of us, as well as an umbrella stroller. We're set for a few days at least.

"Are you hungry, Bella?"

It was a struggle to pull her away from the dollhouse, but she's coloring now in the family room. "Nini, too?"

"Nini, too." I already have the second plate ready, and I'm wondering if I ought to prepare a third for Connor.

"In a minute," she says.

Back at the Shadowlands, I probably would have had to insist she eat *right now* because we likely would have had somewhere to be—the Westlake School, Mini Musicality, Dr. Russo's office, or the IVF center—but there are no deadlines here. The only thing we have to do here is wait.

Wait to see what other leads come in. Wait to see if someone happens across Micah's body.

Guidry says that if my husband considered an overdose of benzodiazepines as a way to off himself, chances are his body would turn up in a bathtub somewhere.

I shudder at the similarities to the situation with my mother, remembering the day she stepped into a tub with water running . . .

My knees buckle every time I think of it.

First Mama, then Micah, drifting off to nothingness in a filled tub.

Why? Because he lied to me? Because life got too big for him?

The man who cha-cha-chad me around the kitchen in the last hours of our life together wouldn't have committed suicide.

But what if he'd snapped?

It wouldn't be unheard of, would it?

There were things I saw my mother do in frantic states, only to listen to her deny the actions later, when she seemed more reasonable, calmer. And she wasn't lying. She really didn't know she'd done or said the things I'd witnessed.

She was crazy. Unless I was mistaken.

Dr. Russo told me there wasn't enough evidence to suggest schizophrenia. And even the doctors she saw while I was growing up disagreed. Not all of them were convinced that she had trouble determining what was real and what wasn't. Besides, she knew enough not to talk about the voices she heard, so in effect, those doctors could have been right.

She said the voices told her to kill me . . . maybe that's why she killed herself.

But is it possible that the delusions were mine? That *I* was the crazy one? That I only imagined her episodes?

The day revisits me now, finding her that way . . . *in the bathtub.*

Is there any way I could've killed her?

Is there any way I could've killed Micah?

Do I just not remember?

For a few seconds, I stare at the two small plates I'm preparing . . . for one child and one imaginary friend.

I'm doing the right thing. Dr. Russo said I should play along.

"Time to eat." I set the plates atop the table. Bella will come when she comes. And if she doesn't come, she doesn't eat until lunch. She'll learn. "Window closes in ten minutes."

She looks up at me, her crayon stilled on the page. "What window?"

"If you don't come to eat in ten minutes, I'll clean it up, and you'll have to wait a long time for another snack."

"Okay." With crayons and paper in her hands, she get ups and approaches the table. "See?" She lays the paper next to Nini's plate. "Here's Connor and Brendan."

I glance at the paper. She's drawn two figures who appear to be boys. "Are they twins?" I ask.

"Uh-huh."

"How old are they?"

"They're little."

"Little like you? Or littler?"

"Yes, Mommy." She gives me a slow blink, as if she's irritated that I asked, and picks up her fork, with which she stabs at a strawberry.

Little boys.

Twins.

Could it be she's drawing the boys in the photographs? The boys who used to live in this house?

"Does Nini know Connor and Brendan?"

"She knowed them once."

"Did they live here, Bella? In this house?"

"They lived in your tummy."

I nod. "Okay." So she's talking about her brothers that were never born. But why now? After all this time?

"Mommy? Is Daddy with my brothers now?"

I brush hair from her forehead before it collides with her fruit. "I don't know where your daddy is."

"He's at God Land."

"Bella, *we're* at God Land. Daddy isn't here."

She takes another mouthful. "He'll come."

Her declaration stops me, midbreath.

The cat's collar jingles as he rubs up against my legs. I push away Papa Hemingway and concentrate on my daughter's matter-of-fact expression. She's talking as if what she's saying is as commonplace as hello or goodbye.

"He'll come?"

"He said he'd come see me."

"Bella, when did he say that?"

"When he kissed me bye-bye."

I narrow my gaze at her. "Bella? Did Daddy *plan* to leave? Did he *tell* you he was leaving and that he'd come back for you?"

She talks through a mouthful of berries: "Nini says he leaves and comes back."

"Okay, but what did Daddy tell you?"

"He told me bye-bye. And see you soon."

Should I buy into the theory that my daughter foresaw her father's demise? That she's talking about her unborn baby brothers because she's communicating with their souls?

Do I trust that my husband was simply saying goodbye to our daughter before he left for a few days?

The smoking man on the fairway . . .

The moment Bella looked out the window, back at the Shadowlands, she told me she was going to be with her father. Had she seen the smoking man and assumed he'd come to get her?

The brown sedan following me . . . had the driver come to take my daughter to meet Micah?

The cat nudges me again.

I surrender and pick him up. "What do you need, Hemingway?" I look into the cat's green-gold eyes. He squints at me, as if I'm an idiot, as if I can't see what's directly in front of me.

There are few gnarls in the cat's fur. I haven't come across a cat brush in this place, but I'll put it on the list of things to buy the next time I hit a store.

"I like this cat," I say.

"Me too. But he makes Nini go *achoo*."

"Should we keep him?"

"Cats make Daddy *achoo*, too." She imitates a sneeze.

"Really?" If it's true, it seems odd that he'd allow one in the house. Come to think of it, I sort of remember him thwarting conversations about getting any pets. "Is that right, Papa Hemingway? Do you make Daddy sneeze?"

I turn over the tag on his collar, where his name is lettered. JAMES BROLIN.

"Nini goes *achoo*, and Daddy goes *achoo*."

"Because of *this* cat? Bella, did you meet this cat before?"

She shrugs. "Nini meeted him once."

All signs point to Bella's being here before: The bedroom, the clothing in the closet, the pictures of the house she'd drawn before we arrived. And now this cat.

I think of the phone call I received at the Shadowlands house, the whispering caller warning me to *listen to your daughter*.

Bella wanted to come to God Land.

Detective Guidry insists my husband's death has yet to be confirmed. Either Micah is reaching out to Bella from beyond, or he planned an escape from our life and has carefully planted clues to lure us here. But why would he do such a thing? What does he want from us?

And this cat . . .

Why did Christian Renwick call this cat Papa Hemingway if its name is obviously James Brolin?

Chapter 31

November 26

The past couple of days, I've begun with a phone call to my mother-in-law. I want to clear up any confusion between us and explain why I'd tell her Micah was dead if the fact has yet to be confirmed.

She hasn't answered. But today, I dial again and again and neglect to leave messages.

I think back to what Guidry hinted: Micah disclosed he had a secret, and that if I learned of it, I'd be angry. Angry enough to kill him, but I'm not going to capitalize on that detail.

If Micah shared something with his mother, I deserve to know what it is. Besides, I'd like to know for certain about the allergy to cats. I want to know if Shell knows anything about Micah's carrying on with Natasha. I want to know about Shell's friend Gabrielle. I want to know what the hell happened between Micah and Mick and the money.

And . . . I pull from its small box the blue-stone ring I stumbled across in the safe-deposit box. With all the confusion of that day, the three-day trek down to the Keys, and everything that's happened since we arrived, I forgot about it. But I found it at the bottom of my purse, and it sprung even more questions . . . questions his mother might know the answers to, if he confided in her.

So I keep calling.

On my sixth attempt, Shell picks up: "Stop calling me."

I'm too stunned to reply for a few seconds. "Shell, it's Veronica."

"I know who you are. My God, do you know what you've put me through? To tell me my son is *dead* when—"

"Shell, two men came to my house and *told* me he was gone. I didn't just—"

"Listen. I know you know more than you're telling."

"I know your son had a double life," I say. "I know that now. But if you think I know what happened to him—"

"Not only do I think that, I think you're *responsible* for whatever happened to him. The police told me about Bella confessing your plan to her teachers."

"My *plan*? Shell."

"Two-point-five million dollars. Christ, a girl like you—never more than a twenty in your pocket until you met my son—it must be like winning the lottery."

I stifle a sob. I want to tell her I didn't know about the life insurance, but I can't catch my breath.

"And all that bullshit about wanting to come to the lake for Thanksgiving," she says. "Did you think I wouldn't notice when you didn't show up? Did you think you'd just make your way down to Key West? Then sail to Switzerland or wherever you managed to buy your house overseas and disappear? With *my* granddaughter?"

"Listen to me. Please."

"I'll listen if you tell me what happened."

"But I don't *know* what happened. And that's the honest-to-God truth."

"The truth will come out eventually. It always does. I ask you, as a mother. End my suffering. God forbid, if anything happened to

Bella, you'd need to know about it, wouldn't you? *Please.* Tell me what happened."

"I don't know. You have to believe me. You have to trust me. You know I love your son. More than anything."

"You know the last person I'm inclined to trust? The person who has to remind me to trust her."

I pull the phone from my ear for a second. I can't bear to listen anymore. When I bring the phone back to my ear, however, I hear the worst of it:

"You won't be raising my son's daughter. Not if I have anything to say about it."

No, no, no, no, no. She wants to take Elizabella away from me.

"I love you," I manage. "Someday, you'll realize you're wrong about me."

I hang up.

Chapter 32

November 27

God, it's warm. It's probably not more than mid-eighties, but it's an oppressive heat. There's barely a breeze today, inland from the shore, and I've just spent an hour in my kitchen. My dress is sticking to my back, and my hair is out of control in this humidity, even when tied back.

With a chicken casserole balanced in my arms, my cell phone in its case dangling off my wrist like a party purse, I walk past the emptied in-ground pool in my backyard, toward the gate at the farthest corner of Goddess Island Gardens. Bella runs ahead of me, then doubles back and circles around me—she's making me dizzy—and we pass through the gate.

I pause at the end of the path and scrutinize the houses, most of which seem to be a single story or a story and a half with dormers, their grounds abundant with foliage. Christian said he lived in the pink house.

Did he mean the peach house with the mint-green door? Or the white one with the pink trim? I look up and down the street. There's a pinkish house down the road a piece, but didn't he say *right through the gate*? So which is it? Peach? Or pink trim?

Bella tugs on my dress. "Mommy, let's go."

I opt for door number two. It has a charming covered front porch, with a dormer situated above it and shuttered windows. There's a small tree, or maybe it's a bush, rooted near the single step up to the porch, and its leaves bear etchings—autographs, sketches of shapes. It appears that where pen or pencil—or fingernail?—scrapes the thick, sturdy leaves, the chlorophyll dissipates, leaving a yellowish tan impression.

Interesting. I wonder if all visitors who have crossed this porch have left their marks here. I take a quick inventory of the names etched onto the leaves. No Natasha, as far as I can tell.

I knock on the door. Rock music—indie pop, or alternative, at least—sounds through the door.

"Go inside," Bella says. "Hot out here."

"We will if he answers." I'm starting to think I chose the wrong house, but a millisecond before I turn around to make my escape, a girl, about eighteen, with silvery purple hair and pale-blue eyes, cracks open the door.

"Can I help you?"

"Ummm . . ."

She stares at me.

I stare back at her.

Elizabella grips my elbow.

"I think, actually, I have the wrong house. I'm sorry." I'm just about to take a step off the porch, when she says, "You're looking for my uncle Chris."

"Christian Renwick?"

"Yeah. One second." The girl with purple hair steps away.

A moment later, she appears again, this time as a blonde. I blink hard. Either the heat is getting to me, or I really am starting to lose my mind.

"Let me take that for you." She holds open the door, and I unload the casserole into her awaiting arms. "Come in. Are you joining us for dinner?"

"Oh, I don't think so. I just wanted to ask your uncle . . ." I take a step over the threshold onto brilliant white tile painted in a geometric pattern of blues and yellows. Bella hangs back. I step to the side. "Come on, Ellie-Belle."

A voice from within the house: "Do you like blocks?"

I glance to see a clone of the girl holding my casserole dish—the one with the purple hair. I do a double take. One is to my right, blonde and smiling, and one is crouching at Elizabella's level, tucking a purple tendril behind her ear, now asking if my daughter likes crayons.

"Oh, you're *twins*." I breathe a sigh of relief. I'm not losing my mind after all.

"Sorry about that," the blonde says. "Andrea still likes to freak people out."

"Well, you do look very much alike."

"Thus, the hair. It's exhausting correcting people all the time. I'm Emily."

"Veronica Cavanaugh. I live . . ." Do I live there now? I clear my throat. "I'm staying in the house through the alley."

Emily tosses her head toward the innards of the house, which is bright and airy. "C'mon in."

Bella sticks by my side, but when Andrea pulls out a bin of crayons, she inches across the room and decides to trust the girl with the purple hair.

"It's okay," I tell her. "Go ahead."

I follow Emily around a corner.

Christian is in the kitchen, feet propped up on a bright-blue table—it steals my breath for a second; Mama once painted our table that same blue—situated beneath a window, laptop open in front of him. He's staring out the window, massaging his chin—cleanly shaven today—and appears to be deep in thought.

"Hi, Uncle Chris."

"Hey, there." His feet come down from the table, and he makes a move to stand up when he sees me.

"Sorry to drop in like this," I say.

"You met my nieces." He nods at Emily as she puts my casserole on the counter and leaves to join her sister and Elizabella.

"Yeah. They gave my head a little bit of a whirl. Thought I was see-ing things for a minute there. With the hair . . ."

"They've been pulling that prank since they were in kindergarten. They're good girls, though. They're taking a gap year. You ever hear of such a thing?"

I start to nod. Lots of kids do it now.

"They take a year off, spend some time living in different places. So I thought . . . why not fly them in for the winter? Let them enjoy the weather."

"Nice."

"And with the holiday . . ."

I feel a frown coming on. Holiday? "Oh, that's right. Tomorrow's Thanksgiving."

"Thanksgiving"—he chuckles a little—"is today."

"Today?"

"Mmm-hmm."

God, I've lost track of the days since we've been here. "Wow, and here I am dropping in on you on *Thanksgiving*. I'm sorry I—"

"This island has that effect on people." His smile brightens his eyes. "Don't worry about it."

We've been here a week now. If I hadn't caught sight of that brown sedan in my rearview mirror, I wonder if we would've made it to Plum Lake. How different our lives might have been, if we hadn't found sanc-tuary here. Would we be sharing turkey with Shell and the father-in-law I've never met? Would she have allowed me to explain my side of the story, had we been standing face-to-face? Or would she have turned us away, considering she assumes I'm hiding something? Or worse, that I'm responsible for her son's disappearance.

"Hey, you're welcome to join us, if you don't have plans," Christian says. "Just me and my nieces."

"I couldn't impose."

"What's to impose? We're just having squash—can you imagine requesting *squash* for *Thanksgiving*? But that's my Emily—and whatever bakes for thirty minutes at three fifty."

I feel a blush creeping over my cheeks. I didn't make the casserole to finagle an invitation to dinner. Surely, he doesn't think so, given I didn't even know what day it was until he told me. "I . . . in return for dinner at Fogarty's, I thought I'd . . . it's just a simple casserole."

He nods. "Thank you."

"Well, you didn't have to pay our tab."

"Just seemed like you'd had a rough few days. Someone did that for me once, when I'd had a rough go, so I thought I'd pay it forward."

"Speaking of rough days . . ."

Bella's giggle silences me, as it reverberates throughout the house. I find myself smiling. Only a child can find happiness in the midst of this muddy river we're trudging through.

"You want to take a walk?" he asks. "They're good with kids, have younger sisters, a lot of experience babysitting."

"I don't know if she'll allow it, but . . ." I take another peek into the adjacent room, where Bella is playing well with my neighbor's nieces. And truthfully, I don't want to leave her.

My conversation with Shell yesterday still has me feeling raw and vulnerable. And Guidry really shook me up with all his talk about overdosing and drowning.

And then Bella's odd commentary, the things she knows . . . the man with the cigarette.

The thought of letting her out of my sight long enough for some-one to swoop in and steal her away from me . . .

"Or we could talk here," Christian suggests.

"I was just wondering . . . the cat."

"Hmm."

"You called him Papa Hemingway, but his tag says . . ." Now that I'm in the thick of this inquiry, I feel a little foolish, accusing my neighbor—a man who selflessly purchased my dinner our first night in town and flew his twin nieces out to the island during their gap year—of lying. Would a man so generous be snooping around my house and inventing reasons to be there? I'd guess not, but I've been wrong and fooled before.

"His name is James Brolin," I say.

"You notice he has six toes on his left front paw?"

"I have, but . . ." I don't see what that has to do with anything.

"He's a Hemingway cat. Cats at the Hemingway estate sometimes have six toes."

"Okay."

"Hemingway named his cats after famous people, so six-toed cats on this island . . . people honor the tradition."

"Oh."

"But I think if you're going to name a cat after a famous person, why not name the cat after the man who started the tradition? I call all six-toed cats Hemingway."

I suppose it makes sense. But something is still off.

I think of the automatic feeder in the laundry room.

The few days' worth of soiled cat litter in the art studio.

The matted fur on the cat's back.

Either Christian is the worst cat sitter of the century, or he never had reason to be in the house.

And if he wasn't really cat sitting, why was he there?

"I don't mean to accuse." I take a deep breath. "I'm just trying to figure out what happened before I got here, so if you wouldn't mind, level with me. You weren't really there to take care of the cat."

"I was actually. Every once in a while, I refill the feeder, clean up after the little guy . . . oh. I didn't get to it that day. You came, and I left before . . . I'm sorry you walked into such a mess."

"It's fine. I don't mind changing the litter. I'm not worried about *that.*"

"I'm sure you're capable, but to be honest with you, I've been busy, and I didn't expect her to be gone this long."

"Do you know the names of the boys—Tasha's boys—who were living in that house?"

He shakes his head.

"Do you know any of the neighbors who might've?"

"I'm sorry. I don't know many people here. It's a touristy city. People come and go. Some stay a week, maybe less. Lots of houses on this street are rented by different families week to week. Hard to keep up."

"But Tasha asked you to watch her cat? You don't know her children—"

"I met the little girl in the garden. Mimi-something-or-other. It was short for something. I never met any boys."

Frustration builds inside me. How is it he can't know anything about the woman who'd impose upon him to watch her cat? Indefinitely?

I pull my phone from its case, the strap of which is still looped around my wrist. "Maybe you can tell me . . ." I start swiping the screen, flipping through pictures until I land on a picture of Micah and our daughter. "Have you ever seen this guy?"

He takes the phone from me, licks his lips, and studies the screen. He glances up at me, but our eyes meet for only a moment before he redirects back to the picture. "This is your husband?"

"Yeah."

"Oh." His brow crinkles, and he's about to look me in the eye, then averts his glance back to the screen.

A funny feeling swirls in my gut, as if my stomach is an empty gum-ball machine, slowly being filled, ball by ball ricocheting around my innards. And my cheeks are flaming hot.

"I'm sorry." I take my phone back.

"Why are you sorry?"

"You know him. You've seen him. And you don't know me, but here I am making you tell me . . . considering what you've been through—with your wife, I mean. I'm here forcing you to give me the worst possible news, and—"

I shut up but can't stop shaking my head in disbelief. I open the picture of Natasha that Claudette sent. "Is this Tasha?"

He studies the picture for a second. "Looks like her."

I dab at budding tears. "I'm sorry, but I don't know what's up or down anymore."

"Yeah, I've been in touch with that emotion." Christian massages the back of his neck.

"Was he, you know . . . did he look like he was happy?"

"I don't want to speculate as to someone else's happiness. How would I know if someone—"

"No, I need to know."

"You want to know if he was acting like a father with someone else's kids."

"Yes."

Christian's nodding. "Yeah, he did. I'm sorry."

"Thank you." I breathe through fresh tears. I wish I could stop the tears from falling. Crying isn't going to change anything.

Micah's been physically gone now for fifteen days.

But I wonder when I truly lost him.

Tasha's daughter is older than Elizabella.

Was Micah ever truly mine?

"You okay?"

"Come to think of it . . . yes. It's the first definite answer I've gotten, and it helps."

"That's one way to look at it."

"It means my life in Chicago was a lie, and I may as well start fresh, and since I don't have anyplace else to go, I may as well start here. I have a house, and it needs a lot of work, and as soon as I figure out where to buy paint on this island, I'll get right on it."

He slides his hands back into his pockets. "This may be an island, but we're not savages. We have Home Depot."

I laugh and wipe away the tears I'm still holding at bay. "Obviously."

"So maybe I can help you get there, if you can help me with something."

"What's that?"

"It's Thanksgiving. I have no idea how to cook a squash."

Chapter 33

I've never had a Thanksgiving alone.

Micah and Natasha stepped in to celebrate with me the very first holiday season after my mother's passing. Some years, we ate turkey sandwiches from the Second City Deli and canned cranberry sauce. The first year we opted to toss a bird in the oven . . . the memory resurfaces now: Some football game on television, all of us in flannel pajama pants and T-shirts, and taking turns basting. Micah: *Christ, it'll be midnight before we eat.* Natasha: *Golden Dragon delivers, you know.* And so we ordered Chinese food.

Somehow, all the tumultuous holidays of the past, those I'd spent with my mother, seemed to melt into prehistory the moment Micah and I started our own traditions.

Bella laughs. I flinch a little when I look up from my plate and find her offering a spoonful of mashed squash to the purple-haired twin, oblivious to the fact that her father—of his own choosing or not—has landed her mother in an inextricable place, wedged between anger and fear and held captive with the fingers of worry and threat.

I want to walk back through the alley, hole up in Goddess Island Gardens, and have a good cry. I even feel like crying myself to sleep—complete with a face-in-pillow, limbs-flailing tantrum—a la Elizabella at her angriest.

But . . .

She's not at her angriest right now. In fact, right now, she might be the happiest she's been in weeks.

Mashed squash, barbecued chicken skewers on the grill, and of course my basic chicken casserole, recipe courtesy of Claudette Winters, litter the table. Remnants of a rock performance happening somewhere on the strip drift on the breeze, settling into our little party, lit with tiki torches and strings of pineapple lights and the last of the day's rays.

"Nini lives in my hair," Bella is saying to the twins. "But my brothers look the same. Like you guys."

My glance darts from my glass of white sangria to my daughter, who tasted the squash because Andrea said Bella could feed her like a baby if she would. Who knew such a silly bribe would work?

With a heaping spoonful ready to go down Andrea's hatch, she says, "Connor's silly, but Brendan's shy. They like airplanes, like Daddy does. Nini likes mermaids and dolphins, like me."

"I'm with you," Emily says. "Who doesn't like mermaids and dolphins?"

"Well"—in goes the squash—"Nini thinks Daddy likes dolphins, too."

"I want to go swimming with dolphins," Emily says.

"Me too," Andrea says. "Would you like to swim with dolphins, Ellie-Belle?"

Bella is nodding enthusiastically. "Nini says yes!"

Out of the corner of my eye, I catch Christian's smile. He's leaning back in his chair, swirling the sangria in his glass, obviously proud of his nieces.

And I'm impressed with the way Bella has opened up to them.

———

She's heavy in my arms, and half-asleep, but we've already stayed too long.

The sun is about to sink over the horizon, and the breeze is bordering on cool now, although even calling attention to that fact seems silly, seeing as it's probably thirty degrees back home. And it's not less than sixty here tonight.

"I'm happy to carry her down the alley for you," Christian says.

"Oh, I've got her, but thanks."

"Sure?"

"I'm used to it."

But he walks alongside us, even past the gate and onto my property, past the empty pool.

"Thanks again for tonight," I say.

"Thanks for the casserole."

"No problem." A few steps later, when the silence is near deafening, despite that band continuing to play blocks away, I say, "Nice night."

"Yeah. Pretty typical around these parts."

"Yeah." I don't know why I feel the need to fill the quiet; it's just as awkward to talk as to walk on in silence.

When we approach the house, I'm zapped into a time warp that brings me back to high school dates and all the drama involved. Is there a certain way I should be acting?

"You have my number," he says. "I'll help you get that pool up and running in no time."

"I do. And thanks . . . for the help with the pool, for everything." For rolling with the punches with my quirky three-year-old. For not asking me to explain my intermittent tears during dinner and my silence after.

"Well, if there's anything else I can do . . ."

"You know a lawyer?"

He grins and gives me a wink. "Criminal? Have you done something I don't know about?"

"No." I laugh. "Family." Although to be fair, I've been thinking of seeing a lawyer who might cover both bases.

"Yeah, I know a lawyer. I'll get you his name and number."

"Thanks."

I manage to insert the key into the back door, open it, and cross the threshold.

Christian backs his way off the rear porch and, smiling, gives me a silent wave as I close the door.

Papa Hemingway is instantly there to greet us, brushing against my legs, wrapping his serpentine tail around my calves.

And then I catch it: the hint of Dolce & Gabbana The One Sport hanging in the air.

I concentrate, inhale deeply.

The skin on my arms puckers with chill bumps.

I'm not imagining it.

Elizabella sighs in her state of near slumber and murmurs, "Daddy."

Chapter 34

I don't know why I'm afraid. If Micah's here, that's a good thing.

I wouldn't have wanted him to hear me ask about a lawyer, and I wouldn't have wanted him to see Christian walk me home.

Maybe that's why my heart is thumping like mad.

Even though my arms ache to the point of numbness, I can't fathom letting go of my daughter.

I carry Bella through the family room, past the kitchen, and into the laundry room. I turn on lights as we go, clearing each nook and cranny.

No one here, no one there.

No one hiding in the alcove beneath the stairs.

My legs tremble as I climb the stairs.

Tears burn my eyes, as the scent of my husband's favorite cologne grows stronger and stronger with every step.

I enter every bedroom, open closet doors, bathroom doors. I shove aside shower curtains and open linen cabinets, and if I could find a way to look under beds with a sleeping child in my arms, I would do that, too. I crouch as best I can and lift bed skirts. The beds in the boys' room are on pedestals with drawers beneath, but just to be sure, I yank comforters off the mattresses.

Clear, clear, clear.

I hold my breath as I enter the master bedroom, where the scent of Sport is strongest.

But I don't find him here, either.

"Micah?"

No answer.

There's not a wrinkle in the duvet. Not a single impression of a foot in the area rug.

I carefully lay Bella on the bed and curl up next to her.

Tears fall silently to my pillow.

He's not here, but I didn't know until now just how badly I wanted him to be waiting beyond the door for us. As angry as I am with him, and despite all the secrets he withheld, all the babies he's kissed while I've been shooting my system full of fertility medications, he'll always be part of me.

And he's gone.

Yet the scent of him lingers in the air.

"I miss you," I say to no one as I drift off to sleep. "You have to come home."

Love you, Nicki-girl.

"Love you, too."

Am I imagining things? Wanting him so badly to show up that I'm conjuring him out of thin air?

But he seems so real, almost tangible, as if I could reach out and touch him in the empty spaces around me.

Logically, I know it isn't possible, but he's here with me, as if he's part of my aura, part of every inhalation, part of every breath of breeze off the Atlantic, where the plane went down.

The plane he wasn't flying.

The plane in which his body wasn't found.

I used to smell Mama in the air, too.

After she died.

Chapter 35

December 4

Here on this island, days pass, one into the next, in a slow, steady, eighty-some degrees. More hours of daylight means more fruitful hours for a woman with too many items on her to-do list, and tackling that list helps me take my mind off Micah's secrets, which are slowly revealing themselves.

It feels like a violation of someone else's privacy—Natasha's—but I comb through every detail of every item I pack, on the off chance it will tell me something about her life these days . . . and in turn, something about my husband.

Sometimes, I'll come across some trinket, and it'll leave me tumbling back in time to the days Natasha and I were inseparable. Rollerblades remind me of skating down Lake Shore Drive, eating street-vendor hot dogs while rolling our way along the path. She always asked for ketchup, although everyone knows a true Chicago dog doesn't come with ketchup.

You're saying the rest of the city is wrong, I said.

Wrong about ketchup? Yes!

I've tried again and again to reach her through social media, but she hasn't even opened the messages I've sent. I wish she'd left her number with Claudette. If only I could reach her, I might know more about what happened to Micah.

Where is he?

Why did he go?

In the early mornings, when I'm still asleep, I sometimes feel him with me. But then the warmth subsides into resentment.

He must know the suspicion he's putting on me by staying away.

He must not have loved me the way I loved him.

Sometimes, when I allow that realization to swallow me, when I'm feeling sorry for myself, I sit at the potter's wheel, failing pot after pot, and stare out the window long enough to imagine the Florida blooms withering, the landscape turning gray and misty, the sky clouding over in a permanent winter. When I blink away the glaze in my eyes, however, everything is vibrant and purple and pink and yellow again, and I forge ahead.

Boxes filled with another woman's belongings find their way to the garage, seemingly of their own volition. I pack a few, carry a few out, and the next I know, half the garage is filled, and hours have passed, and Elizabella is happily riding her new tricycle—sometimes chasing Nini, sometimes with Nini in pursuit—around the roundabout drive. She smells of sunscreen and ocean air, always, and she seems to sleep better at night. Since our arrival, I haven't discovered her in the midst of a tea party at three in the morning, and it isn't because I've removed toys from her room—*Thank you, Dr. Russo*—but because this place agrees with her, and she with it.

From my seated position on the front porch steps, with a glass of iced tea sweating on the planks beside me, I watch her ride around and around. I'm suddenly aware that despite all the motion of the past few weeks, we're standing still, in a sense.

Is Micah out there somewhere? When the police locate him, will I be preparing divorce papers or planning a funeral? Both options are equally abhorrent. I'm perpetually on a pendulum, and we can't keep swinging back and forth like this. At some point, we have to move on. We have to live normal lives.

The lawyer Christian referred me to suggested I file for divorce. It's better to distance myself if he's involved in something illegal. Without a definitive answer as to what happened to Micah, the insurance company isn't going to pay out even the small policy we purchased shortly after we married. Without a divorce decree, I can't collect child support, should Micah resurface one day.

I would've been better off had he divorced me. The legal system could have protected me through the process. But because he disappeared, I'm out of luck. The authorities can't make a man support his child, if they can't find the man.

The saving grace is that I own this house. I found the closing documents in a drawer in the kitchen. Along with the power of attorney I signed over to my husband, there's a refusal of homestead rights form. Micah signed it at the closing, so he has no legal claim to this property. The lawyer said this house should be free and clear of any of Micah's debts. Translation: it's *mine*, and Micah thought to protect it the moment we purchased it.

I can make things work here if I can find a job. I haven't worked in almost five years, and it took a while to get a permanent position out of college, so I have a whopping three years of experience on my résumé. Plus, the island is less than seven and a half square miles. Employment opportunities have to be limited.

But the funds from the safe-deposit box are dwindling with every trip to Home Depot, and debts in Chicago are accruing. I have to find something.

"Nini, faster!" Elizabella should be in preschool. She should be socializing with real children, not with made-up ones who live in her head.

I snap a picture on my phone to commemorate this moment. She's happy.

Normally, I'd forward the picture to Micah and maybe his mother, but under the circumstances . . .

Shell thinks I'm responsible for Micah's disappearance. I've stopped trying to connect with her. She'll come to her senses when she stops blaming me. I can't send her a casual text until then.

Well, why not?

Maybe an incoming text will jump-start some activity on Micah's phone. Knowing he won't answer hasn't stopped me from calling every day just in case.

I forward the picture of Bella to both of them on the same thread.

The moment I send it, however, I realize it might look bad. Guidry all but accused me of being in touch with my husband—he thinks I know where Micah is, that I'm going to meet up with him in Italy, Switzerland, or wherever else he was searching *with my log in* for houses.

I dial Guidry's cell phone.

"Mrs. Cavanaugh," he says. "Good afternoon."

"Hello, Detective." I wait for him to accuse me of something, but when no accusations come, I continue with my reasons for calling. "Do you have any news?"

"I'm following up on the boys' names you offered up last week. There is no record of any children with the last name of Cavanaugh or Markham in the Key West school system."

I'd told him about Bella including Connor and Brendan in her games, as well as my theory that she met a little girl named Mimi and is mispronouncing it as Nini. The longer things carry on without Guidry finding answers, though, the more I'm certain he's going to accuse me of sending him on a wild goose chase.

"I'm searching birth records here," he continues. "And in Florida. It took some time, but I may have hit on something."

"Good. You'll let me know?"

"I'm e-mailing Key West PD. Officer Laughlin should be by some-time this afternoon to show you what I've got."

"Okay."

"The other searches are proving more difficult. We've followed up with real estate agents in Europe, but there are no records of a Micah Cavanaugh inquiring about properties. Still no word on any uniden-tified John Does in the tri-state area, and I'm still waiting for more details about whether he applied for employment in Europe. But as far as whether anyone has confirmed sightings of your husband since he left . . ."

I'm holding my breath, hoping against all that's holy that someone has seen him.

"We have none."

I release the breath. "I want you to know I texted a picture of Bella to Micah's phone and to his mother's. I thought if either replies . . . you know, maybe it'll tell us something."

"Let me know what happens."

"I will. But if Micah's choosing to be gone, he has a good reason, and Shell won't take my calls."

After a pause, Guidry clears his throat. "You wouldn't, by any chance, want to tell me what business you had at a lawyer's office, would you?"

Every time he hits me sidelong with something like this, it makes my head spin.

"I told you I'd have eyes on you," he says.

"I saw a lawyer, yes."

"You're looking to get your ducks in a row." The words alone aren't terribly accusatory, but based on his tone, he may as well have said *you're covering your ass, aren't you?*

"Is there any question in your mind," I say, "that whatever hap-pened to Micah, he's put me in a difficult position? That whatever Micah is doing *now*, it's pretty apparent that what he was doing *before* is unacceptable? I have to protect myself. Whether he's setting me up or whether he's left me for another woman. Technically, I don't even have a home to go home to because my father-in-law owns it. No matter what comes to pass, I have to protect my daughter."

"That's valid," he says. "I finally got a track on that phone call you got . . . the caller who told you to listen to your daughter?"

"Yeah?"

"Turns out"—he coughs a dry cough—"the number has a Key West area code . . . and it's registered to you."

"What?"

"The number is—"

"No, no, I heard you. But how is that possible?"

"Did you know you can sync a phone line with a computer and generate calls even if you're not holding the phone in your hand? You could've made that call to yourself."

I feel a sickening drop in my gut.

A dramatic pause precedes "How are things at *God Land*?" There's a sarcastic lilt and an emphasis on the name of the house, which tells me he isn't merely wondering how things are going.

Great. I wonder if I forgot to tell him the house I didn't know I owned ended up bearing the name of the place my daughter insisted her father had gone. If he's had eyes on me, I'm sure the detail has found its way back to him by now. No wonder he thinks I'm hiding something. My truth is stranger than fiction.

"I'm hanging in there."

And I realize it's true. Elizabella ventures farther down the driveway, calling to Nini to hurry up. She's still in my sight, not anywhere near the road, but she's inching farther from the house. I stand to follow her.

"When are you planning to come back, Veronica? Maybe we could discuss this in person. Or are you making a clean break from the life you led here?"

Who could blame me if I was?

"Considering Mick owns the place in the Shadowlands, and you already had a second phone, with the Key West area code, established in your name—"

"*I* didn't establish anything. Do you think I would call myself, knowing you could trace the call's origin even if I'd blocked the number, then report it? Why would I do such a thing?"

"To convince me you were scared? To give yourself good reason to leave town? Who knows."

"You think I'd go through all the trouble of—"

"The call originated through a cell tower immediately to the south of the Shadowlands. The mobile number is registered to your name. What am I supposed to think when you skip town *after I asked you to stay?*"

"I'm not avoiding you." I'm pacing on the driveway now. "I'm making the best of a shitty situation, but of course I'll come back. I have to at least clean out my closets, don't I, before my father-in-law sells the house? Or is the bank entitled to take my socks, too, when they assume ownership? I'm sure you've been through the place top to bottom by now. If I were hiding anything, you'd know."

He's silent.

"Did you find my Xanax?"

"No."

"So he must have taken it with him."

"*One* of you took it, if you insist it was there. Have you received any more calls from the blocked number?"

"No."

"I'll let you know if we come up with anything," Guidry says. "In the meantime, if you think of anything else you maybe forgot to tell me . . ."

I look up again, to catch sight of my daughter, but all I see is her tricycle, overturned, wheels spinning, abandoned on the driveway.

I drop the phone.

Chapter 36

She was right here.

Where could she have disappeared to in the blink of an eye?

Her weeks-old commentary revisits me now: *I'm gonna go be with Daddy.*

"Elizabella!"

This happened at Centennial Park, too. Right before my world imploded, I lost sight of her.

"She's okay," I say to myself, but I'm not convinced. "She's okay. She's okay." She *has* to be.

If I don't see her in a second or two, I'll call the police. She's on an island. She can't go far.

But could someone leave with her? By boat maybe?

"Bella!" My throat is raw from screaming, and my vocal chords vibrate. "Bella!"

I hear her in the distance: "Daddy, Daddy, Daddy!"

The modicum of relief at hearing her voice quickly trips back into panic when I realize that if he's here, he may want our daughter more than he wants to be back in my life. At the bend in the drive, halfway between my front door and Elizabeth Street, beneath the archway, I spin in every direction, praying for a glimpse of her high ponytail, her pink-and-white sundress. "Bella!"

"Not Daddy, not Daddy!"

Oh no. Who has my baby?

"Elizabella!"

A moment later, her shrieking giggle rings in my ears. "Again, again!"

"Bella!" I scream.

"We've got her."

I turn toward the voice behind me and see Christian Renwick approaching up the sidewalk near the road. Several paces behind are his nieces, Emily and Andrea, each holding one of Bella's hands, playing one of her favorite games: "One, two, three, *fly*!"

I brush past him and run to my daughter, who rebounds into my arms after landing. "Mommy!"

"Bella, you can't run away like that! You can't just—"

She shrieks again and plants a sloppy kiss on my cheek. "Saw Daddy," she whispers.

I brush her hair from her cheeks to look her in the eye. "What did you say?"

"I . . . saw . . . Daddy."

"What? Where, Bella? Tell Mommy."

"I think she may have mistaken me for . . ." Christian's words trail off when I meet his gaze. "She came running after us, yelling for her father."

I close my eyes to get my bearings and take a few deep breaths to calm the beating of my rampant heart. I try to picture Micah, but for the first time since I met him at Lollapalooza when I was twenty years old, I can't remember his face, can't remember his eyes, his lips. The only face that enters my mind is one I just saw: Christian's.

Could Bella have mistaken him for her father?

They're roughly the same height, same build, and now that Christian seems to be shaving his face on a regular basis, maybe a three-year-old could draw some parallels.

I try again, will myself to picture Micah's face. Just as it comes to me, it's gone.

How is it possible that I could be forgetting all the details that make him Micah? And so soon? Think, Veronica. Think about him. Make him stay.

Stay with me . . . stay some more . . .

I hear his version of "Sway," nearly feel his offbeat cha-cha.

I have to remember him for our daughter.

After another deep breath, I get to my feet with Bella still in my arms.

"Down," she says.

Reluctantly, because all I want to do is hold her close, I put her down.

"Looks like you could use a drink," Christian says.

I probably could use more than one.

"I'm heading out to the Rum Barrel tonight," he continues. "Pretty good band playing. Want to join?"

"Oh. Thanks, but I've got Bella, so . . ."

"I've got nieces," he counters.

"We don't mind taking her for a while," Emily says.

Bella swings between the twins again, and for a few seconds, I fixate on the sight of it. One, two, three . . . fly. Like double-dutch jump rope, it's definitely a game you need partners to play. And I no longer have a partner. It's just Bella and me.

"Your daughter seems to like the girls," Christian says.

"Listen, I appreciate the invitation, but I have so much to catch up on . . ." Starting with a phone call to Guidry. I just hung up on him at the height of his accusations. I can't imagine *that's* going to go over too well.

"Anytime you want to tackle that pool, you let me know."

"Yeah, all right. Thanks. Maybe next week?"

A smile slowly spreads onto his face. "Yeah."

"I hate to take you away from your writing."

"Writing?" Emily giggles.

He gives his niece the hush sign, an index finger pressed to his lips. "Em's right, actually. I haven't been too productive lately. Maybe you can help me with that."

I hear my phone ringing. "Rock-a-bye baby . . ." A quick spin in place, however, doesn't reveal its location. Where was I when I dropped it?

"Here you go." Christian's located my phone a few paces away. By the time he retrieves it, it isn't ringing anymore, but I know from the ringtone: it was a call from the fertility center.

He locks me in a staring contest that probably lasts only a few seconds but feels like an era and a half. He probably saw the name on the caller ID. Great. That's all I need for him to know that my life is even more complicated than he originally thought.

In the periphery: "One, two, three . . . fly!"

"Come on, Veronica. How long have you been doing this? All on your own? Christ, have you even slept through the night since the accident?"

I still haven't filled him in. I haven't told him there were no federal agents, that Micah might be alive. I shake my head. "I couldn't possibly . . ."

"I'm giving you permission. Let yourself off the hook for an evening. Just . . . tell me you'll think about coming out tonight," Christian says.

"Okay." I close my fingers around my phone when he slides it into my hand. "I'll think about it."

He gives me a nod. "Good. You know where it is?"

"Front Street, right?"

"Don't look now, Veronica, but you're almost a local."

I crack a smile and turn to walk back up the drive. "Come on, Bella. Let's get some food in that tummy."

"Chocolate pudding?"

"Sure." I glance up at the archway through which we're about to pass.

GOD LAND GARDENS

I look over my shoulder at Christian. "You wouldn't happen to have a ladder?"

"Sure do."

I'm going to take the letters down off the arch.

I don't want to be at God Land anymore.

Chapter 37

"He was in the trees," Elizabella says. "He called my name."

"Are you sure?" I open my wedding album and prop it up on the kitchen countertop. Micah's smile zaps me in all the places that have gone dormant since he left.

The trust I had in him, the devotion and dedication we shared . . . If I went back in time to do it all again, I wouldn't change a thing. Everything we endured resulted in our daughter, but if I knew it would all turn out like this, would I have walked down that sandy path to the shore of Lake Michigan, where he awaited me with a wedding ring? Would I have agreed to love him, had I known I'd have less than a decade of forever?

"Yes, Mommy. I saw Daddy, and he gave me a hug. He kissed my nose."

"Well, that's a nice treat, then."

"I miss my daddy."

"Me too. But now is snack time." With Elizabella seated at the table with a pile of scrap paper and a box of crayons, I dole out pudding cups.

"For Nini, too?"

"Yes." I put out an extra. One for my daughter and one for the apparition.

I wonder if Dr. Russo was right. Maybe the imaginary friend bit is a sign of Bella's creativity. If Mimi is a real little girl, as Christian Renwick seems to think, and if Bella met her here in Key West, she's placing characters she knows—including her father—into situations in her head. And if Guidry can learn more about Connor and Brendan—if they're the twins in the photos—it would be one less thing to worry about: maybe she isn't talking with alternate personalities or demons in her head . . .

"Mommy has to make a phone call."

"Call Daddy!"

My heart sinks a little. I've been calling him every day, just to hear his voice on his voice mail. The phone doesn't ring; it goes straight to his recorded message. "He won't answer, baby." I dial the fertility lab instead.

"River North Fertility Center."

"Veronica Cavanaugh, returning your call." I put out spoons for Bella and Nini. As the call is transferred, I take a seat at a counter stool.

"Mrs. Cavanaugh, I was calling because the credit card on file for the storage fees won't go through."

Of course it won't. "What is the storage fee?"

"We're storing two embryos in cryogenically—"

"I know what it's for. I mean, how much?"

"For the *embryos*, your husband opted to pay month to month, which is a little more expensive, but then you can implant at any time and you aren't paying for the entire year if you don't need storage."

"Okay."

"The embryos were batched together, so it's one hundred fifty a month for the two. If you wanted to pay annually, that's fifteen hundred. As for the sperm—"

"Wait. I'm still unclear as to why we're freezing sperm. I'm not sure that's necessary." Although . . . now that he may be gone, this stuff could be the last specimen of Micah Cavanaugh Jr. ever procured.

Brandi Reeds

"Your husband elected to do so, Mrs. Cavanaugh."

"I'm sure he did." And I guess it makes sense. If he had to be on a flight—what flight? On what plane?—when it was time to batch, we would've needed his sperm to fertilize. "Okay, how much to keep the sperm frozen, too?"

"Same. One fifty per month or fifteen hundred per year. Your husband has been paying annually for that, but the payment just came due."

Do I need the sperm if I have two embryos?

If the embryos fail, there's a chance I can batch another round of eggs, and if Micah isn't here for the fertilization, I'll need the sperm on hand. I stop midthought. For years now, my focus has been on propagation, increasing our numbers.

But . . . why continue?

I'm tempted to tell her to thaw and destroy everything.

But one glance at Bella silences the logical forces in my brain. Loving a child isn't rational, and those embryos could be my children. And I want a big family, for my sake, for Bella's. Lowering my mother into the ground with no one by my side but the paramedic and cop who'd come to answer the call had been devastating. I want better for my daughter.

"The trouble is, if the card isn't working . . . I'm out of town. I can mail a money order. Can it wait a few days?"

"The amount is already three weeks past due, and we have only a sixty-day grace period before it's out of our hands. We've been attempting to reach your husband, but—"

"I'm sorry the credit card failed, and I'm sorry my husband hasn't been in touch with you, but he hasn't been in touch with anyone in nearly a month. He's missing, presumed dead."

"Oh. I hadn't . . . I didn't . . . I'm sorry."

"I'm sure everyone at your center feels sort of like God, giving couples the impossible gift of children, but you *work* because of *people like me*. Your policy gives me sixty days grace. I still have some time. I just told you I'd pay the amount due if you'd only tell me what I owe!"

I hear the clicking of keys. "Three weeks late is three hundred dollars for the embryos and three hundred dollars for the specimen. But if you pay any later than tomorrow, you'll have an additional two hundred dollars in fees. If you prefer to pay cash, I have to charge you annually. Fifteen hundred each. That's three thousand for both the embryos and specimen."

"Plus late fees," I confirm. "Thirty-six hundred?"

"If you pay by tomorrow."

"And then I'm good for a year?"

"Yes, ma'am."

"I'll be in touch."

"Might I transfer you to reception so you can make your next appointment?"

I hang up.

"I know, Nini," Bella's saying. "Mommy's mad."

"I was mad at *them*, Ellie-Belle," I say. "Because they were being mean."

"Nini says you can't help it. People are just mean sometimes."

"Nini is very smart."

The "Rock-a-bye Baby" ringtone echoes throughout the kitchen. I'm sure it's the reception staff at River North Fertility Center, attempting to book another appointment.

Although I can't think about it right now, I answer the call.

"Mrs. Cavanaugh, I'm sorry for the confusion. It appears the storage fees for Mr. Cavanaugh's specimen are up to date. The charge came through after my system updated. I apologize. Storage is still due for the embryos."

"How is *that* possible?"

"The charge just now came through."

"I heard you. But . . . how?"

"You must have updated the credit card or—"

"No, I didn't. Which card is it on?"

I hear the clicking of computer keys in the background. "I'm sorry, Mrs. Cavanaugh. Your name isn't on the financial clearance form for this particular specimen. I can't disclose."

I hang up even more frustrated—is anything easy in the world of infertility?—but then I think. I didn't pay the fee. There's only one other person who might've. I dial Guidry. "Hi, it's Veronica. Can you follow up on something with our fertility clinic? Find out who paid the storage fees for Micah's specimen. Maybe you'll find my husband at the end of that trail."

Chapter 38

I dragged a child-size table and chairs—two, of course; Nini needs one, too—from "Nini's bedroom" to the driveway. Bella colors there, while I balance too many feet off the ground on Christian's ladder and pry the remaining letters off the archway. I'm going to paint the arch, too. The top trim pieces will stay white, but the rest of it I'll coat in the same pale yellow as the house.

"I know, Nini." Bella chatters incessantly to her invisible friend. "But that's what Daddy said."

I stop what I'm doing and listen harder.

"I *told* you," she continues. "When he came to see me. He said we *could* swim with the dolphins." She reaches for another crayon. "But I love my daddy."

Despite the mid-eighties temperature, a chill pricks the back of my neck. Slowly, carefully, so as not to disrupt my daughter's chattering, I climb down from the ladder and inch closer.

"He says it's a house even *bigger* and *prettier* than this one. And I could get a new dollhouse."

"Bella?"

She startles when she hears me.

"When did Daddy say that?"

"Oh." She brushes a stray coil of hair from her forehead. "He said it when he kissed me bye-bye."

"When did he say that?"

"I *told* you, Mommy. I . . . saw . . . Daddy."

"That was Mr. Renwick. With Emily and Andrea? When you were riding your bike?"

"Yes, Mommy." She's exasperated with having to explain it to me again.

"And he gave you a kiss goodbye?"

"In my head."

"*In* your head? Or *on top* of your head?"

"On my nose."

"On your nose."

"Yes, Mommy."

"Are you sure?"

"Nini and I are coloring." She doesn't want to talk about it anymore.

"Bella, this is very important. You said Daddy came to God Land. *This* is God Land. *We* are at God Land."

"Daddy's not here anymore, Mommy."

"You just said you saw him. So he's like Nini?"

"Yes. Like Nini. Except Nini is in my hair."

"Excuse me?"

I turn around to see Officer Laughlin standing next to his parked bike, under the archway.

"Veronica Cavanaugh? Officer Laughlin, Key West Police—"

"Yes, I remember."

"Lake County asked me to drop by to get your read on something." He hands me a few pages of printed material.

I glance down at the fruit of Guidry's investigative efforts.

But quickly, after I register only a few words here and there and focus on the MICAH JAMES CAVANAUGH JR. in the one place I'd hoped it wouldn't be, I return my gaze to Laughlin's. "Does this mean . . ."

I glance down at the dates on the paper.

He doesn't have to answer.

I don't even have to ask the question.

Chapter 39

I'm sitting at the potter's wheel, my fingers coated in wet clay, watching earthenware spin.

There's no denying it now, no way to explain it as a misunderstanding or misinterpretation: the boys in the pictures I've packed away are my husband's sons. Born eight weeks before Elizabella, in Wisconsin, not far from C-Way airport, where Micah's car turned up.

I think I remember Micah taking a longer trip in my third trimester. Perhaps he went to be with the boys' mother—someone named Gabrielle—for the birth.

What if he intended to leave me for her when she turned up pregnant with his babies? What if very quickly after he learned of her pregnancy, I was expecting, too?

I wonder how Natasha Markham fits into this mess.

I scrape this crock off the potter's wheel and place it with the others on the shelf. I look to the kiln. So far, I've been hesitant to use it. But what do I have to lose? I open its heavy door, which is on the top, like a lid.

I place two vases, ones that have dried, into the cavern and close the lid. I pull the lever to lock it and turn up the temperature to cone four—it's the setting the guy on YouTube used—set the timer for four hours, and turn the machine on.

I migrate to the kitchen and check on Bella, who is napping on the sofa in the next room.

All is quiet.

It feels as if the walls are closing in on me, as if I'm suffocating here. It's ridiculous. The place is large and airy.

But this place is also a reminder of Micah's infidelity.

Starting tomorrow, I'm making drastic changes. And I'm starting with paint. Instant gratification, instant visual improvement.

Mama used to say that.

I remember the day she dipped a paintbrush into a can of cobalt blue. She'd mixed the paint with plaster dust to give it a chalky, matte finish, and in no time at all, our table looked brand-new. I can do that sort of thing here, and my life will be brand-new, too.

If Micah were to materialize before me right now, would I throw my arms around him? Or would I take Claudette's advice, slap him good across the cheek, and make him pay?

I reach for my phone and dial Claudette.

She answers instantly. "Honey, I've been so worried. What's going on?"

"I can't begin to tell you." I spy the bottle of rum Christian dropped off to welcome us to the island that first night. Dare I have a drink? I fill her in on the computer searches, on Guidry's theory about the Xanax. I tell her the men that came to tell me Micah was dead weren't really federal agents.

"So . . . he might be somewhere out there?" she asks. "No wonder that cop looked at me funny when I told him about the night we found out Micah was dead."

"If he's out there, he's in way over his head."

"You know, I told the detective this . . . that taller one came back after you left. He was poking around, looking in the windows. And I started thinking that maybe I'd seen him around the neighborhood before. Before the whole thing began."

I think of the cigarette on the eleventh fairway. I wonder how long they've been watching me. And why.

"There's more. Suffice it to say you were right about Misty Morningside, and now they say I have motive."

"I knew it! I knew she wasn't here for *you* that day. I could see it in her eyes. She wasn't mourning for your loss. She was mourning her own."

"You might be right, but that's not the only woman I'm talking about." I give her a quick rundown about the boys' birth certificates. "Their names are Connor James and Brendan Micah. Their mother—not the redhead on my doorstep—is *Gabrielle*."

"I *knew* it!"

"Their father? Micah. James. Cavanaugh."

"I'm assuming not Senior."

"You got it."

"In the middle of the night, I'd wake up for a glass of water, and there he'd be: your husband, walking the streets, chatting on that damn mobile phone. But I never *dreamed* he'd be stupid enough not to prevent *other children*."

I pinch my eyes closed. "Yes, he kept a lot of secrets."

"Do you think that's why he's gone? Because of these other kids?"

"Maybe. But who are these men, then? The ones who told me he was dead?"

"Maybe they're his friends. Maybe he was trying to leave without owning up to anything. Maybe he figured if the world thought he was dead, he could start over."

My phone blips with an incoming text.

It's from Shell: You have Bella?

Of course I have Bella. Where else would Bella be?

Unless . . .

I sent the picture of my daughter to both Shell and her son. Could she have assumed she was replying to Micah?

Chapter 40

It's a possibility, Guidry says.

When you're struggling with infertility, these words give you hope . . . sometimes an undeserved sense of optimism. But now that I'm struggling with a search for the truth, these words instill only an unnerving sense of frustration.

It's a possibility that Shell has been in touch with her son. It's possible Shell assumed Micah sent the picture of Bella.

Until the detective manages to talk with her again, and until he secures her phone records, there's no way to know for certain.

It's a possibility Micah is looking to connect with our daughter, but unlikely he's looking to flee with her. If that's what he wanted, Guidry rationalizes, wouldn't he have taken her with him when he left?

It's possible Micah wants to be presumed dead.

It's possible he's dead already.

It's also just as possible, in Detective Guidry's opinion, that I know where my husband has been the past twenty-three days since he last kissed me goodbye. I've lost track of time, which isn't hard to do in Key West. Guidry hasn't found anything connecting a seven-year-old child named Mimi, or Nini, to my husband, and there's no telling who Tasha is, if not Natasha Markham. But he did say he'd been in touch with my college roommate on a lead he wouldn't share with me, and he said he'd give her my cell phone number and ask her if she would please call me.

I twist my wedding band, but it's still too tight, although I've lost about five of the pounds I packed on since we began IVF. A yank and a tug later, all I have to show for my efforts is a sore finger. I let out a growl.

"Mommy!" Bella giggles. "Silly Mommy."

What a terrible few weeks.

I can't take it anymore.

"Bella? It's time to take a bath."

"No. We're *coloring*, Mommy."

"You've been coloring and getting dirty all day. It's time to take a bath."

"I know, Nini," Bella says. "Mommy's always mad." Her tongue appears at the corner of her mouth as she scribbles a black mass over her drawing. "Me too, Nini. I wish *Mommy* left and *Daddy* stayed."

"What did you just say?"

"Daddy loves us," my daughter sasses. "Not like *you*."

"Elizabella, Mommy loves you more than anything. You know that."

"Daddy's better at hugs, better at games, better at coloring, and better than *you*! I wish *he* stayed and *you* left!"

"You don't mean that." It comes out more as a wheeze than a sentence.

"Yes! I! Do! I hate you!"

I lunge at her, rage bubbling inside me so wildly that I feel it vibrating in my joints.

Bella flinches, a look of disbelief and fear in her eyes.

I tear her from the table, kicking and screaming.

"Want Daddy! Want Daddy! Want Daddy!"

I charge up the stairs and all the way down the hallway, through her room, and to the shared bathroom. I plant her on the closed lid of the toilet and turn to fill the tub.

She's shrieking now, as if in great pain.

"Ellie-Belle, calm down!"

"No! No calming down! Want! My! Daddy!"

"You know what?" I'm screaming now, too. "I want your daddy, too. Just once, I want *him* to handle you at your worst. I want *him* to spend more than three hours alone with you to see how *he* might measure up in your head when he starts to lose his patience. If I left him to deal with even half the shit he's piled up around me, he'd be long gone! He couldn't handle this! He couldn't handle *you*!"

I bite my lip and wipe tears from my eyes as I turn to look at my daughter, who is shaking and white.

And I'm responsible.

Instantly, I try to pull myself together, but the sight of her little body huddled atop the toilet only drives me to unravel even further. Tears sprout from my eyes like April showers, and I'm sobbing, a rumpled mass of bad mother on the cold mosaic tile floor.

"Bella, I'm sorry."

She flinches when I reach for her.

I sniffle over tears. She's just being a little girl. I'm supposed to be the adult. I'm supposed to take a deep breath. I'm supposed to count to ten before I erupt. I'm supposed to place blame where it belongs. I'm supposed to remember she's a sweet and precious gift, even when she's sassy and unmanageable, and I'm supposed to rise above it and teach her with a better example.

I remember when Mama was always a sniveling, screaming mess, when I was her verbal punching bag.

I'm losing my mind.

The water from the faucet is thundering in the tub, bringing me back to the here and now.

"Bella, I'm sorry." I lay down on my back in the middle of the bathroom floor, hands covering my eyes. Deep breaths.

"Bad Mommy."

"Yes, you're right," I tell her. "Lately, I haven't been very good. But you have to listen, too, and lately, you haven't been very good at that, either."

She's cuddled at my side now. "Sorry I didn't listen."

My arms curl around her tiny frame. "I love you, baby girl."

"I love you, too, Mommy."

Christian was right.

I'm not doing myself—or my child—any favors by staying cooped up in this house all day and night. I have to get a job. Elizabella has to start back at school. We have to move on.

"I'll get in the tub now," Elizabella says.

"Thank you. And when you're squeaky clean, let's go see if Emily and Andrea can come sit with you."

For a second, she's silent. Then she offers: "And do one-two-three-fly?"

I nod. "If they don't mind."

She presses a sloppy kiss to my hot cheek.

"I love you," I say one more time.

Chapter 41

Christian said he'd be at the Rum Barrel, but after a quick pass through the first floor, which boasts a plethora of Philadelphia Phillies memorabilia, and a quick scan of the second, I don't see him.

The upstairs section of the Rum Barrel is somewhat enclosed, but farther from the staircase stands an open-air veranda, where a band plays. The sign out front referred to the music as cantina hits; funny, it sounds more like a Billy Joel cover band than a group of Marley wannabes, despite the maracas and steel drums.

A sense of homesickness rushes through me. I practically ache for Old Town, for the street festivals in midsummer—Micah's favorite time of year. I gravitate toward the sound of the music, as if I'll be miraculously passing through to Chicago—and turning back the hands of time—by the time I reach the platform.

An empty table occupies an inconspicuous place near the speakers in the corner, so I take it. Out of the way. Near enough to the amplifiers that no one would dream of speaking to me—or at least expect me to answer any questions.

No one would dream of approaching me.

Micah would, a voice in my head chirps.

It's true. He would've. He *had*, as a matter of fact. It's how Natasha and I met him. In Grant Park. At Lollapalooza. Amid screaming guitars and Nine Inch Nails.

I'm sorry, ladies. I can't hear a word you're saying.

We didn't say anything.

I'm sorry. I can't hear a word you're saying.

My thumb instantly searches for my wedding band.

Still there.

I bite my lip in frustration. Why couldn't I have continued to live in oblivious happiness?

"Welcome to the Rum Barrel." The server shouts so I can hear him. "Will anyone be joining you?"

I shake my head. I fear, if I try to be heard, I'm bound to lose my voice.

The waiter lifts the laminated drink menu a few inches off the table, only to put it back down. "May I interest you in one of our drink specials?"

The band plays the last few notes of a song with flourish, and the vocalist croons "Tah-dahhhh!" as if he were more magician than musician.

I'm grateful not to scream. "Mojito." After a pause, I add, "Please."

Behind me: "Nice choice." Christian.

He places a half-gone pint glass on my table. "Mind if I . . . ?" He's already pulling out one of the aluminum stools at the table and helping himself to a seat.

"Anything for you, sir?"

My neighbor looks to the waiter. "I'll have another Frogman."

I raise an eyebrow at the name of the beer. "Sounds appetizing."

"Try it." He gives the glass a little shove in my direction.

I sip. It's okay. Flavorful. Too bold for a girl whose occasional, if not rare, beers consisted of Miller Lite big mouths at Comiskey Park. "I'll stick with the mojito."

"Anything to eat?"

"Fritters," I say without thinking. Every establishment on the island offers conch fritters, and thus far, I like the ones from Sloppy Joe's best. I ordered their carry-out once last week.

"Look at you," Christian says as the server retreats. "Ordering before you even look at the menu. It's almost like you live here."

"Hardly." I narrow my gaze at him. "I'm still learning my way around."

"Well, kudos to you. You're blending in. Even sporting a bit of a tan, thank God. I swear, your skin probably glowed in the dark the day you got here."

The drummer starts tapping out a beat.

"So. Veronica. Did you come to see your favorite neighbor? Or is this a happy coincidence?"

"If I didn't know you had books to write and waves to surf in the morning, I might guess *you* followed *me*."

"Your daughter is with my nieces, I presume."

"Yes. They're godsends, those girls. Bella threw a tantrum tonight."

"Kids'll do that."

"She actually told me she'd rather *I* were gone instead of her father."

I don't tell him the real reason I'm here, don't tell him about the birth certificates.

I don't tell him about Gabrielle, about Natasha.

I don't tell him Micah might not be dead, that he might be with another woman.

I'll bet Micah and Gabrielle used to come here together. Or Micah and Natasha. Or when—if?—he stopped seeing Natasha in order to start seeing Gabrielle.

Had I known then what I know now, I may have years ago stalked places they'd been together, if only to catch them in the act. So I'm doing it now, too many years too late, but it still feels necessary. Call it closure. Or psychotic obsession.

I drain the mojito more than halfway in not more than a few sips, and I don't care that it's going to go straight to my head. I don't care that I'll pay for it tomorrow or that doing so with a three-year-old will be hell on earth.

"Do your nieces nanny during the day?" I stab at the mint leaves in my glass with my straw.

"You feel like getting a little insane tonight." He takes another sip of beer, leaving a mustache of foam on his upper lip for the breath it takes to lick it away. "I'd offer to help with your daughter, but she still takes a while to warm up to me."

"Don't take it personally. She prefers the voices in her head to real people."

"Nini."

"Yes. Nini."

The server appears out of nowhere. "Another drink, ma'am?"

Christian regards me for a second before suggesting, "Why don't you just bring us a pitcher?"

"A pitcher?"

"Shitty day," he says. "Let's get wrecked."

"I don't mean voices, like *voices*," I say. "She isn't crazy or anything. Nini is an imaginary friend. Perfectly normal."

"I know imaginary friends."

Of course he does.

"Have a few myself." He thumbs over his shoulder. "Meet Tweedledee and Tweedledum."

I study him for a minute. "Can I ask you something?"

"It's intensely personal, I hope."

"Sort of, I suppose." I wait a beat or two. "My daughter. She's been saying things that aren't quite on par with things an imaginary friend would tell her. I mean, blaming the spill at Fogarty's on Nini, fine—"

"She actually blamed that on *you*."

"Whatever. You see what I'm getting at. Blaming Nini for things that get her into trouble . . . I understand that. But she *knows* things. The day before everything happened with my husband, she told her preschool teachers that her father went to God Land. And then, I show up here, at a house, which to be honest I didn't even know I owned until after he was gone, and there are letters missing on the archway, so the place is labeled God Land. And she keeps saying she's seen him. Even after I tell her that she saw *you*, not her father, she insists."

He's staring intently into my eyes.

"I guess what I want to know is . . . do you believe in ghosts? Clairvoyance? Because I don't know how else to explain the things my daughter knows."

A tiny line forms between his eyes. His thumb worries the scar on his opposite hand. He thinks I'm crazy.

"I think . . ." He takes a sip of Frogman. "I think things happen in this world that we can't always explain and understand. I think children are more susceptible to experiencing the unexplained because they haven't been taught to rationalize yet. They're not programmed against believing in ghosts. And who knows? Maybe *every* imaginary friend is a ghost. Who the hell are we to say they're not?"

Why couldn't Micah have said something like that when I'd approached him with the subject? *Let's call Oprah. She'll know what to do.*

"She's beautiful, your Bella."

I take another sip of mojito. "Every miracle is."

"I suppose."

"I know every mother says stuff like that, but in my case, it's true. Do you know what I went through to get her?"

He sort of shrugs, but I'm talking again before he has a moment to respond. "Fertility drugs up the yin-yang." Suddenly, it feels good to be yelling over the music. "You stop your life for it. They say you have to be in for a blood draw at ten-o-six at night? You go at ten-o-six at night. They say you need to have an ultrasound before seven in the morning? You go. They say you need a special drug and that you need to take it before the pharmacy opens in the morning? You go across the state line to Indiana, where the pharmacy opens an hour earlier, on eastern time, and you put everything else on hold if you have to. You shell out three hundred dollars per dose. You just *do it*. And there's no guarantee it'll work."

He's chewing on his lip, looking at me as if I've lost my mind.

Maybe I have. "And *then*, all these women, all around you, they have no trouble getting pregnant on their own, and they rub it in your face, as if there's obviously something wrong with you, as if you're not good enough, and they're having children with your husband, *with a married man*, but you're the one not worthy."

Finally I shut up and draw another few sips of mojito up my straw.

"Well, she's gorgeous. Whatever you went through to have her, it's worth it."

"She's challenging sometimes."

"There are worse things than a headstrong daughter. That bullhead-edness will come in handy when it really counts, you know? She's not going to be taking any shit from any man, I promise you."

She's so unlike me, I realize. "I don't know where she gets it. I've been a doormat. All the things happening right under my nose . . ."

"Maybe you're trusting." He pats my hand twice, then quickly withdraws and places his hand back on his sweating pint glass, where it belongs. "It's not a bad thing to be trusting. The trouble comes when someone takes advantage of that trust. Shame on *them*. Not us."

Us?

"That's right." I cover my mouth, but it's too late to suck back in all the words I'd spewed, which sounded, in hindsight, as if they applied to Christian, as well as me. "Your wife."

"*Ex*-wife."

"I'm sorry. Here I am, going on and on about being a doormat. I didn't mean *you* were a doormat, too. I wouldn't say something like that. You . . . you're obviously so much more together than—"

"And I know what you mean about all these women having babies—even if they shouldn't. My ex . . . she had someone else's kid, and I thought it was mine. Can you imagine? I'm there for the midnight ice-cream cravings, rubbing her belly as it grew, there in the delivery room, there for two a.m. feedings, then one day, a DNA test takes it all away from me."

"Oh God."

He takes a healthy gulp of the Frogman, draining the last bit from the glass, then exhales a long, drawn-out sigh. "Yeah, nothing like being a father for sixty-five days, and then suddenly, it's all over."

Our pitcher arrives, but I don't acknowledge the server when he tells me our fritters will be up shortly. I can't stop looking at the rugged man across the table. Can't stop imagining his falling in love with a baby, counting his toes and fingers, waiting to be called Daddy. Can't stop imagining him falling to pieces when he realizes it was all an illusion.

"Marriage? Over. Fatherhood? Over. Life as I knew it?"

"Over," I say with him.

He meets my glance. "Fuck it. Life deals you shitty cards sometimes. What are you gonna do? Fold? Naw, you gotta play, right? No matter what."

"Absolutely." I think of my mother, folding with a handful of pills. Checking out. But she didn't stop there. After I found her in time and they pumped the poison out of her stomach, she only slashed back harder the next time—at her jugular.

She left me to scrape myself up off the floor. I'd played. I'm playing now, too. I reach for the pitcher of mojito and the spare glass the waiter brought with it. I top off mine and fill the second. The red lights from the stage reflect off the glasses and the liquid in them, like stained glass windows. "To being dealt better hands." I raise my glass.

He raises his. "To lessons learned with the cards we hold."

"To *hard* lessons learned."

We clink.

We drink.

Claudette was right. This behavior—the cheating, the lying—is inexcusable. And if I'd learned of it before Micah flew his proverbial plane into the great beyond, I wouldn't have been half as forgiving as Claudette was of Brad after Misty Morningside.

Who am I kidding? I love him. I couldn't have left him. Despite the evidence of his betrayal, despite the fact that he's gone now, I love him still.

I hear the memory of Micah's whisper in my ear: *I love you, too, Nicki-girl.*

I feel the beat of his cha-cha in time with the music from the stage: *rock, step, cha . . . cha . . . cha.* The cha-chas never at the right tempo but rather at one beat per cha. Wrong. So wrong. But so Micah.

"Dance?"

"What?"

Christian is on his feet, palm up in invitation. "You're practically dancing in your chair already."

Am I? "Mojito effect."

"It's good. I like it." He juts his chin toward the dance floor. "Put it to good use."

"I couldn't possibly—"

"You're already doing it! That is, if you want to call whatever it is you're doing dancing."

"I'll have you know, I can hold my own out there."

"Looks like you want to prove it."

"You're on." I take another long, cold sip of mojito. And then I take my neighbor's hand.

I hold my frame, follow his lead.

And soon we're spinning and cha-chaing through the crowd on the dance floor.

It's effortless. Fun.

And he's a good dancer.

This is what it was supposed to be like, taking classes with Micah. But he never caught on.

Rock, step, cha-cha-cha.

Rock, turn, cha-cha-cha.

Chris smells of pale ale and some cologne that carries a hint of evergreen. His strong arms guide me around the dance floor, and for the first time since Micah left to give some mysterious executive from a fictitious company a ride to New York, I feel as if someone might catch me if I fall.

Images flash in my mind: Christian's feeding Papa Hemingway, his bringing Elizabella a frozen treat at Fogarty's, his mashing squash for Thanksgiving dinner, his lugging over a ladder at a moment's notice.

He turns me into the cuddle step. Rock, step, cha-cha out of the cuddle.

Memories of day-to-day life with Micah interject: his scooping ice cream, his rubbing my pregnant belly, his piercing into my body on that last night . . .

And suddenly, everything is hazy and sweaty.

The music throbs in my veins.

Rock, step, cha-cha-cha.

And I'm feeling it again, as if it's actually happening. Sex with Micah. Deep, passionate, as if he were making love as much with his mind as with his body.

I allow my eyes to close, to sink into the feeling. To picture him as I want to remember him forever: between my thighs, connected to me on a thousand levels.

A shiver runs up my spine.

I lean into him, finesse a kiss onto his lips, which part slightly.

His tongue brushes mine.

Frogman.

I gasp.

I imagine Micah on the edge of the dance floor, watching it all. Shame cloaks me in red—heat in my cheeks, heat on my neck, heat in my *pants*.

But I'm still kissing him.

Christian.

Not Micah.

My neighbor backs off before I do, a stunned, maybe stupefied look on his face, as if he's not sure that what just happened really happened.

Did it?

The fingers on his left hand are still linked with those on my right, but slowly we part as he heads off the dance floor.

At the last second before he drops my hand, he curls his fingers around mine, and he gives my hand a tug: a subtle invitation to follow him.

Chapter 42

Christian veers toward the table—our conch fritters are there waiting for us—but I keep walking past, toward the staircase that will take me out of the Rum Barrel and out of this awkward situation.

I duck into the ladies' room. One step past the door, as I'm staring at my reflection in the midst of carefree vacationers and happy-go-lucky visitors, Christian is right there, holding the door open for a pair of women who are exiting and on their way back out to the party.

The hidden boundary between men and women obviously doesn't deter him, even in a place with a skirted stick figure on the door.

"What are you going to do?" He presses his lips together and narrows his stare. "You going to avoid me? Walk around me forever? The island's not that big, sweetheart, and what just happened . . . well, let's just say it's not too terrible."

I splash cold water onto my face. "It's the rum. I'm sorry. I shouldn't have—"

"But you did. *We* did. What're you going to do?" He touches my elbow, and I turn toward him. "Pretend it didn't happen? Because I have to tell you, trying to forget it or even trying to *pretend* to forget—"

Our lips crash together again, and after a second or two, the kiss comes to a close. I'm not sure how it happened, but . . . *damn.*

"There," he says. "We're even. You made a mistake, then I made a mistake, and now we're even."

My hands are pressed to his chest; his arms are draped casually around my body. I can't look him in the eye.

"Nothing to be ashamed of," he says. "Blame it on the island, on the mojito, on the dancing."

"It's just that . . ." I'm a clumsy idiot at the moment, tripping over my words as surely as I'd trip over my feet if I tried to walk around him right now. "If anything else happens . . . not saying that's what I *want*—"

"You're saying you *don't*."

"I'm not saying that, either. I mean, look at you. You've been the best neighbor anyone could ask for."

"So have you."

"And you're sort of nice to look at, you know?"

"Sort of?" His brow crinkles, and the corners of his lips turn up in a combination smile-slash-smirk.

"And after the day I've had—after the *months* of fertility shots and timetables and . . . everything else . . ."

"Veronica."

"It wouldn't mean anything, and after what you've been through, you *deserve* it to mean *everything*, and—"

"Veronica."

"What?"

"Let's eat our fritters. Have another drink. Maybe dance a little more. We don't have to solve all the world's problems right here, right now, in the ladies' room."

Another patron comes in.

"Come on." He juts his chin toward the door. "It's getting crowded in here."

At the corner of Front Street and Simonton—with one, possibly two, too many mojitos under my belt—I grab Christian's elbow to steady myself as I pull the flip-flops from my feet. "My feet are killing me."

"Well, what do you expect, walking around on three-dollar slabs of rubber?" He smooths an eyebrow with the pad of his thumb. The streetlamps catch the raised flesh on his hand, and in my slightly inebriated state, I nod in its direction. "What happened there?"

The hint of a smile appears on his lips. "We're going to have a personal conversation?"

"Are you kidding?" With the straps of my flip-flops tucked over my fingers, I step off the curb, toward the ocean, to my left. "We've had at least ten of those tonight."

"Elizabeth Street is this way." He slides his hands into his pockets and twitches his head to the right. "And that's debatable."

I indicate left. "The beach is this way. Would you believe I haven't so much as *seen* the beach since I've been here?" I've been texting with Christian's nieces all night. They've sent pictures of my daughter mid-games, mid-snacks, mid-drawings, and finally, asleep. I know Elizabella is in good hands, and while I may have sucked down more mint-infused rum than I need, it's still early.

He shakes his head a little and lets out a chuckle. But he follows me across the street and past the gate of some fancy-looking hotel.

"So . . . do you want the story I usually tell about how I got the scar? Or do you want to know the truth?"

"Does any girl ever tell you to lie to her?"

"All right, I'll tell you both versions. You get to decide which really happened."

"Are you going to tell me if I guess right?"

"We'll see. Story number one: I'm in the middle of a fistfight. You know the one. With the asshole who knocked up my wife."

"You broke his nose."

"Right. But the real story is why. He came at me first, like I told you. But what I didn't tell you is that he came at me with a weapon."

"A weapon," I repeat.

He shrugs. "Of sorts. Automatic nail gun. We were in the midst of a home improvement project. The guy was our general contractor. He came at me, and I"—he demonstrates with a hand up—"I blocked, and he shot."

"So you broke the guy's nose with a nail sticking out of your hand?"

"Yes, I did." His elbow grazes against mine as we walk. "But to be fair, I hit him with the other hand."

"That's pretty unbelievable."

"You think so?"

"Sorry. I do."

"Okay. Story number two: It's after the split with my ex, and I'm out on a blind date at one of those chop-chop-at-the-table Japanese grill restaurants. The chef is there, doing his thing, and suddenly, one of the knives goes flying. It's heading straight for my date. And I'm thinking, I can't let anything happen to her, or she won't go out with me again, right?"

"You're thinking about all of that as the knife's flying?"

"It's one of those situations where you sort out your thoughts later. But long story short: I bat the knife down midair." He shakes his head. "At least that's what I *thought* I did. She's screaming, and some other guy at the end of the table passes out, and I look down, and the knife is sticking straight up out of my hand."

"That really happened?"

"I don't know," he says. "Did it? But it *would* explain why I'm thirty-four and retired. Those national chain restaurants have some decent insurance. Also might explain why she never went out with me again, but I digress."

"You saved her life."

"Eh." He shrugs, as if what he proposes he's done is no big deal.

262

"You took a knife for her, and she wouldn't go out with you again?"

"I don't know if that's the *reason*, but no, she didn't."

"What a bitch."

"Are you saying that if I took a knife for *you*, you'd go out with me again?"

"Well, considering this isn't a date, I don't know if I'd go out with you *again*, but—"

"But we danced . . . you bought my drinks. How is this not a date?"

I stop walking before we hit the ocean, but the surf rolls up on the shore to tickle my toes anyway. "I didn't pay the tab."

"Huh. How about that?"

"Did *you* pay the tab?"

He shrugs. "They know me. I'm probably the only Phillies fan on this island. They'll bill me later."

For a few moments, I'm astonished that I was too lit to remember to pay for my dinner—and I most certainly am feeling a little on the warm and dizzy side—and I'm feeling a bit like a degenerate. But when he starts to laugh, I realize he's kidding.

After drink number three . . . or four . . . I asked for the check and went to the ladies' room—alone this time—and when I came out, he was waiting there, offering to walk me home. *Of course* he paid the tab. "That's twice now," I say. "You didn't have to do that."

"Maybe I want another casserole."

"Because the first one was so incredible."

"If I'm being honest, I'm not that big on casseroles. I prefer to drink my carbs, to tell you the truth. And I don't much like the idea of having you indebted to me, but I do like the idea of getting to know you a little better."

A wave of guilt washes over me with the next ripple of the Atlantic tickling my toes. Am I a married woman? Or a widow? The impermanence of my situation is mind-numbingly irritating. I don't know if I should be mourning Micah or hating him. Probably, I should be feeling a little bit of both ends of the spectrum, regardless.

I take another step farther into the squishy, white sand and realize my husband has probably walked these shores with another woman.

"I'm saying it because I think you need to hear it," he says. "I'm on your side. You've got a friend in me."

"I've never had many friends." The moment the words cross my lips, I wish I could rewind time and take it back. It sounds so pathetic, so woe-is-me.

"I don't believe that for a second." The way he's looking at me . . . as if he believes I can hold my own, as if he's been fooled by the mask of confidence I wore the day I strode right up those plantation-style steps at Goddess Island Gardens and proclaimed to belong there.

I can't deceive him anymore. He doesn't deserve it. Or maybe he does—what do I know?—but I know I don't want to be the one to do it. I can't be responsible for anyone feeling as wretched and uncertain as I've been feeling since Micah's secrets began revealing themselves to me.

The wind catches my hair and flutters it over my forehead and into my eyes.

Christian brushes the windblown mess aside. "Your daughter looks so much like you."

I soften for a second. He's practically daring me to leave all the ugly truths of my life behind for the night, but I'm afraid I'll only start believing in illusions if I do that.

"She's beautiful," he says again.

My cheeks warm with his flattery. If he thinks my daughter looks like me, that must mean he thinks I'm beautiful, too. "Thank you."

"Whether you have friends or not—"

"I don't. It's true."

"I wouldn't mind being one."

"The only friend I ever had—the only one in my adult life, anyway—was my college roommate, and I ended up stealing and marrying her boyfriend."

He shrugs. "Well, you married the guy. You weren't just filling a vacancy."

"A rationalization."

"But a valid one."

"What is it with you? I'm trying to tell you I'm a terrible friend and—"

"You're a terrible friend because some girl had trouble letting go of a guy who didn't want her? I don't buy it."

"No, I'm a terrible friend because I have trouble investing. And now, after everything with Micah, I'm only going to have even more issues." I gauge his reaction, but he offers only a no-big-deal shrug in response.

"Most of us have some sort of issues."

"True." I take in the span of the beach. The moonlight reflecting off the waves. The foam of the tide lingering on the sand. The boats lolling at the pier. I scan the names lettered on the hulls: MERMAID, JOANIE, AZUL . . .

Blue. "Micah used to say friends were silver and gold," I continue. "Ironic because we didn't hang out with anyone. Never got close to anyone. I had friends when I was younger, in high school, but they were up here"—I float a hand at eye level—"on the surface. I couldn't afford to get close because of how things were with my mother."

Realizations hit me like a roundhouse kick across the jaw.

"That's why Micah chose me," I say slowly. "He couldn't have pulled this shit on Natasha. He needed someone vulnerable, someone broken." I meet Christian's gaze.

Micah needed someone who could fall into him to the extent she'd lose herself.

And I most certainly did that.

"Don't sell yourself short," Christian says.

"No, it's true. I'd just been through a god-awful few years with my mother, and it was always just Mom and me. And . . . she wasn't well. My mother . . . she wasn't normal."

"How so?"

I'm going to tell him, I realize. Maybe it's the alcohol, or maybe it's just that not telling Micah everything didn't exactly work out as expected. I never told my husband the whole story. He never knew Mom had attempted an overdose. He never knew she'd tried to blame me when her attempt failed. He doesn't know about the very bitter end, either, because I didn't know how to broach the subject; and it turns out he didn't know how to tell me a lot of things, too. But I take a seat on the beach and allow myself to enter the twisting, coiling corridors of my history. And I begin to tell him what I lived through.

It happened slowly. So slowly that I can't pinpoint a moment when I knew she was different. But it started with the jewelry.

"The jewelry had faces. Those faces had mouths, and when those mouths opened, the most terrible thoughts were spoken, but only Mama could hear them."

It's all so vivid, as if I'm spiraling through dimensions of time and space, and I'm there again, or she's here.

The ocean becomes a window.

The waves are the table at which she worked so diligently on the beautiful pieces of artwork that wormed into her brain like parasitic assassins.

And I feel her all around me, whispering:

He wants me to kill you, kill you, kill kill kill kill . . .

Chapter 43

Christian's fingers curl around my hand. "You poor kid."

"I'd try to explain it to her," I say. "I'd remind her that she made the jewelry, that the jewelry wouldn't be here if she hadn't meticulously placed every crystal into every prong. The jewelry couldn't make her do anything she didn't want to do, but eventually, I guess I realized that she *did* want to do it. I wasn't enough for her. I couldn't bring her back when she'd already gone off the deep end."

I see her drowning in my mind, slipping deeper and deeper into the tub, while the water overflowed, creating a freshwater sea over the hexagonal ceramic tile, splashing against the pink pedestal sink.

I'm so deep in the memory that I feel the lukewarm water soaking from the hallway carpeting into my thick, cotton socks as I near the bathroom door, hear the splash of the overflow as I step onto the tile.

"I found her," I say. "They say I saved her life. I pulled her out of the water, gave her mouth-to-mouth . . ."

My fingers pressed into my mother's soft, waterlogged skin—she felt like a velveteen sponge—as I fought against the weight of her and lugged her out of the tub. She landed facedown with an enormous, thundering *thud.* But I'd gotten her out in time, breathed life back into her.

I'd wrapped her in blankets and rocked her, barely conscious but breathing, until the paramedics arrived.

They praised my efforts. Called me a good girl. Thanked God I'd gotten there in time.

But she hated me for it. The voices hated me. They hated the doctors who prescribed the medicine to silence them. They knew how to play the game. Stay quiet, stay hidden until the doctors let her go home.

I'd told them about the voices, but Mama denied it. The doctors turned their microscopes on me after that. Mama lied for those voices. She chose to honor the voices, even if it meant sending me upriver. I think they knew something was wrong in her head, but as it turned out, there wasn't enough time for them to diagnose it.

"It was almost as if she wanted them to think *I* was crazy. She wanted them to think the voices were in *my* head, that it was *my sickness* that drove her to what she used to call a simple case of the blues. She accused me of letting the water run in the bathtub that day. She said she'd fallen asleep after drinking a tea I'd given her."

"You gave her tea?"

"I wasn't even there, but she planted the seed. They did toxicology tests, to see if I'd drugged her, and they found traces of a sleeping pill. She said I'd turned on the faucet with the intention to drown her. She said I'd saved her because I had second thoughts about killing her." I shiver with the memories, but I'm too numb with them to cry.

"How old were you?"

I'd just turned seventeen, but admitting that makes it seem either more pitiful, or as if I would've been more capable of actually carrying out the acts she'd accused me of. "It's just something that happened. Just something I survived. I'm not asking anyone to feel sorry for me."

"No one's pitying you," he says. "But I'm telling you . . . that is batshit wrong, and it shouldn't have happened to you."

It's pretty unbelievable, actually—maybe more unbelievable than his stories about acquiring the scar on his hand—and it does sound as if I'm fishing for sympathy. So I go with details. Details make the story harder to dispute. "Just a few weeks later, when they were still reviewing my psychiatric evaluation, she came at me with a kitchen knife. But at the last second, she turned the blade on herself. I didn't see it happen."

But I can conjure the picture of the knife in her neck. I see, as clearly as I see the stars reflecting off the waves, the blood spurting like a geyser.

"I was hiding from her, but when I heard her fall . . ." There's nothing I can do to change the picture in my mind. "She was already gone by the time I came out of the closet."

"I'm sorry."

"My prints were on the knife."

"Of course they were. You lived in the house. She came at you."

"There was an investigation."

"You were cleared. Obviously."

"Doesn't change the fact that it happened. That I spent a year in a county home, trying to prove I wasn't crazy. Or that the life insurance company didn't want to pay out, first because I was under investigation, and second because once I was cleared, her death was ruled an apparent suicide." I bite my lip. "But they eventually paid, and I got enough to put myself through school. I met Micah, had Bella, and now, I'm going through the same bullshit I survived back then. So that's that."

"And you think that makes you vulnerable?"

I shrug a shoulder. "Makes me something."

"Maybe he chose you because he knew you could handle it."

"What?"

"Look, I don't know what's going on with Micah, but . . . you survived it all once . . . at *seventeen*. All this time, you're thinking he chose you because you were more vulnerable than Tasha. What if he chose you because you're *stronger*?"

I face him now. The night wind musses his too-long hair. His gray-green eyes reflect the light of the faraway lampposts.

"No one survives what you've been through if she's not strong," he says.

Does he really believe that?

Or does he have ulterior motives? It wouldn't be the first time some guy said something amazing to get a woman into bed.

But does it even matter?

It's not as if it was his idea to come here. He offered to walk me home. I brought him here. I sat down in the sand and started telling him things I don't usually discuss with anyone.

Not even Micah knows about the faces in the jewelry. Even if I'd shared a few gruesome details of my mother's suicide and her attempts prior, with my husband, he doesn't know the police once suspected me of involvement in her death.

Unless . . . what if Micah found out, and that's why he's running? In all my accusations about *his* deceiving me, have I forgotten that I married him without sharing the biggest secret of my life?

Yet I told Christian after a few rum concoctions.

And he's still looking at me as if he respects me, as if he'd still like to get to know me, as if he still considers me a friend.

"You said before . . . maybe you didn't admit to believing in ghosts, but you didn't tell me you didn't," I say. "So maybe you don't think it's out of the question."

"Nothing's out of the question," he retorts. "Do you believe in God?"

"No, really. Because sometimes, I swear I see Micah out of the corner of my eye, or I smell his cologne, and I swear he's there. It's so real."

"Well, that could be God as much as it is a ghost. But either way, who am I to tell you what you saw or didn't see? What you experience or don't?"

And suddenly, the urge to know him—*to know him, know him*—overcomes me, too.

He licks his lips, and I imagine they must taste like the elixir that stole my inhibitions this evening.

I don't know the last time I thought of another man in this capacity or even if I ever thought of anyone other than Micah this way.

Micah, whose name is embossed on birth certificates alongside a Misty Morningside named Gabrielle.

Micah, whose life has become as foreign to me as distant lands I'll never see.

Micah, whom I'm not sure I can forgive or forget.

I'm not thinking straight, or maybe I'm not thinking at all, but I don't care about regret, revenge, or reconstitution. All I know is the concept of gratification leaves me hungry.

I lean into my companion, land my lips on his, and before I know what's happening, we've joined the other pairs of shadows on the stretch of shoreline. We're part of the scenery, like the lovers vacationing at the resorts dotted along the coast. My back is against the sand, and Christian's hand—the one marred with the scar—is on my hip, and his tongue is brushing against mine.

It's wrong.

But I *want* it. I want to feel real. Like a woman. Not like a shell in which to implant and nurture embryos that won't develop.

I nudge a knee between his legs.

Feel the heat of his breath on my lips. His warm hands on my body. His thumb daring to brush along the contour of a breast.

I shiver with anticipation of letting go of the chaos . . . if only for a night.

The trill of a phone startles me.

Christian lets out a breathy laugh, but he keeps kissing me. "You should get that."

"Go ahead," I say against his lips.

"It's not mine," he says between kisses. "It's coming from your purse."

So it is. I unzip my purse and yank out my cell phone.

My fingers instantly tense.

"Oh my God," I manage to say.

The call comes from a blocked number.

"Hello?"

A whisper, familiar only because I've heard it before, answers me: "I see you."

"Who is this?"

The caller is still whispering: "Veronica?"

"Yes."

"I'm watching."

"Who is this?"

Click.

Chapter 44

"You're sure?" Christian asks his niece.

I hear Andrea's voice, filtering through the speaker on Christian's phone. "I'm looking at her right now, Uncle Chris. She's sleeping on the sofa."

"Is the door locked?"

She asks her sister: "Emily, is the door locked?"

"Lock the door!" Christian says.

"Okay, already. It's locked. What's going on? Should I call the police?"

"Just don't let anyone in."

"Obviously."

"We're on our way back."

By the time we arrive at my place, I've lost my sandals—maybe I left them on the beach—and my feet are killing me. I've heard the girls insist that my daughter is fine, but I'm not convinced, won't be convinced . . . not until I'm holding her in my arms.

This is my punishment. I shouldn't have been doing what I was doing on the beach. I shouldn't have been enacting revenge for Micah's irresponsibility . . . let alone allowing Christian Renwick to take part in it with me.

The entire run back from the beach has exhausted me, and I don't even think about the sand I must be trailing in with me until after I unlock the door and after I'm seated on the sofa, cuddling my safe and sleeping little girl.

Whatever effect the mojitos had on me, it's gone now, slapped out of me with the fear of losing everything.

"What happened?" Emily's asking.

Christian's explaining, but everything happens in a fog, in the distance.

It's almost as if I'm tuned in only to the sound of Elizabella's yawn and the sweet sigh she emits as she tosses her arms over my shoulders. She's fine. Thank God, she's fine.

I hear the police in the periphery, but I can't focus on what they're saying.

I stroke her baby-soft hair and rock her in my arms. I kiss her warm, rosy cheeks and study her, as if memorizing every detail of her face.

Members of the KWPD walk through my house, while another takes notes from here in the living room, as if keeping an eye on me.

What's the crazy lady going to do next?

But I didn't imagine any of it. It happened. Christian was there when I answered the phone. He knows—and maybe Key West PD will assure Detective Guidry—that I couldn't have generated that call.

Emily and Andrea sit on the floor opposite me, trading glances. If twin telepathy exists, I'm sure they're sending each other messages about me. Maybe they'll take their uncle aside and urge him to sever all ties with me. It might be good advice.

The officer stationed in the room with us asks questions: Any idea who might've called? Did you recognize the voice? Has anything like this happened before?

In the interest of furthering the investigation, I answer the questions, but I know my answers will only serve to put more suspicion on me. No one can help me. History keeps repeating itself.

I have no doubt Detective Guidry will find a way to trace the call—just like the one before—back to me. Because everything leads back to me. Just like after Mama died.

My prints were on the knife.

Her blood was all over my body.

The mix of emotions I experienced back then stirs in my heart now. Never had I known I could love someone and fear for her, fear because of her, worry for her, and despise her all at the same time.

It's the same way I now feel about my husband.

Between horrific scenes of my past, I tune into the present, hear the police inquiry and my answers, as if I'm watching the whole thing on the nightly news:

Yes, we'd been drinking.

No, not so much that I could have hallucinated.

Yes, I'd told Christian about Micah.

Yes, I'd originally told him my husband had died.

Christian's going to think I lied to him because it's apparent now that Micah's death is not confirmed. I should have updated him. I should have told him sooner. He's going to think I'm hiding something—especially after I just spilled my guts about my mother.

I knew there was a reason I shouldn't have told him about my mother. But I can't help that now. It's probably just as well. Let it end between us before it really begins.

I tighten my grip on my daughter. She's the only one who matters.

"Veronica."

I shift Bella on my lap, but I can't stop looking at her even long enough to acknowledge whoever is speaking to me.

"Veronica?"

I glance up when I feel a hand on my shoulder and see an officer standing over me. The twins are gone. I assume their uncle left with them. I didn't have a chance to thank him or to pay the girls for their time.

"We've looked through the house, made sure everything's safe," the officer says.

I nod.

"Call us if you need anything else."

I take the cue and, with some minor struggle to shift my daughter in my arms, manage to stand and lead the police force to the door.

I thank them.

I lock the door behind them.

I take a deep breath and start to climb the stairs when I see Christian, very much *still here*, lingering in the hallway with Papa Hemingway in his arms.

"You've been through enough today," he says, lowering the cat to the floor. "You want me to carry her?"

Just as I'm about to refuse the offer, Bella reaches for him. The moment he unburdens me, a strange dichotomy settles into my skin. It feels good to accept the help; relief relaxes my shoulders, my lower back, and I feel as if I might fall into a deep, deep sleep at any moment. But at the same time, I feel inadequate, as if I should be able to do it all alone but again have failed to prove I can.

All along the walk up the stairs, I keep my gaze pinned to Bella's cheek, resting naturally on Christian's shoulder. If I squint just right or if I let my mind play tricks, I can convince myself I'm seeing Micah on that last night before he disappeared, carrying our daughter up to bed.

I've watched the scene a million times in my mind since then. There has to have been a clue, a hint, as to what his plan had been. When he said goodbye, was there anything in his voice, in his embrace, in his eyes, that said that particular goodbye meant forever?

I direct Christian to Bella's room, where he transfers her to her bed.

"You okay?" he asks.

I shrug. "Sure." What else does he expect me to say?

For what feels like an eternity, we're staring eye to eye.

"You feel alone," Christian says. "Like you've been doing it all on your own, with no one to help you."

Accurate.

"I'll make you a deal. If ever you feel that frustrated again, and you start breaking things again . . ."

I feel the heat of embarrassment creeping up my neck, still sheepish that I lost control and destroyed every picture frame lining the shelves.

"I'll come help. And not because you kissed me tonight, but because that's what friends do."

"I'm not crazy, right?" I finally say. "I mean, you heard the phone ring, too."

"Yeah." He leans against the wall and massages the scar on his hand. Another awkward silence fills the hallway for the space of a few seconds. "But, Veronica, you've been through a lot the past few weeks. You must be exhausted."

"You think I imagined it."

"No."

"You do! You think I heard a whisper when really it was just static. You think my imagination is getting the best of me."

"Is that what *you* think?"

"I don't know what to think anymore. I just feel like the whole world is out to prove I'm off my rocker."

"*I* don't think that," he says. "You don't know me too well yet, but when you do, you'll know that you should never presume to know what I think. That's when communication fails: when people start making assumptions. Don't infer I feel something based on something I never said."

"Well, the police are inferring it, too."

What if all of this has been in my head? What if none of it's happening at all?

What if Micah's out there, while I dare to cross a line with Christian Renwick on beaches and in bars?

There are too many parallels hanging between the known and unknown.

Twin boys. She gave birth to them; I miscarried them.

My name is on the deed of this house; her things are in this house.

Bella talks about Nini.

Christian remembers a Mimi.

It's almost as if I've been sharing a life with this woman because she was sharing a life with my husband.

And the kiln in the studio . . . I keep wondering if it's there to invite me to tap into an artistic side—*creativity runs in families,* Dr. Russo said—and lately, I've been creating.

Is there any chance Gabrielle is part of me? Is my sense of self, my soul, splintering into pieces? Have I been seeing things, imagining things, hearing things for a terrifying, yet wholly explainable reason?

Would I know if I weren't listening to my conscience but to voices no one else could hear?

The need to see the pictures of the children, to hold the boys' birth certificates in my hands, comes on like a monsoon.

"Sometimes cops don't think about what you're going through," Christian says. "It's their job to push to find answers, but that doesn't mean they think you're crazy."

"I'm not so sure."

"I am." He presses a kiss to the crown of my head. "Get some sleep, pretty lady. We'll talk more tomorrow."

I don't want him to go. I know he can't stay, but . . .

"If you need me, just call."

I watch him walk out the door. I lock it behind him.

Chapter 45

December 5

For the first few hours, it wasn't too much of a trick to stay awake. My heart didn't cease pounding with adrenaline until long after the police left with a full report of things I know happened tonight but can't prove.

But now that the numbers on the clock are gradually morphing their way from two to three, my eyes are growing heavy.

I can't imagine how I'm going to function tomorrow, but I fear that if I sleep, something terrible will happen. Something irreversible.

Another cup of coffee, another glass of water.

It's impossible to sleep when the urge to pee is ever present.

But I can't drink anymore. My stomach is starting to gurgle and churn.

I left a message for Guidry; if the mysterious call from the blocked number originated from Key West, I'll know someone is following me, even if he and his team still prefer to think I'm trying to pull some sort of trick.

Sitting upright in Bella's bed, with her asleep, snuggling at my side, I almost feel peaceful. My eyelids grow heavy.

I feel the rise and fall of Bella's chest, and I try to sync my breaths with hers. She's part of me, and I'm part of her. I won't let anything happen to her. I'll stand up for her in a way Mama never stood up for me.

Mama . . . an ethereal feeling settles into my skin, my bones, as if I'm hovering in a place between dark and light. A feather on air, I drift through the coils of memories I keep locked away.

She's on the floor, blood pooling beneath her head and spurting out of her neck, her lips twisted into a grin, and her eyes cold and open. I hold her limp body in my arms, staring down at her as if I can will life back into those eyes.

Eyes like amber stones.

A blink later, her body becomes my babies'.

The sheets are sticky with miscarriage and death.

Bella!

I startle and gasp, a sob lodged at the back of my throat.

Caught in a hammock of sleep paralysis, I can't move, can't open my eyes to prove to myself that it's just a bad dream.

I feather a finger over her cheek.

Warm.

Alive.

And then I smell it—the fading scent of cigarette smoke—and I see, in my mind, the glow of an orange light on the fairway back at the Shadowlands.

I struggle to draw in a breath, but I can't breathe over the asphyxiating sensation, as if fingers of smoke are curling around my throat.

No, Micah. Don't do it. Don't take her away from me!

Micah, Micah, Micah.

If I concentrate, can I bring him back?

Slowly, I expel the smoke from my mind.

Gradually, it fades, giving way to Dolce & Gabbana The One Sport.

Drifting through the air on a surreal breeze, accompanied by the crickets and humming from the lampposts outside.

I smell him, practically feel him sitting next to me.

"Nicki-girl."

I flinch.

And suddenly, he's there—Micah—sitting on the edge of the bed and cupping a hand over my feet.

He's whispering, something about *blue*.

I taste rum on his breath.

Suddenly, I'm back there, on the wet sand, kissing a man I hardly know. The things I did last night are irreversible.

"Blue what?" I draw in a stuttering breath. I can't stop shaking. "What?"

Chapter 46

I open my eyes when Elizabella's shriek of laughter rings in the air.

"That's so funny, Nini. Do it again."

Micah.

I gasp and sit up. I'm in Bella's room, in her bed.

She's seated on the floor, a scattering of plastic teacups and doll-house furniture surrounding her. A teddy bear sits on the swing in the corner of the room.

Of course, Micah isn't here.

It was a dream. It must've been.

I fell asleep—obviously—and dreamed Micah had come back to me. My head whirls.

"Bella."

"Nini, Mommy's awake!" She catapults from the floor into my arms and plants a kiss on my lips. "Hungry."

"Okay, baby. Give Mommy a minute."

She squirms off my lap.

I inhale deeply, testing the air for any trace of Micah. I still feel the warmth of him, the comfort of his arms around me, but there is no physical evidence that he's been here.

My head is aching, and my bladder feels as if it's about to burst. I think to ask Bella if she remembers seeing her father last night, just to confirm that no matter how vivid, how real it felt, it didn't really happen.

"Brendan, *don't!*"

But maybe there's enough going on in that head of hers. I can't confuse her; I can't put ideas into her head.

I close my eyes for just another few seconds to savor the feeling of Micah in my arms; however illusory it was, it warms me, fills voids he left behind.

I swing my legs off the bed and stand on numb legs. A wave of nausea washes over me. I stumble my way to the toilet and kneel at the commode.

It's a side effect of my hormones balancing out after I'd taken such extreme doses in an attempt to conceive. And now that the first menstrual cycle after retrieval has passed, the elevated hormones are wreaking havoc on my system.

Or maybe this time, it's the price I pay for a good mojito.

Vomit splashes into the toilet, but Bella's still there behind me, chattering about Brendan and Connor and Nini. Her lack of reaction to my throwing up is also a side effect of IVF: my daughter is so used to seeing me toss my cookies it doesn't bother her to see it.

Now, in the light of day, all the demons of yesterday seem impossible. It was just a bad day. Too many things hitting me all at once. I don't know who called me on the beach. But I have to stay strong, have to move on. Have to trust that Guidry and his team will do what they're supposed to do.

I flush the toilet.

I'm feeling a little better.

"You know what we're going to do today, Bella?"

"Go to the park with Connor and Brendan?"

"We're going to probably *see* a park, and maybe we can play at one. But first, we're going to look at some schools."

"No school." She crosses her arms over her chest and sticks out her bottom lip so far I fear she'll trip on it.

"We won't even go inside. It's Saturday. We're just going to look."

"Just look?"

"School can be fun, Ellie-Belle. Your other school . . . not so much, right? But that's why we're going to look and spend some time playing there first. Before you enroll."

"No school."

"You can help Mommy choose the school this time, and maybe you won't go every day, but you have to go."

She's emphatically shaking her head.

"One step at a time. Brush your teeth."

"Nini says no."

"*Mommy* says yes. Remember what we talked about yesterday? About listening?" I hand over her toothbrush, and she reluctantly climbs the steps in front of her sink. She brushes as I count aloud the number of times her brush passes over her teeth.

We then walk the length of the hallway to the master suite, where I splash water onto my face and brush my teeth and pull another sundress over my head. A lovely breeze passes through the open window over the claw-foot soaker tub. I turn into the breeze, which carries the scent of jasmine vines and summer. "Let's have breakfast on the porch," I suggest.

"Nini, too?"

"Nini, too."

Before I get breakfast together, I enter the studio and cautiously test the exterior of the kiln. While it's been off for at least twelve hours, it's finally reasonably cool. I learned yesterday that the metal sides of this appliance could pass for a radiator, even hours after the timer goes off. I don't know if it's hot to the touch at that point, but I didn't want to learn the hard way. I unlock the lever and lift the lid.

My weird, amateurish creations are a whiter gray now. But they're sturdy and solid. No longer brittle.

I did it!

I created oddly shaped ceramic coffee mugs. Or flowerpots. Or topless canisters.

My victory is short-lived, as a sinking feeling returns to me.

I smell something burning. And while I suppose it's to be expected—this kiln at cone four had to have gotten pretty hot to have morphed clay into something unbreakable—should the scent of fire linger?

There's an ashy residue at the bottom of the kiln, a fine dust. And some larger flakes, like paper incinerated.

Is something still burning? I can't risk a fire hazard.

And wouldn't that be just my luck? I try my hand at the arts, and it results in devastation? If I burn the residence I own to the ground, Bella and I will truly be on the streets.

I follow my nose to the floor, where the odor grows stronger.

Soon, I'm on my stomach, with my cheek to the travertine floor, peering beneath the kiln, which stands on four legs, like a piece of furniture.

There's something beneath it, something rectangular, which I fish out.

I gasp when I realize what it is: two bundles of cash, now singed and blackened.

I peel away the layers; bill after bill crumbles in my hands.

I feel sick.

A few of the bills at the bottom of the first stack are salvageable and many in the second. A partial Ben Franklin stares up at me. Smiling. Smirking.

My eyes tear up. If these charred blocks were bundles of hundreds, I just ruined $10,000 per bundle. Given about half the second bundle is in decent condition, I figure I've burned $15,000.

Wait. The ashy flakes in the kiln . . . they're similar to the flakes crumbling off these brittle bills.

I scramble to my feet to compare the residue within the kiln to that in my hands. The matter is too consistent for me to assume it's a coincidence.

"My God," I say aloud. "How much did I burn?"

Worse yet, if these are hundreds . . .

Jesus, is this *my* money? From my safe-deposit box? Did I, in one of my sleepless, out-of-my-mind moments, think hiding this money in a kiln I couldn't possibly ever use was a good idea?

I tear out of the studio and fly up the stairs.

I yank my suitcase out from under the bed and unzip the top compartment, where I've been storing the cash.

"Oh, thank God." It's all there. Whatever I've yet to spend is still right where I left it, along with the mysterious velvet box that holds the blue-stone ring.

My relief quickly fades, however, when I consider what that money might have been.

Did I just incinerate the money Micah stole from his father?

The money feeding some illegal operation, for which his employment with United terminated?

Hell, even if I just burned money someone hid there for a rainy day—mattress money—it's still disturbing.

I lean back against the wall and shove my suitcase back under my bed with a measured kick.

God, Micah. What kind of mess did you leave me in?

For a moment, I allow myself to sink into the feeling of being in his arms again. I know it was just a dream, but it keeps haunting me. For a brief moment in the middle of the night, somewhere between sleep and wakefulness, I was kissing him. And what did he say? Something about the color blue.

Just the power of suggestion, I'm sure. Mama's blue table, the boat docked near Simonton Street Beach . . . it was named *Azul*. Blue flowers, blue skies, blue waters. The blue-stone ring . . . why on earth did he have it?

"Mommy? Nini and I are hungry."

I look up to see Elizabella standing in the doorway.

That's right. I was getting breakfast together before I was distracted. I wipe tears from my eyes. "Me too, baby."

She approaches with some hesitation but ultimately wiggles her way onto my lap and rests her head on my chest. "Mommy's okay?"

"Mommy's okay." I kiss the top of her head. "Come on. Let's get some yummies for that tummy."

After a quick gathering of fruits and breads, which is all I have left in the kitchen, Bella and I migrate to the back porch. Papa Hemingway winds about my legs.

"Good morning."

I turn toward the voice, which I recognize as Christian's.

He's climbing out of the pool, a caulk gun in his hand.

"Hello." I place the melon and croissants on the round table.

"How are you feeling this morning?" Christian nears.

I drop an arm around my daughter, answer my neighbor—"I've been better"—then turn to Elizabella. "Say hello to Mr. Renwick." I'm about to add that she allowed him to carry her to bed and tuck her in last night, but it suddenly feels too familiar a thing to say.

Maybe after I landed a few kisses on his mouth, I shouldn't worry about being too familiar.

There are many things about last night that I ought to just forget. Dreaming about Micah won't bring him back. And kissing Christian Renwick won't make the dilemmas in my life disappear.

"Where's Emmy and Andri?" Bella climbs onto a chair.

Christian shades his eyes from the morning sun. "Playing tennis, I think."

"See them later?"

"Maybe," I say.

"Rough morning?" He approaches the porch and wipes a glob of caulk onto his shorts. His smile is casual, inviting.

"Well, I don't usually drink that much."

"Evident."

"Evident, huh?" I assume he's referring to my repeatedly kissing him.

"Are you all right? Last night was rather"—he tilts his head from side to side—"intense."

I suppose that just about covers it—from the heated kisses on the dance floor to my massive freak-out after the mysterious phone call on the beach. "Bella, eat some cantaloupe."

"Chocolate pudding," she says.

I ignore her counter-offer and push her chair a smidgen closer to the table. Her hair is an unruly mop, and yesterday's dirt still encrusts her fingernails. I'm acutely aware, now that I think about it, that I must look rather mussed myself.

"I sort of remember something about hair of the dog. I'm contemplating a shot of that rum you left on my porch—"

"Rum?"

"Maybe in a glass of orange juice or something."

"Veronica, I didn't leave you any rum."

"It was on my front porch. The day I got here. I assumed you'd left it."

"Not me."

Who could it have been, then, who left it? But before I can ponder too long, he's talking again:

"So I was worried about you last night. There we were on the beach, you know . . . and I'm thinking you're a free woman—not necessarily that you're *ready* to be one—and then . . ."

Our gazes lock.

I don't know what to say.

"So you want to fill me in? Or do you want to leave me here, filling in the blanks on my own?"

He probably deserves an explanation, but what would I say? I'm a person of interest in my husband's disappearance? Is that what I am?

I open my mouth to explain, but this situation is nearly inexplicable.

I clamp up and turn to the table, where Bella has acquiesced to a wedge of melon. "Have you had breakfast?"

"No. But I brought you a coffee." He points to the porch railing, where a collared cup awaits. "I figured you might need it."

Is he for real? If things were different, I might want to bottle him and sell him at the farmers' market in Old Town. Maybe it's true, what they say about southern hospitality. "Thanks." I haven't had a cup of coffee since before Micah and I began our crusade with in vitro fertilization, long before Elizabella was conceived and born, but I remember the long nights Natasha and I crammed for finals with mocha roast at the ready.

Screw it. For the first time in forever, I'm not trying to get pregnant. I deserve to start living. I draw in the scent of it.

"It's just black," he says. "I wasn't sure how you—"

"I don't take coffee, period, usually. But I'll make an exception today."

"So you don't usually drink alcohol. You don't usually drink coffee. Do you have *any* vices?"

"I'm thinking of investing in a few."

"I did the same during a rough patch after the drama with my ex. Careful, or you'll find you *like* vices."

"Actually, lately, I've been doing a lot of things I don't normally do. Pottery, painting, installing glass inserts into cabinet doors . . ." *Burning bundles of money. Kissing strangers.* Lord, it's been a destructive twenty-four hours.

I hand a napkin to Bella, who has yet to take her eyes from our neighbor. "You're already working on the pool?"

"I stayed most of the night, keeping watch, on your porch."

I do a double take and pause to study him. "You didn't sleep?"

"I was worried. Under the circumstances, I figured I should . . . you know . . . you were pretty shaken up. So just in case."

He spent the entire night on my property? Outside?

I should thank him. Or I should tell him to drop the caulk gun and walk back through the gate. Option two is probably smarter. It's either better for me because he's turning into something of a stalker, or it's better for him to stay away from the crazy lady in the big yellow house.

Then again, if Christian really was here most of the night, he can confirm whether or not we were alone, whether or not he heard or saw someone enter the house.

"Did you see anyone?" I swallow over a dehydrated lump in my throat. "Or hear anything?"

He begins to shake his head.

"I had this dream, and it was so vivid, so—" I shut up. There's something in the grass, not far from where Christian is standing.

It's a cigarette butt.

The police didn't find any evidence of a smoker on the property when I called them. But I know I saw the glow of a cigarette shortly after we arrived that first night. I know I saw the same thing on the fairway back home. I know I caught the stench of it last night, too, right before my dream about Micah.

And there's a cigarette butt on the ground. In my yard.

Christian's gaze follows mine, and I think he probably sees it, too.

"We should talk." He rubs the outside of his elbow with the hand that was pierced either with a nail gun at the end of his marriage or with a knife at the onset of an underdeveloped date.

Yeah, we probably should talk. But what could I say to make sense of any of this?

"You want to see what I'm doing here? In the pool?" He's already climbing down the steps into the massive cement crater in my backyard. He travels down the gradual slope, farther into the deep end.

Despite Bella's protest, I follow him, stopping at the edge of the empty in-ground pool. I opt to sit, as if dipping in only my legs up to my shins. This way, I can keep an eye on my daughter while I try to explain things to the man I slammed into last night.

"So." He stops somewhere around four and a half feet deep, near a tiny crack in the tiling, which I assume is what he's been caulking. "You don't know where your husband is? Technically, you're still married?" The way he's looking at me . . . very say-it-ain't-so.

I break eye contact and busy myself with rubbing at a speck of paint still coating the cuticle of my left thumb. "Before I got here, two men came to my house." I try again to look him in the eye, but humiliation draws my gaze right back to my hands. "They said they were FBI agents, and they *told* me he was gone. Dead. You heard about the small plane crash off the coast of Florida last month?"

He shrugs. "I don't watch much television."

"Well, they said it was his plane, and I had no reason not to believe them because Micah's a pilot. Or he was. And he was supposedly flying for Diamond Corporation, only maybe he wasn't—I don't know. I don't know anything anymore. And it turns out the children who lived here, in this house, they're *my husband's children*."

"Is that why you're here?" Suddenly, he's right in front of me. His hands fall atop mine. "To figure out what kind of a man your husband was? Or, as the case may be, *is*? Is that why you're spending time with me? Because you think I know something about the people who used to live here?"

"You don't seem to know anything about them."

"Right."

"So obviously . . ." I glance up at him again. There's no nice way to say what I'm about to say:

I like him. I just can't get involved right now.

Not that it's apparent that that's what he wants. I kissed him first, after all. And if I tell him I can't even think of a relationship . . . not only because I don't know where Micah is, but because I'm a mess right now . . . isn't that rather presumptuous? Doesn't it sound as if I'm assuming that he wants me in that regard?

Sorry, lady, you read me wrong.

"I had a dream last night," I say. "At least I think it was a dream. Micah came back."

He squints at me but rubs a thumb over my fingers in what I perceive as encouragement to continue.

"And I know now that our marriage was a lie. I know he had these secrets, so I wasn't sure I wanted to let him close to me last night, but it felt good to have him there. Despite all the evidence around me that I never really knew him, that he obviously didn't respect the institution of marriage, I was happy to have him there. But a second later, I was waking up, and he was gone again. So it couldn't have happened. Right?"

He shrugs a little. "I guess we can talk about that instead."

"I'm not avoiding the subject. I'm trying to tell you how crazy things have been."

"You should have told me what you knew."

"If I'd known what was going to happen between us last night, I absolutely would have. But it all happened so fast."

"You're a person of interest in his disappearance."

I give a reluctant nod.

The heat of his hands radiate into me. "Spouses usually are."

There's a tickly sensation in my nose, and my eyes begin to tear up. God, can I get through *just one day* without feeling as if I'll forever be fragmented?

"You're right," I say. "I should've told you. But whatever happened to Micah . . . I didn't have anything to do with it."

Christian presses his lips together and sort of nods.

"Still . . . a girl keeps wearing her wedding ring, and her husband's not dead . . . it's got to mean *something*. We were on the beach and—"

"I can't take it off."

"I understand. I just wish you'd told me."

"No. I mean it *won't come off.*"

"Mommy!"

Instantly on my feet, I quickly realize we're not alone.

Chapter 47

"Veronica." Lake County Detective Jason Guidry—flanked by Officer Laughlin and two other Key West PD officers I don't recognize—stands a few feet away, hands in pockets, as if he teleported there. "Got a minute?"

Elizabella flies off the porch and into my arms. "Daddy came," she whispers in the hollow between my shoulder and neck. "He came. He came."

"Bella . . . what?" I try to look at her, but her face is buried against me. "What did you say, baby?"

"No, no, no. Down."

Guidry clears his throat. "Looks like you've been keeping busy."

"I've been doing some work on the house," I begin. But then I realize the detective is nodding at my neighbor, insinuating my extracurricular activities might concern another man.

Christian extends a hand. "Chris Renwick."

The detective meets him in a handshake.

"He was feeding the cat for Tasha," I begin, but I quickly shut up. Maybe it looks even worse that I was just holding hands with a guy I met a few weeks ago. Even Papa Hemingway is giving me the stink eye.

"I need to speak with you alone." Guidry flips open his pocket-size notebook.

"I'll, uh . . ." Christian thumbs toward his house. "If you need me, you know where to find me."

The cops and I move toward the porch. Instinctually, I opt to enter the house. It's better to keep whatever is about to happen out of the public eye. I lower Bella to the floor.

She kisses me on the cheek and sits down at her table of art supplies in the family room. Representatives of the KWPD help themselves to seats on the wicker sofa and begin making small talk with my daughter, who does not reply.

"So it must be pretty bad, if you came all the way here." I must be channeling Claudette Winters's inner hostess because I fill a glass with ice, then water, and place it in front of the detective, who looks beyond warm in his long pants and collared shirt.

"*You* came all the way here," Guidry counters.

"That's what I mean. I came because it was bad." Papa Hemingway/James Brolin nudges me with his nose. "So what happened?"

"We treated your husband's car with luminol. Do you know what that is? It's an agent used to detect the presence of blood at a crime scene. We spray the scene with luminol, and if there's any blood, even if the crime scene has been cleaned, it glows blue."

I raise a brow.

"Your husband's car lit up like the Fourth of July."

"So there was blood in the car."

"There's indication of it, yes."

"Was it his?"

"We don't know yet. But if it is, it might explain why the license plates were switched on the cars: it's easier to see a license plate than a VIN. We're looking for Illinois plates I FLY 3, and we find the car more easily than searching for a long line of tiny numbers on the dash.

So we found the plate but on a car reported stolen. Whoever switched the plates needed to buy some time. A delay in connecting the scene to your husband might be beneficial to whoever might have killed him."

The wind is temporarily knocked out of me. *So he might be dead.* "Okay." I glance at my daughter—I don't want her to hear this—but she's happily coloring.

"But certain things can also give us false positives, such as excessive cigarette smoke in an enclosed space, and a car would certainly qualify. So while the tests are being done, and before I definitively go on thinking it's blood . . . Have you ever known your husband to be a smoker, Veronica?"

Is there any way he could have hidden it from me? "No." But lately, I've been wondering. The glow of the light on the fairway . . . the butt in the grass this morning . . .

Was I so wrapped up in fertility treatments that I didn't notice my husband had picked up a habit?

An officer on the wicker says, "Do you know where your daddy is?"

I interject: "Please don't interrogate my daughter about—"

"My daddy came to see me last night," Bella announces to the officers keeping her company.

"What did you say, Bella?" I meander toward her.

She points to her drawings. "He says we're going to be by the dolphins."

My innards go hollow under the pressure of Guidry's stare. I ask Bella for clarification: "Have you ever been by the dolphins?"

"*No*, Mommy. Nini goed there once."

"With your daddy?"

"That's what he said."

"When did he . . . Bella, when did he tell you that?"

"I *told* you, Mommy. He kissed me bye-bye on the nose again."

"Something you want to tell me, Veronica?" Guidry clicks his pen open and closed.

I spy the bottle of rum on the countertop, its blue ribbon daring me to numb the pain. How much rum could make me forget? How much could distort my reality?

Was it a dream? Or was Micah here? And who put the rum on my porch, welcoming me to the neighborhood, if not Christian?

I rush to the back door, throw it open, and lunge toward the grass, where I saw the cigarette butt. Maybe they can test the butt for saliva samples and prove it's Micah's.

Or maybe it isn't. Maybe it was someone else smoking out here last night, every night for all I know, but even then, the police will know I'm not crazy, that I'm not putting crazy ideas into my child's head.

I have to find it.

On my hands and knees now, I rake through the blades in search of what I know I saw. What I'm sure Christian saw, too.

But whether or not it's here now—What happened to it? Did a gecko run off with it?—I know it was here five minutes ago!

Or maybe I really am seeing things, hearing things.

Maybe I really am losing my mind.

"Mommy?"

Seeing me like this must be frightening for Bella.

All of this must be terrifying.

What will happen to my daughter if I'm really crazy?

"Veronica." Guidry places a hand on my shoulder. "If you don't talk to me, we don't get to the bottom of this."

Maybe I'm crazy. Maybe I'm not.

Maybe I did something in a fit of rage that I don't remember.

Or maybe I'm a victim of circumstance.

The only way to make it all stop is to tell Guidry everything I can possibly think to tell him. Even if I know it's going to make me look crazy, even if I know it'll make me look guilty.

"I had a dream." I wipe away tears with the back of my hand. "At least I thought it was a dream. But then, considering what Bella said . . ."

"Maybe someone's putting ideas in her head."

Through tears, I meet the detective's stare. "You think it's me. That *I'm* putting ideas into her head."

"You think it's Micah," he counters, deadpan.

"Do you think there's a chance he was here? That he's running from something, and he's trying to lure me to run with him?"

"Anything's possible." Guidry nods. "Tell me why you ask."

"My dream. Micah was in it. He kept saying something about blue. About the color blue."

"Blue."

"And Shell . . . maybe she knows where Micah is, maybe she knows he's coming for us. I keep going over it in my mind, and we *grieved* together on the phone when I told her he was dead, but when I first told her about Micah's being missing, she was sort of casual about it."

"Casual?"

"If anyone had called me with the news that Bella didn't come home, I would've been halfway to the airport and on my way home, but Shell was *rational*."

He nods.

"And my neighbor, Claudette . . . she sent me a picture of Natasha Markham on my doorstep. I haven't seen her since *college*, and she showed up right after Micah left. She told Claudette she'd left me a message, but when I called the voice mail at Shadowlands, there weren't any messages. *None.* Not even a telemarketer. Someone must have retrieved the messages and deleted them."

"Micah?"

"Or someone trying to follow his trail. Someone with access to the house. And his name is on those boys' birth certificates . . ."

"I'm sure that was a hard thing to face."

"And I keep thinking I'm seeing someone smoking outside. It happened here. It happened back home."

"Can I get a description?"

"Of what? A shadow? The little round orange flicker of light you see when someone inhales through a cigarette? If I could *describe* him, I wouldn't be worried that I'd *imagined* it. And the whispering caller . . . that's *twice* now it's happened to me and—"

"Mmm-hmmm."

"And this morning, I opened the kiln—"

"The *kiln*?"

"There's a kiln here, yes, which is weird enough on its own. But I tried to make a few pots, and this morning, when I opened the kiln, there was ash. And I found charred bundles of money under the kiln, so I'm scared now. What if I burned the money Micah stole from his father? Or what if he stashed it there to pay debts? I mean, he didn't have a job, right? So where'd all the cash come from?"

"I'll need what's left. It might be traceable."

"There's not much, but I put it aside for you. And he'd been using his father's social security number, at least to buy a house, right? All of this . . . it has to mean something. Why would he hide all this cash? Why would Bella *say* these things? That her father came back for her, that he's taking her by the dolphins? It doesn't make sense unless she's seen him."

Daddy said Nini goed there once.

"We need to find Nini," I tell Guidry.

"You think your daughter's imaginary friend has something to do with this."

"Yes."

He sighs and shakes his head in muted exasperation.

"I think Nini is a real little girl. I think Bella met her with her father at some point, and the only way she can make sense of this confusing situation is to bring the most relatable part—a little girl—with her wherever she goes. A few days after we first got here, she started talking about Connor and Brendan. Then you sent Laughlin over with birth certificates for Connor and Brendan. You need to find out if Gabrielle had a daughter. Even if she isn't Micah's daughter, Elizabella might have met her at some point. Or Natasha Markham. Does she have a little girl with red hair?"

"First"—Guidry shakes his head—"Natasha does have a little girl, so there's a possible correlation there."

"Have they been here? To this house?"

"From time to time, yes."

I remember Micah's mocking my concern over our daughter's imaginary friend. And if he knew Natasha was spending time here and if he introduced Bella to Natasha's daughter . . . Would he rather I fear I'm crazy—or that our daughter is—than explaining? But I wouldn't have understood. How could he have told me he'd been seeing his ex-girlfriend?

"Second," Guidry continues, "Gabrielle and her two sons—Micah's sons—died in the plane crash off the coast of Florida."

My fingers are numb.

"Seems they, too, spent time on this island from time to time."

I think of the art supplies, the kiln, and my reluctance to believe Natasha might have had any occasion to use these items. But if Gabrielle was here, maybe she *did* use these things.

"Veronica?"

I snap out of it and meet Guidry's gaze. "Who was flying the plane?"

"That's a good question. Only three bodies were discovered. Could be the pilot parachuted out. Could be the pilot's body is lost at sea."

"Whose plane was it?"

"An even better question. The make and model match the one you sent pictures of, but we can't trace the registration. There was no flight plan registered, so it seems the plane took off from private grounds. It appeared in the ocean out of nowhere."

"They're . . . Gabrielle and the children. They're dead?"

"Yes."

"And whoever claimed to be working with the federal government assumed my husband was with them when they died, and they notified me he was gone."

"It's possible. But it's more likely they concocted the story of his death to see where you'd lead them."

"It's possible then that whoever they are, they want what he left behind." An intense urge to hold my daughter, to never let her go, practically aches in my arms. "And if Micah's been here, it's a pretty good bet they know where to find us."

Chapter 48

An intense urge to flee the island only subsides when I realize that if someone followed me from Chicago, it's likely he'll follow me wherever I go from here. Guidry brought my mail with him, courtesy of Claudette Winters, because he didn't want to make known the address of Goddess Island Gardens even to her.

Guidry says he's going to stay in the area for a while. He's asked the Key West police force to double the patrols along Elizabeth Street. But other than that, it's business as usual. He won't say it, but he's watching me like a hawk watches a squirrel. He's waiting for me to screw up, or he's waiting for someone to find me.

Among credit card statements and utility bills, none of which I have had the nerve to open, is correspondence from Natasha Markham. It's a blank-inside card, a picture of a field of daisies on the front. Her message is simple, written in the instantly recognizable, no-nonsense block letters:

I'M SORRY FOR WHAT YOU'RE GOING THROUGH.

WE SHOULD TALK.

—N

Her phone number appears at the bottom right corner of the card.

I dial.

It rings and rings.

She doesn't answer.

Chapter 49

December 7

It's a pattern these days: a lot of hype followed by a stretch of relative normality.

After I received the strange phone call on the beach, and all that followed that night and the next day, I've changed the locks.

The days edge closer to Christmas, and I'm another week closer to D-day with the embryos at River North Fertility Center. I call to tell them I haven't forgotten about the storage fees. They'll have my decision by the end of the week.

Another coat of paint here.

Another box out to the garage there.

Another blob of clay tossed onto the potter's wheel and transformed into some new formation.

Guidry took the charred bundles of cash and cleared the ash from the kiln, so I'm free to use it again, should I get more adept at this art form.

I find a Jimmy Buffett CD on a dusty shelf. I slip it into a player in the art studio and get ready to work. But I'm not sure I should pack these things away. They aren't mine, but if Gabrielle won't be coming back for them . . .

I've grown accustomed to spending time in the studio. There's comfort in the solitude, in the things I create within it. The cat butts my shins with his head. I pick him up and snuggle him as I look around. Now that I know Gabrielle won't be coming back for her things, I feel less urge to get rid of them. She and I have something in common—something more than our sleeping with the same man. We both lost Micah's twin sons. She died along with her children, and I felt like I was going to die when I miscarried the boys.

I wonder, and not for the first time, if Micah, like Gabrielle, is a victim of foul play, if his body will eventually wash up on the Atlantic coast. Or if Micah arranged the plane crash, if he flew out to the ocean with the bodies, then parachuted out of the plane—D. B. Cooper style. What if living a life so outrageous that he needed two identities to do it became too much for him to handle? Add to the mix whatever secrets he shared with Natasha, the mess of my unexplained infertility, the money, and the debt . . . would he have done something drastic to escape it all?

The fourth finger on my left hand itches beneath my wedding ring. I place the cat back on the floor and twist at the band. It still won't slip over my knuckle.

I go to the kitchen, lube my finger with dish soap, and tug at my wedding ring until my finger hurts, but it still won't budge.

My pool stands dormant, in the same state in which Christian left it a few days ago, when Guidry showed up with the news about Gabrielle and her sons' death in the plane crash.

And when Christian left that day, he stayed gone. Maybe because I haven't been honest with him or maybe because all of this is too intense for a guy who spends his days paddleboarding and tapping out words on a laptop. Either way, I suppose I can't blame him. But I'm going to try to make it right. I'll apologize, at least, for my secrecy.

"Ellie-Belle." I dry my hands on a towel and glance at the new television I purchased so Bella can watch the plethora of Disney DVDs Gabrielle left behind. "Come on, baby. We're taking a walk to see Emily and Andrea."

"After the movie?"

"Now."

Her eyes light up.

"Excited to see Emmy and Andri?" I ask.

"Can we play one, two, three, fly?"

"We'll see."

The autograph tree near the door now bears the markings of Emily and Andrea on its leaves. While we wait for someone to answer the door, I busy myself perusing their sketches and the artful ways they wrote their names.

"Hi!" It's the one with the purple hair. She's still in her pajama bottoms, but she looks alert enough that I don't think I woke her.

"Hi, Andrea." I squeeze Bella's hand in a subtle reminder for her to be good. "Is your uncle free?"

"Yeah. Come on in."

"One, two, three, fly?" Bella asks.

I look down at her. "Bella, you don't have to always play that game—"

"Sure. Let's go find Em." Andrea juts her chin toward the back of the house. "He's writing." After a roll of her eyes, she continues, "I'm sure he'd love the interruption."

As I near the back bedroom, I hear him humming—a Jimmy Buffett classic. The door is half-open. "Knock, knock." I nudge the door open a bit more when he doesn't answer.

He's standing at the window, shirtless, staring out at his rear garden. "Hi."

He turns toward me, one thumb hooked into a belt loop and the other grasping a coffee mug. A look of surprise registers in his eyes but quickly mellows. "Hey." One corner of his lips turns up in a grin.

Contagious.

I feel a smile coming on, too. "It's funny. I was just listening to Buffett."

His warm, bare chest melts against me, and he cups my face in his hands, kissing me.

"I told myself not to crowd you." He rests his forehead against mine and whispers at my lips. "I figured, let you come to me. God, it took you long enough."

"I wasn't sure you'd want to see me, after . . ." Out of the corner of my eye, I see papers strewn about a desk situated next to the door, not far from where I'm standing. Pictures. Of Micah. His boys. A dark-haired woman. "What are you—"

He seals his lips over mine again, effectively shutting me up.

But I keep my eyes open. Addresses in Plum Lake, Wisconsin, in the Dominican Republic . . . satellite images: A red circle in the Atlantic Ocean, I assume where the plane went down; an overhead view of the house in the Shadowlands. And an image of Goddess Island Gardens.

"Chris, wait."

"I'm hungry. You hungry?" He steers me toward the door.

I pull his body tight to mine and steal another glance at the desk.

A notation scrawled onto a scrap of paper: *owes Diamond Corporation 5M.*

Diamond Corporation! I'm about to ask what he knows about it, but half a breath later, I realize he's researching my life. Is he writing a book about my predicament? Using me to get close to the story?

I'm about to accuse him, when I see a cigarette stubbed out on a small saucer at the corner of the desk. It looks like the same type of cigarette I saw in my yard, with an amber-colored butt and a white shaft. I suppose that could describe most cigarettes, but . . .

It hits me.

He's one of them.

He's following me.

How else would he have this much information—more than Guidry has—unless he's part of the scheme to make my husband disappear?

That kiss was a cover; he was trying to distract me from seeing his work.

The twin nieces and surfing and paddleboarding and beach-bum wardrobe are part of the cover, too.

It's why he doesn't have any concrete information about the people who used to live in my house. It's why he didn't know the cat's name. It's why he couldn't give me a straight answer about the scar on his hand. He's in on it.

It's why he doesn't really write.

I trusted him. I told him things I've never told anyone.

"Hmm?" He traces the contour of my cheek with the pad of his finger.

My heart is banging in my chest.

He plied me with rum. He knew I'd sleep eventually after that much to drink. He admitted he'd been at my house all night long. He must have come into Bella's room. I thought it was Micah. But I detected the scent of cigarette smoke that night, too, and there's a cigarette butt on his desk.

Did he plan to take my daughter? I slept with her in my arms the night I'd sworn Micah had visited. No one could've taken her without taking me, too.

Bella's declarations of the past—*I'm gonna go be with Daddy*—haunt me now. She said it after we saw the figure on the golf course.

It's possible Christian is working with whoever was smoking on the fairway.

And then, the phone calls: *Listen to your daughter.*

I listened. I came to God Land. In coming here, have I fallen into some sort of trap?

"Veronica?"

Gabrielle and her sons are dead.

I can't assume it's a coincidence that someone's after me, too.

He cranes back a bit, as if studying my whole face at once. "You okay? You're shaking."

"I had a cup of coffee this morning. Jittery."

"You eat yet?"

"I'm starving," I say.

"Yeah?"

"Let's grab the girls and hit Sloppy Joe's for an early lunch."

"Joe's isn't even open yet."

"They will be, by the time we're all ready," I blurt. "Good fritters. Maybe the best on the island."

He narrows his gaze, tucks a coil of my hair behind my ear. "Better than Turtle Kraals? Don't think so."

I force myself to speak more slowly. "Never been there."

"Right up Margaret Street." Now he's raking through my hair, holding it in a bunch at the nape of my neck. The act could morph from a loving gesture to a vicious yank in a moment. "But Kraals might be more appropriate when it's just the two of us. They have this drink . . . a mind eraser, let me tell you."

I'm staring into his eyes. I force a smile and breathe through it. "If I didn't know better, I'd swear you're asking me out."

His smile brightens. "Maybe I am."

"I have to turn off my sprinkler, and I have a few errands to run in town." I pat him on the chest. "I'll let you get dressed and meet you at Joe's." And just in case I'm not convincing enough, I press my lips to his in a quick peck. "Say, half an hour? Forty-five minutes?" I back out of the room, and once the door is closed, I rush to the living room, where Bella is playing with Christian's nieces.

"We're going to lunch." I catch Bella in the midst of one, two, three, fly.

"No lunch," Bella protests.

"We have to let Emily and Andrea get dressed and ready, Bella, okay?"

"No lunch!"

"It'll be fun, Bella," Emily says. "Where are we going?"

"Sloppy Joe's."

"I love their burgers," the twins say in unison.

"We'll meet you there," I say. "I have to change, and . . . my sprinkler is running, and . . . I have to stop on the way for a few things. We're meeting you there. Right at the corner."

The teens are wide-eyed, tracking my movements.

"Okay," one of them says.

"Are you all right?" the other asks.

"Just in a hurry."

Despite my daughter's protest, I keep her on my hip all the way down the alley, past the gate, and through the yard. As soon as I have my cell phone in hand, I unlock my screen to dial Guidry.

I'm looking over my shoulder the entire time.

The detective's voice mail picks up. I leave a message as I enter my house. Buffett emanates from the left corner of the place, but I let it play. I gather a few things—DVDs for the car, paper and crayons, clean clothes out of the dryer—and shove them into a beach bag. We might have to disappear for a while in order to stay safe. "My neighbor," I say. "Christian Renwick. He's been watching me. He has addresses: the house on Plum Lake, the Shadowlands, something in the Dominican. I think he's working for Diamond Corporation. Call me back. Bella and I have to get out of here. We're not safe."

I grab my car keys and my stunned daughter.

"Leaving God Land?" she asks.

"Yes, baby."

"No. You said lunch. With Emmy and Andry."

"Later, baby."

The next call I place, when we're already heading toward Truman Avenue to get the hell off this island, is to the Key West Police Department.

I'm doing what they asked. I'm calling them when I'm leaving.

I keep an eye on the rearview mirror all the way past the first bridge to Cow Key.

Chapter 50

A few islands up, we settle in a hotel and wait for a call.

I pace the length of the room while my daughter colors at the table.

"Nini wants to go swimming."

"No, baby. We have to stay here." I peek out the drawn curtains every once in a while. The desk staff said they'd let me pay in cash and wouldn't run the card I'd had to leave "for incidentals," but I'm nervous. Is simply leaving a card at the desk enough to tell the world we're here? Is it enough to draw people I don't trust to whatever-Key-this-is and threaten our safety?

Guidry has yet to call me back, but I take that as a good sign. He's probably following up on Christian Renwick, and I know the Key West Police Department is on it, too.

When the phone rings, naturally, I pounce on it, but the name in the caller ID gives me pause. Do I want to take a call from Claudette Winters right now?

Maybe she knows something. "Hi, Claudette."

"Honey, are you *ever* coming back?"

"Well . . ."

"Micah's parents have been across the street all day, clearing his things out of there. I mean, maybe you appreciate the help, but if it were *me*, I'd rather be doing it myself."

"Wait. They're at my house?"

"Yes. Box after box of things are coming out of there."

I suppose it's not shocking they're getting it ready for sale.

But given Shell's odd text message—You have Bella?—it's just as likely they might even be clearing whatever evidence the cops may have missed to help their son disappear forever.

We'll know more soon enough, once Guidry and his team comb through Christian Renwick's shrine.

A sense of dread drops in my stomach. Why did he have to turn out to be one of the bad guys? I *liked* him. I liked his nieces.

Or maybe . . .

Is there any way he *is* writing a book about me? And if that's all it is, could I possibly forgive him for not telling me?

I shake the nonsense from my head.

If he were an author, he wouldn't know more than the police. And the information sprawled on his desk . . .

Is it true that Micah owes Diamond Corporation millions of dollars?

And he supposedly stole money from his father a decade ago . . .

Who did I marry?

"Micah's father is clearing the house," I say. That means they don't expect us back. Or at the very least that they don't want us back.

"There's already a buzz about the house."

"Really."

"I told you when you bought, the Shadowlands is *very* desirable, so maybe it's good that they're spending the time, but I thought you should know."

I wonder if Guidry knows what Shell and Mick are doing.

My phone blips with another call. It's the Key West PD. "Claudette, I have to go. The police are calling."

"Honey, call me, all right? If you're not coming back, I'd like to arrange a time to visit. The kids would love to see you and Bella."

"Sounds good." As I click to answer the incoming call, I realize I'm actually looking forward to seeing her. "Hello."

"Mrs. Cavanaugh, this is Officer Laughlin, Key West PD."

"Yes."

"Listen, I don't how to tell you this, but we followed up on the residence in question—Christian Renwick's, did you say?—and it's vacant."

My spine goes limp. I practically slump to the floor. "That's impossible."

"It's *furnished*, ma'am, but it's rented as a furnished house. It's been vacant for a little over two months."

"But you saw him . . . the guy that was at my pool the other day. And the night I got the call on the beach. You saw him."

"I saw *somebody*, yes, but—"

"Are you sure you have the right house? Off-white. Pink trim. Blue table in the kitchen."

"Yes. It's vacant. Went through it myself. I spoke with the owners. It hasn't been rented since early October."

"The owners. Christian Renwick owns the house."

"No, a Roberta Marley owns the house. If you search the address, it'll take you to a vacation rental site."

But he was there. I saw him writing in the kitchen. I ate Thanksgiving dinner on his back patio. He kissed me in the den a few hours ago.

"It's safe for you to return, ma'am. We'll have someone patrolling regularly, and we can better ensure your safety here than wherever it is you've run to."

Unless I imagined it all.

Chapter 51

By the time we return to Old Town, Goddess Island Gardens is as calm as the wafting ocean breeze. One would never guess the frantic occurrences of this morning.

I wonder if everything suspicious is as much a fabrication in my mind as an imaginary friend. Did I conjure Christian—in all his feigned perfection—as a means to help me cope with the unthinkable things happening in my life? Could I have been so distraught over losing Micah that I brought myself into an alternate reality?

But what of Christian's nieces, whom Bella has been drawing consistently since we met them? Andrea, with purple hair; Emily as a blonde. They, too, seemed too good to be true. Would eighteen-year-olds, on a gap year, be willing to spend their free time with my bossy three-year-old? Is it possible for a parent with delusions to pass the same visions onto her children?

Is Elizabella seeing people that don't exist simply because I tell her they're there?

Mama tried to make me see things from her point of view, but I never budged from reality. The state clinics declared me sane, even though she told the authorities I wasn't right. I always thought she was simply good at convincing them of her sanity, but what if it's the other way around? What if I managed to convince them of mine?

Or is there another explanation for Christian's sudden exodus?

Could he have packed everything he owned, and everything his nieces brought for use during their gap year, and cleared out in less than an hour?

I mentally retrace the past twenty-four hours.

I was feeling guilty for neglecting to tell Christian the truth about Micah.

Bella and I paid him and his nieces a visit—at the very house that is now vacant, the very house Laughlin claims has been vacant for months.

Andrea answered the door, her vibrant purple hair voluminous in the humidity.

We entered. Bella wanted to play one-two-three-fly.

All of this I could've imagined, I suppose.

But wait.

The autograph tree.

Emily and Andrea added to the leaves others had decorated. They wrote their names and drew pictures. If their scribbles are still there on the leaves, I'll know I didn't imagine them.

Bella is tired; she needs a nap. But I buckle her into her stroller and take the long way around, down Elizabeth. By the time we turn left on Southard, my daughter is asleep. I continue to Christian's place on Love Lane.

There, next to the front door, is the tree.

And on the leaves are signatures:

Emily

and

Andrea

And several others, as well, in different handwriting. This lends credence to the house being a rental for vacationers.

I look more closely. One of Christian's twin nieces wrote GAP YEAR! on a leaf and the date of their arrival. They got here a few days before I did.

I'm not crazy . . . unless *I* decorated the leaves. Unless *I* wrote the girls' names in varying fonts.

I'm about to turn around and walk home, when something catches my eye: a leaf from the tree, discarded on the porch. On it, someone wrote *Miss You, Bella*. Only it doesn't match the handwriting of Emily or Andrea.

It looks, actually, like it could be Micah's.

Chapter 52

My phone is ringing by the time I bolt the door behind me.

"Detective Guidry." I'm near tears of relief to see he's finally returned my call. "You have to follow up on my neighbor. His name is Christian Renwick."

"Do you have a minute? I'm out front."

I'm already on my way to the door.

A minute later, the detective is seated at my table. Eight-by-ten glossies occupy the space before us.

I'm looking at one of the photographs. "Yes," I say. "That's him. He said his name was Lincoln, and he was an FBI agent. He told me my husband was dead."

"He has ties to Diamante, stationed in the Dominican Republic."

"Diamante," I repeat. "That's the business account Micah transferred money from."

"Yes. It's a legitimate company. Once one of the biggest in international shipping."

"If his name was on the Diamante account, are you telling me Micah *owned* a legitimate shipping company? If it's legitimate, why would he lie about flying executives around the globe?"

"Diamante paid Micah, according to the transfers, up to four, sometimes five, times the going rate for carriers. Either he was transporting something illegal, or he was laundering the money they obtained from illegal goods. Those carriers are of another class they call *de azul.*"

"*Azul.*"

"You know the term?"

"No, but there's a boat docked at Simonton Street Beach. It's called *Azul.* It means 'blue.'"

"Micah could have been a blue-status carrier—responsible for transporting high-risk shipments."

"Micah said something about blue in my dream, but . . ."

"You don't know anything about this?"

I shake my head. "Nothing."

"And you've never been to the family's lake house in Wisconsin?"

"No."

"Yet you took off, planning to drop in, on a father-in-law you'd never met, for the Thanksgiving holiday."

"Shell invited us. I told you that."

"Instead, you show up here. Your daughter starts talking about Connor and Brendan *before* I send over the birth certificates."

"Yes."

"Yet you claim you didn't know about the boys—"

"I didn't!"

"Until Laughlin gave you copies of the birth records."

"Right."

"And the boys' and Gabrielle's remains were in the plane that crashed off the coast. They died before they ever got on that plane. Their lungs were filled with lake water, not salt water. Venture a guess as to which lake we're pinpointing?"

"Plum Lake?"

"That's right. Traces of benzodiazepine were found in their systems. Drugged, then drowned. We're guessing it happened sometime in the days before you claim your husband left or shortly thereafter."

He's looking at me as if he expects me to say something.

"Your neighbor says she picked up your daughter from preschool two days before your husband left."

"Yes."

"So you're unaccounted for that afternoon."

"I had an appointment with the fertility clinic. We batched oocytes."

"Your husband was with you?"

"Yes. They fertilize right after batching. He had to be there."

"And the clinic. They'll confirm the appointment?"

"Of course."

Guidry's staring me down again. "And the days following the batching? Anyone account for your presence then?"

"Claudette. People at the preschool."

"But not consistently."

"Never not for fourteen hours in a row, which is the minimum it would have taken me to drive up there and back."

"Even overnight?"

I hold his stare. I didn't do it.

"And no one can account for Micah," he says. "We know that."

"You think Micah did it?"

"I've got a dead woman who had a relationship with your husband. Two dead boys fathered by your husband. Access to benzodiazepine and death by drowning. Indications you're attempting to purchase a house out of the country, and you've already gone against my advisement in coming to Key West. Not to mention your prescription for Xanax that was recently refilled, according to your pharmacy."

"Wait, what? But I didn't refill it. I didn't! I didn't like taking it. So I never took it. I wouldn't have to refill it."

"How tall are you, Veronica?"

"Five-eight."

"What do you weigh?"

The question takes me aback. No one should ask it and expect an answer. But he blinks at me expectantly.

"Your license says one-thirty-five."

"I gained a few pounds with treatment."

"Gabrielle was five-one. Weighed ninety-five pounds."

"Good for her."

"You could overpower someone of that size."

"I *could*. But that doesn't mean I *would*, detective. I couldn't fathom doing something like that."

"Yet this isn't the first time you've been accused of doing something like that."

"I was a kid," I say, voice breaking. "My mother was sick. She did it to herself, and the county record will confirm it."

He nods, still not breaking his deadpan stare. "Benzos in a bathtub."

"Yes." I know this doesn't look good. "And later with a knife."

"Uh-huh. The knife did the job?"

"Yes." I can't look away. I don't want to give him any reason to think I'm not being truthful. I have nothing to hide.

"Tragedy seems to follow you."

"Maybe Diamante killed Gabrielle and the boys?" I offer. "Because Micah owed them money?"

"Could be." He bites on his lower lip for a moment. "In that case, you and your daughter would be in real trouble but—"

"Someone followed us toward Wisconsin. I *told* you this. That's how we ended up here. And the guy who lives through the alleyway—at least I *thought* he lived there—he's working with them. He was in the house—possibly searching it—when I arrived. It might have only been a matter of time before . . ." I shudder with the thought. I let him in. He carried my daughter to bed. He could've hurt us.

I think of the notation on Christian's desk. *Owes Diamond Corporation 5M*. He knows Micah owes big money.

"The luminol test . . . turns out it wasn't a false positive. There *were* traces of blood found in Micah's car," Guidry says. "It's his blood, but it appears to have been staged. The patterns aren't consistent with a body bleeding out."

"He staged his death? To escape debt?"

"Or it's a ploy to collect the life insurance."

"I didn't know about the insurance policy," I remind him. "And how would I get blood from my husband to spill into a car that I had no idea where to find?"

"I don't know. Give me another scenario. How do *you* explain all this?"

If Lincoln works for Diamante, and if Christian Renwick is working for them, too, they're after me for the money Micah owes. Because I had access to the safe-deposit box. Because I'm the beneficiary of an exorbitant policy. Because I'm squatting in a house where Micah might have stashed millions of dollars.

A chill runs up my spine. "Did I burn up five million dollars in the kiln?"

God, if I did . . . there's no getting it back. If I'd known, I would've handed the money over, no questions asked. But now the money is gone.

I look Guidry in the eye. "If I were in on this for the insurance money, would I have burned up twice that amount?"

"Good point."

I flash back to a night filled with mojitos and dancing and kisses tasting of Frogman ale. *"Azul,"* I remind him. "It was the name of a boat at the harbor by Simonton Street Beach."

His notebook is out. "When, again, did you see this boat?"

"Maybe it's Micah's boat. Or Micah was on the boat. Maybe he was watching me. And then I got the phone call on the beach." I don't iterate that it's possible he wanted to stop what was about to happen between Christian and me on that beach.

Suddenly, more pieces of the puzzle fall into place. "Maybe Micah was trying to lure us here, to where he stashed the money. He planted the seeds with Elizabella before he left. She knew he'd be going to God Land because he told her. How else do you explain her telling her teachers he was at God Land? I'll bet he's the one who called me, telling me to listen to my daughter. He was trying to get us down here."

It makes sense. Elizabella ran off at Centennial Park, then claimed Nini thought she saw Micah. She claimed to see him near this house. He was *in the trees*, she said.

But if he was at first trying to save us, my recent behavior could have changed his mind. God, what kind of wife grieving her husband would *do* the things I considered doing with Christian? Leaving aside Micah's own hypocrisy, have I made myself expendable in his eyes?

"And now, because I don't have that much money here at this house, we're in danger."

Shell—texting Micah accidentally on the thread I began—is clearing the house in the Shadowlands. Ready to sell it. Ready to hide whatever evidence the police may have missed. She knows more than she's telling. I can't imagine the Shell I know supporting this kind of activity, but I can't imagine Micah being involved in anything like this, either.

"The insurance money won't pay out without a death certificate," Guidry says. "And I'm not about to declare Micah Cavanaugh dead."

"I'll prove to you that I don't know anything about any of this Diamante business. That I had nothing to do with Gabrielle and her boys drowning. That I don't know where Micah is."

"Nini, dolphins can't live on land." Elizabella belly laughs. "You're so funny."

I share a glance with Detective Guidry. "Are you going to check out the boat? Or are you going to keep wasting time, pointing your finger at me?"

"I'll send someone to check out the boat. In plain clothes. You sit tight."

"I don't feel safe here."

"I've got eyes on you here. This might be the safest place for you."

If that's true, it's not saying much.

Chapter 53

"Nini!"

Elizabella's shriek and subsequent laughter, filtering in from the hallway, jars me from a fitful sleep.

"Ellie-Belle!" Another little girl.

This voice doesn't belong to my daughter. And I can't deny I heard it.

I catapult out of Bella's bed, where I've been sleeping for the past four nights since the beach incident, and trip on the toys strewn about the room on my way toward the hallway.

Silence.

I listen hard for a second or two, but when I hear nothing, I wonder if I imagined the second voice. As I make my way toward the stairs, I call to her. "Bella!"

"Nini!" Her voice echoes up the stairs.

"Bella." I reach the staircase.

"Where's my daddy?" my daughter asks. "He came to kiss me at night night. Kissed me on the nose."

"Bella!" I'm halfway down the stairs now.

Elizabella's pudgy hands are pressed to the window in the foyer; and outside, another little girl is pressing her hands to the glass, too.

I scoop up my daughter.

"Mommy! It's Nini!"

Now that my daughter is secure in my arms, I brave a glance out at the porch, where a little girl is smiling and waving.

Bella slobbers a kiss onto my cheek. "She came out of my hair to visit today!"

There's no mistaking the child's red hair.

A second later, I see her mother: Natasha Markham.

She's staring at me.

I stare back.

She looks as put together as I must at the moment: Her eyes are red and puffy, and her hair is knotted in a messy bun atop her head. She's wearing navy-blue sweatpants and a gray tank top with a red stain—ketchup, maybe—dribbling over her right breast.

But there's certain relief in her expression the moment our eyes meet.

I shift Elizabella in my arms, balancing her on my hip, and turn the dead bolt and open the door.

My ex-roommate practically falls over the threshold and into my arms.

Despite her grip on her daughter's hand, she throws her arms around me and, sobbing, buries her head into my shoulder.

"Natasha, how did you—"

"I'm sorry for just showing up, but I didn't know if you'd be here, and your car's not here . . ."

"It's in the garage."

"And my key doesn't work."

Her key?

"I changed the locks."

"I haven't known what to do or where to go. Someone's . . . it sounds crazy, but I think someone's following me. I told the police, but they seem to think I know something I'm not telling them."

We share a knowing glance.

"You too?" she asks. "What's Micah mixed up in?"

I want to ask her what business it is of hers, but instead I usher her and her daughter into the house and engage the dead bolt behind them. "You should've called. I could've . . . We could've compared notes and—"

"Veronica."

I look her square in the eyes.

"Is he dead?"

Chapter 54

"I got your card." I pour a strong cup of mocha roast and top it off with a healthy spill of cream. Just the way Natasha likes it. It's been a while, but being with her is comforting, in a sense, as if we'd never ripped our friendship to pieces for the sake of a man. We'd clicked right away as freshmen, and I wonder if there isn't something magnetic in our systems, something that pulls us together.

Yet there's a wall standing between us. Secrets.

I clear my throat. "I did call but . . ."

She takes a sip of the coffee and dabs a tissue at her eyes. "I got your message."

"I wish you'd called back."

"I couldn't risk it. Maybe I've been paranoid, but I'm pretty sure my conversations haven't been private lately. I let the battery on my phone die so it couldn't be tracked."

I have a million questions about how much she knows, but Natasha seems so sad, *devastated* actually, that I don't think she's equipped to answer at the moment, and I don't know where to start, anyway.

While my first instinct is to be irate with her assuming nature—he's *my* husband, after all, and she's unraveling as if he's always been hers—I've never seen her so vulnerable and crushed before. Even after she caught Micah and me together all those years ago, she'd stood her ground. She'd looked at me with an expression of disappointment in her eyes. Something akin to *how could you?* And simply, very logically and calmly, she walked out the door. I moved out shortly thereafter, and we never spoke again.

But now, she's inhaling over tears, breath caught in her throat, and she looks as if she hasn't slept in days.

I cough. "Your daughter. *Nini*, is it?"

"Mimi," she corrects me. "Miriam. After my grandmother."

So Christian was right. The girl in the pictures is Mimi.

"Elizabella seems to know your daughter," I say.

"The girls met back in April." At last, she looks at me—"After the miscarriage"—but promptly refocuses on her coffee. The very mention of miscarriage causes her to hiccup over her tears. "I'm sorry you had to go through that."

"I don't know how I'd be surviving with three children under the age of four at this point if I hadn't . . ." I shut up. "Sorry. It's a stupid rationalization. I would've made do."

"But you're right," she says. "Sometimes even the cruelest things happen for a reason." She catches tears on her fingertips. "I only wish I could rationalize this."

"So you were up at the cottage on Plum Lake then in April." I hope my bitterness doesn't come through in translation. Or maybe it should. Not that I'm deprived due to my never having been to the lake house, but I sure as hell should've been welcome there if my husband was bringing his ex-girlfriends for weekend visits.

"No." She sips her coffee. "We met here. At Goddess Island Gardens."

Curtains part, and sun shines on dark rooms in my mind. I feel my cheeks grow hot with fury, but I bite my tongue. Natasha is confirming what I suspected. All that time spent wondering how my daughter could have foreseen the landscape of this place, puzzling over her knowledge of God Land, over her creation of the mysterious *Nini*. It wasn't just that Micah told her about this place; she was here.

"But Bella knew the plane would be in the water," I whisper.

"Pardon?" Natasha leans closer, her elbows resting on the countertop.

"My daughter . . . before Micah went missing. She said . . . she knew about this house. She drew it. And she knew there was a plane in the water, and then there was a crash . . ." I chew on my lip, trying to decipher, trying to put it all together.

Does this mean Micah knew the plane was going to crash? Is he responsible for the accident?

I open a drawer in the kitchen and pull out a stack of Bella's drawings. I leaf through them. "She drew the crash. She explains by saying this is where the big house is"—I indicate to the left of the drawing I'm holding up, the way my daughter always does when interpreting this particular piece of artwork—"and this is the plane in the water."

"She's talking about the seaplane."

There's a faraway look in Natasha's eyes, as she reminisces about a happy memory she shared with my husband. With *my daughter*.

"We took the kids by seaplane," she continues, "to Dry Tortugas. The plane landed in the water, and Bella was amazed . . ." With a shake of her head and a shiver, she zaps out of her wonderland. "She wasn't talking about a crash."

"Oh."

And Micah knew that, too. He could've put my mind at ease, assured me our daughter was referring to something else. Instead, he allowed me to worry about our daughter's sanity.

The girls chatter over Bella's crayons, a DVD playing in the background.

"So all this time, you've been in touch with Micah."

She shakes her head. "It's not what you think. You know, when Micah and I were dating, I was close with his mother. We stayed in touch."

Jealousy burns inside me. I always assumed Mick was the reason Shell and I couldn't be closer. Little did I know she'd already filled the daughter-in-law position with the woman her son neglected to nail down. "You and Shell stayed in touch?"

"I guess you could say we had a mutual friend, but Shell *adores* you, Veronica."

I study her. I wonder how Mimi's father, if he's in the picture, feels about Natasha's friendship with an ex-boyfriend's mother. She's wearing a thin, silver band adorned with a pear-shaped aquamarine on the fourth finger of her left hand. "Are you married?"

"No. We talked about it, but we hadn't gotten around to it."

I glance at the little girl whose name my daughter has been mispronouncing since they met. She's beautiful, like her mother. Just as Elizabella has been insisting, she's seven. *Not little*, at least to a three-year-old. The longer I look, I realize there are certain similarities in our girls' appearances. Their brow lines, their smiles. *Wait.* "Who's her father?"

"I was in a committed relationship—"

"With my husband?"

Her hand lands atop mine. "And we couldn't have children. Miriam is a miracle . . . courtesy of artificial insemination. But yes," she says. "Not the way you assume, but Micah is her father."

I pull my hand away and try like hell to ward off tears. "So all this time . . . you've been in touch with my husband since college."

"We reconnected a few years after graduation. There was a—"

"He didn't tell me. Why wouldn't he tell me?"

"Veronica, listen. There was a seminar, years ago, at Evanston Northwest. About help for couples who couldn't conceive. Do you remember?"

"No." But I think about it. Maybe I do. We were having trouble. Micah sought a solution to the problem. Maybe Shell suggested we go. Maybe she even *planned* the event. I vaguely remember *something*.

"It was before you were ready to take extra steps. Micah was there. He said he couldn't talk you into coming, but he was there to learn about your options. I was there, too, for the same reason. God, don't you know he wanted children *so badly* with you?"

"And apparently with you."

"We needed a donor," she explains and reaches for me despite my pulling away. "Micah offered. I would've preferred he tell you, but by then, he thought it would be too much for you to handle. It worked on the first try. We were lucky."

And I was very far from lucky.

"Why AI?" I pull a melon from the far end of the counter and select a knife from the block. "Why not just do it the old-fashioned way?"

"Veronica, I—"

"No, Natasha." I lower my voice so the girls can't hear and slice into the melon. "Betrayal is betrayal. And after all we went through—you and I, I mean—you don't think you owed me the courtesy to tell me that you and Micah were creating children together? I'd almost rather you'd given him one last roll than a child, considering all the trouble I was having getting it done."

She presses her lips into a thin line, her weary eyes rimming with tears. "His name isn't on the birth certificate. We didn't anticipate his being involved in Mimi's life; it just sort of . . . happened."

"You kept your distance after Micah and I got together, and I understood that. But to find out, all these years later, that the two of you were sharing a secret of this magnitude . . ." I shake my head in disbelief. *Slice, slice, slice.*

She was my only friend. Losing her was necessary in order to explore a life with the man I loved. And now that I know Micah didn't have to make the sacrifice in reverse, I could scream.

"I wanted to tell you," she says.

"I hate to break it to you, but you're not the only one."

She chews on her thumbnail.

"There was another woman. Her name was Gabrielle. She and Micah had twin boys."

She's nodding. Her tears intensifying. "Connor and Brendan."

Of course she knows about them. Both women came to this house. There were no secrets between *them*. After a breath or two, I continue. "Can you imagine? All these years ago, I signed paperwork, and it turns out I was giving Micah power of attorney to buy this house. I didn't know anything about it, and then I found the deed . . . and then I got here, and the hits kept coming. He'd stashed some hot little number and their children away here, in a house he hid from me. And his name *is* on *their* birth certificates."

She's nodding. "We knew at that point that he should be part of their lives. *Of course* his name is on their birth certificates. He gave us a *family*, Veronica. Gabby and I couldn't have had a family without him."

My heart pounds as realization dawns.

When I was finally ready to consider IVF, Micah knew which clinic to go to because he'd already been there with Natasha, with Gabrielle. Is his betrayal any less because he wasn't sleeping with them, only donating his sperm?

I imagine Micah, Natasha, Gabrielle, and all their children sitting around this table, while I was zoned out on Xanax. It must've been quite a party, the three of them snickering about dumb, clueless Veronica bleeding out while they waited out the miscarriage in Key West.

What an idiot I've been.

"She was a special woman, Veronica. I wish you'd gotten the chance to know her the way Micah did, the way *I* did."

Wait. The way she's talking about her . . .

I replay Natasha's words: she and Gabby wouldn't have had a family without Micah. *A* family. Not *families*.

I meet Natasha's gaze, and finally, I understand.

Gabrielle was Natasha's life partner.

The sperm in storage. It wasn't for Micah and me. It was in storage for Gabrielle and Natasha. That's why it was paid with a separate card—probably Natasha's. It was on a second account. My husband's name was associated with the account. The clinic must have screwed up when they called me to settle the bill. And it explains the coincidence of her twin boys and mine. Assisted fertility often results in multiples.

All this time, I assumed Micah had been in love with Gabrielle, torn between two families. But all this time, Gabrielle was raising a family with my roommate from college. She wasn't in love with Micah. She didn't steal him from me.

And suddenly, I wonder if I stole Micah from Natasha . . . or if he stole me from her.

All the nights she and I spent curled up together, watching television . . .

The way Natasha looked at me, when she learned Micah and I had fallen love . . .

Micah's words from the past resurface: *Losing* me *wasn't the problem for Natasha; losing* you *was.* Was he right? When I was busy falling for Micah, had I neglected to notice Natasha might have been falling for me?

"I loved you," she now says. "I never wanted to hurt you. He kept promising he'd tell you. Kept insisting he would. After you conceived again. After you'd reached your fertility goals. I would've told you myself, but Gabby thought it best to let him handle it. And when he didn't handle it, she appealed to his mother."

"Shell knew?"

"Of course Shell knew. She did charity work at Children's Memorial, right? Gabby was a nurse there; she'd known Shell for years. When Micah and I were dating, we went with Shell to a benefit, and there she was. I think . . . sometimes I wonder if Micah knew what I was before I did. He must have seen the energy between Gabby and me. Maybe that's why he so easily turned his back on me . . . for you."

Maybe.

"Shell agreed with Micah," Natasha says. "It was best not to tell you about the babies. You weren't my business anymore. You were Micah's, and Gabby was mine."

"Gabrielle was up at the cottage because she knew Shell," I say. "Not because she and Micah were screwing around."

"Yes."

"They found lake water in her lungs."

Natasha lets out a whimper. "Yes. And now, they're gone," she whispers. "She was the love of my life. How do you move on, once you've lost the love of your life?"

I'm gravitating toward her. Pulling her into my arms.

"I haven't told Mimi yet about her brothers," she whispers at my shoulder. "How do you tell a child something like that?"

I'm crying along with her now.

"Will you go with me to identify them? I can't bear the thought of going on my own, of Mimi having to be there, and you're the only person I trust now that I'm constantly looking over my shoulder."

"Of course."

Micah had other children.

Micah had secrets.

But Micah loved me.

And I . . .

My mind drifts to a slow, sweaty dance at the Rum Barrel, to heated kisses on Simonton Street Beach. I can't believe I did those things. Especially when it's painfully clear now that Christian Renwick was not what he seemed.

"Veronica." Natasha swallows over a fresh batch of tears. "What's Micah involved in?"

"I don't know."

"Months ago, he asked Gabby to draw his blood," she says. "He gave her a story—something about banking the blood for Bella. Do you know anything about that? Any reason Bella might need a transfusion?"

I don't.

"And she wasn't crazy about doing it and suggested he go to the hospital, but he insisted, and after all he'd done for us, she agreed. She did it for him. Two separate occasions, a pint each time. Why would he request something like that?"

To spill it into his car. To stage his own death.

"Can you imagine?" she says. "I think Gabrielle is up at the cottage on Plum Lake with our sons. Suddenly, she stops answering the phone. I rationalize it. Cell service isn't reliable that far north, and if they're out on the water, they won't be answering the land line. Then there's a plane crash. I learn from the news that Micah's missing, and there might be a link between him and the crash. And I want to go to you, but Gabby doesn't come home when she's supposed to come home, and then there's a report. Three bodies, and not one of them is Micah. The police had a theory: Gabby had been lying to me, that she and Micah were having an affair and that they were running away together. Can you believe that?"

I can. That seems to be their standard explanation for everything. I shake my head in anger and disbelief. Guidry should have told me these things.

"And then, when the autopsy revealed lake water in their lungs . . ." She breathes deeply. "They were murdered, Veronica. *Murdered.* Who would do such a thing?"

"I thought it was Micah," I say.

"He wouldn't . . . no."

"I thought the lies got to be too much for him, and he couldn't juggle two families anymore. But now that I know that isn't what was happening . . ."

"I didn't know what to think, except Gabby and the boys were at the wrong place at the wrong time. But why the request to draw blood? None of this makes sense."

"He spilled the blood in his car," I say, "so it would look like he bled out there."

He even switched the license plate to another car . . . maybe so he could drive to C-Way airport and catch a flight out of there before whoever killed Gabrielle could catch up with him.

But how would someone manage to smuggle three dead bodies onto a plane? There was no flight plan registered; I guess it would be possible to do, if the plane were in a hangar somewhere and not at an airport.

"But why?"

"I don't know." I look her in the eye, and I know for certain now: from the moment she fell across my threshold, we became obligated to each other.

Papa Hemingway jumps into my lap.

"But something big is going on." Quickly, I fill her in on everything I know.

Diamante and *de azul*.

The men posing as federal agents.

The smoking man.

The whispering caller.

Micah's debt and the accusations he stole from Mick and Diamante.

"How much money are we talking?" Natasha asks.

"Too much to fathom," I say. "And I think they're here looking for it."

Our eyes meet, and she covers her gasp with a hand.

"Do you . . . do you know where it is?"

"They're here," I say. "Looking. Looking in Chicago, too."

"Is it here, then? Or back home?"

"It could even be at the lake house."

"But that would mean . . . Gabby and the boys." She swallows hard. "God, if they were looking for the money there and found my family . . . Do you think they were killed because Gabrielle couldn't give them what they want?"

I open my mouth to answer, but I quickly clam up. If it's true, the rest of us are in for the same fate. I can't bear to utter the words.

"But Shell . . . she wouldn't allow that money at the lake house."

I used to think the same thing, but lately . . . "I'm not sure anymore." I tell her about Shell's odd text, asking if I have Bella.

"Do you think she knows where Micah is?" Natasha asks.

I hesitate. "Maybe. When he first went missing, I called her in a panic, but she was rational about it. She didn't fall apart until I told her what the agents said—that he was dead. And then later, when I learned he wasn't, she was *furious* with me and refused to talk to me. *Refused.* She wouldn't listen to my explanation."

"Then again," I say, "everything's *void* of explanation. Even my neighbor . . . he was squatting in a house through the alleyway, and he up and disappeared. Wait. He said he knew you. Christian Renwick."

She shakes her head. "I never met him."

"He referred to you as Tasha. He knew about Mimi." I gauge her expression, but it's clear she doesn't know what I'm talking about. "He said you weren't usually gone this long. He said you asked him to look after the cat."

"We don't have a cat. Miriam's allergic."

Didn't Bella tell me as much?

"And much to Gabby's disappointment, we didn't live here, but only vacationed here twice. Once with Micah and Bella, and before that, for our anniversary."

I frown. "So the pottery stuff . . . it isn't Gabby's?"

Natasha shakes her head. "I think it was here when Micah bought the place."

"The cat, too? This cat was here when I got here. The neighbor said *Tasha* asked him to look after it. Have you ever seen this cat here before?"

She shakes her head. "I assumed the cat was yours."

Simultaneously, Natasha and I look to the table, where our daughters are giggling.

Judging by what happened to Gabrielle and her sons, our daughters' survival—and ours—depends on our finding the $5 million Micah owes Diamante—Diamond Corporation—before Diamond Corporation runs out of patience.

"I'm pretty sure Micah's on the island," I say. "Bella's seen him a few times. I could have sworn he came in the other night."

"If he came for the money, is there any chance he took it? And took off?"

"Maybe."

But I suspect its ashes sit at the bottom of my kiln.

"Maybe I'm naive to consider this, but I wonder if all this was an exit strategy for him. The blood in the car, dropping hints to Elizabella to come here . . ."

"You mean life got too big for him?" Natasha asks. "He wanted out?"

"I don't know. But could he hope I'd collect the death benefit? Could he hope I'd listen to Bella and show up here, so we could leave the country? By boat?"

"I just can't believe he *never* told you *anything*. Think, Veronica. What are we missing?"

Maybe he stashed money in the kiln so he could disappear without us, and if I burned it, he can no longer get out.

And because that money doesn't belong to him, Diamante is coming after it. We won't be safe until they get back what Micah took.

Where else can I find that kind of money to save our lives?

Chapter 55

December 9

It's after two in the morning.

Papa Hemingway snakes around my legs as I follow the sound of Natasha's quiet tears to the back porch, where she sits, overlooking an empty pool.

I scoop up the cat and join her.

She looks up at me. "Girls still asleep?"

"Yeah."

It's a calm night, filled with cricket choirs and soothing breezes, both of which overtake the space between us.

I sit.

After a few minutes, Natasha speaks. "I was working in the city the week Gabrielle and the boys went to the lake house. Miriam had school, but she'd begged to tag along. To think that if I'd let her go . . ."

I know what she's feeling. Near miss. "But you didn't."

"But I had before."

And if Claudette Winters hadn't been there the day Lincoln and his sidekick showed up to convince me my husband was dead, would I have ended up at the bottom of the ocean, too?

Natasha sniffles. "I find myself feeling grateful—"

"Of course you do."

"When I've lost them. They were *my* children, too. And Gabrielle was the reason my world turned."

"But to think Mimi was spared . . . *of course* you'd feel grateful for that."

"But if all of this is really about money . . . If I lost my family, if you lost your husband because of money . . ."

"I can't imagine what else it might be," I say.

"Then they won't stop until they get it."

"No," I agree. "Or until they have Micah."

What I can't figure out, however, is why Micah would've taken that much money. And how Lincoln would've gained access to the Shadowlands and my home, unless he trespassed through the county property, hopped the fence at night, and broke in.

Elizabella's commentary haunts me: *My daddy doesn't know that man in the kitchen.*

I shiver with the feeling of a hundred near misses. I was home every night. Elizabella was home every night with me. To think what could have happened . . .

"There was an incident," I say. "With the kiln." I fill her in on what happened. "If the money was in there, it's gone."

She turns pale and drops her head into her hands. "God, Veronica."

"I don't know how much money we're talking, but that ash was everywhere. I know I lost at least fifteen grand *beneath* the thing, let alone what was actually hidden *inside* of it."

She looks up at me. "What are we going to do?"

"I can't *unburn* it."

"God, Veronica! What are we going to do?"

"I don't know. I didn't know it was there. And if they come looking—if they come looking *again*, I mean—and I can't produce it . . ." Or if Micah came to get it the other night, and it's not here, he can't repay Diamante.

"Shit."

"I've told the police. Maybe they can help. Maybe they'll keep us safe."

"A big gamble, seeing as the police seem to be zeroing in on two suspects," she says. "Me. And you."

"Micah had an insurance policy. Two-point-five million, but Guidry said it wouldn't pay out without a death certificate."

"Gabby had a life insurance policy, too. But it's not much. Certainly not enough to cover what he owes."

"I found some in our safe-deposit box. Fifty grand. I've spent some, but it'll account for something."

"I have a retirement fund."

"You spent more time in this house than I have," I say. "Am I overlooking a hiding place besides the kiln? Unless . . . do you think it's possible Gabby found any of the money and hid it someplace else?"

"Too late to ask her now, but I doubt it." She drums her fingertips against the tabletop. "I'm sure she would've told me if she'd found even a twenty on the sidewalk, but—"

Natasha pulls a pack of cigarettes from the shadows.

I stare at it, mindlessly massaging the cat's head.

She takes a smoke from the pack and lights it. "I just . . . I can't seem to calm down."

I point to the cigarette. "You quit in college."

"Well, after the month I've had, I'm thinking quitting is overrated."

The image of the cigarette butt on Christian's desk haunts me now. Natasha is puffing on its clone.

Could she be the one who's been spying on me?

I kissed Christian Renwick a few times. Did I ever taste even the slightest hint of cigarette on his lips?

Never.

And the butt in the saucer on his desk. There weren't any ashes with it. He wasn't the smoker. He picked it up from my lawn.

He must have known I saw it. And he removed the evidence that someone—a colleague of his?—had been there. But why keep it? Why not throw it away?

He knew too much about the case, but he hadn't been following me. His nieces, as evidenced by the autograph tree, arrived the day I left home, before I even knew I was coming or where I'd end up.

I stare at Natasha's cigarette. She was on my doorstep at the Shadowlands. She knew where to find me here in Key West. There was the brown sedan . . . the one that followed me into Wisconsin. Was Natasha smoking on the fairway? Or could she have been in touch with whoever was?

Whoever killed Gabrielle could have threatened Natasha. I think of the questions she asked tonight. Maybe she's here to gather information . . . for *them*. Maybe she's looking for the money, too.

And I just told her I can't give it to her.

Chapter 56

If Natasha is in on it, I wonder if she's been telling me the truth. About Gabrielle. About Miriam. Could it be the men after the money are using her to get to me?

I stand and back toward the door, Papa Hemingway in my arms, just as a peal of girlish laughter rings out from inside the house.

Natasha groans. "Would you mind getting them back to bed?" She exhales a ribbon of smoke into the air. "God, I just can't calm down."

Silently, because I can't find voice enough to answer, I nod. I place a trembling hand onto the doorknob, and once I manage to enter, I lock the door behind me to keep Natasha out . . . just in case she's not on my side. I can't think straight. I need time to process, time to sort through everything. She showed up at the Shadowlands and then here, but in between she'd disappeared. And she's been keeping Micah's secrets for years. Can I trust her?

It's difficult to hear anything over the pitch of adrenaline ringing in my ears, but I hear a whisper coming from the foyer: "Good girl. You opened the door."

"No." I drop the cat.

At first, I don't see more than a shape lifting my daughter from her feet.

Instantly, I'm by her side, screaming, ripping her from the hands that hold her.

The back door rattles with Natasha's attempts to turn the knob. She starts pounding on the door when she can't. *"Not Daddy!"* Bella huddles in my embrace. "Not Daddy!"

In the shadows in the foyer, the man who held my daughter turns the dead bolt, locking us in. There's another man standing silently behind him—the shorter of the two agents who came to my house with the feigned news of Micah's death.

Natasha is outside. Is she with me or against me?

I glance back at her.

But she's not alone anymore. I recognize the man with a gun to her head: Lincoln.

The faces in Mama's jewelry hiss and heckle in my mind, and suddenly, I'm a teenager again, seeking safety in a seven-hundred-square-foot apartment.

The man in the foyer steps into the light. I catch a glimpse of silver-blue eyes, and although I've never met him, he's familiar.

I hear the echo of Micah's warning in my head, words that illustrated his feelings for his father, on the last evening we shared:

Man's a tyrant. Nicki. No.

"Open the back door."

I cradle my daughter close. My eyes widen. It's perfectly clear to me how Bella could have mistaken this man for her father in the dark. Same build, same square jaw. Same blue eyes. I may as well be looking at my husband, twenty years into the future.

"Not Daddy," Elizabella whispers.

Miriam, suddenly standing at the foot of the staircase, rubs an eye with a knuckle. "Mommy?" Her eyes grow wider when she sees the intruder.

I reach for her. She takes my hand.

My father-in-law leans against the wall opposite me, his frame foreboding in the small space. "If you value her life"—he nods toward the back door—"open the door."

Still, for a good few seconds, I'm afraid to move.

"Veronica!" Natasha screams.

I inch my way down the hallway and through the kitchen and unlock the door. "Stay with me," I say to Mimi. I don't want her anywhere near the gun.

Micah's father comes into the light. "You," he says in the midst of a sigh, "must be my daughter-in-law."

I do my best to nod. "Mick." I think to divert him with a *nice-to-meet-you*, to show him we're family, to hope he recognizes that fact over and above his reasons for being here. But he's no idiot. He knows I realize he wouldn't drop in at this hour, with a gun to Natasha's head, simply to meet me.

The door opens, and Lincoln shoves Natasha inside.

I tighten my grip on her daughter's hand, but Mimi tears away and runs to her mother anyway.

"Where's Micah?" I ask.

"That's the question of the day, isn't it?" Mick says. "Where can he stay out of trouble?"

Italy, I suppose. Switzerland. Where else did Guidry say the computer records revealed a home search?

"He's been sighted here on the island."

"So he's alive?" I dare to ask.

"A lot of that depends on you," Mick says. "On whether you're prepared to tell me what you know. On whether I find him before our business associates do."

"I don't know anything." I'm about to plead my case, but Lincoln silences me when he holds up a prescription pill vial with my name on it. Xanax.

I think of the details Guidry shared about Gabrielle and the boys: traces of benzodiazepine, lungs filled with lake water. I'm guessing disposing of our bodies might be a little easier than getting rid of Gabrielle's. We won't have to be flown to an ocean to get the job done.

Mick waves at Lincoln to take it down a notch; Lincoln pockets the pills. "My son is running. I assume you're following him. The authorities have a car full of my son's blood. Eventually, when he fails to turn up, and when all of their leads take them nowhere, the police will have no choice but to declare him dead, and the insurance will pay the death benefit. Where do you plan to be when that happens, Veronica?"

It feels as if my blood is pooling in my legs. I'm dizzy, and it's hard to focus, hard to formulate a thought, let alone words.

"Considering your history, do you think anyone will question it, if you turn up dead in a bathtub?"

"Please," I say. "Not in front of the girls." The irony is enough to kill me. Despite all my efforts to avoid it, history is about to repeat itself. My child will grow up wondering if there's something she could've done. Wondering why she wasn't important enough, special enough to keep me alive.

"It doesn't have to happen that way," Mick says. "It's up to you."

"I'll cooperate. But I don't know—"

"My son misplaced something valuable. His survival depends on my finding it."

"But I don't know . . ." I swallow over the Sahara in my throat. "Your men told me he was dead, and I believed them. I'm mourning my husband. I don't know where he is or where he put the money, if he put it anywhere at all."

"They were testing you," Mick says. "They knew you'd show up at the bank. They knew you'd leave with money . . . to get it to Micah. So where is he?"

"I didn't—look. I didn't expect to find that much money in the box, and I wasn't getting it for Micah. I was trying to pay the bills. We're in debt. Lots of debt."

He continues, as if I haven't said a word: "I value my son's life, but the value of yours depends on how helpful you're willing to be."

I glance at Lincoln—if I'd let him take the money in the bank that day, would this all have been over then? Not likely—$50,000 isn't a substitute for $5 million. "You can have it—everything that's left from the box. I didn't know he stole from you. The police told me later, but if I'd known . . . Is *that* what this is about? Money he stole from you a decade ago?"

"Tsk, tsk," he says. "Is that what you think of your husband's character? He was honest enough that it took a certain amount of persuasion to bring him into the fold. Fifty thousand, to be exact, planted to make him *look* guilty. His mother assumed he was."

The picture is becoming clearer. Mick staged it to look like Micah had stolen the money. When Micah said he was putting five grand in the deposit box, it was actually fifty.

"I made a deal with him," Mick continues. "I'd drop the charges, and he could keep the money, as long as he did what I needed him to do. And he's been doing it, until recently."

My mind is flipping in circles as I piece together what might have happened. Mick needed someone to transport for Diamante. Micah didn't want to do it, so Mick found a way he'd have to do it. Was that why Micah lost his job at United? Because Mick had him transporting something illegal? After that Micah didn't have a choice but to go to work with his father—what other airline would hire him?

But something still doesn't make sense: "If he did what you wanted, why are we here? What else is going on?"

Mick flashes a lupine grin. "Micah's more of a chip off the old block than I knew. I set you up in that pretty little house on the golf course. Gave him enough to finance more grandbabies. He's been taking money almost since the beginning. Ten grand here, ten there. Sharing my name only made it easier to access the accounts."

I glance at Natasha. If he stashed money in the kiln, where else might it be? Then I look around—$1 million to buy this house.

"Let's consider the money a bonus. But then he disappeared during his last drop, never showed in New York. Money is just money, but there are irreplaceable artifacts. I'm interested in where he stashed the diamonds." He steps forward menacingly. "Particularly the blue diamond."

I shake my head. "The blue . . . what?"

Both girls are sobbing now, as is Natasha, whose temple must ache with the cold steel barrel of a 9mm still pressed there.

I bounce Bella on my lap, the way I used to when she was colicky at a few months old. "Shh . . . it's okay. It's going to be okay."

"You need bait to catch a fish." Mick's lips curl into a sinister grin. "When Shell told me Micah's kids were on Plum Lake, I assumed my men would find *you* there. Not the boys and the dyke."

Wrong place, wrong time.

"And she was wearing a necklace with a blue stone—"

"It's an aquamarine," Natasha whispers.

"A misunderstanding. But things got a little out of hand. Lincoln had the bodies in a plane before my son even got there to tell them where he put the diamonds."

Natasha draws in a stuttering breath over tears.

"The timing was perfect," Mick continues. "I was overseas with an airtight alibi. The other one didn't know enough to save her life. The question is . . . do you?"

I take a deep breath. "If I knew where to find the diamonds, the rest of the money, I'd hand it over to you. You're welcome to search the entire house. Take whatever you find. But I don't know where my husband is. Micah never told me anything about his business. I thought he was flying executives around the country. I had no idea he—"

My cell phone, abandoned on the counter when I grabbed hold of Papa Hemingway, rings.

I glance at it, then at my father-in-law.

But if he's bothered by the fact that Detective Guidry is calling at this hour, he doesn't let on.

He keeps his stare fixed on me, and finally, the ringing dies. "The blue diamond. He wouldn't leave without it."

Natasha's aquamarine ring catches my attention.

Suddenly, it dawns on me: "The ring. I have the ring. It was in our box at the bank. If I give it to you, will you leave? Quietly? I found it, but I didn't know what it was." I swallow hard. "It's in my suitcase upstairs, under my bed. In a blue velvet box. There's some money in there, too."

Mick gives the shorter, silent agent a nod, and the man disappears up the stairs.

We wait.

Natasha's whimper is constant, as if a recording played on a continuous loop.

Bella shivers with tears and buries her head against me.

When the agent returns, he tosses the box in question onto the counter in front of me. "This box?"

With trembling fingers, I open the box.

It's empty.

"And the money?" I ask.

"None," the agent says.

My heart sinks. Micah must have been here again, just as Bella insisted. He must have taken the ring and the money, which means he's not coming back.

And because I can't produce it, and because we're bait on a hook, waiting for a fish that's not hungry, there's no saving us.

"Search the garage," Mick says to his errand boy, who quickly heads toward the front door. My father-in-law then nods to Lincoln. "How about a drink?"

Lincoln holsters his gun.

Natasha instantly gasps in relief.

Lincoln finds two glasses and pours generous shots of my welcome-to-the-island rum. He places one glass in front of me and one in front of Natasha.

I stare wide-eyed at it.

But Natasha gulps it down before I can stop her.

I know what's in that rum.

Benzodiazepine.

And I know now who left it: The man who followed me halfway to Wisconsin in a brown sedan. The man now playing bartender in my kitchen.

"Drink," Lincoln says.

Chapter 57

"It's been my experience," Mick says, "that alcohol lowers the inhibitions. So you drink until you talk. If you don't talk, maybe you sleep. If you sleep, maybe you'll wake up. Or maybe you won't. And you"—he points at me—"have a lot of arrows directed at you, don't you? Your husband has other children. Your husband is worth more dead than alive. Insurmountable debt. Enormous life insurance policy. Motive, motive, motive. The ordeal with your mother—yes, I know more about your mother than my son does—can only serve to prove your culpability, and if you end up sleeping at the end of it all, we'll be certain to plant your empty medication bottle in your hand."

Pieces fall into place.

I think of the rare nights I'd taken sleeping pills, the nights when Micah was traveling, and I hadn't slept in days. I think about the time I woke up, feeling as if someone had been in the house.

My daddy doesn't know that man in the kitchen.

I wonder if the man in the kitchen in Old Town was my father-in-law. I wonder if he came to see what went wrong at United, if that's the night my family changed.

And if Micah's father owns the Shadowlands house, he likely has the gate code out front, so he could have been there, too.

"You've been in my home," I say.

"Just keeping an eye on my assets. Micah was always too much of a loose cannon not to. Always like to know where those assets might be in case I need to use them."

Assets equal me and Bella.

But I made things difficult when I ran.

They figured out where I was going when I exited the freeway in Wisconsin. Maybe it wasn't too difficult to discern, if they knew about this house. Guidry found it pretty quickly. Ownership of a house is public record. Maybe Christian Renwick was here upon my arrival for a reason.

But if he were planted here, waiting for me, why not get to the bottom of things right away? Why not kill me then, instead of weeks later? Unless . . . unless they assumed I would imbibe the rum they left on my doorstep—which I didn't.

"Drink," Mick insists.

"I can't." I shake my head. "Ask your wife. I'm a fertility patient. I—"

"Drink!"

Natasha puts her glass down, empty, and wipes her mouth with the back of her hand. It's only a matter of time before she passes out, which means it's only matter of time before they sink her to the bottom of the ocean.

I can't take a sip.

Bella's face is buried in my chest. "Want my daddy."

Lincoln's gun is out of its holster again, and this time, it's aimed at the back of my daughter's head.

"No, no, no." My hand covers her hair, as if I could stop the bullet if he happened to fire.

"Drink," Lincoln says.

"Drink it," Natasha whispers.

"Okay, okay." I lift the glass to my lips and slowly drain it.

Lincoln, with firearm still aimed, pours another round.

It's clear that eventually, when they know all we can possibly tell, or maybe because we don't know anything at all, they'll allow us to drift off to sleep, thanks to the medication crushed and dissolved in the rum.

And at *that* point, we're as good as dead. And I'll be the scapegoat, suspected of masterminding the entire thing: the death of Gabrielle and my husband's sons; the death of my college roommate, with whom my husband had never cut ties. My prescription medication would be my assumed weapon.

It would look like a murder-suicide. Eerily similar to what my mother tried to pull off when I was seventeen years old.

Mick's men had baited Micah with Gabrielle and the boys, who just happened to be vacationing at the lake house. What if Micah had been on his way up north to warn her? Or even to return the money? But Diamante got there first.

He's been planning his escape since he bought this house, and that's why he put it only in my name—I'm certain of it. I wonder if he really had planned to take Bella and me—maybe after we'd implanted a healthy embryo. It makes sense that he wouldn't tell me his plan, in order to keep me safe—legally speaking. If I don't know anything, I'm not responsible for whatever he's done. But he planted information with our daughter to ensure we arrived in Key West.

Mick doesn't budge, save to nod toward the small glass of rum in front of me.

I don't have a choice. The gun is pointed at my baby's head.

I down the shot.

Lincoln pours another.

The fat cat that lives here meanders back into the kitchen, as if nothing in the world is wrong or out of place.

The cat that doesn't belong to anyone.

The cat with six toes on his left front paw.

Someone lured me down here. Someone wanted the rest of Micah's children, and their mothers, to convene here.

Who would've done such a thing, if not the one person who'd want to save us?

The one person who's been watching me, warning me by cell phone, and interrupting me when I was about to cross the line with another man?

Who else could have known what disasters were about to come? Who could've told Bella to insist on coming here?

Her father.

But that doesn't explain why the cat is here.

Papa Hemingway winds his way through the kitchen and brushes against my legs.

His collar scratches against me, and when he props himself against me, with his paws on my leg, I manage to straighten the tag hanging at his neck. **James Brolin.**

My thumb brushes over an odd buttonlike thing attached to the underside of the collar.

I catch my gasp before I release it.

I massage the cat's head and trail a hand down his back, as if he needs calming down, too. I've gotten most of the snarls out of his fur over the past couple of weeks.

Hemingway cats sometimes have six toes.

Hemingway cats are named after famous people.

This cat doesn't belong here. He wasn't Natasha's. He wasn't Gabrielle's. He's a transplant from the Hemingway house over on Whitehead Street. Someone planted him here to serve a purpose.

The other day, I was listening to Buffett in the studio. The cat was in the studio. I paid Christian Renwick a visit. He was humming a Buffett song.

Was it more than a coincidence? Was he listening to Buffett because it was playing in my house, and he heard it through the bug he'd fastened to the cat's collar?

Suppose Christian was sent here to serve a purpose: to keep me safe. Mick couldn't show up until after Christian had gone.

Guidry said he'd have eyes on me here in Key West. What if Christian Renwick was working undercover, spending the nights camped on my porch? And when I showed up at his house unannounced, and his nieces allowed me into his bedroom, I saw the notes on the case. His cover was blown. He cleared out.

But the house hadn't been rented . . .

Or so the cops *say*.

Or maybe this scenario is only a face in one of Mama's jeweled pins, sticking its tongue out at me, as I swallow the line, hook, and sinker.

I whisper to Elizabella, "It's going to be okay." I follow the statement with something else, whispered at an even lower decibel: "One, two, three, fly." She looks up at me with a confused expression, but nods and reaches for Natasha's hand.

If the authorities are listening, why haven't they come in yet? I get that they need to gather as much information as possible before they pounce in and save the day. But they don't know about the rum. They might not know about the gun. I have to find a way to communicate the dire situation we're in.

Or maybe they aren't listening *all the time*. Maybe they're checking recordings at the end of the day, to see what I might have revealed. If that's the case, they might not hear any of this for several hours, and by then, it might be too late.

Or maybe Buffett *was* a coincidence, and the bug is the work of Diamante.

If that's the case, we're screwed.

There's only one way to find out.

"I've done what you've asked," I say. "I've drank. I've encouraged you to tear this house apart, looking for whatever it is you want. Please. Take the gun off my child."

If ever you feel that frustrated again, and you start breaking things again . . .

I choose to believe it: Christian is on my side. He will come if he hears me.

But I have to pick my moment.

I have only one chance.

And if I'm wrong, there might be no chance at all.

Chapter 58

My glass is already in my hand, full with another double shot of rum, when Lincoln loses concentration and looks away for a split second.

In a liquid motion, I spill my daughter into Natasha's arms—*one, two, three, fly*, she says as she goes—and I throw my glass to the floor and manage to reach the bottle before either of them can get to it.

I crack the bottle against the marble countertop. Again and again. Making as much noise as possible.

Glass shatters and splinters.

The cat bolts toward the studio, but I hope the necessary message was transmitted.

Natasha and the girls are hiding under the snack bar by the time I hit the bottle against the marble a third time.

Mick has me in a barrel hold now, and he's dragging me toward the laundry room.

I'm sure the second agent will be back any second now, hearing the ruckus. I hope Natasha can get the girls out of the house.

My daughter is shrieking; I hear her cries over Mimi's, over Natasha's.

Please let Natasha be on my side.

I kick and wriggle, holding tight to the neck of the bottle, which represents my only chance at getting out of this house alive.

Mick shoves me through the louvered door to the studio.

And only then do I realize he's cut, bleeding at the side of his abdomen. I must have grazed him with the neck of the bottle.

Good. His blood will be in the house, too. More evidence that he was here. No one can convince me it didn't happen, that it was only in my mind.

Papa Hemingway is hiding under the shelves on the far wall. I charge toward the shelves, where my first attempts at pottery sit. One by one, I throw them to the floor.

Crash, crash, crash.

The cat takes off again.

When there's nothing left to break, nothing left with which to summon the man who maybe placed a listening device on the cat's collar, but definitely told me to smash something when I needed him, I point the jagged neck of the bottle at my father-in-law.

Mick staggers toward me.

I swallow over my fear. "This isn't going to go the way you thought it would. So stop. Just get out of my house. I don't know what you need me to know, and I don't know what happened to that blue diamond . . . or the money."

Yet he keeps coming at me. "It's more than the money. It's more than the diamond. I brought him on board, you see. I vouched for him. You could've just drained the bottle of rum when you got here. You would've saved me a lot of trouble.

The sound of a gunshot paralyzes me for a second, and the sonic boom of it rings in my ears.

Elizabella.

The world goes blurry through my tears, and the piercing tone in my eardrums has yet to subside. My knees weaken, and I stumble.

My father-in-law is too close now.

He pulls from its hook the wire tool with the knobby buttons on each end, and seemingly in slow motion, he wraps the device around my neck.

No one comes. Not Christian. Not the cops.

I was wrong.

But so was Mick, if he thought I wasn't going to fight.

Visions of a blue table flash in my mind. Crystals of all shapes, sizes, and colors rain down on me.

My throat constricts.

I can't breathe.

But I elbow and kick and stab with the remnants of the bottle.

"Veronica."

He has me by the wrist.

"Veronica."

My airway starts to open.

When the crystals fade away, reality slowly bleeds into view.

Guidry's there.

Officer Laughlin.

A few other men in blue.

My father-in-law in cuffs.

"My baby . . ." I scramble to my feet and charge toward the kitchen.

Blood pools on my kitchen floor and trails down the travertine in the hallway, toward the front door. "It's not her blood," someone says. "It's Lincoln's."

"Bella!"

"She's out back," Guidry tells me. "She's safe, Veronica."

I burst onto my back porch, where Natasha is seated, cigarette in hand, trembling. She's talking with an officer. "I didn't have a choice. He was going to kill us. When Veronica distracted him, I got the gun away from him, and I shot."

Bella and Miriam huddle at her side, and my daughter leaps at me when she sees me. "Mommy. Mimi says it's okay to be scared."

I press my forehead to hers. "Nini says that?"

"No. *Mimi.*"

She's growing up. She's saying Mimi's name correctly now.

"Mimi's right. But Mommy's here now."

Out of the corner of my eye, I see Christian Renwick, clad in cargo pants and a ripped T-shirt. This time, I see something I've never seen on him before: a holster at his hip and a badge on a lanyard around his neck.

Chris raises his hand—the one with the scar—and offers a wave.

I wave in return.

"Let's get you to the ambulance," Guidry says.

I tighten my embrace on my daughter. Bella presses her cheek to mine.

"The boat," I say. "*Azul.*" For a moment, hope flashes: maybe Micah's still there.

"Impounded. We recovered a cell phone on the boat, registered to your name. Pretty safe to say whoever had access to that boat was the one making the calls."

"Who owns the boat?"

"It's registered to the company, Diamante. Diamond Corporation."

"Micah?"

"Or his father."

"Daddy kissed me bye-bye on the nose," Bella says.

"He was here," I say. "There was a ring he must have taken, along with the rest of the money from the safe-deposit box. Who else would've wanted to lure us here?"

"Renwick suspected he saw him, too."

"What?"

A paramedic is taking my blood pressure.

"Twice," Guidry says. "Once in the morning, during a walk with his nieces. And later that night."

"The night I got the phone call on the beach?"

"Yes."

"Christian saw him? At my house?"

Christian lied to me.

"Renwick also switched the rum left on your porch with the bottle you drank from tonight. We ran tests on the bottle left on your porch. The levels of benzos found are consistent with those in Gabrielle's system. If you'd drunk that rum, you'd be sleeping for a while."

"He said he was a writer. He should've told me."

Guidry shakes his head. "A good undercover man never does. He cleared out when you saw his work."

If Christian hadn't been here, Mick would've come for me sooner. If he hadn't put the device on the cat's collar, no one would have known we were in danger. And if he hadn't switched the rum, I'd be in a deep sleep by now. He saved me three times.

I meet Guidry's gaze. "Thank you for putting Chris on the case."

"Don't thank me." The detective shakes his head and backs away from the ambulance as the EMTs prepare to close the doors. "I didn't do what I told you I'd do. I didn't find your husband."

Chapter 59

December 23

I've given the police every morsel of information I can muster, and they think my theory has merit: Micah was planning to escape his role in Diamante, to escape the insurmountable debt he'd put us in, to escape the web of lies he'd spun in regards to the children he'd fathered without telling me.

He'd spilled his blood in his car to thwart anyone looking for him—both those from the Diamante international shipping company and the authorities—or maybe even to fake his death.

"His plan wasn't to leave you behind. He wasn't supposed to disappear like that. When you told me he was missing, I assumed he was delayed, but that he'd be back for you. So when you told me he was gone . . . dead, I mean . . ." Shell is sitting across from me at Blue Heaven, an outdoor café and bar on Thomas Street, just down the road from Ernest Hemingway's house. She's lost weight since I last saw her, and maybe that's why she looks a little older around the eyes, the mouth. Or maybe she's just weary with the prospect of the legal battle ahead of her husband. "He never wanted you to go through this."

She shoos away one of the Blue Heaven's free-roaming chickens that dares to waddle near our table. "Oh, this place," she mutters under her breath.

I have to admit that when she asked me to meet, I chose Blue Heaven partly because I thought she'd be just distracted enough to give me the upper hand in conversation. On one hand, I smile to see her out of her element, if only because she should know how it feels to be knocked askew without firm grounding. On the other, the woman sitting across from me is the only mother I've had for the better part of ten years.

"You should have had more faith in him," she says. "In the way he feels about you."

"Shouldn't *you* have had more faith in *me*?"

She looks down at the plate of food she's barely touched. "I'm sorry about that, Veronica, but I was hysterical. Think of Bella. If anything happened to her, wouldn't you be irrational, too?"

"Your son lied to me," I remind her. "About everything. You knew what he did for Natasha and Gabrielle, and you chose to hide that from me. You *knew* your husband was putting him in a tough position—"

"I didn't know the extent of that."

"And you didn't wait to hear my side. You thought I did something unthinkable to the man I loved. You were ready to send me to the gallows."

"Veronica, I knew he was in over his head, but Micah said he was getting out. And then he was gone without you and his daughter."

"So you assumed I'd killed him."

"Maybe not *killed* him. But there was so much to consider, given what happened to the boys and Gabby."

"Whom your husband ordered his henchmen to kill."

"But at the time, I assumed the worst: that you'd found out about his deception, that you'd snapped."

"Like my mother?"

She ignores that one. "Mick's going away for a long time," she says quietly.

As for the rest of it? The money Micah supposedly stole? It's phantom money. Diamante kept no records of their illegal shipments. The only evidence of wrongdoing is in the suspiciously high amounts they paid their pilots for the transfer of goods, but it isn't enough to build a case.

"Yes, I know."

"You and Bella are the only family I've got . . . unless Micah comes back."

I nod.

"Can we work through this?"

I truly don't know. "It's a lot to ask me to forget." She turned her back on me when I had no one else.

"I think he'll buy that place in Tuscany," Shell says. "It was just darling."

I stare at her. Does she realize she's just admitted to being in contact with her son since he left? That she just admitted to knowing he was looking at houses overseas?

"I think he'll come for you."

"Yeah?"

"Yes. I do."

"Well, I won't go with him if he does."

Shell pinches the bridge of her nose. "He's still your husband. He never meant for this to happen. He only wanted to take care of you and Bella, to provide for you. Why do you think he took that money to begin with?"

I don't tell her, but I doubt he was thinking in my best interests. Considering Micah's cell phone—the one he'd registered in my name—was found on the boat at Simonton Harbor, I have to believe he was comfortable allowing suspicion to fall on me.

Considering he was in my home and didn't bother to shake me awake and take Bella and me with him, I'd guess he's never coming back.

And he's guilty of worse: although he must have known what had happened to Gabrielle when Mick's thugs descended on Plum Lake, he still risked our lives to use us as a distraction for his own escape.

I wonder if he intended to take us with him but changed his mind because of Christian. I didn't know I was being unfaithful to Micah, but he would have seen those kisses on the beach as unforgiveable. "He's not coming back anyway."

"He'll come for you. For Bella. He's your *husband*."

"He may be my husband. But he's not the man I married."

That man is gone, stolen away by greed and untruths. When I met him, I felt as if he were the only man on the face of the earth that I could ever want. I've learned over the past month and a half just how untrue that is.

In the silence, Shell sips at her glass of wine. "I'd like to see my granddaughter."

"You've got a plane to catch."

"Please, Veronica."

"I'll think about it. I'll let you know."

I pay the tab and walk back through the streets of Old Town, Key West.

I saunter up Thomas to Southard, the sun on my shoulders and ocean breeze in my hair. By the time I pass Whitehead, I've already made up my mind: Shell knows more than she's telling. She hasn't earned the right to see my daughter. And I don't trust that she won't steal her away to wherever Micah is hiding.

Maybe we're the only family Shell has, but she's not the only family *we* have.

Natasha and Miriam are back in Chicago, mourning their losses, but we have plans to get the girls together here in March. We were friends before Micah tore us apart, and while we still have a long way to go, and many fences to mend, we're willing to put in the time.

Claudette and the kids are coming next month for a long weekend.

And Emily and Andrea still have a good eight months before their gap year comes to a close, and they'll be spending some of that time on this island . . . with their uncle, who happens to live on the quieter side of town, closer to the airport.

I stop at the corner of Southard and Bahama, just as I was instructed to do, and I pretend to check my phone.

Guidry is there on a bench, pretending to read a novel. Really, he's been listening in on the conversation I shared with Shell at Blue Heaven. That's right . . . I'm wearing a wire.

"Did you get it?" I don't look up when I ask.

"That tidbit about the house in Tuscany? That'll narrow down the search."

"I'll be in touch." And I continue on toward Elizabeth Street.

Bella jumps into my arms when I step beneath the welcoming arch. "Mommy!"

"I missed you," I tell her, carrying her up the pink driveway.

She gives me a wet kiss on the cheek.

I pay the twins for their time, but they don't leave right away. "Uncle Chris wants to talk to you." Emily grins when she says it. "He's out back."

I enter the house and, after discarding the wire and my shoes, head toward the backyard.

I stare at the blank shelves as I pass through the family room.

No matter that I know the truth about the children whose pictures used to line the shelves—I know now that they were conceived in a laboratory and not in the heat of passion—I can't look at the built-in cabinetry without seeing their faces.

A sinking feeling settles into my bones. The boys are dead.

So much loss, and none of it makes sense.

I'm going to repaint the room and the woodwork and fill the shelves with new memories. The empty shelves only serve as a reminder of all that's gone.

The beaded paneling at the back of the left cabinet looks more askew than it did upon my arrival. I'll have to have it repaired. And I know someone who might be able to help.

I look out the kitchen window, toward the sound of running water, at the man I know as my neighbor standing at the edge of my pool.

Only he isn't my neighbor. He's retired Lieutenant Christian Renwick Brown—he didn't lie about being retired, although he isn't a writer. He's a private detective. He is, indeed, a Phillies fan. And he's filling my recently repaired pool.

I pour two drinks, one for Christian and one for me, and meet him on the porch.

The warmth of the afternoon sun soaks into my skin.

He approaches, rubbing the scar on his left hand.

"Let me guess." I hand over one glass, which he takes. "No knife at the chop-chop-Japanese-grill. No automatic nail gun or fight over the cheating ex."

Chris grins. "Actually, that's exactly what happened. Everything I told you about my ex . . . it's all true."

"And you were shot in the hand with a nail gun."

"Yes, I was. *And* I took a knife in the hand, too."

"Really."

"That's why I do my own cooking, for the most part, and why I don't believe in contractors. They're very untrustworthy."

"In that case . . . I might need some help with repairing the built-in shelves."

"I'll have a look."

"Thanks."

"My pleasure." The way he smiles tells me he really might find pleasure in helping me. "You know, I saw some work in the gallery over on Greene Street."

Heat flushes my cheeks when he mentions seeing my stoneware creations. "Yeah, they're just little . . . you know."

"I bought a few pieces. The pasta bowl, the blue thing with twisty thing. I mean, I don't even know what that thing's supposed to be, but damn. You're talented."

I shrug. It's not a career yet. But it's a start.

"So." I redirect to finish the conversation we started the day I met him. "You said you were a writer."

"I am. I write true crime. Just haven't found a subject worthy enough to finish."

"Are you writing about me?"

"No." He narrows his gaze. "But to be honest, I'd like to."

"And you said, when I first met you, that a Tasha asked you to look after the cat."

"I went with what I knew. I knew there was an ex-girlfriend named Natasha. I borrowed the cat . . ."

I miss the cat, who is back at the Hemingway estate. "I'm thinking of getting another, actually."

"Yeah?"

"Maybe."

"If you let me do the honors, I won't steal one from the Hemingway estate this time."

"You want to buy me a cat?"

"It's Christmas." He shrugs. "Least I can do."

"You won't put a bug on his collar this time?"

"Not this time." He chuckles. "That was a mad scramble, getting that rental set up with two days' notice. There was the cat . . . I even moved his *litter* from the cat shelter on the Hemingway grounds."

"Just so you know, if you'd told me the truth . . . why you were here . . . I would've understood."

"Lying is an occupational hazard sometimes. I'm sorry about that."

I understand. In the scheme of things, these are tiny lies, compared to those my husband told.

"Emily said you wanted to see me."

"Always. What are your plans?"

"I like it here. I'm going to stay." I sip my drink. I breathe in the flora of my gardens. "I guess you were right. This island can swallow you whole."

"Swallowed me long ago. Beats the hell out of winter in Philly." He sips. "But really . . . I was just wondering if you had any plans *for tonight.* Up for dinner at Turtle Kraals?"

"Oh."

"But I'm glad you're going to stay." A slow smile spreads onto his face.

"Me too." I've already renamed the house: *Verità.* Truth. And in finding the truth about the man I'm divorcing, I'm slowly finding myself.

"So," I say. "Dinner."

"People have been known to eat it."

"Just the two of us? At Kraals?"

"I like you, Veronica. From the moment I met you and your untrusting daughter, you were never just an assignment."

"If I can find a sitter, I'm game."

"I know a couple of teens on gap year who might be interested."

"Then it's settled. If Em and Andrea are available, I'm free."

He wipes sweat with the back of his hand. "Let's have a look at these shelves."

Drinks in hand, we walk into the house.

"The panel is slipping," I tell him.

"I see that." He taps his fingertips against it, then presses his palm to it.

I worry at the wedding ring still stuck on my finger. To my surprise, it slips past my knuckle. I laugh a little. "It came off."

As he turns toward me, the panel slips a bit more.

"Look at that." He gives me a nod of approval.

I stand there, stunned, with the ring tucked onto the tip of my index finger. But I'm not focused on what Christian's looking at. I'm not concerned with my ring.

I'm staring at the wall behind the shelves.

"Chris?"

He turns toward the built-in cabinetry.

The hollow space behind the shelves is lined with bound Benjamin Franklins.

"He left it," I say. "I wonder why."

Elizabella's giggle carries in from the front drive.

That's why.

He left it for me and Bella. For Natasha and Mimi.

Visions of a blue diamond ring flit through my mind. The plinking tune of a music box comes to a gradual stop in my memory, and the doors of Fourth Presbyterian close in my mind.

Christian's fingers lace into mine.

"Dinner's on me," I say.

His eyes are wide, and he laughs a little. "So is the cat."

"Again, again!" My daughter's giggle carries on the island breeze.

I have two embryos frozen at the lab with storage paid for the next calendar year.

But Elizabella is more than enough to fulfill me.

The IVF chapter of my life is officially over.

"One, two, three . . . ," Chris whispers. *"Fly!"*

ACKNOWLEDGMENTS

Over the course of a decade or more, this book has grown from a simple tale of infidelity to a story of hope laced with criminal espionage. I thank readers of Veronica's story when it was in its infancy—Mary and Angela and my cousin Kristin—and of course I offer hugs of thanks to those who made this concept a reality.

My agent, Andrea Somberg, latched on to this story from the first mention of Nini. Andrea, I appreciate all you do. Not many writers can claim flawless feedback and utmost attention from their agents. I'm blessed to have you.

To Jodi Warshaw, Caitlin Alexander, and the team at Lake Union: Thank you for seeing the bones of this story at the bottom of the ocean and for lugging them to the surface and helping me flesh them out. I have absolutely loved working with you, and I hope this is the first project of many.

To my English teacher at Antioch Community High School, Miss Janel Maren (with whom I lost touch long ago): You introduced me to Harper Lee and Mary Higgins Clark. In your classroom, I learned to love reading again. You were the first to acknowledge and encourage my ability to manipulate the reader, and I doubt I'd be the writer I am without you.

To Patrick W. Picciarelli: Thanks for always lending an ear and for writing with me. Your voice is in every cop I write.

To Jessica Warman: Your suspense in YA, not to mention your cadence, had me engrossed from *Breathless*. I learn so much from you and appreciate our friendship more than words can say.

To the little girl with the original Nini in her hair: You're a force to be reckoned with. Don't you ever forget it again!

To my brother, who always endures: We're survivors. Keep on truckin'.

To my mother, aunts, and grandmother: Thanks for providing a solid foundation . . . and offering a little crazy along the way.

To my daughters: You remind me that strength comes from within, and you've kept me strong when I most needed to steel. I think you've taught me more than I'll ever teach you. You are treasures, well worth all I endured to have you.

To my hunky husband: I married an action hero. Thank you. For everything. Including your attempt at cha-cha lessons. You're a surge of power—always have been—and Key West will never be the same without us. Let's go back to Duval Street. Save me a seat at the bar while I wander over to Whitehead to marvel at Hemingway's powder room.

ABOUT THE AUTHOR

Photo © 2017 Bella Vie Photography

Brandi Reeds is a critically acclaimed author who writes young adult novels under the pseudonym Sasha Dawn. Her debut psychological thriller, *Oblivion*, was chosen as one of the New York Public Library's Best Books for Teens, recommended by *School Library Journal*, endorsed by the American Library Association, and selected by the 2016 Illinois Reading Council as a featured book.

On her way to becoming an author, Reeds earned her BA in history and English from Northern Illinois University, followed by an MA in writing from Seton Hill University. When not working on her next book, she teaches college English and works as a kitchen design consultant and cabinetry specialist. She's also an avid traveler, reader, and dance enthusiast.

Reeds is a Chicago native (Go, White Sox!) and currently lives in the northern suburbs with her husband, daughters, and three puppies. Visit her at www.BrandiReeds.wordpress.com.

JAN -- 2019
'19

DISCARD

LINDEN FREE PUBLIC LIBRARY
31 EAST HENRY STREET
LINDEN, NEW JERSEY